The Eilat Trap

Nick Cree

Copyright © 2018 Nick Cree
All rights reserved.
ISBN: 9781980670889

For Daniel
May your life be one big adventure

ACKNOWLEDGMENTS

I guess at this point it is usual to have an Oscar style list of names of people who have made this whole journey possible, well as a new and self-publishing author I don't have a huge backroom team behind me. It's just me and a couple of loyal friends who have encouraged me and looked over my work from time to time, more to check on my spelling than anything else., so thanks Neil and Joules for that.
But what I might lack in Backroom staff I make up for in inspiration which I take from the thousands of people who have followed my blog and read my work there. Most of them are themselves ex-volunteers and in the end that was what this book was about and who it was for. The over 350,000 volunteers who went and worked on Kibbutzim in Israel.
Shalom Aleichem
Nick Cree

Connect with the Author

Facebook: https://www.facebook.com/NickCreeWriter/
Read the ISHTAV Blog: https://houseofcree.com/ishtav/
Follow the News: https://houseofcree.com/nickcree/

CHAPTER ONE

The first training shoe did it. It bounced off his head and dragged him from sleep. Billy wasn't ready to face the day so he reached down and pulled the duvet up over his head. The second trainer jarred his elbow. Thrown harder and faster than the last, it caught his funny bone and sent a spasm up his arm.
"Ow, fuck off. I'm awake." Billy didn't even have to open his eyes to know who his attacker was. There was only one person who would venture into Billy's bedroom at this time of the day. It certainly would not be his mother. She would have been up at the crack of dawn and off to her first job as a cleaner, in the fancy five-star hotel in the centre of town. When she finished her shift there, she would then walk to her second job, as a checkout operator at the big supermarket.
No, there was definitely only one person who would come to the flat at this time of the morning and make sure Billy was awake, up, dressed and ready to face the day.
Billy pushed aside the duvet and sat up in bed. Across the room, standing just inside the door, leaning casually with his arms now folded was his best friend Mike.
"Come on sleepy head, let's be having you."
Mike could never quite wipe the smile off his face. Beautiful teeth courtesy of a private dentist shone in his slightly open mouth. His face was still tanned from the two weeks Easter break he had just enjoyed with his family somewhere exotic and hot, and his blonde hair was neatly cut in the latest fashion. He was wearing his work uniform of green shirt and trousers but even these cheap polyester garments looked good on him.
Billy was busy rooting around on the floor for his own uniform bits. He found them where he had discarded them the previous afternoon when he returned home. He struggled into the trousers

which were about two sizes too big and then bent to roll the bottoms of the legs up a couple of turns. The shirt was a better fit but was missing two buttons so it gaped open at the bottom. He tucked the shirt into his trousers and then cinched the whole thing tight with a leather belt. He found his steel toecap boots under the bed and forced his feet into them.

"Make yourself useful mate and put the kettle on. We must have time for a quick coffee before we go."

Mike made a big play of studying his large and rather expensive looking watch and then sucking on his teeth.

"Weeeelllll" He said drawing out the word. "As I already put the kettle on before I came in here and as the coffee and sugar are in the mugs then we might have time to drink half a cup." He turned on his heels and walked out of the room.

Billy caught sight of himself in the full-length mirror hanging on the wardrobe door. His dark hair needed cutting; his dark brown eyes peered out from underneath an unkempt fringe. He was badly in need of a shave and he really did look strangely like a sack tied in the middle. He shrugged his shoulders at his reflection. Any improvements would have to wait until later in the day. He walked out into the hallway, turned left and entered the kitchen.

Nothing was very far away in the council flat he shared with his mother. The front door opened onto a tiny hall with the bathroom on the left. There was his mother's bedroom and the living room on the same side. On this side of the hall, the door to his bedroom stood next to the alcove that served them as a kitchen.

There was not really room for both Billy and Mike in the kitchen space, not if they wanted to open the fridge so Mike did the honours and passed the steaming mug to Billy who led the way into the living room and collapsed on the sofa.

"Don't get comfortable. I wasn't joking. We have about five minutes and then we have to go. I can't have you being late again, Hollingsworth will fire your ass."

Pete Hollingsworth was a bully and their supervisor. He had taken an instant dislike to Billy from day one and done his very best to make life a misery for him ever since. Billy hated the man with a passion but Hollingsworth's position and his greater physical strength meant that all Billy could do was endure the taunts that were dished out to him.

It was not that Billy was bad at his job. A kinder soul might have described him as thorough or methodical. Hollingsworth described him as a lazy, clumsy, useless piece of shit.

Billy had not really got off on the right foot with him. On the first day, he had been trying to make a good impression and had loaded too much onto the forks of his truck. Taking the corner too fast, the top of the load had fallen off and smashed to the ground. Of all the crates that he could have sent to the floor, Billy had to pick one stacked full of expensive crystal glassware.

But for the presence of two senior managers in the warehouse at the time Billy might well have received his marching orders there and then. However, the Managers, fearing injury to staff and a potential injury insurance claim, had intervened to check that no one was hurt. By the time they had made sure there would be no legal repercussions from staff claiming damages at a later date, the whole thing had passed over and Billy had been granted a reprieve on the grounds of beginner's bad luck.

Later, in a quiet moment, away from prying eyes, Hollingsworth had grabbed Billy by the neck, lifted him off his feet, and pinned him up by the throat against a packing case. Billy squeaked with fear as Hollingsworth's sour breath had filled his nose and mouth and his spittle had painted the side of Billy's cheek.

"If you ever pull a stunt like that I will bloody well...."

"Does there seem to be a problem here?" Mike's voice was music to Billy's ear. Never far away, his friend had been alerted by Billy's fearful squeak.

Hollingsworth had returned Billy to his feet and smoothed down the lad's uniform shirt, before stalking off. He had clearly decided that the kind of conversation he wanted to have with Billy wouldn't benefit from the presence of spectators or possible witnesses.

"Thanks Mike," Billy smiled as he massaged the tender spot on his neck. "I'll have bruise there by morning."

"Just remember when the girls ask, the other guy is in Intensive care." Mike punched his friend playfully on the shoulder as the two friends went back about their work.

It had always been like this, right from their very first day in school, when a trick of fate had thrown the two boys together at the same double desk in the first-year classroom. The fate, their surnames, had meant that they sat side by side. Teachers in their school liked order and one manifestation was the class had to be sat in alphabetical order with Paul Adams sat in the first seat inside the door and Trevor Williams the last seat over by the window. In between, in rows front to back the other thirty boys were arranged by surname.

Mike Spencer and Billy Randell were therefore sat in adjacent rows but due to the ancient design of the furniture, their desk was actually a double desk, which they were forced to share. If it hadn't been so their paths might never have crossed.

They came from such wildly different backgrounds. Billy lived with his mum in a small council flat on the seventeenth floor of a tower block in the centre of town. Mike lived up the posh end of town with his father and mother, both professional people in well salaried jobs. Their five- bedroom house was like a mansion for Billy, who stood at the gate in stunned silence, the first time he accompanied Mike home. The family's two cars, a BMW saloon and a little Italian Roadster were parked in front of the double garage. Billy reckoned that his whole flat would fit inside the Spencer garage. It was only the beginning of the surprises. These continued at the rear of the property, where the terraced gardens included an indoor/outdoor pool and a tennis court. This was really the lap of luxury and a long way from anything Billy had ever experienced in his short and rather dull life.

Billy had always been picked on, for his size, for his poor background, for his cheap second-hand clothes.

At the first morning break, Billy and Mike had ventured out into the playground. Billy was unaware that some former classmates from his old junior school were waiting for him. They, apparently, had some scores to settle and it was obvious they were not going to wait until the first day of school finished. They had been planning their revenge all summer long. They grabbed Billy and dragged him off behind the bike sheds and Billy knew he was going to get the kicking of his life.

As he went to the ground and tried to cover his head and face with his arms he was wracking his brains to try and remember why exactly he was getting the full treatment. For the life of him he could not remember what slight or insult he had delivered to earn him this beating. He waited for the first impact. And waited. Eventually he lowered his arms and opened one eye. Gazing down at him was Mike and he was extending a hand towards him to help him to his feet.

"I got your back Randell," he said.

"It's Billy." Billy said, dusting off his threadbare second-hand school sweater and hitching up his slightly oversized school trousers.

That first encounter had taken place nearly a decade ago and all through school the two had been inseparable. Sometimes, late at night, in his bed and in the privacy of his own thoughts, Billy wondered what Mike saw in him. Why did a guy who had everything going for him bother to take care of someone like him, who had nothing to offer?

He never voiced these concerns out loud, not to anyone, not even his mother, who thought that the sun shone out of Mike Spencer's arse. Although she would not have put it quite in those terms.

Mike had been Billy's guardian ever since that first day in school, always at his side, ever vigilant and watchful. It was not that Billy went looking for trouble. It was more the case that trouble came looking for him.

#

The two friends were five minutes early when they approached the punch clock and checked in for their shift. Both punched their cards and placed them in the right slots on the clocked-in side. Billy was pleased to notice that Hollingsworth was standing in the hallway and therefore bore witness to his early arrival. There could be no grounds for any snide remarks later, at least not on any aspect of his timekeeping.

Billy's nemesis was leaning against a wall talking with one of his endless supply of fawning minions who followed him around constantly, ready to do his every bidding. This morning the two were in the hallway casually observing the time clock and checking on people arriving for the day shift.

Hollingsworth was a little under six foot in height with a thinning head of brown hair, which he combed over in a vain attempt to hide his rapidly developing bald spot. He was stocky in his upper body with heavily muscled arms that displayed tattoos, a legacy from his days in the Merchant Navy. He always wore a brown full-length warehouse coat which Billy thought made him look like an old-fashioned shopkeeper. It certainly set him apart from all the other members of the workforce whose uniforms were dark green. The pockets of the coat were always stuffed to overflowing with folded sheets of paper and weighed down with other heavier items so they bagged out of shape. A row of blue Bic biros lined his breast pocket. He was normally seen strutting around carrying a red vinyl clipboard which he consulted from time to time. Hollingsworth also wore Doc Marten shoes instead of the company approved safety footwear and the rubber soles squeaked annoyingly every time he walked anywhere. The only advantage was that the squeaking gave prior warning of his arrival so it was possible, if you were quick and heard him in time, to avoid his attentions.

Billy was not naive enough to think that he would manage to pass the whole day without feeling the sharp side of Hollingsworth's tongue. That day would only come in a week when there were two Thursdays and all the pink elephants were flying south for the Winter, or alternatively Hollingsworth was struck down with some rare and incurable disease.

Imagining what form that disease might take kept Billy occupied until lunchtime.

Every day the work was much the same. The warehouse where the two friends worked was part of a distribution network for a chain of homeware superstores. Pallets of merchandise from wholesalers arrived on one side of the warehouse on lorries, were unloaded and then loaded directly onto lorries bound for the individual stores. Each pallet of goods had a barcode on the side which was read by a scanner on the forklift. The destination bay and lorry number were then displayed on a screen that the driver could read. There was no need for the forklift driver to leave his seat to check the box or pallet details he simply drove the truck, pallet and its contents into the designated outgoing trailer. It was all highly efficient and saved time and ultimately warehouse space.

Occasionally, however, stock was not destined to cross dock, but instead was allocated space in the warehouse and had to be transported there.

Stacking the pallets safely on the high shelves was a job reserved for only the best of the forklift drivers and was therefore not something that Billy got to do very often. Mike, on the other hand was often the first choice for the warehouse runs. If enough pallets were being sent to stock it was possible for Billy and Mike to only meet during their breaks. Today was such a day and when Mike and Billy met for their lunch break in the canteen, Mike was keen to make final arrangements for the evening ahead.

A local band were playing at one of the pubs in the town and as the majority of the band's members were old school mates, Mike felt they should turn up and show their support. Billy who was perennially broke pointed out that until they got paid at the end of the week he couldn't even afford to buy a soft drink.

"Billy you know I would never let you stand there without a pint in your hand."

Billy, who knew all too well, that Mike's father would never allow his son to leave the house without a crisp twenty or two nestling in his wallet, didn't feel like a scrounger. The charity was freely given and never mentioned.

"I will come by the flat about eight." Mike said with finality. He was not going to take no for an answer.

With that decision reached, the rest of the day passed without incident. Hollingsworth seemed to have spent the afternoon closeted in some high-level supervisors meeting, because his menacing presence was noticeably absent.

Billy and Mike were off their trucks, and out the door as soon as the clock hit six. They both felt they owed no debt of loyalty to the company, no one ever suggested paying them for voluntary overtime, and really, they could not wait to get out of the place. Mike had left his bike in the bike shed at the bottom of Billy's tower block so the two friends crossed the town centre together and only parted at the entrance to the tower block.

Billy entered the four-digit code that unlocked the main door and went up in the lift.

He reached in through the letterbox and recovered the door key on its long string and let himself in to the flat.

In the little kitchenette, he opened the door to the freezer. One of the perks of his mother's job at the supermarket was that the staff got the first pick of the frozen goods that were about to pass their sell-by date. Consequently, the freezer in the flat was always well stocked with microwavable ready meals. Billy ran a finger down the available selection and pulled out the one that looked the least unappetizing.

He prepared the packet piercing the plastic cover three times with a fork then placed the plastic dish in the microwave and slammed the door. When the bell pinged a few minutes later he tipped the contents onto a plate, covered the whole thing with Tomato Ketchup, grabbed a fresh fork from the cutlery container on the draining board and went into the living room. He flicked on the TV and plonked himself on the sofa.

The TV had belonged to one of his mother's former boyfriends. Unlike some of her other lovers, this boyfriend had not returned to collect the television when the relationship had ended. This was probably due to the fact that he was serving a five-stretch at Her Majesty's Pleasure in Wormwood Scrubs for his part in an armed robbery. Billy was half expecting someone from the guy's "crew" to turn up any day and reclaim the TV but it had been almost a year now without a sound from him or anyone who knew him.

His mother had dumped the guy just after his arrest and while he was still on remand. She was totally pissed off that the Police had felt it necessary to kick in the apartment door at five-thirty in the morning, hauling her semi-naked from her bed and handcuffing her whilst they tried to subdue their prime suspect by bouncing up and down on his head. The resulting damage to the bed and bedroom furniture had never been paid for.

Susie Randell had ended the relationship, not because of the early morning alarm call from the Police and the damage they had caused but because her beau had lied to her. He had told her that his former life of crime was over and that he was now going straight, but as Billy's mum later discovered he was only going straight back behind bars.

A claim for compensation for damages to the furniture was still outstanding with the Chief Constables office. Naturally the council had footed the bill for the repairs to the front door, but only after Billy's mum had gone down to the local rent office and read them the riot act. Unfortunately, that approach wouldn't work with the local old bill. So, Billy's mum had a wardrobe with a broken door and a bed that canted over at about twenty degrees.

#

Billy was still glued to the TV when he heard the front door of the flat open. It had to be Mike as Thursday Night was Bingo Night and his mum would not be home before eleven.

Mike spent enough time with Billy to know that the door key was reachable through the letter box. Billy was on his feet when Mike walked into the room.

"You ready to go?" Billy greeted his friend with a smile.

"Not before you have had a shower and washed your hair, changed out of your work uniform and made yourself look presentable." These harsh words, even delivered with a smile, might have tested the strongest of friendships but Billy knew deep down that his friend had his best interests at heart so he went through to his bedroom, found his least dirty jeans and his freshest smelling t-shirt, crossed to the bathroom and took a quick shower. The shower gel was one of his mother's particularly pungent floral varieties and as Billy used it for both body and hair it was necessary to douse himself with aftershave afterwards to regain any shred of machismo. He walked back into the living room in a cloud of Blue Stratos and watched Mike visibly pale as he caught a whiff.

"Lucky we have a bit of a walk to get to the Half Moon." Mike said with a wry smile and a shake of his head.

Billy grabbed his wallet although he knew there was little in it except IOU's and the odd bit of fluff. Mike handed him two fivers which Billy placed in with the papers. At least it would look like Billy was paying his way. Billy's silent look of thanks was all Mike expected and the two left the room, went out of the flat, across the hall and rode the lift down to the ground floor.

Out in the street the two friends turned right and began to climb the hill towards the pub. Mike was unusually quiet so Billy was prattling on trying to fill the void. Eventually he gave up and the two continued on their way in morose silence. Billy wondered what was bothering Mike and why he was so quiet but as their boots crunched on the gravel of the footpath Billy was at a loss over where to start interrogating his friend. Experience taught him that whatever was troubling Mike would come out in its own time and when Mike was ready to discuss it. So, Billy put his head down against the cold wind, pulled his jacket tight around his body and walked on.

They reached the pub and joined the queue for the live music venue. The doors were about to open and there was a good sized crowd waiting to be admitted.

They both leaned on the wall as they waited for the bouncers at the head of the line to dispose of the usual liggers and guest-listers. Those whose names were on the list were admitted those who had not made the grade were unceremoniously dismissed to the back of the queue. Whether they opted to join the queue and pay like everybody else or stomped off in self-righteous disgust, the Security staff really couldn't have cared less.

"Listen Bill I've got something to show you:" Mike was reaching for the pocket of his bomber jacket and extracting a plain brown envelope.

"What's that the results of your pregnancy test?"

"Open it and read it." Mike handed him the letter.

Billy didn't like the serious tone in Mike's voice so he opened the envelope flap with a degree of trepidation. He extracted the single folded A4 sheet and flipped it open.

The top of the page, the letter head, was a series of squiggles that looked like some kind of ancient script. If he had to guess he would have said the text was Middle Eastern in origin. Billy was not stupid. Far from it. He could easily have been accepted to one of the better Universities if he had bothered to apply. His exam grades had been good enough to get him in, but he knew that his mother could not afford to pay for him to spend the next three years of his life effectively earning nothing. He scanned past the foreign script to where someone had helpfully written something in English.

"Kibbutz Representatives" The rest of the text was a letter addressed to Mr Spencer congratulating him on having been accepted into the program and how they were looking forward to welcoming him to their country. Billy held the letter up by one corner between his finger and thumb.

"What's this?" His facial expression suggested he was expecting either the letter to burst into flames or turn into a snake and make a lunge for his heart.

"Come on Bill. I told you about this months ago. I am going to a Kibbutz at the end of the month."

"A Kibb-what?"

"A Kibbutz, it's a kind of agricultural collective where everyone lives together and shares the work"

"You mean it's a commune full of fucking hippies. Where exactly is this commune?"

"It's in Israel."
"Israel? Isn't there a fucking war going on down there?"
"No there isn't a war going on." Mike's tone was defensive now.
"Well a lot of people still get killed down there, blown up, shot at or stabbed."
"It's not as bad as you think."
"Sounds pretty dangerous to me. Any roads, when did this all come about."
"Come on Billy, you remember Carmen?"
"Everybody remembers Carmen, she made sure of that." Billy's face took on a lecherous expression. "She was the original good time that was had by all."
"Well she was over there a few years back and had a superb time. She couldn't stop talking about it, so I decided to give it a try. Look I told you this about three months ago when I put in the application."
Billy wracked his brain trying to remember the conversation but it was just coming up a blank in his memory.
"So, when are you leaving? Wait a minute the end of the month, that's next week."
"The flights on Tuesday night. My dad is taking me to the airport so if you want, you can tag along and wave me off properly."
"Fucking hell Mike, you're really going through with this?"
"Too right my old son, nothing here for me right now. Fed up to the back teeth with Hollingsworth and his cronies. Going to be great telling him where to stick the job tomorrow."
The two friends had reached the head of the queue now and Billy had turned towards Mike and was about to say something else when the Bouncer cut across him.
"You two clowns coming in, or are you gonna stand there all night?"
Billy turned back to face the Bouncer, a witty comment on the tip of his tongue but the guy was as big as a house and his stern, piggy eyes told Billy he was not to be messed with. The curly wire going from his earpiece and disappearing under his black nylon bomber jacket made him look impressively efficient, like some Secret Service Agent on Presidential Protection duty. He had hands like small hams and arms like small tree trunks folded across the front of his jacket.
"Well," he said. "What's it to be? You coming in or not?"

"In," said Billy with a wan grin and the two friends passed the doorman and entered the venue.

Mike flourished a tenner to pay their admission fee, handing it to the girl sitting behind the small table and both lads got their hands stamped from the ink block. The crescent moon, in black, shone for a moment as the ink dried.

The interior door of the venue swung open briefly and the noise of a tuning guitar escaped only to be cut off as the door swung shut again.

Mike pushed the door open and they both went in, making a beeline for the bar and joining the crush to get a drink.

When they both had their pints in hand they went towards the back of the room and stood by one of the pillars. Mike was surveying the crowd looking for familiar faces, Billy was silently contemplating the approaching separation from his best friend.

The Half Moon Live, as the venue advertised itself, was nothing more than an oversized wooden shed built onto the side of the Half Moon Public House. Funded and largely constructed by the local Irish Republican community, the place had served as a venue for fund raising dances and discos during the dark days of the troubles in Northern Ireland, with all the gate receipts and a large percentage of the bar takings going to the cause.

With a change of management in the Pub and a change of climate in the province the place had reinvented itself and, in the process, become a more mainstream live music venue, with local bands using it to try and drum up support for their fledgling careers.

The toilets were a favourite hangout for the local drug dealers, with the security staff generally turning a blind eye to their business dealings, in return for a slice of the profits Billy suspected, and there always seemed to be some kind of fight towards the end of the night. At one time there had been a ring of tables and chairs around the central dance floor but these had been removed, for safety reasons. In any conflict they were the first items to be broken up and then deployed as weapons. Now the venue was standing room only or leaning room if you included the walls and the pillars that held up the roof.

The roof itself leaked after any heavy rain shower and there were often puddles of water on the floor. The place was probably a fire hazard and a death trap but it was popular amongst the youngsters and was to remain so until the place burnt to the ground a few years later. The cause of the fire was later determined to be faulty wiring, although arson by an embittered band who had been denied payment by the management, was the popular story told by the locals for many years afterwards.

The subject of Mike's imminent departure was put on hold as their friends began to congregate and the first band of the evening took to the rickety stage.

This was their first outing as a band and after the appalling way they performed most likely their last, at least until after a few more rehearsals. The lead singer had stormed off stage before the band had come to the end of their last number and the bassist looked like he was ready to do physical harm to the lead guitarist. It was something Billy had witnessed many times in the past and was sure he would see again in the future, while there were still young hopefuls anxious to take a first step on the rickety ladder of success.

The houselights came on while the stage was cleared of the support band's equipment and then the lights dimmed again. In the darkness the suspense was tangible as the audience awaited the arrival, on the stage, of the main band. There was the occasional whistle or catcall audible above the general hum of excitement from the audience.

The main band were determined to make an entrance and they succeeded. A piece of intro music blared out from the PA and then the fun really started. A great cloud of smoke enveloped the stage and bright white spotlights blinded the audience.

Someone among the band's entourage had obviously thought some pyrotechnics would add that extra professional feel to the start of the show. Unfortunately, they had forgotten to clear this with the venue management. The result was quite spectacular. As the first fireworks detonated the security team came racing into the hall, fearing that their worst nightmare had just come true and either a terrorist bomb had detonated inside the venue or a gunfight had broken out.

There were red faces all around as realisation dawned and order was quickly restored with the men in earpieces retreating to their place by the main door, muttering into their microphones and shooting evil looks at the band on the stage, who, blissfully unaware of the uproar they had just caused were halfway through their first song.

The noise of the music and the crowd made meaningful dialog impossible so it was not until they had left the venue to walk home that the conversation resumed.

Billy, who had been unusually quiet all evening, had been thinking about what to say and had formed an opinion. If Mike was leaving then so was Billy. All he needed to do was find a way to pay for the trip.

When they had said good night to the last of their friends and were alone again this was exactly where Billy resumed the conversation. Mike stopped in his tracks and looked at his friend.

"Are you serious? You want to come along?"

"As a heart attack mate."

"God, I wish you had said that when I asked you the first time."

"You never asked me."

"Yes, I bloody did. We were sat in your living room watching TV."

"Well I don't remember that."

"Anyway, you can't just suddenly decide to join me. You have to go through the application process and be accepted."

"How long is that going to take."

"About a month."

"And how long are you planning to stay there?"

"I don't know until I get there. Could be three months might be more."

"Well then I could be with you in just over a month if I send an application to them tomorrow."

"Tomorrow's Friday Billy and nobody Jewish works on a Friday."

"Well Monday then."

Mike was fighting with himself. He knew in his heart there was one very good reason why Billy would not make it to Israel. It was a simple matter of finance. The return ticket alone would cost nearly three hundred pounds and the Kibbutz Movement expected all volunteers to have sufficient funds to support themselves for a limited time. Billy would be lucky if he could scrape together a hundred quid all up, straight after pay day.

Mike didn't want to be the one to point this out to his friend, not at this point in time anyway. The pair of them had consumed a few beers and emotions could run high once alcohol was introduced to the equation. Mike had fought with Billy in the past. It would have been impossible to have been friends for a decade and never

disagreed about something. But deep-down Mike knew this was neither the time nor the place to start an argument. All he could do under the circumstances was to go along with his friend's ideas and then maybe at some point in the next few days drop a subtle hint about the overall cost of the venture.
They parted at the front of the tower block as usual with Mike retrieving his pushbike and cycling off into the night.
Billy's mum was still up and sat glued to the TV when he entered the living room.
"Hi Mum, I am going to Israel."
"Don't be daft that's the other side of the world."
"I am going mum, just you wait and see."

.

CHAPTER TWO

Billy was not totally naïve. He knew that the cost of a trip to Israel was outside his limited budget. Mike's supposition had been right. Even after payday Billy could probably scrape together a hundred quid at the absolute tops. He had no savings and no rich parents or relatives to tap for a loan. His mother struggled with two jobs to pay the rent and the bills. Billy, of course paid his way but even so it was always tight at the end of the month. Billy's weekly wage from the warehouse was often all they had to tie them over until the Supermarket salary was paid into his mum's bank.
Billy had absolutely no idea where his father was or what he was doing. Billy's father had left home when Billy was only three, leaving his mum to cope with raising him alone. Mother and son had heard nothing from him since. For all Billy cared the bugger could be dead, and given the amount he had drank, he probably was.
He had not been a good father, perpetually unemployed and according to his mother, permanently off his head on drink or drugs. When Billy's mum had eventually turned off his money supply he had disappeared into the night, never to be seen again. His legacy had been a mountain of debt that left Billy's mum virtually penniless for years afterwards. Billy seriously doubted his father was about to ride in on a white horse and provide a solid financial solution to his current predicament. If anything, it would be the total opposite. Billy knew that he was going to have to solve this one on his own.
The next day at work Mike was full of himself. It was a Friday, and it was payday and he was about to drop a bombshell in Hollingsworth's lap. He was also proudly showing off his airline ticket, which had arrived in the morning post.

Billy grabbed the ticket and studied the details, making a mental note of the flight number and the airline, departure time and arrival. When he had a moment to himself he committed the details to a scrap of paper.

At lunchtime, he made a lame excuse about having to run an errand in town and took himself off to the travel agents. In the shop, he waited to be served and then handed over the scrap of paper.

"Can you tell me if there are any seats available on this flight?"

The girl behind the desk smiled at him and started to tap away on the keyboard of her computer terminal.

"Is this a return ticket?"

Billy shook his head. "No just one way."

After an age of keystrokes, she studied the results on the screen in front of her.

"There are two seats still open on the flight, one in economy and one in business class. I assume you want the economy seat?" She glanced up and took in Billy's cheap polyester uniform.

Billy nodded his head. "Actually, I just want to know what the ticket will cost. I haven't got the money with me to pay for it."

"Well, let me see. If you add in the departure tax and the Israeli airport tax then the total cost for the ticket, one way will be two hundred and seventy pounds."

Billy gulped at the cost but managed to splutter a thank you. As he left he checked the opening times of the shop and saw that they were open until six the following evening.

He worked out he had just over 24 hours to find about eight hundred pounds. As well as the ticket, he would need to get himself some new clothes and a suitable travel bag, and he thought he might treat himself to a small portable stereo and still have enough to pay for his return ticket and have some spending money while he was away.

As he walked back across town sucking on a can of coke he considered his available options. There was only really one option available to him and he knew that he would have to act tonight. With this in mind he returned to the warehouse to find that word of Mike's departure had got out and all hell had broken loose in the loading bay.

It had taken less than the allowed one-hour lunch break for him to venture to the travel agent and back but in that time, war had been declared.
It seemed that a chance comment overheard by one of Hollingsworth's henchmen had got back to the man himself and he had found Mike and faced him down about his imminent departure. Mike had been waiting until the afternoon to hand in his notice but now at just after one it was already out on the company grapevine.
Hollingsworth was not happy that he had been kept in the dark and he had also guessed that Mike's resignation was exactly what it was intended to be, an attempt to shaft him. These two things had caused him to fly into a rage and confront the young man.
Therefore, when Billy walked back into the loading area, shrugging his shoulders into his work jacket with the horrible yellow high-viz sleeves, Hollingsworth was facing off to Mike across a pallet piled up with cardboard boxes and shrink wrapped. Voices were raised and words were spoken in anger. Fists were clenched and being shaken in faces.
Billy stood rooted to the spot as he watched two of Hollingsworth's sidekicks emerge from the shadows and close in behind Mike. They both made a grab for him and secured his arms. Hollingsworth, now seeing his adversary was restrained and immobilised emerged from the safety of the far side of the packing crate and closed in menacingly. Mike was struggling, hopelessly to free his arms but the two were hanging on tightly.
"You, my little rich kid, are going to get what we up towners call a real fucking over." He reached into his pocket and pulled out a huge bunch of keys.
Billy didn't need to use his imagination to know what a mess those keys would make of Mike's face. He had seen it often enough around the Tower blocks. Either held between the fingers of a clenched fist or used like a medieval flail if the chain was strong enough, the sharp edges of the keys would tear the soft flesh of the face open in ugly wounds. Mike was going to need medical treatment and would probably bear the scars for the rest of his life. Billy was not about to let this happen to his best mate.
Out the corner of his eye he spied a shovel left leaning against a pillar. It was used to sweep up rubbish, like a long-handled dust pan, but it was the right size and weight for what Billy had in

mind. He grabbed the shovel and with an animal-like howl launched himself at Hollingsworth. Billy swung the shovel in a high arc above his head using the force of his forward movement to add momentum to the weapon. He aimed for the soft pink circle of flesh that was visible through the comb over.

The blade of the shovel connected with the back of Hollingsworth's head with a deep resonant clang, like the ringing of the doomsday bell. Blood shot out of his targets nose and splattered the ground in front of him. The two henchmen fearing they might be the next victims let go of Mike and scarpered out of the loading dock, baying like frightened wolves.

Mike was massaging his wrists as he bent to check on the body on the floor at his feet. Blood was flowing freely from Hollingsworth's nose and dribbling out of his slack mouth, forming a glistening puddle on the floor.

"Have I killed him?" Billy asked nervously.

"You could have, that was one hell of a swing. But no, I think he is just stunned."

As if to confirm Mike's prognosis Hollingsworth let out a slow moan and moved his hand to the back of his head. Still partially face down in his own blood he turned his face to the side and opened an eye. His first sight was of Billy, still clutching the shovel in both hands, like a weapon.

"No," he moaned, "Please don't hurt me." He began to cry like a baby and curled up foetus-like into a ball, covering his head with his arms.

This was the tableaux that greeted the Operations Manager, Mr Scarman when he entered the loading dock a moment later. Hollingsworth's two henchmen had beat a hasty retreat in the direction of his office, hoping to recruit reinforcements to employ in the battle to save their leader. When Scarman had heard, the words spade and kill uttered in the same sentence he had leapt up from his desk, spilling the cup of soup he had been enjoying into his lap, and run the fifty yards from his office to the loading dock. He was not the fittest of individuals and even a short distance sprint had raised his heart rate and caused him to breathe much harder.

He stopped about ten feet from where Hollingsworth was curled up on the ground sobbing with Mike knelt beside him. These two he could ignore, neither looked particularly threatening. The third

member of the tableaux was the clear threat. He was dark and brooding with an evil glint in his eye, wielding a large shovel which was clasped across his chest like a weapon.
"What the blue-buggery is going on here?"
Everybody started to talk at once and Scarman was forced to take a deeper breath and scream at the top of his lungs.
"SILENCE".
This had the desired effect and everyone fell quiet.
"Will someone help poor Hollingsworth to his feet if he can stand or get him a chair if he can't. And you," he pointed an accusatory finger at Billy, "put that damn shovel down now. And will someone get me a paper towel." The soup had soaked one leg of his suit trousers and Scarman wanted to dab the worst of it off before it stained and he was forced to have the whole suit dry-cleaned. One of the henchmen handed him a length of green paper towel and Scarman half walked, half hobbled across the loading bay while cleaning the residue of Tomato soup off his leg. The whole incident had put him in a very bad mood.
Billy let go of the blade end and grounded the shovel but was reluctant to let go of it completely in case he needed it again to defend himself. Mike took his place by his friend's side and left the two henchmen to help their leader to his feet.
Now Hollingsworth realised he was not in danger of imminent death or further injury, some of the old swagger was coming back. He shrugged off his two helpers and stood, all be it rather shakily on his own two feet.
"Mr Hollingsworth would you be so kind as to explain what the devil is going on here."
"Well sir I was attacked with a shovel."
"Now wait a minute." Billy began to object.
"SILENCE." Both men turned on Billy and yelled at him in unison. He took a single step back in surprise. Mike put a hand on his arm to steady him.
"Leave it," he whispered, "they don't want to hear our side of the story."
Mike proved right in his estimation. Hollingsworth told his version of the truth omitting to mention anything about the two henchmen holding Mike or his threat to "really fuck" Mike up, and certainly making no mention of the large bunch of keys. Scarman listened, his face darkening with anger at every word, still dabbing

ineffectually at the soup stain. At the end, he could no longer restrain himself and he cut across his subordinate.
"An unprovoked attack with a deadly weapon and employing deadly force. There is no alternative but instant dismissal. Son go get your coat. There will be a letter sent to your home address explaining your rights and the terms of your dismissal, but I want you off the site in ten minutes' flat. And you might be getting a dry-cleaning bill for my suit as well."
Billy dropped the shovel with a clang and ripped off his work jacket and slung that to the floor beside the shovel. He saw the satisfied look on Hollingsworth face as he walked past him. Billy pulled his fist back a little as if he was about to lash out and attempt to throw a punch at his supervisor's face and was delighted when the man recoiled, flinched and closed his eyes.
Billy laughed manically as he strode from the loading dock to the locker room to collect his coat.
Five minutes later he was strolling through the gate of the compound. He had tossed his Identity badge at the security guard on the way past his hut and when asked had told the guy on duty that he had just clocked Hollingsworth with a shovel and been fired for his trouble. The guard had smiled and muttered, "Good on you son. He's had it coming."
He had barely made it out the gate when a loud whistle stopped him dead in his tracks. Only one person he knew whistled like that. He turned to see Mike running across the yard towards him
"Wait up Billy."
Billy stood still until his friend had caught up with him.
"Are you not working the rest of the shift. They are one driver short now."
"They are two drivers short now. I laughed once too often at Hollingsworth and he said he thought I was owed the extra hours off for time worked in lieu."
"You what? He never did."
"Look already news of events has spread through the warehouse. Everybody wants to shake you by the hand, kiss you or buy you a drink, and in some cases all three at once."
Billy shivered as he recalled the crew he had until just recently called work colleagues.
"Actually, thinking about the guys in the warehouse moving in for a kiss makes me want to puke."

Mike laughed out loud.
"I think it was the girls in the shipping office who were talking about dishing out the kisses."
"Great. I get fired and now they all suddenly get the hots for me. I couldn't get one of them to even give me the time of day when I was working there."
"Ah but now you are a real-life hero. And by the way I owe you one mate. Those guys could have really fucked me up and screwed my plans into the bargain. So, thanks mate."
"I don't think you owe me anything you have been bailing me out of scrapes since day one. This is the first time I have had a chance to repay the favour."
"Consider all debts cancelled and let's go drink a toast to our freedom."
The two friends made a bee-line for the nearest public house and downed a couple of pints each. After they had slaked their thirst they were sat at a table when the subject came up of Billy's future.
"I can have a word with my Dad and see if anyone he knows can use a forklift driver. I am sure he will be prepared to help out when he hears about how you stepped in to save his son."
"Thanks Mike I appreciate your help. I guess I am going to need it."
The incident this afternoon and its inevitable outcome had been the final decider for Billy and as he had strolled out of the Warehouse and across the yard he had made his decision and now it was just a question of putting his plan into effect.
He knew that Mike would never approve so he would have to lose Mike for a couple of hours in order to carry out his plan. That would not be too difficult to achieve. It was nearly three and already they had consumed a couple of pints. Billy would suggest that they take a break and reconvene in a pub in the old town later on in the evening. There might be a few of the other people from work there and Billy might actually get bought a drink or two for his heroic act this afternoon. He was daydreaming now about one of the secretaries who worked in accounts sliding her hands through his hair as she moved in for a kiss.
"Billy, Billy, Earth to Billy." He was back in the present and Mike was standing up and waving an empty glass at him.
"You want one more for the ditch?"
"Yeah I can manage one more."

Mike went up to the bar to get fresh drinks and Billy went back to review his plan.

On paper, it was not the smartest move he could make, but in the short time available to him his options were severely limited. He knew that the repercussions could be serious in the long run but hopefully by the time anyone realised what had happened he would be long gone and hopefully far away.

The two decided this would be their last drink for the afternoon and when they had emptied their glasses they went their separate ways. Mike had not brought his bike with him this morning so he went straight home from the pub. They had already arranged to meet in the Red Lion later that evening. This was the pub favoured by most of the crowd that they worked with as well as a fair few of their former school mates and the girls who had attended the associated girl's school. The Catholic Founders of the two schools and the Board of Education had felt it best if the young were educated separately although Billy had heard a recent rumour that due to falling numbers of Catholic children the two schools may be forced to join together in order to stay open at all. That would have some of the founding Fathers and Reverend Mothers spinning in their caskets.

#

Billy didn't go straight home he made a detour to the tower block across the road from his own. Billy approached the electronic concierge and paused for a minute. He knew the floor he wanted but he couldn't remember the exact flat number. The block was laid out on the same plan as his own so the flat number he required was between 73 and 76 as it was on the 19th Floor. He only had four numbers to choose from, so he picked the middle number and punched it into the keypad. The intercom buzzed and an aggressive voice answered.

"Wot yer want?"

"I'm looking for Delchie."

"Whose looking for Delchie?"

"Billy Randell."

"You Suzie Randell's kid?"

"Yeah I am."

"Come on up."

The door buzzed as the lock was released and Billy pushed his way into the lobby and called the lift.
He started having second thoughts on the way up.
Delchie Matthews and his crew were very naughty boys. If there was an illegal racket going on in this neighbourhood they were in on it and probably owned it. They controlled the prostitution, the gambling and the drugs on the whole of this side of town. But Billy wasn't interested in getting high or getting laid. All the illegal businesses and syndicates generated plenty of dirty cash and as a side-line Delchie Matthews ran a loans business. He was in other words, a loan shark. He loaned money in cash and you paid him back through a bank transfer thus laundering and cleaning the money in the process.
Billy's mum had used Delchie's services a few times in the past to tide her over, hence the reason she was known to his doorman. Of course, his mum had paid Delchie back on time but there were stories whispered in quiet and frightened tones about what happened to people who defaulted on the loans or didn't pay them back on time. This was what was causing Billy to have second thoughts. This crew were truly frightening and there was nowhere a man could go to hide from them. Except Billy concluded, maybe on a Kibbutz in Israel.
For this was in fact Billy's masterplan. He would borrow the money from Delchie Matthews for a month, buy the ticket in the morning and leave the country on Tuesday. He admitted the plan had severe weaknesses and as the lift wheezed to a halt on the 19th Floor, Billy nearly pressed the G button to return the lift to the ground floor. But the doors opened and instead he strode into the hallway.
Across from him the door to flat 74 was ajar so he walked across and pushed it open.
"Hello, anyone at home?"
The thick waft of Cannabis smoke that overwhelmed him brought tears to his eyes. He altered his breathing in order to keep his wits about him and to prevent him from choking.
The first thing that struck Billy, as his eyes adjusted to the fog of smoke in the room, was that the flat was laid out differently to his own dwelling in the tower over the way. For a start most of the interior walls and doors were all gone so the place was just one large open space. The windows of the living room area and the

main bedroom were covered by heavy dark curtains and instead of the usual domestic furniture there were office desks and other business furniture scattered around the room. This space was obviously a place of work rather than low rent council owned accommodation. The only nod towards relaxation was the presence of two large leather sofas in one corner and a huge TV set which was running with the volume turned down low.

There were a handful of individuals lounging around the place with their feet up on desks and other furniture. They seemed, to Billy's untrained eye to fall loosely into two categories. The thinkers and the doers. The thinkers, distinguishable by their smart trousers, suits and shirts were clearly the decision makers, the management team. The doers were the hired muscle, in jeans, t-shirts and leather jackets. They were the enforcers, the persuaders, the leg-breakers. Almost to a man and irrespective of their attire, they looked like a scary bunch.

One of the guys in suit trousers and a shirt swung his legs off the desk and came over to where Billy was waiting.

"You Billy Randell?"

"That's me." Billy nodded

"Come in, take a seat. Delchie will be right with you."

Billy scanned the room and noticed that the main man was not present at the moment. He had never met the man in person, but anyone who lived on this estate knew Delchie Matthews by sight. Billy sat down in the chair that he had been shown to and waited. He didn't have long to wait. A curtain was pulled back and Delchie Matthews entered the room.

Through the curtain, Billy caught sight of the space beyond and realised that he was looking into the flat next door. Delchie's operation occupied the two adjoining flats with the second space clearly set aside for accommodation. Though he only got the briefest of glimpses he caught sight of a large four poster bed with black sheets and pillowcases.

Billy started to wonder how this whole set up was possible and was just arriving at the conclusion that money must be changing hands in order for the local housing authority to turn a blind eye, when Delchie arrived in front of Billy with an outstretched hand.

"Wow, Suzy Randell's little boy is all grown up now."

Delchie's handshake was firm, the palm dry. Billy felt the hard metal of three large rings biting slightly into the soft skin of his own palm, which he hoped was not too sweaty.
Handshake over Delchie took his place behind the largest desk. Billy had a moment while Delchie seated himself to study the man. He was probably in his mid-thirties and looked tanned and fit. He was wearing an expensive looking charcoal grey suit over a white cotton t-shirt. His blonde hair was cut short but in a fashionable style. Apart from the rings on his fingers, the only other jewellery on display was a diamond ear-stud and a rather expensive looking wristwatch. Delchie sat back in his desk chair and studied Billy across the desk.
"You know I don't think I have set eyes on you since you were about seven years old. That was the last time your mum came to see me about a loan. How is she coping these days?"
"Well she has two jobs, but she is managing." Billy realised too late that the enquiry had not been into his mother's financial situation, but more into her general health. He tried to cover it up by adding. "She is well enough."
Delchie chose to ignore the first statement but responded with a nod and a "Good" to the second.
"You must be out of school now. I hope you are working and paying your share."
Billy just nodded, not trusting his voice to what could later be taken as an outright lie. If he didn't mention his recent sacking then he felt it could not be used against him and he knew that Delchie wouldn't lend him a penny if he thought there was any danger that he couldn't repay the loan if full.
"So to business. What brings you to my humble place of work? I know you are not a stoner so it won't be drugs. Maybe you got a grudge you want us to help you with? Or is it that old chestnut money?"
With each of the options Delchie held up a finger.
As the last digit extended Billy nodded his head.
"So you found yourself a little short and you've come to see your old mate Delchie for a loan?"
Billy nodded again.
"What-cha want the money for?"
Billy had not been expecting twenty-one questions. If he had thought it through carefully, even in the lift on the way up he might

have expected some interest in what the loan was for. Obviously, he could not tell the truth. Even the dumbest of loan sharks would not give him one red cent if he told them he was planning to skip the country on Tuesday and he knew that Delchie was far from stupid.

Billy decided to wing it and pray.

"I just got fired from my job today and I know the job market is dodgy at the moment so I thought I might set up on my own. Delivery driver like. The money is for the deposit on a second-hand van".

He looked over at Delchie afraid for a moment at what he might see in his eyes. The green eyes that stared back at him were clear and emotionless.

"You got any contracts lined up yet?"

Billy took a moment before answering. He could maybe invent a couple of imaginary customers and it would take a man with Delchie's connections about ten minutes to prove him a liar, or he could tell his version of the truth. He went with the truth.

"Not really, but I am hoping if the price is right people will come to me."

Delchie nodded. Clearly, he was pleased that Billy hadn't spun him a story about being a millionaire overnight.

"Well my old mate if the price is right I might have a few delivery jobs that I could bung your way. Just to get you started. Whatcha think?"

Billy guessed that this offer could be a poisoned chalice. Anything that Delchie wanted delivering was probably illegal from the outset, either contraband like drugs, or illegal due to the fact that it had been liberated from someone else's possession.

He thought for a moment. To reject Delchie outright could cause offence and maybe lead to a refusal. Against his better judgement, he nodded his head agreeing to the offer.

"Good," Delchie seemed satisfied with the answer. "So how much you need. A set of decent wheels are gonna set you back a bit. A couple of grand maybe?"

Billy thought for a moment. He was gonna do a runner owing Delchie Matthews two thousand pounds. If he said no, he could manage with just a thousand then, again, the suspicions might arise. He had no idea how much a second-hand van might cost and guessed that the man sitting opposite him had more idea of the prices in the used car market. He guessed that if Delchie was proposing to lend him two thousand pounds then he had better accept, simply to avoid suspicion. And then another thought occurred to him. He realised that if he was careful and left some of the money in the bank at least he could offer to repay some of the loan should his plan fail, and he did not manage to get clean away. In the end it might be the difference between a beating and serious injury.

"Yeah, I guess a couple of grand would cover it." Billy tried to sound nonchalant but every fibre of his being was screaming and the adrenalin was making his heart pump faster.

Delchie looked over at one of his lieutenants.

"Stevie get the man his money. I will write up the contract."

Stevie was one of the other suited and booted individuals. Clearly a lieutenant and someone Delchie trusted if he knew the combination to the safe.

While Stevie went off to another room to collect the money, Delchie drew a pre-printed form out of a drawer and began filling in the blanks.

There were only a half-dozen boxes on the form and by the time Stevie returned with a pile of banknotes Delchie had completed his task.

Stevie placed the notes in the middle of the desk. Delchie checked the bindings on the notes to see what he was lending out and then when he had the final count he filled in the last box on the form, swivelled it around and pushed it across the desk. At the same time, he pulled out a wicked looking stiletto and popped out the blade. He tossed the blade on the desk and straight afterwards a goose feather. They both landed in the centre of the paper contract on the middle of the desk.

"Right if you could just open a vein for me, dip the quill in the blood and sign the bottom of the form."

The instructions were delivered completely deadpan, with no emotion showing in his face. The silence around the room told Billy that this was a serious part of their transaction. He picked up the knife and pulled up the sleeve of his shirt, starring at the blue vein that was pulsing at his wrist. He gulped and moved the point of the blade closer.

"Naaaaaahhhh. I was shitting with you." Delchie's eyes were now alive with mirth, and behind him Billy heard one or two guffaws of laughter from the assembled crew.

"We do that for kicks. Sorry kid." He looked over at his crew. "I do believe the kid was going to do it." As if this was the cue they had all been waiting for, all the men in the room burst out laughing.

Billy's ears burned at the humiliation. Maybe, he thought to himself it is good that I am about to skip the country with this money. At least for once in my life I will have the last laugh.

Delchie tossed a Bic biro across the desk.

"Here sign with this."

Billy scribbled his signature in the space at the bottom of the contract, noticing ironically, that the biro contained blood red ink. From out of another drawer in the desk Delchie produced, of all things, a McDonalds take away bag which he opened and placed the money inside.

"No point in drawing attention. Nobody's gonna nick yer takeaway."

He rolled the bag shut, just like they did in the restaurant and placed it on the middle of the desk.

Billy looked at the bag and then at Delchie. Was this it? Were they finished? Could he just grab the bag and walk out?

He hesitated, waiting for some signal from the man that their business was concluded.

Delchie had sat back in his big chair and steepled his fingers under his chin.

"Is there anything else I can help you with, partner?" There was a heavy emphasis on the last word that made Billy squirm a little inside. He was very careful not to let it show on his face.

"I can't think of anything right now." He almost stammered

"What about your recent labour problems is there anyone we could maybe teach a lesson on your behalf?"

This set Billy thinking. Could he really stoop so low on the human scale? He was sitting here surrounded by a room full of mad men, who at a word from him would go and gladly mess up Pete Hollingsworth. The man had been the bane of his life for the past year or so and to be able to get even would be a huge personal victory. The question was would Hollingsworth receiving a beating make Billy feel better as a person?

He had to admit to himself that the answer was no it would not make him feel better. He was on the point of saying thanks but no thanks when he thought about the next poor sad sack that fell under the control of Pete Hollingsworth and the misery that the poor guy's life would become as a result of this situation. In reality he might be helping someone he didn't know and would never be likely to meet, but somehow that made it worthwhile.

Billy made his decision and told Delchie exactly what he wanted to happen. He even stressed he wanted the guy hospitalised for a short period but not crippled for life and gave his reasons, his personal justifications for wanting the beating to happen. He was hoping that by stating his reasons out loud it might make him feel better about what he was asking for. It didn't. And his personal justifications were of no concern to the man sitting opposite or the rest of the assembled group in the room. They just wanted an excuse to do someone harm and this lad sitting there in their midst had just given them a golden excuse.

Delchie listened for the duration of Billy's spiel and then nodded his head.

"Very noble of you my son. Consider it done. You happen to know where the bugger lives?"

Billy happened to know the address off the top of his head and as he recited it, Delchie wrote it down on a piece of paper.

"Right well we will take care of that for you. And I will be in touch with you at the end of next week or you can contact me when you have the van and are ready to do some work."

Delchie stood up and picked up the McDonalds bag in his right hand, at the same time he extended his left hand towards Billy. Billy stood up too and seeing the outstretched hand offered his own. The two shook hands and Delchie handed over the money. With the transaction at an end Delchie almost immediately lost interest in Billy and started talking over his head to his followers. Billy sensing his presence was no longer required beat a hasty retreat in the direction of the door and out into the hallway. The lift opened as soon as he hit the down button and he took a step forward and hit the button for the ground floor.

Almost as soon as the door closed and the lift lurched into motion, Billy felt his knees go weak and his head start to spin.

What the fuck had he just done? What had he let himself in for? He was intending to rip-off one of the craziest people this town had ever given birth to. And for what?

He barely managed to stagger the hundred metres from the base of Delchie's tower over to his own block and then up to his own floor and apartment. He collapsed face down on the bed in his room and placed a pillow over his head as he let out a slow moan of despair. He knew he was a dead man walking

.

CHAPTER Three

The effect of afternoon drinking combined with the rush of adrenalin he had experienced whilst visiting Delchie Matthews had put Billy to sleep, the sound of his mother arriving home woke him up. She called out from the hallway as she let herself in the front door.
Billy sat up and tossed aside the pillow. His eyes fell immediately on the McDonalds bag, lying on the chair where he had dropped it. He did not want to have to explain the money to his mum so he leapt off the bed and scooped up the bag, threw it in the bottom of the wardrobe and slammed the door, turning around just in time to see his mum enter the room. The guilt must have been apparent on his face but his mother misinterpreted it.
"Aren't we getting a little old to be hiding porn in the wardrobe?" Billy probably turned an extra deep shade of red at such an accusation from his own mother.
"It's not porn Mum, I swear."
"Well OK. I will be annoyed if you have some good stuff in there and are not sharing it." She winked at him mocking his discomfort, before she burst out laughing, turned on her heels and left the room. Over her shoulder she called back, "Are you going out tonight?"
Billy was still spluttering and trying to regain the power of speech after his mother's little outburst, but he did manage to croak, "Yes we are all meeting at the Red Lion later."
"How much later?" his mum asked, "It's nearly eight-thirty now."
Billy glanced down at the alarm clock, the one he never set because Mike always came by to wake him up. The angry red numbers blazed back at him. 20:24.

Billy was changed and out the door before the clock made it to eight-thirty and he half ran, half jogged across the town to the Red Lion.

The main bar was packed with people he knew and it took him several minutes to find his way through the crush to where Mike was holding court. Along the way, he noticed several sympathetic looks from people and the odd hand reached out to pat him on his back or grab and squeeze his arm or shoulder.

It took Billy a few moments to realise what was happening. All these people, some who had known him since that very first day in school had heard the news about Mike's imminent departure and were offering him their sympathy, as if he was losing a friend forever. At one-point Billy wanted to stop, stand on a chair and shout out to the assembled throng, "Stop with all the compassion, will you? I am going with him."

But Billy knew that one idle comment at this time could easily get back to the ears of Delchie Matthews and he would probably spend the next month in a hospital bed, not on a farm in Israel.

When he finally located Mike holding court at one of the large circular tables in the very back of the bar people automatically scooted over to make room for him to sit down and join the group and someone handed him a pint of lager.

Mike was in the middle of explaining the reasons behind his decision to leave the country and go travelling and what he was expecting to happen over the next few weeks. The whole Kibbutz experience was familiar to many of the assembled audience. Some of them had other friends, older siblings or other family members who had made the trip and had stories they could offer although they were all of the "I have heard" anecdotal variety. These recollections came from right across the experience spectrum. Everybody around the table seemed to know someone who had ventured over to Israel and done the "Kibbutz Thing" so all seemed to be qualified to offer a name of a particular settlement and their relative or friend's opinion of the place. Some could offer more detail and even go as far as to relate stories of happenings among the Volunteers. As these stories were told and opinions were offered, Billy noticed a pattern developing.

Some people had clearly gone there and loved the place and others had gone there and returned quickly with horror stories about the conditions. Billy found that his pessimistic nature made him pay more attention to the negatives, as experience had taught him that this was all he could expect from life. So, although he joined in laughing at the funnier stories told, and particularly the ones that concerned excessive drinking or practical jokes, he made a mental note about all the awful things too.

And it was these that he returned to later on when he lay awake in the early hours of the morning. In the dark stillness of his bedroom Billy lay on top of the duvet. He could not sleep, not because he wasn't tired, every fibre of his being screamed out for sleep, but because his mind was working overtime. He was processing the information he had received during the evening and sorting through it, filing it away in various places. He was, at the same time making plans about how to deal with some of the more extreme situations he had heard about. Were there steps he could take before he left home, to diminish the impact of some of these incidents?

A third string of thoughts consisted of mentally composing a list of items he would need to purchase the following day to take with him and in the light of some of the episodes he had heard about, that list was becoming longer by the minute.

It was ironic that the negative aspects of the imminent adventure were the ones that had left the greater impact on Billy and while stories of primitive living conditions in buildings that in the UK would have been demolished and where the bathroom facilities were third world in standard, the whole place infested with rats, cockroaches, killer spiders, snakes and scorpions, should have filled Billy with a strong desire to forget the whole exercise, he found he was instead compensating for them and trying to find solutions.

The other negatives he could deal with. They were mainly in the areas of food standards and work. The cynics were quick to point out that the food was inedible, well they had maybe never tried to eat some of the things Billy had cooked in the past, and the work was like slave labour. Again, they had probably never had to work at some of the heartless and depressing jobs that Billy had endured since leaving school.

So, as he lay there, Billy managed to convince himself that with a plentiful supply of insect repellent and bite cream, a moderate supply of luxuries like Jam, Marmite and Tea Bags, he could easily endure the three months "in hell" that some of the nay-sayers had been describing.

#

He must have dropped off at some point because the alarm woke him at eight AM sharp and he threw off the covers and leapt out of bed. He had a long list of things to accomplish today and he was keen to be about his business. His first job was to assess the size of his problem.

While in the pub the previous evening Mike had been brandishing around the "Introduction to the Kibbutz Experience" pamphlet for all to see. Billy, feigning a genuine interest in Mike's future had managed to secure the loan of the glossy brochure and sufficient time to read and make mental note of the contents. Among the information contained in the list had been a recommended list of items that the new Volunteer should bring with them.

He could not remember every detail of the list but working from memory he now wrote his own list and tried to sort through his own possessions to find what he had and what was missing and would need purchasing.

The first item on the list had been a plentiful supply of light-coloured t-shirts. Billy sorted through all his drawers and the dirty linen basket and assembled all his t-shirts. He had never considered his choice in t-shirt colours before but as he stared at the sorry pile in front of him he noticed a particular theme running through the items. They were mostly black or dark in colour. The predominance of band "tour" t-shirts ensured this was the case and although one or two of the "Alternative" bands had been alternative enough to sell white tour t-shirts the dominating colour was black. He felt that one or two could be dark in colour as the sun wouldn't shine all the time but the pitiful pile that he put on the bed told him that a trip to a store selling t-shirts was on the cards for today. Likewise, he didn't own a single pair of shorts of any description. The last time that Billy had worn proper shorts was when he was a schoolboy of nine. He had made the move to long trousers as soon as was allowed by the school authorities and with the exception of a pair of football shorts he had worn in physical education he had never worn shorts since. He did possess one snazzy pair of Bermuda style beach shorts but despite searching everywhere he was unable to locate them. He sat on his bed and thought long and hard and then he realised they were probably somewhere at Mike's house as the last time he had worn them had been the previous summer when Mike had thrown a poolside party. Given the clandestine nature of his plan to join Mike on this trip he couldn't very well swan round there and ask for them back. Instead he added Bermuda shorts to the list of items he would need to buy. The letter had recommended a couple of pairs of ordinary shorts as well so he added those to his shopping list underneath the Bermudas.

Next on the list had been a pair of good strong boots. Those Billy had in abundance. The majority of his footwear could be classed as "good strong boots". So, Billy selected the pair that looked like they might last the longest and chucked those on the bed. By the time, he had added underwear and a thick sweater, to wear on cooler evenings, he was just about finished with what he possessed currently that would be suitable to take with him.

The small, sad pile of items would just about fill a supermarket carrier bag. Billy knew it was time to go shopping.

But first he needed to take all the clothes he was taking with him and get them clean.

At the local parade of shops there was a laundromat and he dropped by to see them.

He was never sure exactly when the place opened and closed, if indeed it ever closed, but every time he passed the place, night or day, the windows were steamed up and opaque with condensation and the machines were on and turning.

Janice, the woman who owned the place was an old friend of his mother and she greeted him as he walked in the place.

Like a million laundromats the world over, the temperature inside the place was a dozen degrees higher than that outside. In the winter this gave the place an inner warmth and a cosy feel. In the summer the place became like a Swedish sauna. On days like today it was merely a comfortable change in temperature.

The clientele, this early in the day, were few in number and generally uninteresting. An older man was sat at one end of the bench reading one of the red-top newspapers. At the other end of the wooden bench an elderly lady was engrossed in her crochet work. The third occupant caught Billy's eye for a moment. She definitely looked out of place here. The quality of her clothes spoke to a different social class, certainly one that could afford to own a washing machine and tumble drier. She was clearly out of her element and was perched on the edge of one of the plastic chairs that faced the large tumble driers. She was glancing around her every few minutes, as if she was expecting to get mugged at knifepoint.

As Billy drew level with her he smiled at her but rather than helping to reassure the woman it seemed to have the opposite effect. Billy glanced in the drier as he passed and saw the tell-tale white of a duvet spinning there. This explained everything. The presence of several others, still wet, in a plastic bag on the floor told Billy that she was here only to use the driers as her own drier at home could not handle the bulk of the heavy bedding when it was wet.

At the very back of the shop stood the owner. Janice had probably been a stunner as a young lady, but now in middle age, the peroxide blonde hair, heavy makeup and false eyelashes made her look slutty. Under her yellow uniform coat, she was dressed as if she had just returned from a night at a Seventies disco, her ample, orange perma-tanned cleavage encased in some sort of spandex boob-tube and her abundant hips and legs in tight black leggings. On her feet she wore white sandals, her fire engine red toe nails peeking out of the open end. One arm was heavy with costume jewellery bangles, the other, hand cocked was holding a lit cigarette, which she puffed on from time to time.

He had sorted his clothes into two piles, colours and whites and handed the two bags over to Janice.

"Can you do these as a Service wash today?"

"Aw come on Billy, what's the rush? You know Saturday's are my busiest day."

"Please Janice as a favour." Billy didn't want to have to go into details with Janice as she was renowned in the locality as the source and supply of all gossip and whatever she knew was quickly known throughout the local community. Billy knew that telling her anything would be the same as taking out a huge advertising hoarding on the side of one of the tower blocks.

"All-right as it's you, put em out the back and I will do em later on this morning. They will be ready after lunch."

"Thanks Janice I owe you one?"

"Yes, you certainly do young man." She winked seductively at Billy.

Billy had the good sense to blush as he made his excuses and left the place.

The travel agent was empty as he pushed open the door except for the young assistant who had answered his query the previous day. She was pretending to work while scanning the pages of a fashion magazine as the doorbell pinged when Billy entered. She looked up apprehensively, probably expecting the store manager, while attempting to push the magazine off the desktop and into the waiting maw of her handbag.

"Good Morning, how can I help you?" She smiled at Billy and then he saw recognition in her eyes.

"No wait. I remember you. You were here yesterday. No, don't tell me. I will remember. It's what I am good at." She paused for a moment searching her memory.

"Got it." She exclaimed with obvious delight. "It was yesterday lunchtime, you were asking about flights to Tel Aviv. Am I right?"

Billy nodded his head unsure how to answer this apparent gushing enthusiasm. Either this girl was interested in him, which he doubted, or she led such a humdrum life spent mostly booking all-inclusive packages to the Costas, the Balearics or the Greek Islands that his enquiry had been rather unusual, at least unusual enough to have been memorable. This, Billy felt, was the more logical explanation.

"Er, Yes, that's right." Billy fished in his pocket for the now very crumpled piece of paper with the flight details scribbled on it and handed it across the counter.

He watched the girl as she input the details into the travel computer system.

She looked up and they made eye contact and she smiled again. Billy began to study the young lady as she bent over her keyboard. Yesterday she hadn't struck him as anything particularly special, just another mousy-haired shop assistant type. But today there was something different. Her hair, yesterday in a tight bun was now let down and cascading to her shoulders in rich glossy dark curls. Her face was artfully made up to highlight her eyes, now freed from the heavy rimmed spectacles of the previous day. Her clothes had also been carefully picked. The skirt was figure forming in all the right places. She must be going straight from work to a function somewhere and not have time to go home and change.

As he leaned on the counter he looked down and was instantly aware of the open neck of the young lady's blouse and the visibility of white lace and soft pink flesh. He immediately looked away anxious not to be caught staring. He looked around the rest of the shop but his eyes were drawn back for a second glance conscious that his heart rate was slightly elevated and his palms were sweaty. He looked away again and wiped his hands on the front of his t-shirt.

After a few more minutes the assistant was finished with her keyboard work and ready for him.

She asked his name and address and input all his details into the computer before she took his money and printed out his ticket and folded it into one of their cardboard ticket holders and handed it over to him.

"Have a fantastic trip and come back and tell me all about it when you get back."

Billy paused for a moment searching the young ladies face for any trace of mockery, but her face was open and showed no sign of ridicule. This confused Billy even more and he struggled to find his tongue.

"Er yeah OK."

"Make sure you do." She smiled "So tonight will be your last Saturday night in town. Have you got any special plans?"

"Not really. Might just go to the pub."

"Really. Which one is your local?"

"The Red Lion up the Old Town."

"OK well I might see you there later."

This last sentence floored Billy completely. As the girl smiled at him he managed a weak smile back before she turned to serve the next customer. Billy had been so enthralled with the young shop assistant and her enthusiastic attention that he had not even heard the shop's doorbell go and jumped as he realised there was someone else waiting to be served.

He pocketed the ticket and left the shop in a welter of embarrassment.

Did that mean she was going to be at the Red Lion pub anyway, with a group of friends or was she coming to the Pub to see him

specifically. It was too late to go back in and ask for clarification, he would just have to wing it tonight and see what happened.
His next planned stop was on the other side of the town centre but along the way, as most of the shops were now open for business he ambled in and out of the various clothes shops looking at t-shirts and shorts, short sleeved shirts, polo shirts in the whole rainbow spectrum of colours, adding by small increments to his inventory of new clothes.
By the time, he reached his destination he had two large carrier bags from a leading men's clothing store containing all his purchases.
The Worldaway Sports and Adventure store was a large double fronted shop located on one of the side streets away from the main pedestrian shopping area of the town. Some wag in the store management had played on that fact because a hand drawn sign in the window proclaimed, "We are off the beaten track so you can go there in style."
As an advertising slogan it was pretty weak but Billy got the point of the joke and if there was any doubt about what the shop had to offer, then the displays in the windows gave enough inspiration to the would-be adventurer.
The first window display had two mannequins posed in an alpine environment with fake snow on the ground and both the male and female figures dressed head to foot in foul weather clothing. As well as the large igloo tent that was precariously pitched at a forty-five degree angle up the internal wall of the window display, the rest of the rocky diorama was scattered with every piece of equipment a couple venturing into an alpine environment could ever possibly need, from a small pocket compass, through a rather groovy looking gas cooker and cooking utensil set that packed together into a container the size of a large cake tin, to a range of rather cosy looking sleeping bags, in a large range of bright colours, that were hung from the branches of an artificial pine tree.
The second window contained a similar rugged display. Another mountainous and snowy backdrop had the mannequin couple posed artfully in what looked to be half a canoe. The rest of the accessories scattered around comprised everything our adventurous couple might need to turn a journey by canoe into more of a five-star cruise on an ocean liner.

Billy took a moment to absorb all that the window displays had to offer before he pushed the door open and entered the shop.

It was not a particularly warm day out and Billy had pulled on a jacket before he left the flat, but entering Worldaway he got the impression that the temperature had dropped another ten degrees. Obviously, this was a marketing ploy by the management who felt that in order for the customer to appreciate the full value of their wonderful range of alpine clothing one should at least have the opportunity to test them in sub-arctic conditions.

Billy pulled his jacket closed around him and ventured further into the store.

On all sides the clothing carousels were hung with heavy weather clothing in a range of dazzling colours, rain clothing, fleece tops, with and without hoods, ski jackets and trousers. The wall displays were hung with tents, sleeping bags, skis, snowboards and posters of rugged looking men and women in a range of outdoor locations from the high alps to the beach.

As Billy stood in the middle of the store he looked carefully for the section of the store that might cater for his particular needs. He was sure that while the majority of the clothing on display would keep him extremely warm he didn't think it would be relevant in the hot desert environment of an Israeli summer. But while there were large colourful and helpful signs with words like Ski and Climb and Canoe on them, he could not see anything which said Desert or anything close. He decided to approach the staff and ask for some help.

He could see three shop assistants in the general area of the sales desk so he made his way in their direction. As he got closer one of the assistants stood up and addressed the other two.

"Who wants a coffee?" He collected the mugs and disappeared towards the back of the store.

The other two were engrossed in other tasks, one was cross-referencing a paper document with some data from a computer screen the other was stood with a phone pressed close to his ear. Both seemed to want to ignore Billy, but Billy had plenty of time so he waited patiently, figuring that if he waited long enough in plain sight then someone would eventually take pity on him and offer him some assistance.

The three assistants were all about the same age as Billy and he figured that given their wan and pasty complexions, none of them

had ventured further than the south coast of England. He figured there had to be someone else, someone more knowledgeable about all things travel related, a manager or senior assistant. Billy hung around the sales desk until the coffee maker returned. He placed the three mugs on the countertop and then clearly as there were nothing else that could occupy his time he turned to Billy.
"How can I help you today?"
This totally took Billy by surprise and he had to focus for a moment to remember exactly what he had come here for.
"Er. Yeah, I am looking for a sleeping bag."
"Certainly sir. Right this way." The assistant led the way towards the back of the shop where the wall display contained an artfully arranged display of sleeping bags, the zips partially undone and the bags folded open like a bed turned down and ready for climbing into. They all looked very inviting to Billy.
At floor level the shelves were piled high with all the sleeping bags rolled up and in their carry bags.
The assistant reached the centre of the area and turned around to face Billy.
"So what sort of sleeping bag are you looking for?"
Billy was about to answer the cheapest, but then he remembered the money from Delchie that was burning a hole in his pocket. Knowing money was no object and knowing absolutely nothing about sleeping bags he threw the question back at the assistant.
"Which one would you recommend?"
This invitation seemed to please the assistant who welcomed the chance to show off his fledgling knowledge of sleeping bags gleaned at a recent manufacturers training course. He didn't really know that much, but what little knowledge he had he wanted to be able to share. He launched into a long and very complicated sales spiel about comparative tog ratings and how the higher the number was so the thicker the bag was and as a result the warmer the bag was. He was even able to quote relative temperatures and which particular tog rating would ensure the user was kept warm and comfortable at minus temperatures.
When the sales assistant had reached the dizzy heights of minus thirty Celsius Billy put up a hand to stop him.
"I am actually going to Israel so I need a bag that will do well in much warmer climates."
That seemed to completely knock the sales assistant off course.

"Does it never get cold there?"
"Well I guess it must get cold in the Winter?" Billy didn't know for certain but he felt sure it might get a little cooler at night in the Winter.
"How cold?" The sales assistant was desperate to get back to a place where he felt comfortable and where his recent training could kick back in again.
Billy blew out through his teeth.
"Not that cold I guess." He really didn't have any clue. "I was kinda hoping you might be able to help me out with that."
The two young men stood for a moment both wracked by indecision and neither wanting to lose face by admitting they lacked the knowledge.
Billy broke first.
"I guess I should take a bag that is somewhere around the middle, not too hot and not to cold."
As soon as the words were out of his mouth Billy realised too late that he was sounding like he was in a bad version of the fairytale story Goldilocks and the Three Bears and he cringed inwardly. The sales assistant had clearly missed the literary reference and instead had moved to the section of shelves that contained the sleeping bags in the range "not too hot and not too cold."
"Any particular colour?"
Billy chose one in a dark blue.
He added to the purchase of a sleeping bag a rather fetching under mat and rain cover before they moved over to the section of the shop that contained back packs and rucksacks.
Here again it seemed that most of the items on sale were more for going up a mountain with all kinds of groovy loops and fixtures for safety ropes and ice axes, things that Billy could not see himself ever needing in a desert environment.
But again, they settled on a compromise. It was a large pack but there were special fixings for the sleeping bag and the mat on the outside, so they would not take up space inside the pack.
Billy paid cash for the items and got a small day pack thrown in as a bonus gift. He put everything together and packed his bags containing his new clothes inside the rucksack before slinging it on one shoulder and heading back across town.
On the way back to his flat he stopped in a sports shop where he managed to pick up a couple of pairs of Bermuda shorts and a sun

hat that he felt didn't make him look like a complete prat. Standing by the till waiting to pay his eyes were drawn to the carousel display of sunglasses. He didn't possess a decent pair so while he waited patiently to be served he tried a few pairs on using the small mirror to check the effect. Deciding that a certain pair worked he added them and a case to the pile and when it was his turn he placed the pile on the counter with the sunglasses balanced on the top. More cash exchanged hands and the new items were packed into the rucksack along with his other clothes.

His last stop had been planned from the start and his route around the town centre had been laid out so this would be his last stop before heading home. On this, the last parade of shops before the end of the shopping centre was the town's main electronics superstore.

When he had worked out the finance for the trip he had made provision for the purchase of a small personal stereo. Now with the extra funds from Delchie he could afford to raise his sights a little. He spent some time browsing in the portable stereo section, checking out the prices and reading the features cards of each of the individual items.

He had read in Mike's letter about the poor security offered on the Kibbutz and their recommendation that Volunteers didn't bring expensive items like stereos, watches or cameras with them. Billy had never owned a camera or for that matter an expensive watch, and his cheap watch would definitely only be attractive to the most desperate of thieves.

But then again, he had never owned his own stereo, always relying on a small transistor radio for the music in his life. His mother owned a record player and a cringe worthy collection of compilation albums from companies like K-Tel and Ronco. Billy, like most kids his age, had a pile of cassettes, mix tapes, often given as love tokens, but they had sat on the window ledge in his room gathering dust, never removed from their boxes.

Now he eyed up a particularly sleek looking cassette player from the Sony Corporation. It was white, so it stood out from all the others in the department which were the standard black. He checked the price tag one more time then swiped one of the tickets off the display and went to the cashier point to pay and collect his purchase. With the bag containing the new stereo in one hand and the rucksack over his shoulder he was on his way towards the exit when something made him stop dead in his tracks. It was if the money in his pocket was acting like a magnet and without realising it he found himself in front of the camera display.

He was not a photography expert, not even an interested amateur but he felt a desire to at least attempt to document their time away. There were some quite cool looking compact cameras, at reasonable prices. He settled on a model that the sales assistant assured him was fool proof which suited Billy down to the ground. He also bought a case and a dozen rolls of film. The whole lot fitted nicely into one of the external side pockets of his rucksack and he re-shouldered the rucksack and set off for home. He was not totally stupid so he took a circuitous route home and approached his apartment block from the opposite direction in order to avoid any prying eyes or casual observation from Delchie's block. He made it back to the safety of his own bedroom without meeting a soul.

He dumped his rucksack and headed off to collect his washing from the laundromat and when he returned with the two bags of washing he laid out everything on the bed and began to pack his rucksack. He managed to get everything into the large rucksack and he still had some space in the top for more stuff. He stood the new rucksack in the corner of the room and chucked a blanket over it to conceal it from prying eyes.

After he had finished he rustled up a cheese sandwich and went through to the living room. There was a light flashing on the answer machine so he pressed the message play button.

The single message was from Mike. He explained that his parents had decided to throw a surprise going away party for him and invited all the family. He was hoping that like most family parties the whole thing would be over by early evening and he could meet up as they had arranged.

Billy wiped the message and sat back to watch an afternoon of sport on TV.

\#

He was still on the sofa when his mum got back from her shift at the supermarket with two bags of shopping. As they were putting the contents away in cupboards and the freezer she asked Billy about his plans for next week.

"Mrs Turnbull was in the store today and she says you were given your marching orders on Friday."

"That's right mum. I had an argument with Hollingsworth."

"You threatened him with a shovel" His mum had a note of disapproval in her voice.

Billy was relieved that the busybody Mrs Turnbull's source had not known the full details of the attack with the shovel.

"Son, why did you go and do a thing like that?"

"He was about to beat up Mike."

"I bet Mike was more than capable of dealing with it himself and he didn't lose his job I bet."

"No mum, he quit. That's why Hollingsworth was going to do him in. He had two of his men holding Mike and he was about to key him. That's why I lashed out"

As Billy watched his mum turned a strange shade of white. He didn't know whether it was because she had imagined the damage that might have been done to Mike's face or the fact that her own flesh and blood had attacked someone violently with a shovel. His mum took a deep breath and swallowed before she continued.

"Why did he quit?"

"Because he is leaving on Tuesday and going to stay on a Kibbutz."

" A Kibb. what?"

"A Kibbutz, mum, in Israel."

"And I suppose you are going with him."

"Yes mum as a matter of fact I am."

"Who put this stupid idea in your head. I thought Mike had more sense."

"It wasn't Mike's idea for me to go. He doesn't even know yet."

"Doesn't know what?"

"That I am going with him."

"And who is paying for all this globetrotting?"

"I am mum."

Billy wanted the conversation to end now. He did not want to have to explain where he had got the money for the trip from. He knew that his mum would never understand and even though she had used Delchie herself in the past she had always borrowed money with the full intention of paying it back, not skipping the country. He knew that would be the next question out of his mother's mouth so he was relieved when he heard the doorbell ring.

It was a relief that would be exceedingly short lived.
Billy opened the door and was confronted by a Police warrant card held by a very angry looking policeman in plain clothes.
"I'm Detective Sergeant Harrison," he thumbed over his shoulder at the second person standing slightly behind him.
"This is DC Smith, we want to ask you a few questions about last night. Can we come in?"
Billy didn't get chance to read the details on the warrant card before it was whipped away but it looked authentic enough for him to stand back and allow the two officers to pass him.
The looming presence of two detectives and Billy made the small hallway exceedingly cramped and an uncomfortable place to conduct an interview.
"Do you want to go through there." Billy waved in the general direction of the living room.
Harrison led the way followed by Smith and Billy brought up the rear. By the time, he got in the room his mother was on her feet trying to rearrange cushions on the sofa and tidy up the general detritus that was always left lying around. Billy thought she looked like a junkie trying to hide her stash during a raid and that thought bought a slight smile to his face. He was still grinning a little when the two officers turned their attention on him.
His mother had offered them both seats on the sofa, Billy had taken an armchair and his mother had shuffled off into the Kitchen to make some coffee.
Billy got his first chance to size up the two. He couldn't call them policemen because one was clearly a woman, although that had not been clear at first in the dim light of the hallway. Now with space and distance and a little perspective he could see that although the lead detective, Harrison was a man, his assistant DC Smith was a woman. Not an overtly attractive woman, but a woman nonetheless.
She was wearing baggy beige trousers and a badly shaped jacket, like a combat jacket, but in a rather drab beige colour rather than combat green. On her feet, she wore heavy Doc Martin shoes. Her hair was mousy and cropped in a tight bob. She wore the merest trace of makeup. Billy wondered if her almost masculine appearance was an attempt to secure her position in a world dominated by macho males.

Harrison looked to be one of those men's men. He was wearing a cheap suit and a grotty shirt with a polyester tie which showed obvious signs of a pie and mash lunch. Although he looked young, his hairline was clearly heading north at the same speed as his waistline was heading south. He probably still had enough youthful vigour to turn out regularly for the Police Rugby team and a slight blue tinge on his cheek from a fading bruise suggested that he had either recently played a game and caught a stray elbow or had caught a stray fist in the course of making an arrest.

The two detectives were in turn taking a moment to size up Billy. They knew why they were here and neither of them could quite believe that this wretched individual sat opposite them was responsible for the damage they had just witnessed first-hand at the hospital.

The Detective Inspector leading the enquiry had been asking the questions and the two witnesses had both been adamant in their testimony. As work colleagues they were able to describe the violence that had taken place the previous afternoon at their place of work and they were able to name a name. Harrison and Smith had been dispatched here to interview the "prime suspect."

DC Smith had extracted a note pad from her pocket and was poised with a pencil to take notes. DS Harrison was also consulting his notebook keen to get some detail of the coming questioning correct.

"Now Billy," he started in a familiar and matey fashion, "We are making enquiries about a very serious incident that took place between 10 and 10:30 PM last night. Can you tell us where you were at that time?"

Billy who had leaned slightly forward at the start of the question, tense, because after all this was the Police and they were interviewing him, relaxed visibly and sat back in the chair.

"I was at the Red Lion Pub in the Old Town."

"Can anyone verify this?"

"Well I was with a group of people that varied in size from twenty to thirty throughout the evening but most of them will confirm my whereabouts."

Billy noticed a look of disappointment flash across Harrison's face. He had clearly been hoping that he could bang Billy up in a cell and effectively wrap up their investigation tonight and enjoy the rest of the weekend free.

"So you never left the Pub? Not even to go down the chippy?" Harrison was clearly clutching at straws.

"No I was in the Public Bar all night."

"What's this all about?" Billy's mum had returned carrying a tray full of coffee cups, a milk jug and sugar bowl. Out in the kitchen with the kettle boiling she had missed the opening questions but she was keen to get up to speed as quickly as possible.

"Mrs Randell, we are following up some serious allegations made against your son."

"What sort of allegations?"

"Allegations of assault."

"Assault? Billy? Be serious." She snorted as she handed out the coffee cups. "Who is he supposed to have assaulted?"

"A Mister Hollingsworth."

Billy's mum stopped dead, her hand poised over the sugar bowl, the spoon in her hand started to shake slightly scattering the contents all over the tray.

"But that was…" Her voice tailed off into silence. She did not want to offer the Police any extra information.

"Yes Mrs Randell. We know about Billy's altercation, the one that took place yesterday at work. But this is more serious. Last night between ten and ten-thirty someone beat Peter Hollingsworth to within an inch of his life. It was brutal attack with a weapon or weapons and the poor guy will be in hospital for a month and may never recover the full use of his legs. He will certainly not be working for several months. At first the doctors only gave him a fifty-fifty chance of survival. So, we are taking this assault very seriously and given that witnesses have already come forward to tell us about the incident yesterday afternoon and a spokesman for the company has confirmed that Billy was sacked following yesterday's altercation. He has fallen into place as a number one suspect."

"But he said he has witnesses." Billy's mum knew enough about the criminal justice system to know that Billy was in deep trouble. As weapons had been used the Police would have little trouble proving that there was intent beforehand and that put the whole case into the more serious bracket where sentences could go as high as life imprisonment.

"If his alibi holds up then that will be the end of it." DC Smith had spoken for the first time. She could obviously sense the panic and

desperation that was creeping into Mrs Randell's voice. Her
intervention, however humane, did not sit well with the Detective
Sergeant who shot her a withering look before continuing.
"We will need the names of those witnesses and addresses if you
have them."
"If it's the usual crowd you can find them most nights in the Public
Bar of the Red Lion. Isn't that right Billy?"
"Yeah. Most of them will be there tonight I should think."
Billy was now growing in confidence. Knowing that the incident
the previous afternoon had been eclipsed by events last night and
that there was no likelihood of the shovel attack now amounting to
anything was a relief. That Delchie's justice had been so swift and
so devastating however filled him with fear on a whole new level.
He realised that Harrison was asking him another question and
focused on what he was saying.
"...subject can you think of anyone else who had a grudge against
Mr Hollingsworth?"
Billy didn't even pause to think before he opened his mouth.
"Where would you like me to start. The guy is an arrogant prick
and a bully. Anyone who had the misfortune to work for him could
be in the frame."
"You do realise you are not helping your case here."
"I didn't do it and I wasn't there."
"Betcha would have liked to watch though?"
"On no Detective. You are not catching me out that easily. I had
my differences with Hollingsworth and I had my reasons for
clouting him yesterday afternoon. But that was as far as it goes."
Billy knew there was one person he could involve who would back
up his story. Mike had been the reason behind the altercation at
work and had been with him the entire evening. In addition, Mike,
coming from the smarter end of town would be a more credible
witness in Police eyes than a kid from a tower block in the middle
of a sink estate. Just the mention of Mike's name and the supply of
his address would be enough to get Billy off the hook, but
involving his best friend at this time might put a stop to Mike's
travel plans and Billy was not prepared to take that risk.
Harrison drained the last of his coffee and stood up. DC Smith
took her cue and replaced her half-drunk coffee on the table and
stood up as well, replacing her notebook in the pocket of her coat.

"We might have a few more questions for you in the future. So, don't leave town."
This parting shot from Harrison merely confirmed that Billy had been right to keep Mike's name out of the picture, at least for now. If he was going down he was not about to take his best friend with him. Billy Randell might not have had much in life but he was always fiercely loyal to his friends.
Mrs Randell saw the two detectives out and returned to the living room.
"You heard them Billy. You can't leave town now."
"Mum I am going on Tuesday and that is that."
He went off and shut himself in his room. After about ten minutes he threw on his coat and headed out. He went to the only bookshop left in town and enquired if they had any tourist books on Israel. They did so Billy bought one and then headed off to the park to sit and read up about his soon to be adopted country.

CHAPTER FOUR

The noise from inside the bar of the Red Lion was something tangible as Billy approached the door. The throbbing of the heavy bass from the music could be felt under the breastbone and the windows of the public bar seemed to be pulsing in time with the beat as if the building itself was alive and breathing.
The stultifying heat could be felt as he pushed his way through the heavy door and into the large room
The place was packed, wall to wall with gyrating bodies. Everyone seemed to be yelling at each other to make themselves heard over the pounding beat of the mobile disco in the corner. The strobing multi-coloured lights caught faces in the darkness, making ugly monstrous masks of people's features. The whole place stank of beer, sweat and perfume. Billy wondered if this was the vision of hell that Dante had seen when he had been writing Inferno. It certainly came close for him.
As he pushed his way through the crowd to the bar he wondered if the two policemen had been in here earlier to look for witnesses. He certainly noticed a few faces that had been here the previous evening and in fact were probably here most evenings if the truth be told. The landlord's son Jeff was on duty behind the bar and he smiled in recognition as Billy made it to the front of the queue. Billy tapped on the lager pump and held up a single finger. Jeff did the honours and placed the foaming glass on the beermat. Billy handed over the banknote and waited for the change. When Jeff returned with the change he bent over the pump and yelled in Billy's ear.
Over the noise from the Disco Billy heard the words "Dad" and "Lounge Bar" Jeff also nodded in the direction of the other bar in the rear of the building to emphasise the point.

Billy made his way to the Lounge Bar stopping to greet the odd friend on the way.

In contrast to the Public Bar, the Lounge Bar at the rear of the pub was almost genteel. It was only half full with punters and they seemed to be all sitting and making polite conversation, drinking Gin and Tonics, Wine by the Glass or tankards of Real Ale instead of cheap lager by the Pint. As soon as he entered the room Billy spied Jim Edwards, the patron and landlord of the Red Lion over at a corner table. There were two older gentlemen sitting with him. Edwards looked up and seeing Billy waved him over.

"Hello Billy, how are you this evening?"

Edwards had served time in the Army before mustering out to go into the licence trade and he had retained his overall military build and bearing since leaving the service. His hair, although now turning grey, was still closely cropped in the military fashion and his RSM's moustache was smartly trimmed and impeccable. He was, as usual, smartly dressed wearing a shirt and tie, the sleeves folded over just enough to show the military tattoos on his thick forearms. He dressed in this fashion even on the warmest summer day when everyone else went for t-shirts and shorts.

He had been landlord of the Red Lion for the best part of the last twenty years and didn't look like leaving any time soon.

He was a totally fair landlord, treating his young clientele in the same way he had treated the young soldiers in his charge with a mixture of fierce discipline and avuncular kindness. He didn't tolerate any trouble in his Pub and knew the exact price of every fixture and fitting. If something got broken by a customer they were asked nicely to pay for the damage and if they coughed up in full, the incident was forgotten. If they argued they were barred from the place and never allowed back. Very few people got barred and incidentally very little was ever broken or damaged.

Billy stood before the table feeling like a boy summoned to the office of the head teacher.

"I am OK Mr Edwards."

"Just wanted you to know I had a visit from the Police late this afternoon. They said they are conducting enquiries into an assault and you were a suspect. Is there anything you want to tell me about ?"

"There's not much to tell. They came to the flat this afternoon and asked me loads of questions about my whereabouts last night. I told them I was here for the whole evening and they said they would have to check. I thought they would check later when most of me mates are here."

"Well they won't be bothering your friends. They spoke to Jeff who was able to confirm your story. Was it Pete Hollingsworth who got beaten up?"

"Yes it was."

"I heard about that earlier today. Apparently, he was out walking his dog when he got jumped by a gang of thugs who attacked him with baseball bats. He took a real beating."

"If the Police knew it was a gang why did they just come looking for me?"

"Every gang has to have a leader Billy."

Billy had never seen himself as a gang leader and the looks he got from the two others sitting at the table with Edwards indicated they agreed with Billy's assessment of himself.

"Well it's all sorted out now. I can't have Plod traipsing in and out of here all evening. It's not good for business, upsets the customers."

Edwards stroked his moustache for a moment as if he had something more to say but he remained silent.

Billy stood there looking awkward, unsure if that was the end of the matter.

Edwards looked up and saw he was waiting to be dismissed.

"That will be all Billy. Go and enjoy yourself."

"Thanks Mr Edwards."

Billy returned to the Public Bar and joined his friends. It seemed that word of Hollingsworth's fate was now public knowledge and a few people stopped Billy to ask him about it. Half of the enquirers wanted to shake him by the hand or clap him on the back for standing up to Hollingsworth the previous afternoon. Some of the girls even went so far as to hug Billy tight or plant a kiss on his cheek. The other half were seeking details of the second, more serious, attack. Billy accepted the praise and kisses but denied vehemently knowing anything about the second incident. He was not sure that he was totally believed which he found a little worrying. He was, however, enjoying being the centre of attention for a change. In the past, he had never had problems being accepted as part of the group, but that was all he had ever amounted to. Just another one of the herd. Now for the first time in his life people were coming up to him and greeting him, Billy Randell, the individual.

The highlight of the evening was when the shop assistant from the Travel Agent sought him out. He took a few moments to recognise the young lady when she approached and stood in front of him. He struggled for a moment trying to place her among his acquaintances. Then it suddenly dawned on him exactly who she was. He looked past her to see if she had friends with her but there was no one obviously lurking close by.

"Hello Billy." She mouthed at him and smiled.

He bent down so his mouth was beside her ear.

"Hello there," he had noticed her hands were empty of a drink. "Can I get you a drink?"

She pulled his head down so that she could shout in his ear.

"Can I have a half of lager?"

Billy knew that further verbal communication was going to be ponderously slow and with the volume from the Disco, a bit hit and miss, so he just nodded his head and offered his hand.

It was taken and the two of them headed to the bar.

Jeff met him by the pumps and Billy tapped the lager pump and held up one finger. He then made another gesture where he brought his finger and thumb almost together. It worked and he received a Pint and a half of lager. He paid and handed the smaller glass to his companion.

She nodded her thanks and then waved her hand indicating she wanted to speak to Billy again. He bent his head down so she could speak directly in his ear.

"Is it quieter in the other bar?"

Billy nodded his head as an answer.

Now it was the girl's turn to take Billy by the hand and lead him through into the Lounge Bar.

As the heavy door closed behind them it cut out the majority of the noise from the Disco and the other hubbub coming from the Public Bar.

"That's better." The girl said as she walked over and took a seat at one of the empty tables.

"Don't you like loud music." Billy joined her taking a chair opposite.

"I love it. I love to dance, to lose myself in the music. But it is not very conducive to having a conversation or getting to know someone."

The last part of the sentence left Billy with a warm and fuzzy feeling all the way down to his socks. No one had wanted to get to know him in a very long time. And no one he knew used words like "conducive". He was definitely smitten. Then he remembered he was leaving town in three days' time. Any friendship would have to be brief by nature. He wondered whether he should mention this, but decided that bringing up the subject of his imminent departure would only dampen the mood and after all she was in full possession of the facts as she had sold him the ticket earlier in the day. It was not as if any deception was taking place.

"I haven't seen you in here before. Are you here with some friends?" Billy was conscious of the fact that they had made a hasty exit from the Public Bar and that maybe there would be people worrying about where their friend had disappeared to.

"No, I am here on my own tonight. Being brave and adventurous."

Billy was about to ask something but then suddenly realised he didn't even know the young ladies name.

"You have an advantage over me. I had to give you my name to put on the ticket but you never told me yours"

"Jo, well Joanna, but everyone calls me Jo."

"Then Jo it is." He stuck his hand out across the table and they shook hands. "Pleased to meet you." Her hand felt warm in his and soft. He released it, reluctant to prolong the physical connection for too long and appear creepy.

He was rewarded with an even bigger smile from across the table. They talked for an hour finding out about each other, like any couple on a first date, although all the way through Billy was trying to figure out if this was what it was, given the circumstances and his imminent departure. He didn't want to jinx the evening by bringing the subject up and Joanna acted like she didn't care about it so he just let it ride.

Eventually after a few drinks they went back to the Public Bar and had a bit of a dance and Joanna proved to be a very provocative dancer, constantly dancing in close and grinding her hips on Billy's thigh. She was flushed and exhilarated when they took a break and returned to the other bar for some refreshment.

In the corridor between the two rooms she grabbed Billy's arm, spun him around and planted a warm, wet, opened mouth kiss on his lips. Billy responded and was rewarded with just the tip of her tongue spearing into his mouth. The kiss only lasted a few moments but it was enough to raise Billy's pulse to racing pitch. He was sorry it had to end, but realised they were in a very public place and someone could come along at any moment.
Joanne was clearly pleased with the reaction her kiss had provoked.
"I look forward to the next one." She said with a sly wink as she turned and pushed open the door to the Lounge Bar.
The evening was progressing nicely in Billy's opinion and he had even forgotten to miss the presence of his wingman. Guiltily he realised he had not thought about Mike for several hours. As if the thought was enough to summon him, suddenly he was standing there by the side of their table.
"Evening Billy. You gonna introduce me to your new friend?"
"Oh hi Mike." Billy tried to keep the disappointment out of his voice. "I thought you were tied up at a family party?" He made brief introductions all round and then waited while Mike went and got fresh drinks for all of them.
"That's the thing with family parties," He said when he returned with the three drinks.
 "Where the young and the old are invited they have to get home to bed and as soon as the first group leave so the rest of them follow in quick succession. And anyway, I wanted to come down here and celebrate my last Saturday night in the country."
"Are you leaving too?" Joanna asked "Where are you going?"
"I am off to Israel on Tuesday."
Joanna opened her mouth to speak but Billy cut across her.
"And we are all going to miss you when you're gone."
Billy was trying to catch Joanna's eye to shut her up. He didn't want her blurting out something about his own imminent departure. He wanted to break that particular piece of news to Mike when they were alone, or better still when they both got to the Airport on Tuesday and it was it was too late to do anything about it.
But Billy's wishes on that front were not to be granted. In hindsight, he couldn't blame Jo. They had not known each other long enough to be able to take visual cues from each other, and he

had certainly not mentioned to her that his ticket purchase was to be kept a secret.

"Oh, that's nice are you travelling together?"

"I wasn't aware that Billy was going anywhere, except to the local Job Centre, now if Billy has been spinning you some story about how he is jetting off on some big adventure then I apologise for my friend's behaviour and I will have words with him later. I am the one setting out on a life changing journey." Mike's voice was full of mock seriousness. But Joanna was not to be deterred.

"He is not spinning any story, I sold him a plane ticket this morning."

There it was. Billy's secret was out in the open. Mike took a moment to process the information he had just been given.

"Could you give us a moment alone?" This was Mike to Joanna.

"No. I am staying right here." Joanna was clearly perceptive enough to realise she had put her foot in it, but all credit to her, Billy thought, she is not going to run away from her mistakes.

"This is likely to get heated and ugly," Mike warned in a menacing tone.

"Oooh I just love heated and ugly." Joanna rolled her eyes back in her head in mock ecstasy.

"Well don't say I didn't warn you."

"I won't." Joanna was definitely in no mood to be cowed by Mike. She reached across the table and took hold of Billy's hand, squeezing it supportively.

She made no attempt to remove her hand and neither did Billy. Mike glanced down at the hands clasped on the table in front of him and suddenly burst out laughing.

"This is all a wind-up, isn't it? Come on Billy-boy, you have put this young lady up to this.?"

"No Mike this is not a wind-up. I sold Billy a one-way ticket to Ben Gurion this morning."

It might have been the school-mistress tone of voice that swung it for Mike but he suddenly turned very serious.

"For fucks sake Billy. What have you done now?"

"Bought a ticket on the same flight as you."

"You can't just buy a ticket and turn up Billy. It's a lot more complicated than that. You have to go through registration, selection, interview. There are forms to be filled in and all that admin crap. You can't just waltz up and go ta-dah and expect to be welcomed with open arms." Mike voice was starting to crack, not with anger but with despair. He didn't want to pour water on his friend's plans but knew he had to introduce a healthy dose of realism into the whole affair before it was too late.

Billy's attitude was by sharp contrast defensive and was mirrored with the way his head sunk forward as he raised his shoulders. His voice was flat and monotone.

"Why not?"

"Because, numb nut, that's not the way the program works." Mike's tone had softened and he smiled at his friend. "Anyway," he continued, "Where did you get the money to buy a plane ticket?"

"I borrowed it." Billy was still on the defensive. He did not like to have his ideas destroyed in this way.

Mike, surprisingly, did not follow up on his line of questioning on where Billy had acquired the money and for that Billy was grateful.

"So, you bought a ticket on the same flight as me, on Tuesday?"

"Yes, I did, there were only a couple of seats left." Billy offered the last as an excuse for why he had not discussed it first with Mike.

"You know they might not even let you into the country?"

Joanna had been listening to the exchange and watching the body language of both friends, whilst remaining silent but still clinging on to Billy's hand. Now she felt qualified to speak.

"Why ever not. If he has a valid ticket and a valid passport and funds enough to pay for a return ticket then they cannot refuse his entry unless he has a criminal record or has been expelled from the country before."

Billy listened to Joanna and nodded his head as she made each of the points, although maybe he should have shaken his head at the bits about criminal record and being expelled as he had done neither of these. Overall, though, he agreed with Joanna's points. Mike, ever realistic, knew that he didn't know enough about the subject to argue the point further, whereas a professional in the travel industry might possess a greater knowledge of the facts, so he just acquiesced and backed down. Billy guessed that the subject was not closed but merely put on hold to be resurrected at another point in the near future when the two friends were alone. For now,

though, Mike seemed to just shrug his shoulders and then simply changed the subject.
"I am not going to spend my last evening arguing and fighting with you I have hugs, farewell kisses and much more to collect. Who is up for a dance?"
As one they finished their drinks and pushed away from the table, making their way noisily into the Public Bar.

\#

Much later Mike found Billy and Joanna locked in the close embrace of a slow dance. Mike had a young blonde clinging to his arm. She looked barely a day over eighteen, was clad in tight satin-look jeans, knee-high boots and a crop top that showed ample quantities of naked midriff. Her blonde hair was scraped away from her face and captured in a ponytail. Her blue eyes, emphasised by a little too much eye makeup, had the outward appearance of innocence but this was not reflected in her gaze which was old and cynical beyond her years. She knew what she wanted and right now that was a night of passion with Mike.
He had other ideas though.
"Billy-boy, we are just off up the high street for a kebab and then I need to find a cab." He nodded at his partner. Billy read the message in his friend's eyes. He was going to get something to eat and then send this young lady on her way. He was clearly not in the mood for complications this close to his departure.
The young lady, unable to see Mike's expression clearly, thought she was on a promise, because she began to tug impatiently at Mike's elbow, trying to drag him towards the door.
"See you tomorrow?" It was a question.
Both Billy and Joanne replied in unison.
"Yes."
Mike missed the significance of the answer as he was dragged out of the Bar. Billy didn't.
"Does that mean what I think it means."
Joanne kissed Billy lightly on the end of his nose.
"It does. Get your coat stud, you've pulled."
Billy wished he could be as stoic as his friend, but for him this type of occurrence was so rare, that when they came along he felt it was churlish to turn them down.

They walked arm in arm back across town to Billy's flat exchanging passionate kisses as and when the mood took them. Billy was hoping that his mother, true to her usual form, would be at a lock-in with her drinking pals at her local pub. This was her usual practice on a Saturday night and fortunately tonight was no different.

On the rare occasions that Billy did bring a young lady home, his mother was very relaxed about it, even if the young lady stayed the night. She had raised the subject of sexual partners, much to Billy's embarrassment, a few years ago and had delivered her homily on what she expected from Billy.

The rules were very simple and straightforward. If a girl was drunk then they were to remain partially clothed. He must always use protection or some form of contraception, and the girl was not allowed to raid her underwear drawer in search of clean underwear in the morning. They were three rules Billy was happy to comply with, and there was no way that Joanna was anything close to drunk.

The ride up in the elevator was one long passionate kiss. It was the first time they had been totally alone away from prying eyes and Billy felt the heat was turned up a notch or two as a result of that privacy. They could not keep their hands off each other.

The lift door opened on Billy's floor at just the wrong moment and they were lucky to avoid tumbling to the ground. They both managed to right themselves and Billy crossed the hallway and fished out the key from the letterbox.

The hallway of the flat was dark, a sure sign his mother was not home. Billy flicked on the light and closed the door behind Joanna. She took this as a cue and launched herself at Billy tearing at his jacket and pulling up his t-shirt to kiss and lick his stomach and chest. Billy went back against the wall with a thump, feeling his body respond.

Then Billy was overtaken with a sudden panic and pushed Joanna away from him. She stood there, her hair a little dishevelled with a look of confusion on her face.

"I just need a minute." Billy was consciously aware of the state of his bedroom. The packing exercise had not gone too well. There were piles of clothes everywhere but particularly on the bed and the whole room could benefit from a thorough deep clean. There was no time for that but a quick gathering up of clothing, clean and

dirty, followed by the dumping of the whole lot in the bottom of the wardrobe would improve the room.
He went through and bent to collect the first of the items.
"Clear the bed, the rest can wait."
He turned around to see that Joanne had spent the twenty seconds his back had been turned to remove her outer garments and she was leaning provocatively on the door jamb clad only in her underwear. Her skirt and blouse clasped in her hand.
"I like the mess. It proves you didn't set out tonight to get laid. If that had been your intention then you would have tidied up the room before you left home."
Billy smiled at Joanna's logic although he felt that Mike, if he had been there would have disagreed with her. Mike would have pointed out that complete tip was the default setting for Billy's room whether he felt he was on a promise or not. Then he stopped. Why was he thinking of Mike at a time like this?
He dumped the armful of clothes he was carrying on the adjacent chair and turned to take Joanna in his arms.

#

Several hours later he awoke. In the light from the bedside lamp he saw that Joanna had managed to locate her knickers amongst the confusion of clothing that lay scattered around the bedroom. No mean feat considering that as well as Billy's own mess, their own clothes had been tossed aside in the earlier frenzy to get naked. She was sleeping on her back with one arm behind her head and as she breathed so her hips rose giving him an enticing flash. He was riveted by the sight and jumped when a voice spoke behind him.
"It won't bite if you are nice to it." Joanna giggled. "Particularly if you are nice to it like you were earlier." Another giggle escaped her lips.
Billy looked up and moved to claim his prize. This time things were a little less frantic and in Billy's mind more pleasurable.
The next time they both woke up the sun was streaming through the half-opened curtains casting a band of warm white light across the room.
Billy was conscious of his morning breath so he pushed the covers aside and sat on the edge of the bed to struggle into his shorts. He

stood up and turned around, looking down at the semi-naked figure in the bed.

Joanna responded to the movement by stretching her body, a movement that highlighted all of her major assets.

"I will go and make us some coffee." Billy nodded in the direction of the bedroom door.

"That would be great." Joanna had recovered the duvet cover from the floor and pulled it over her to cover her nakedness.

Billy was lucky the kettle was recently boiled so he only had to spoon some coffee into cups add some water and put some milk and the sugar bowl on a tray.

He re-entered the room and saw that Joanna was now sat up in bed and was intently studying the book Billy had bought about Israel. She glanced up at him.

"Really serious huh? You even bought the tourist guide."

Billy nodded and placed the tray on the only available free space, the corner of the writing desk.

"Do you take milk and sugar?" He asked over his shoulder.

"I like my coffee, the same way I like my men. Strong and sweet."

Billy looked at his scrawny upper arms and thought he hardly fitted that description, but maybe in his case Joanna had made an exception.

He stirred the sugar into the mug and handed it handle first to Joanna.

She murmured a thank you and carried on reading for a few moments slowly turning pages. She was obviously just looking at the glossy pictures, no one could read that fast.

Billy sat on the bed and watched her as she read and drank her coffee. With her tousled morning hair, she looked vulnerable and extremely sexy. And she was still semi-naked and in his bed. He was just contemplating making another move on her when she flipped the book over, open but face down on her lap and looked up at him.

"Man cannot live by coffee alone. Do you fancy going out for breakfast, my treat?"

"Only if you promise to put some clothes on." Billy grinned and was rewarded by a having a pillow lobbed at his head.

They both dressed and headed across town to a restaurant that served good breakfasts. Billy was surprised by how hungry he was until he remembered he had burnt a few calories in the night.

As if she read his thoughts Joanna looked up at him, but her expression was serious and not smiling.
"About last night."
Billy felt the food in his stomach do a barrel roll. He definitely didn't like Joanna's tone of voice, and he really didn't want to hear what was coming next.
"I have a confession to make, I have not been totally honest with you Billy, and I am sorry."
"Well if last night was about not being honest, long may it continue." Billy was trying to make light of things and Joanna smiled her appreciation.
"I know what you are trying to do Billy but just let me finish before you say anything more."
"OK." Billy braced himself for the worse.
"When you walked in the shop the other day I took an instant like to you. You were the total opposite of most of the people I see in the shop and you were heading off on a real adventure. That made me like you even more. When you left, I began to wonder if you would really come back like you promised and because I hoped you would I made an extra effort to look good for you today and you noticed. And because you looked twice I thought I would try and take things further and ask you out on a date. At the last minute, I lost my nerve but at least I managed to find out where you would be last night and that was enough. And last night was everything I had hoped for and more but here is the problem. I already have a serious boyfriend".
"Blimey," Billy was genuinely shocked by that particular revelation. On his list of possible reasons for this particular serious conversation, that particular revelation was not even in the top ten.
"Understand me Billy, I didn't want to hurt you."
"I am more worried right now about your boyfriend wanting to hurt me." The look of mock terror on his face was enough to make Joanna burst out laughing.
"It's lucky I am leaving the country on Tuesday."
"Yes as he won't be back in town until next weekend so you will be long gone by then."
"That's a relief." Billy mock mopped the sweat from his brow.
"Listen Billy, I mean what I said, I didn't want to hurt you."
Joanna had reached for his hand across the table and squeezed it.
"So, is this it? The Last Supper or in this case Breakfast."

"Well that's up to you. I have no commitments today or tonight so if you want to spend time with me I will be happy in your company. I need to go home and change but I can meet up later on."

"Later on, would be good. I need to try and track down Mike first and talk to him. Can I call you later?"

Joanna scribbled her number on a napkin and handed it to Billy, then paid the bill as she had promised, kissed him passionately on the lips and left the cafe to catch her bus.

Billy finished his coffee and then left the cafe too heading back to the flat and his showdown with Mike.

CHAPTER five

Back at the flat Billy's mum was nursing a hangover and was in no mood for conversation so Billy took himself off to his room to read his book about Israel and wait for the summons from Mike. He was expecting a phone call instead he got a personal visit.
When his bedroom door swung open he was expecting his mother instead it was Mike stood in the doorway, hands thrust deep in the pockets of his denim jeans.
"Hello Billy." Mike's tone was flat and he was not his usual chippy self. Billy placed the book face down and gave his friend his full attention.
"I want to apologise for last night. I was out of order."
"It's all right mate I understand. No need to apologise. I probably took you a bit by surprise".
"Yes you did."
"Look I wanted to tell you myself in person. I guess it just slipped out."
Mike smiled and winked. Billy got the gist of what Mike was thinking without any more words passing between them.
"Well I was a little taken aback by your announcement. I never thought you were that interested in foreign travel."
"Well to be honest I have got fuck all to keep me here now. No job, no best friend. So why not give it a shot?"
"That's the spirit. I am sure we can work something out when we get to the Airport on Tuesday morning. When I went to the selection day the organisers were saying there was a shortage of Volunteers throughout the country. It seems it is not as popular as it was a few years back. Something to do with the trouble that is going on down there at the moment."
"Yeah I have just been reading about it in this book." Billy tapped the spine of the book in his lap. "It's a very interesting read."

Billy put the book to one side. He was anxious to show off his new purchases to Mike and they spent the next half an hour unpacking and re-packing Billy's rucksack and going through what they should take in terms of food staples like tea and biscuits, spreads, like Marmite and Marmalades. They made a final definitive list and set out for the local corner shop to see what they could buy and then splitting those items up so they would have equal weight in their packs.

After this they retired to the Red Lion for lunch and from there Billy phoned Joanna and asked if she wanted to meet up later as they were going to be in the pub for the regular Sunday Night Quiz competition.

Joanna said she would join their team but pointed out that while she was Okay on Geography, useful if you worked in a Travel Agents, Okay on History, she knew nothing about Sport or Politics. Billy said he was sure that she would do fine and to be at the pub by seven-thirty.

\#

On Sunday nights, the Public Bar of the Red Lion was taken over by a clientele that was radically different from its regular patrons. The possibility to win a large cash prize in a General Knowledge Quiz brought out the closet intellectuals and couch potatoes. The plethora of bottle-top glasses, long greasy hair and Iron Maiden and assorted other heavy metal, Band T-shirts made the public bar of the Red Lion look more like the main bar of its equally imaginatively named neighbour, the White Lion, which was the traditional hangout of rockers and nerds alike.

Jim and Jeff Edwards didn't care about the length of your hair or the motif on your t-shirt. For them it was all about the money and punters in a pub on a Sunday night were a bonus so they ran the quiz night knowing they would attract said punters in droves on a night when traditionally people stayed home with the family or eased up on the alcohol intake ahead of a Monday morning start back at work.

And the more punters taking part the bigger the bar take but also the larger the cash prize so it was a ourobouric or self-perpetuating event.

Tonight, was no exception as Mike and Billy entered the pub the place was already full. There were only a couple of tables left unoccupied and already the banter had started between the regular teams. Although most of it was friendly the atmosphere was a little like the champions taking their place in front of the army before the main combatants clashed and yelling insults at the opposing side.
Most of the taunts involved wrongly answered questions from previous encounters. Some of these gems of general knowledge were on the far side of obscure. Who really did make a habit of knowing who won the women's basketball world cup final in 1964? Although the answer to this was for any given year between 1953 and 1990 a fifty-fifty guess between the Soviet Union and the USA.
Billy and Mike were in a team with three others who were already at their table, pints and pencils at the ready. Billy did the honours at the bar and then joined the others. He kept one eye on the door, waiting and hoping that Joanna would show her face.
The quiz master, a teacher friend of Jeff the barman was already going around taking names and collecting the entry fees from the players when Joanna stuck her head around the door.
She caught Billy's eye and motioned for him to come over. She led him outside to the street and then turned to him.
"Are you OK?" she asked
"Yes I am fine, how are you?"
"I'm fine. I have just been thinking about you all day. Especially after our conversation this morning. I feel guilty."
"Why?" Billy looked puzzled and this confusion showed in his voice.
"Because of what happened last night."
"If you are guilty about what you are going to tell your boyfriend when he gets home then I am sorry. If you are guilty about what happened between us then don't be."
"Really? You aren't mad at me."
"No Jo, I am not mad at all."
"We are OK then?"
"More than OK." Billy reached out and touched her.
The contact of hand on wrist sent a shiver down Joanna's arm and she moved close into Billy and he opened his arms to welcome her.

The kiss was long and passionate still holding some vestiges of the passion from the previous night. When they broke apart they were both a little breathless.
"Well I guess nothing has changed on that front then." Joanna gave a wicked smile.
"Let's go inside and see if we can't win the quiz tonight."
"Have you ever won the quiz before?"
"Never, but there is always a first time and I feel in a winning mood tonight." Billy's grin was lecherous.
"Easy Tiger, save something for later."
They pushed open the door and entered the bar together, holding hands like newlyweds.

#

By the time the quiz had reached the halfway point Billy was confident of most of their answers. The half time break gave the competitors a chance to visit the bathroom and to get more beers from the bar. It was not like a conventional sports fixture where tired, exhausted muscles gained a respite and recharged for the second half of the game, unless of course you considered the brain as a muscle.
In the first half of the quiz there had been two questions that referred to Israel. The quiz master had clearly been briefed about Mike's impending departure and made reference to it when he was asking the question. Mike had been clueless over the answers to both questions but Billy, having spent time reading the book about Israel was able to answer both questions with ease. Mike was slightly miffed with Billy's performance and had gone to the bar more than a little disgruntled.
Billy was left at the table with Joanna, the other team mates had left to use the facilities. Joanna was jealously guarding their answer sheet, her arms crossed over the top of it as it lay, face down, on the table.
"I never took you for a Jew lover." The voice sneered behind Billy. He spun round on his bar stool and came face to face with an expansive beer gut barely contained by an Aerosmith T-Shirt.
"I beg your pardon?" Billy spoke to the T-Shirt
"You heard. I never took you for a kike, a yid, an Israel Apologist."

Billy looked up at his antagonist.
His clothing marked him as one of the visitors from the other place. Dirty jeans, the faded and washed out heavy metal band t-shirt, the bad complexion, the long straggly unwashed hair all rounded off with heavy framed geeky nerd round bottle top glasses. This one also had particularly bad acne and fat full lips that were moist with spittle.
"I don't know where you get that from."
"You were pretty quick with the answers to those two questions. Something you would know if you only saw things from the Israeli point of view."
"What on earth are you ranting about?"
"Well there are two sides in this conflict."
"Conflict? What conflict?"
"The repressive regime, the Occupation of the Territories, Israel's fascist government and their attitude towards the Palestinians. It's State sponsored terrorism."
That afternoon Billy had ploughed his way through a couple of difficult chapters in his Israel book. He had never been much of a history fan but the writers had encouraged their readers to "stick with it", as an understanding of, where Israel was in the timeline of the Middle East, and in the overall history of the region was crucial to understanding many of the facets of modern Israeli society.
Billy had stuck with it and now felt more than equal to arguing the toss with some Grebo who had never ventured further than the end of Southend pier.
"If it's State sponsored terrorism you want to discuss, where would you like to start? Shall we take Israel backed by the US, or Hamas backed by Hezbollah and Iran? You choose." Billy spat back acidly in response.
Having rationally asked where they would like to start the discussion and then offering to debate the Israel and American side first Billy had shown a maturity which his opponent had clearly underestimated. It showed Billy was not going to leap to defend Israel and allow his assailant to recount all the facts that he had read in the press and thus win the argument by sheer volume of data. Billy's confidence left an impression that there was a spectre lurking and that maybe Billy knew some "facts" of his own about the links surrounding Hamas, something he had no knowledge of

and felt in no position to defend. In the end, he snorted and turned on his heels and stomped off.

Joanna put an arm on Billy's wrist to calm him but found that Billy was already calm.

"That was amazing. You dealt with that so well."

Mike had observed the whole incident from the bar and wanted to know what had been said when he returned to the table.

Joanna filled in the details while Billy sat there expressionless but secretly pleased at the wonder in Joanna's voice.

"Billy boy," Mike slapped his friend on the bicep, "When did you become an expert on all things Israel? Two for two in the quiz questions and I think we may have the edge there if what I have heard in the break is anything to go by, seems like nobody has a clue about the answers and some of them are complaining to Jeff about that choice of topic. And now to cap it all, you step up to debate the whole Middle East question with some nerd from the White Lion."

"I've just been reading this book." Billy offered as an answer.

Mike looked over at his friend and the reality suddenly hit him. Billy was not joking about coming to Israel and he was also forced to acknowledge that Billy, for the first time in all the time he had known him, was actually deadly serious about something. He resolved that he would have to do all in his power to make Billy's wish come true. But that was a battle for another day and another arena. For now, they had the second half of the quiz to complete and the question master was calling the teams to order.

\#

At the end of the second half of the quiz after the scores were tallied up the winners were announced. Mike and Billy's team had triumphed by a single correct answer. Of course, there were ribald comments about the whole thing being a "fix". That happened every time one of the home teams were victorious. On this occasion though it got a little bit out of hand with a colossal argument breaking out at the bar involving Aerosmith T-Shirt man and a couple of his team mates.

They were protesting about the inclusion of questions about the state of Israel. They started to hassle the bespectacled quiz master who quickly fled for safety behind the bar. Voices were raised in anger and insults traded across the beer pumps until Jeff, the landlord's son, arrived and took his place beside his friend. His raised voice cut across the whole room.

"If you are not out of the pub door in sixty seconds you will be leaving via one of the windows."

Jeff folded his treelike forearms across his chest leaving the protagonists in no doubt that he had the upper body strength to carry out his threat.

There were a few grumbles and further threats as the disgruntled losers left the pub, but with their departure things quickly calmed down and returned to normal.

After the winners' pot had been shared out and the balance spent on a round of drinks for the victorious team people started to leave. Mike told Billy that he was due to have lunch with his family the next day but he would be around in the afternoon as he was going to complete the last of his packing. They made an arrangement to meet up and Mike left.

By closing time there was only Joanna and Billy left in the bar. Jeff was putting chairs up on tables so Billy took the hint, downed the last of his pint and stood up. He helped Joanna on with her coat and the two left the bar.

"What happens now?" Billy was trying to sound casual but every nerve in his body was tingling.

"What do you want to happen?" Joanna was acting all coy.

"I think you know the answer to that, but I will understand if you say no."

"Why would I do that? I had a great time last night."

"Really?" Billy could not hide the surprise in his voice.

"Yes Billy, I did. Do you think I would be standing here with you now, hoping that you will invite me back to your flat, take me to your bed and make love to me again if I didn't?"

Billy was grateful for the poor lighting outside the pub. It meant Joanna couldn't see the colour that shot up his cheeks, although she was probably standing close enough to feel the heat from them.

#

Joanna left in the early hours of the morning. Billy called her a taxi and then waited downstairs in the lobby, shivering in his socks, until the driver arrived and collected her. Their final kiss was long and very passionate and just about enough to beat back the night chills. Billy struggled back upstairs and collapsed into the messed-up bed and fell instantly asleep.

The sun shining in through the gap in the curtains hurt Billy's eyes when he finally opened them. With no Mike and no work, he just turned over and placed the pillow over his head to shut out the light and went back to sleep.

When he did finally struggle back to consciousness he looked over at the alarm clock and saw that the red numbers told him it was nearly ten.

He sat up in bed and rubbed his eyes before pulling on a pair of tracksuit bottoms and a t-shirt and shuffling into the kitchen.

His mother had left for work but there was note propped up on the kettle. He opened the piece of paper and read the note.

"Dear Billy, I am not sure if you will be home when I finish work tonight but I would like to see you before you leave, if only to say goodbye and good luck. I know things were not working out for you here at home so I can only hope you have more luck wherever you end up. Please find a moment to write to me and let me know you are OK. I don't need to know where you are just that you are OK.

And remember you will always have a home here if you need one.

Love you always Mum xx

Billy read the note a second time and noticed that the last few words seemed smudged as if something had been spilt. He realised that the smudges were in fact his mother's tears. She had been crying when she wrote the note.

At that moment, he knew he would have to come by after seven tonight to say a final farewell to his mother.

He made himself a cup of coffee and took it back to his room and then sat in his bed reading more from the book on Israel.

With little or nothing else to do he decided to unpack and repack his rucksack, just to make sure he had not forgotten anything crucial. After this was completed he had his last frozen cottage pie and watched afternoon TV until Mike phoned him and summoned him to his house.

Billy called a taxi to come and collect him then had a final look around his room to make sure he hadn't forgotten anything, picked up his rucksack and his day pack and made his way down in the lift to wait for the taxi. As the taxi sped away from the base of the tower block Billy got the distinct impression that he might not be seeing this place for a long time. He caught sight of the looming presence of the adjacent block where Delchie Matthews and his team of thugs were located and shivered. He clutched the day pack on his lap close and whispered a silent prayer of hope, that everything was going to work out in the morning.

#

At Mike's house the place was in total uproar. Both his Mother and Father had taken time off from work and together with other members of the extended Spencer family were preparing to bid farewell to the son and heir. Like the departure of some monarch on their annual progress Mike was sat in the middle of the maelstrom as people shouted reminders of things that he needed to take with him.

Billy stood to one side and took in the scene. For him this was what it meant to be part of a family, to be loved and cared for. It was not that he didn't feel loved by his mother but it was a different kind of love, a more hands-off approach, where Billy was left to fend for himself both emotionally and physically. It had been that way as long as Billy could remember and it was only when he was around Mike's family that he realised things could be completely the opposite.

Mike's mother was collecting food items together and pushing them into the top of what was already a heavily stuffed kitbag whilst one of Mike's uncles stood over the bag ensuring that the zipper would still shut.

Mike's father was the first to notice Billy stood in the doorway and beckoned him in to join the fun.

As Billy entered the Kitchen he caught Mike's eye. Mike grinned first then pulled a face that said "I don't really need all this fuss". Billy shrugged his shoulders and grinned back.

Mike's father was by Billy's side to help him off with the rucksack and set it down by the door.

"Travelling light?" he smiled.

Mike's dad was always smiling. He had good teeth that shone when he smiled, and he had plenty to smile about.
Mike's dad was successful and everything about him reflected that success. His blonde hair was cleanly styled and although he was going slightly grey at the temples that just added to his confident, paternal air. His chest hair where it curled out of the V-neck of his polo shirt was also tinged with grey, although the heavy natural tan, the product of sunshine not a tanning studio was also evident. He was wearing tailored shorts, but unlike many men of his age he looked good in shorts as his legs were well muscled from hours spent on the tennis court or the golf course.
"Darling you could take a lesson from Billy here. He has not packed the kitchen sink" Mike's dad indicated the lightness of Billy's pack by lifting it high above his head with one hand before replacing it lightly on the floor.
Mike's mother looked up from her place squatting on the floor before the open maw of Mike's kitbag.
She brushed a stray lock of her blonde bobbed hair from her eyes and smiled at her husband. She was simply dressed in a sleeveless summer dress, plain in design and powder blue in colour. It looked good on her because like her husband her limbs were lithe, muscled and well-tanned. She wore little in the way of jewellery, a wedding band and a women's Rolex, the partner to her husbands.
"Come on Martin, be helpful instead of just standing there flinging brickbats."
Billy wondered what a brickbat was. Relieved of his pack he ventured over to where Mike was sitting.
"Are you ready for the off?" he asked.
"I am but I don't think my parents see things the same way. I have enough food with me to last me a year."
"Nothing perishable I hope, you won't be able to take that through customs at Ben Gurion."
"Don't tell me you read that in your book."
"Well as a matter of fact yes...."
"Don't worry Billy," Mike's mum had overheard his comment. "It's all dry goods or stuff in tins and jars. Anyway, since when have you become an expert on all things Israel."
Billy was about to answer but Mike cut him off.
"He bought this stupid book the other day and has been reading it non-stop."

"That stupid book won us the quiz last night". Billy pointed out just the slightest trace of annoyance showing in his voice.
"Touché". Mike grinned at his friend and stood up from his chair. "Let's get a couple of beers and retire to the den. I need to put the finishing touches to a couple of mix tapes and I want your advice. Are you stopping here for the night? We need to leave pretty early tomorrow to make it to Gatwick in time."
"Yeah, I know. I need to pop back to mine to say goodbye to my mum but that shouldn't take too long".
"I guess you will be coming with us in the car."
"If that's not a problem, and if you have room for me with all this stuff you are taking."
"Hey, hey don't you start." Mike's mum wagged a finger at Billy. "You will be walking to Gatwick if you are not careful."
"Sorry Mum." Billy sheepishly grinned at Mike's mum and her smile told him he had been forgiven and there would be a place for him in the car.
A couple of beer's later and the play lists were completed to both Mike and Billy's satisfaction and Mike's mum called them down for dinner. After the meal, Billy made his excuses and left to say goodbye to his mother. Mike agreed to meet him in the bar of the Red Lion for a last pint or two before their departure.
When Billy got home the flat was in darkness. He went through to the kitchen and found another note from his mother propped up against the kettle. He looked at the clock on the cooker and saw it was only just after seven, so he was not late. He unfolded the note. It was short.

"Can't face goodbye. Write me soon. Love Mum x"

Billy cursed under his breath. He was not going to chase around the town looking for his mum. He flipped the note over and scrawled on the flip side.

"Disappointed. Take care, will write when I have an address, Bill x"

As he walked back towards the Red Lion he thought, not for the first time in his life, about the total contrast between Mike and him. It went far beyond anything to do with wealth or position. There

was a fundamental difference in their whole life experience. Was it really any wonder that Mike had turned out the supremely confident winner when he had the love and support of his family. Was he always destined to be the loser purely because he had a family that didn't give a shit about him. If there was one thing he was determined to change in his life it was that he was going to stop being the loser all the time and instead become a winner.
.

CHAPTER SIX

A dull ping tone caused Billy to look up from the page of his book. He noticed the seatbelt sign was lit. For those passengers who were not so observant the co-pilot came on the PA and announced the fact to the passengers and the crew that the Pilot had started their descent into Ben Gurion and they expected to be on the ground in fifteen minutes.
Billy, who had managed to secure a window seat looked out the window and saw that they had indeed come down from their cruising altitude and the sea below looked much closer and the ships sailing there were much larger than the small dots he had seen earlier in the flight.
This was the first time in years that Billy had been on an aircraft and he had taken his lead from Mike who was a more frequent flyer. He was sat in the aisle seat and had sat with his seatbelt fastened throughout the whole flight so Billy did the same.
He looked across at his friend now. Mike was still dozing fitfully and although Billy had also taken a short nap on the flight for the most part he had been too excited and too tense to sleep. He had spent the time reading his tourist book and glancing at the in-flight magazines.

#

The tension had started earlier at Gatwick after they had said goodbye to Mikes parents and pushed their luggage trolley into the Terminal building. Billy was pushing the trolley and Mike was in charge of navigating to the right check in area.
The area set aside for the Tel Aviv flight was on its own at one end of the Check in hall, in an area roped off from the rest. Within this area there were metal tables set up and teams of individuals in

white shirts and black trousers who circulated around among the tables.

Billy and Mike joined the queue and were eventually called forward to one of the tables.

There were two of these white shirted individuals waiting for them, one male and one female.

"Please put your bags on the table." The girl spoke first, her accent was vaguely foreign to Billy's ears.

"May I see your tickets and passports." The male extended his hands towards Mike to collect the travel documents.

The guy flicked through the two passports, pausing briefly at the photo page to compare the pictures with the people standing opposite him. Satisfied that they were genuine he then examined the two plane tickets.

"Is this your first trip to Israel?" he asked

"Yes." They replied together.

"And what is the purpose of your visit?"

"To stay on a Kibbutz," said Mike.

"Do you have an introduction letter?"

Mike sorted through his document wallet and then offered the piece of paper from the Kibbutz Office.

The security officer opened the letter and read the text.

"Kibbutz Tel Boker, it's a very nice place."

Billy wondered whether the guard actually knew of the place or whether he would say that for any destination.

"And you?"

"I want to work on a Kibbutz too."

"Do you have your introduction letter?" The guy stuck out his hand expectantly.

"Er no I don't."

"You have forgotten your letter?" This time it was the girl who spoke and there was a harsh edge to her voice. She was obviously going to be playing 'Bad Cop' today.

"Not exactly." Billy mumbled.

"What do you mean?" All trace of friendliness was now gone from her voice.

"I never got a letter of introduction."

"Well that could be a problem." The guy had intervened cutting across the girl.

She turned on her male counterpart and delivered an angry stream of words which Billy assumed was Hebrew. The two moved away from the table and exchanged words. Watching the two it was obvious that there was some disagreement between them over what should happen next. After a few moments, the two stalked off.
"Way to go Billy boy. I guessed you might have a problem."
"I think we both have a problem. They just walked off with our tickets and passports."
"And my letter of introduction as well."
Billy tracked the two of them through the crowd until they disappeared through a door.
With nothing better to do than wait Billy sat down, cross-legged, on the floor. Mike was a little more anxious about the disappearance of his documents so he stood drumming lightly on the table top with his fingers.
They didn't have long to wait. Ten minutes did seem like an hour but that was all it took before good cop and bad cop emerged from behind the door. Mike kneed Billy in the shoulder.
"They're back."
Billy stood up and brushed himself down, composing himself to hear his fate. The two arrived back at the table and the guy gave them back their papers.
"We have spoken to the administrator on your kibbutz and they have agreed to take your friend. All we need to do is make sure you have the necessary money with you".
The woman security officer remained silent but as she looked Billy up and down she sniffed the air. It was clear she thought that she had won and that Billy would not possess sufficient funds to pass this test.
"How much exactly will he need?" Mike was already reaching for his money belt.
"It's OK Mike I got this."
"In Israeli Shekels about 2,300, in English pounds that's about two hundred and fifty pounds."
Billy reached in his pocket and pulled out a roll of bank notes. He slapped them down on the table.
"That should cover it. I think there is about three hundred quid there. But don't take my word for it, you can count it if you like."
"Christ Billy where did you get that kind of money from?" Mike spluttered in amazement.

"I earn't it." Billy was stood back looking the two security officers squarely in the face. They were both looking at the wad of notes on the table and wondering if they should pick it up and count it or take the young man's word for it.
In the end they decided to believe Billy and the guy nodded at Billy indicating he should put the money away. Billy jammed the roll of notes back in his trouser pocket and left his hands there. The two security guards looked at each other before the woman spoke.
"Please wait here." The two stalked off. They went over to two of their colleagues and exchanged a few words before they headed off to another table and another passenger.
"What do we do now?" Billy asked.
"We wait and while we wait you can explain where you got all that cash from. You never got that kind of money from working.?"
"Simple. I borrowed it."
"From who?"
"I think you mean from whom?"
"Don't sass me Billy Randell, you know what I mean."
"I had a word with an old friend and he agreed to lend me some cash. I was not going to let you go swanning off on an adventure on your own and I couldn't afford to pay for it out of my own savings. Beside what else was I going to do? I lost my job saving your ass."
"You don't have to remind me of that." Mike pulled a face.
"OK here's the deal. I won't ask you where you got the cash from and you don't mention the problem with Hollingsworth. Oh yeah on that subject did the Police come back to you?"
"No they apparently spoke to the Landlord at the Lion and he gave us both a rock-solid alibi so I guess they must have gone off pursuing other leads."
"Who do you think did that to him? I heard he took a pretty brutal beating."
"I dunno," Billy lied, "but there were enough people who hated his guts so I guess it was long overdue. The Police have got their work cut out working through a list of potential suspects. A list of his enemies must be the size of small telephone directory."
Billy was leaning against the table with his hands in his pockets when two more security officials turned up.

They were asked more questions about their intentions for travelling to Israel and what they intended to do if they had time off from the Kibbutz, where they intended to travel within the country and if they had plans to visit other Middle Eastern countries apart from Israel.

Most of these questions the boys both answered honestly. That they had no plans except to go and work on the Kibbutz and they had made no firm plans beside that. Their answers seemed to satisfy the two security officials as they were eventually released to put their luggage through the x-ray scanners and over to the Check in desk.

As they left the roped off area and headed towards the British Airways check-in desk Billy cast a last look around the rest of the passengers who were going through their own interrogations. Some of them seemed to be having an easy ride, laughing and joking with the officials whilst others were clearly getting the third degree with the contents of their bags strewn out over the metal table tops. Billy wondered what these individuals had done to warrant such close attention. It looked like once the search was complete the security personnel left the unfortunate individual to re-pack their own luggage. Billy murmured a silent word of thanks that they had not been subjected to such a rigorous screening. He glanced at Mike's large kitbag on the luggage trolley in front of him wondering secretly how they would have ever got everything back into in and the zip closed again.

After they had checked in, disposed of their heavy bags, and collected their boarding cards, they had passed through the Airport Security and on into the Duty-Free shop. They had made a few purchases there and then gone down to the gate and boarded their flight.

Now five hours or so later they were preparing to land and face the next hurdle of their journey. Billy was not totally convinced that any arrangements had been made for his inclusion on the list of candidates accepted to Kibbutz Tel Boker but he was not prepared to let Mike go off on his own so he was girding himself mentally for another battle.

#

Billy glanced out the window as the plane crossed the coast. It was his first sight of the Israel, in the shape of Tel Aviv and he was surprised by what he saw.

He had read in the book on Israel that the city of Tel Aviv was a modern thriving metropolis but he had not expected to see a skyline full of high-rise buildings, streets choked with traffic and parks and green areas thronged with people. Maybe the pictures in the book had deceived him but he was expecting more of a desert outpost with sand strewn and dusty streets, areas of desert encroaching at the fringes and more of a frontier town vibe. Tel Aviv was the polar opposite.

The pilot flew on across the city before performing a steep banking turn over the city rubbish dump and lining up to land at Ben Gurion.

Neither Mike nor Billy were prepared for the furnace heat that greeted them as they left the aircraft to descend to the waiting buses.

Sweat instantly broke out inside Billy's shirt and he hastily removed the jean jacket he was wearing. Mike had on a denim shirt, with a t-shirt underneath and he quickly unbuttoned the shirt and freed the t-shirt from his jeans.

Mercifully the bus waiting to take them to the terminal building was also air-conditioned so the discomfort was only brief.

When the first bus was full it pulled away from the side of the aircraft and headed for the Arrivals hall.

When the stewardess had passed through the cabin just before landing she had handed out landing cards. Mike had told Billy to fill out the form and then slot it into his passport by the picture page. This was to ensure that the Immigration Officer stamped the visa stamp on the landing card and not on a page in the Passport. The officials were quite happy to do this and it would prevent problems later on if they needed to use the Passport for entry to a country not on politically good terms with Israel, like any of the Arab countries. Billy could see the sense in this so he handed over his passport to the young lady and she duly stamped the landing card and Mike and Billy went through to the Arrivals hall and baggage reclaim.

It was mid-afternoon and the Baggage hall was heaving with people. Everywhere he looked Billy noticed a different group. On the one side, there were the religious types, everything from Orthodox Jews in their sombre black suits with their fedora hats, to

Priests and other Christian clergy in similar attire but with white dog collars showing at their throats. There were nuns in habits of colours ranging from white, through blue, grey and even black, some with elaborate head gear, some bare headed.

There was also a large group of what appeared to be refugees with all their worldly possessions packed into large plastic holdalls and cardboard boxes, which they piled in precarious heaps on their luggage trollies.

There also seemed to be quite a few other volunteers in the Arrivals Hall collecting rucksacks, tote bags and even the occasional suitcase which were slung over shoulders or loaded onto the available luggage trollies. After collecting their individual pieces of luggage from the conveyor belt these groups all clung together in loose knots hoping not to get separated from each other. Mike and Billy had shunned the company of the other volunteers on their flight although they had been easy enough to pick out as they all waited in the gate area to board the flight in London. Now they knew they would have to join up with the group as they had to board the transport provided to take them to the Kibbutz. Outside where the arriving passengers met the general public it was even more chaotic.

As the doors slid open and Billy and Mike walked out there was an endless sea of faces leaning expectantly over the metal railings anxious to catch a first glimpse of either returning relatives and friends or try to identify the charges they were here to collect from among the throng.

Things were made more complicated by those new arrivals who felt they had to make a show of bending down and kissing the pavement, thus acknowledging their joy at returning to or elation at finally arriving in, their promised land.

Billy was so intent on scanning the crowd for any sign of a driver holding a sign with the name of the Kibbutz on it that he only narrowly missed tripping over one elderly lady who had prostrated herself on the floor in front of him. He apologised as he stepped around her and was greeted in return with a beaming smile and some words, which might have been, 'no problem' in what sounded like Russian but could have been any of the other Slavic languages.

Mike grabbed Billy's arm and pointed. Over to one side was a bearded fellow with a pair of mirrored aviator shades on top of his head, holding a sign with the words Tel Boker on it.
"I guess that's our ride there."
Just ahead of them two girls, both of them pasty white, were already introducing themselves to their driver and he checked their names off a list and then pointed behind him to a place where they should wait until all the arriving volunteers were assembled. Mike and Billy were next up. Mike offered a hand and received a strange look in response.
"Hi we are volunteers from England."
"Names?"
Mike supplied the two names and the guy checked his list and then looked up.
The guy took a moment to size the two friends up before sniffing loudly.
"I don't like English volunteers, you are all lazy drunks." The words, delivered in vaguely accented English, caused both the friends to take a step backwards.
"Go over there and wait with the others."
Billy and Mike wandered over to where the two girls were waiting by an advertising hoarding that ironically bore the words "Welcome to Israel".
Mike was clearly shocked by the reception from the Israeli.
"Well that was a shocking generalisation." He declared in a loud voice.
Billy was more philosophical in his approach.
"The guy might have had a bad experience with Brits. We have been known to misbehave when we are abroad."
"It might be nice to get a chance to prove him wrong."
"I am sure we will get the chance and anyway, we are hardly staggering around vomiting into plant pots, are we?"
Mike smiled. He was happy his friend was with him and seemed to be maintaining a positive outlook on life.
"I wonder if our Israeli friend is always so forthright in his greetings?"
There were eight people already assembled by the hoarding. They all looked up as Mike and Billy arrived and a few embarrassed smiles were exchanged and a few casual nods of greeting. None of them seemed the worse for drink but no one seemed to want to

break the ice. There was an overall air of Anglo-Saxon reserve as they all stood around and waited for their driver to come and collect them.

A couple more volunteers came over to join the group before their driver, satisfied that he had collected all of his passengers came to join them.

He studied the clipboard for a moment then looked up and took a headcount. They two numbers didn't agree because he visually checked them twice before singling Billy out.

"What's your name son?"

"Billy Randell." Billy replied

"You're not on my list."

"I know. I was a last-minute addition". Billy couldn't think of a simpler way of explaining his presence in the group. "The guys at the Airport in London said they had called your people and it was OK for me to join the group."

"That's not the way it works."

"They said I could pay the registration fee directly to you." Billy added, hoping that the bribe of cold hard cash might swing the decision in his favour.

It clearly gave the guy a moment's pause for thought.

Billy was already reaching for his wallet from his backpack. He hoped that producing some real money might prove that he was serious and seal the deal.

The sight of a thick wad of brand new twenty-pound notes seemed to do the trick.

The guy scribbled some numbers down on his clipboard and then held the board up for Billy to read.

There was a column of numbers on the left-hand side of the board and what looked like a spider scrawl and a series of squiggly lines and dots on the right-hand side. Billy realised he was looking at a tally list. The squiggly lines were the items, written in cursive Hebrew and the figures the corresponding costs. Billy was only really interested in the bottom line figure. It would have been nice to know how that figure had been reached, but right now was not the time to ask for a breakdown in English. The figure at the bottom was not unreasonable so Billy counted out the notes and handed them over. They disappeared with amazing speed into the blokes back pocket. Billy secretly wondered if they would ever reach the right people. He didn't care and he was not about to ask for a written receipt either.

With the transaction, out of the way and the money safely out of sight their driver turned to more practical things.

"I have a minibus parked over in the car park so we need to carry all of your stuff over there and load it onto the roof." He didn't offer to help anyone, even the women one of whom seemed to be struggling with a very heavy suitcase. He just set off at a fast walk in the direction of the car park. To get there, they were forced to cross the, very busy airport approach road. This was their first introduction to Israeli drivers. Even when they tried to cross at a pedestrian crossing the flow of traffic continued.

The only concessions seemed to be that the drivers slowed down when they reached the crossing. None of them bothered to stop. The only time the traffic came to a complete standstill was if the road ahead was blocked by sheer weight of vehicles, and then the cacophony of horns was deafening. It didn't seem to matter that the driver ahead was unable to move, a suspension of forward movement meant the driver of the car, bus, taxi or van just leant on the horn. With the heat, the dust, the fumes from the engines and the noise it was truly a Tartarean version of hell.

Entering the parking garage was like crossing into Elysium by contrast. It was cooler out of the sun and the only noise was the occasional squeal of car tyres on the concrete.

Their driver headed towards the stairs and Billy saw the looks of desperation cross the face of the people who were wheeling suitcases.

It was only a single floor to climb and working in relay teams they were able to help everyone with their cases up to the next level. It served two purposes, it forced them all to work together and it forced them to communicate. In that respect, it was a superb ice-breaker and by the time they had arrived at the minibus they were all chatting like old friends, exchanging details of their origins and their reasons for embarking on this great adventure.

As they approached the minibus in the parking garage two figures detached themselves from the shadows and came towards the group. Billy didn't like the look of either of them. They were dressed in cut-off shorts and vest tops and both had long and untidy hair, one dark and the other a dirty blonde. Their faces were both hidden behind massive mirror shades. They looked like

beggars or thieves so Billy did a quick physical check of the whereabouts of all his valuables, covering his pockets and holding on extra tight to the straps of his small backpack.
One casually took the dog-end of his cigarette out of his mouth and exhaled a cloud of smoke, before flicking it to the floor and crushing it under his barefoot.
That made Billy wince but seemed to have no effect on the smoker.
The dark-haired one spoke to their driver and it was quickly clear that these two knew each other. Billy relaxed a little. They were both talking in rapid Hebrew and their exchange took a couple of moments. At the end of the exchange dark hair turned to blonde hair and spoke in English, and much to Billy's surprise, with what sounded like a London accent.
"Well little bruv, you heard the man. A SAS flight touched down a few moments ago so let's go back and see if we can find some more. You remember what SAS stands for?"
"Scandi's are Sexy." They high fived each other.
The blonde noticed that Billy was watching them.
"How are you doing? Welcome to the nuthouse. You have to be mad to work here and it doesn't help." He smiled at Billy.
"Hi." Billy said a little taken aback at being singled out.
The others had moved closer to the minibus and were stating to hoist bags and suitcases up onto the roof.
"Where you from?" the dark-haired guy asked.
"Just outside London and you?"
"We are both Londoners." He pointed to both of them.
"So what are you doing?"
"We are about to head off to comb the queues at Arrivals looking for any volunteers not assigned to a Kibbutz, who want to join our happy band. It's a good way of getting to them before they get into the system and get sent somewhere else. It's not strictly legal but everyone does it."
"And we better go," the blonde cut in, "or all the good ones will be gone."
"You want to come with?" the dark-haired guy asked. "It's a good way to get in first with the cute looking girls, make a good first impression and all." He grinned.
"Yeah why not?" Billy tossed his rucksack in Mike's direction.
"Mike, can you make sure this gets on the roof."

Mike, who was engrossed in conversation with a cute strawberry blonde, waved his hand in acknowledgement. Billy shouldered his small pack and set off in pursuit of the two.

Back in the sunshine Billy delved in his pack and pulled out his shades and the three crossed the road together.

"Well if we are going to be working together then maybe we should introduce ourselves. I'm Stig and this is my little brother Dingo. And before you ask, it was different Milkmen." Stig fielded the obvious question about their different hair colour.

"I am Billy, Billy Randell."

"Actually, having you along with us might help to convince people we are genuine and not just scam artists. A newly arrived volunteer, perfect. Work shirts on?" The question was addressed to his brother who produced two blue shirts out of a small bag he was carrying over one shoulder. The two brothers pulled on the shirts, instantly transforming themselves from vagabonds into a passing impression of two Kibbutzniks.

Stig lit another cigarette before offering the packet to Billy who declined.

"Don't smoke?"

Billy shook his head.

"Wrong answer. From now on you do. You get five free packets of smokes per week and these can be used to get favours from people. My advice, take them, you can always give them away if you don't want them."

"To us," chipped in his brother

They had arrived back at the Arrivals gate and the two brothers started to scan the crowds.

"Anything in particular I should be looking for?" asked Billy

"Lost looking blondes with rucksacks is always a good place to start."

"Or anyone who is not walking slowly studying all of the signs people are holding up. Those people are probably being collected and are already assigned to a Kibbutz."

"If you try to recruit them we could be in a whole heap of trouble."

"Oh and Billy, don't get sucked in by the lost looks. The first rule is they carry their own bags."

Billy tipped two fingers to the side of his temple to show he had understood and received a wide smile in return.

The three waited until it became clear that the SAS flight had cleared customs and immigration and the first blonde-haired passengers began to emerge.
The three of them did well and managed to recruit four Swedish girls who were travelling together and seemed pleased not to have to go through the lottery of the Kibbutz office in Tel Aviv. Although they hadn't known each other before they left Sweden they had, in the short period they had been together, seemed to have become inseparable. So, a promise of one destination for them all and a minibus waiting to whisk them away was more than enough to convince them to follow the three lads back to the parking garage.

#

Back at the minibus things were organised and the luggage all stowed, apart from the bags belonging to the four new arrivals. These were quickly hoisted onto the roof and everyone sorted themselves out with a seat. inside
Billy noticed that the new arrivals were all taken on one side and their names added to the manifest. They also handed over their referral letters. He also noticed that no money changed hands. He wondered whether he should say anything about this but decided that he didn't want to jeopardize his chances of staying together with Mike and from what Stig and Dingo had been telling him, about the potential lottery that awaited him if he went to the Kibbutz office in the centre of Tel Aviv, there was a strong chance he could end up anywhere in the country.
With everybody seated the minibus negotiated a path out of the parking garage and through the endless stream of traffic leaving the Airport. In a short while they were out on the open highway and heading south to their new life. Stig and Dingo were riding up front with the driver who had now been officially introduced as Yossi. He was, according to the two lads, the Volunteer Leader. This meant he was responsible for the well-being of the Volunteers on the Kibbutz as well as assigning them to their rooms and to their work duties.
The two lads, despite their obvious English heritage seemed to get on well with him and teased him constantly both in Hebrew and in English and he seemed to accept their teasing good naturedly.

Billy whispered to Mike out of the corner of his mouth.
"I think that the greeting we got was more for effect than anything else."
"I wouldn't be so sure. I am not about to test the water. I am definitely going to keep my nose clean for the first few weeks."
"Agreed. It wouldn't be too hard to give him a positive impression of us Brits."
"I don't think he has had one up until now."
"Well we can always be the first."
They were both determined that they would set a good example and their determination lasted almost as long as the journey back to Tel Boker and the time it took for them to be assigned to their room.

\#

The journey from Ben Gurion to the Kibbutz reminded Billy of a school outing. There was plenty of chatter in the back of the minibus as people introduced themselves and told their stories. Billy spent the first part of the journey listening intently but as soon as the minibus left the city limits he was captivated by the scenery outside.
As the countryside unfolded before him Billy got his first glimpse of the country that would be his home for, he hoped, the next few months.
Once they had reached the outskirts of Tel Aviv Billy was instantly amazed at how fertile the land looked. On either side of the highway as they drove south the landscape was dotted with fields and orchards. The dark green of the Citrus Orchards was in sharp contrast to the almost white of the desert rock and where the orchards and fields ended then the true nature of the land was revealed. This barren moonscape made testament to the miracles that the Kibbutzniks and Farmers had performed in taming the land.
In several places Billy was able to witness this miracle in the making as the fields were in the process of being irrigated the upright heads of the irrigation pipes scattering their water in rainbow arcs across the growing crops of cereals.
At one point the grumbling over the rising heat in the back of the bus prompted one of the braver newcomers to enquire whether

there was any possibility of turning on the Air conditioning. This was met with a short answer from their driver.
"You want Air-con, open the windows."
So they did and the next time they drove past one of the fields being irrigated they all got to hear the tell-tale rat-tat-tat of the impact springs on the sprinkler heads. It was a new sound to Billy and one that he would forever after equate with Israel.
The drive to Tel Boker from Ben Gurion took them about an hour and things were just beginning to become uncomfortably hot in the back of the bus when Yossi finally slowed down and turned off the main highway and onto a smaller road. None of them noticed the sign at the junction but the lettering in both Hebrew and English said simply "Tel Boker".
Five minutes later at just before six in the evening Billy drove, for the first time, through the gates of Kibbutz Tel Boker.
He could see from the back of the minibus that the gate and perimeter fence were heavy duty, designed to deter even the most ardent attacker. The fence, a little over two metres in height was topped with rolls of razor wire on angled iron brackets, and the gate was a seriously solid construction in wrought iron and steel that rolled back to allow vehicles to enter the settlement
There were several armed guards in military uniforms, on duty around the gate, most of them carrying rifles or machine guns. The whole effect was slightly disconcerting to the newcomers and prompted more than a few comments about Military Bases and Prison Camps.
Billy watched the two brothers in the front seat and noticed that when one of the armed guards came to inspect the occupants of the mini bus he greeted the two of them with a huge smile, a spoken greeting and a tight handshake before he turned to indicate the gate could be opened. This then rolled and clanked its way open enough to allow passage of the mini bus through and on into the Kibbutz itself.
After the Militaristic nature of the front gate the interior of the Kibbutz could not have been of a greater contrast.
Leafy shaded walkways crossed and re-crossed the settlement interspersed among lush green lawns and flowerbeds laid out with an eye for shape and form. The tarmac road wound its way past stark white and gleaming blocks of rooms and houses with small private gardens surrounding them. Even the blocks of communal

rooms looked neat and tidy with individual solar panels and large water heaters perched precariously on their roofs. Mike noticed Billy looking at the rows of rooms.
"They look okay don't they. Look quite comfortable, and if I am not mistaken those rooms have their own bathrooms and showers. Looks like we will be living in the lap of luxury."
It was just unfortunate how wrong Mike eventually proved to be. In a split second, as if they crossed some magical line, the scenery outside the window changed. Instead of leafy green trees and well-tended lawns they saw scrubland and old wizened olive trees. The mini bus ground to a halt outside some dilapidated buildings with heavy steel doors and boarded up windows. Yossi and the two brothers jumped out and threw open one of the doors.
A large folding table, piled high with sheets, blankets and piles of clothes was manhandled out into the daylight and the three started to issue the bedclothes and the traditional blue Kibbutz work clothes to all the new volunteers.
Once everyone was in possession of their new clothes and bedding they were formed up and marched through to the Volunteer blocks and each was directed to one of the vacant rooms on the block. Billy and Mike were sharing a room after a last-minute change to the planned allocation was carried out.
The room was hot and smelt vaguely of dead animals but it was clean, if a little basic in its fixtures and fittings. Each of them had a metal bedframe with a thin mattress on the top and a metal cupboard to keep their clothes and personal items in.
Billy sat on the end of his bed and looked over at Mike.
"Hardly the Hilton but I have stayed in worse places."
Mike was fiddling with the insect grill that had come away from part of the window frame.
"I'd like to know times and dates."
Billy thought he detected a note of despair in Mike's voice but when he looked again his friend was smiling broadly clearly relishing the prospect of roughing it for the next few months. Mike sat down and then lay down on the bed wiggling his shoulders to try and get comfortable.
"You know what Billy-boy. This will do fine."
Billy lay back on his own bed imitating his friend's actions. The bed was not as comfortable as his bed at home but then he had no

reason to expect it would be. He didn't think he would have any trouble sleeping.

#

Almost as soon as their bags hit the floor in the room it seemed that a party started outside at the front of the block.
Billy was all for raging off and joining in the fun but Mike wanted to unpack a few clothes, make up the beds and generally get things organised so the two friends got some of their clothes stowed away and other bits and pieces unpacked. They both took the time to change into clothes more suitable to the heat before they wandered down to where the party was.
At the end of the block of rooms there was an open area where someone had lit a fire. The fire pit was ringed with stones in an area of beaten flat sand. Around this area there were several large ragged looking sofas and armchairs, most of which were occupied by scruffily dressed, well-tanned young people. Music was blaring out from a couple of old hi-fi speakers. One was lashed to the concrete upright post that supported the roof of the veranda that ran along the front of the block, the other was wedged in the fork of two tree limbs. The stereo system pumping out the music was hidden away in one of the rooms.
All the volunteers were talking together, laughing and joking. Most of them had either a bottle of beer or some other drink in one hand and a lit cigarette in the other.
One or two of the Volunteers were standing around and helpfully pointed Billy and Mike in the direction of the large plastic bucket that contained cold bottles of beer and some very large blocks of ice.
"Help yourself, the openers on a string."
Mike and Billy took a bottle each and opened them and then they both took their first sip of Israeli beer. The label said Goldstar and they both agreed it didn't taste bad and best of all it was cold and refreshing and went down well. After the heat of the minibus journey it was what both of them needed.
They joined the others and space was made on one of the sofas for them to sit down.
They introduced themselves and were in turn introduced to everyone sat around the fire, a list of names they had no hope of

remembering. Billy looked around the throng seeking out the two volunteer brothers from the trip from Ben Gurion. They were nowhere to be seen so he asked after them.
"Stig and Dingo? They are working right now, they work in the Dairy so they will be milking cows until midnight."
Billy didn't think he would still be at the party at midnight but to his surprise he was, and it was still going strong when the two brothers arrived.
Things seemed to turn up a notch with their arrival. The music got louder and the drinking got more intense. The beer was replaced by hard spirits and even a few people started dancing.
Someone offered Billy a glass of a white coloured liquid that smelt strongly of aniseed.
"What's this?" Billy asked.
"That my dear boy," came the reply in a rather clipped public schoolboy accent that sounded genuine, "is the queen of the world, the most magnificent, ha-Arac."
Billy sniffed again before putting the glass to his lips and tasting a sip. It was a strong spirit but not altogether unpleasant to taste. More to the point there seemed to be several bottles of this mixture going around among the guests with everyone filling up their glasses as the need arose.
At one point each of the new arrivals was asked to take part in an initiation ceremony. This involved drinking a glass of the fiery spirit, mixed with orange juice down in one long swallow. It was a difficult task and not all of the newcomers acquitted themselves admirably, but then not all of them took up the challenge. As an ice-breaker it was pure entertainment.
At some point Billy noticed Mike was talking to the same girl he had been chatting to at the Airport and they seemed to be getting along well, very well.
The stronger drink was beginning to take its toll and inhibitions were beginning to disappear out of the window. Several couples were making out around the place and a quick glance confirmed that Mike and his new friend were one of those couples.
Billy panicked. Where would he sleep tonight if the room was occupied? How would he know if the room was occupied? They had not arranged any signal, like a towel hanging on the door handle. He was distracted from his worries by the arrival of the four Swedish girls that they had collected at the Airport earlier.

They arrived as a delegation wanting to complain that the noise from the party was keeping them awake, and from their beauty sleep. One charmer said out loud what most of the guys were probably thinking. Any of those four could go a few nights without sleep and still be stunning to look at.

This flattery seemed to mollify them and after a quick conversation in a language that sounded like expectorating to Billy's ears, they decided that if they couldn't stop the party they might as well join in, much to the delight of the males around the fire. Drinks were provided and places made on the sofas for the new arrivals. One of the girls made a beeline for Billy, probably as a face she recognised and sat down next to him.

The presence of this Nordic beauty was enough for Billy to completely forget about Mike so the next time he looked around there was no sign of his friend. Billy found that he didn't really care as he was too wrapped up in this new experience of chatting to someone who spoke passable English, but with a very sexy accent, who had the most amazing sapphire blue eyes, a body that would have shamed a super model, and most surprising of all seemed to be really into him.

This much was made clear to him when other guys tried to muscle in by offering cigarettes or drinks or trying to just cut in on the conversation, Katarina, for at last, he had managed to discover her name, would either just ignore them or politely tell them to buzz off.

The hours flew by and people either went to bed or passed out where they fell and eventually Billy got the feeling that Katarina was beginning to flag as well. She barely managed to stifle a couple of yawns. Despite the fact that as new volunteers they would have the following day free, Yossi had informed them that there would be a tour around the Kibbutz starting at 10:00. Before the tour there would be a special welcome breakfast in the Dining Room, so it might be a good idea for them to get some sleep. He suggested this to Katarina who agreed with his suggestion. She stood up, a little unsteady on her feet, and walked over to where her friend, and Billy guessed, her roommate was chatting to two other girls.

A brief exchange in Swedish took place and the two disappeared off. Billy had hoped for at least a "goodnight" from Katarina, if not a good night kiss or hug. Katarina had been very tactile throughout the evening, always holding onto Billy's forearm when she spoke to him or touching his shoulder and his cheek. It had all seemed very encouraging to him. Maybe, he thought to himself, he had not made such a good impression after all. He set about making himself comfortable on the sofa. Since the party had thinned out by now he had the whole sofa to himself. He didn't think it would get much colder and there was still a bit of residual heat from the last embers of the fire.

He lay back on the sofa and looked up at the canopy of stars overhead. Deep down he didn't mind sleeping out under the stars. He noticed how, with the absence of street lights, the stars seemed much brighter and the sky seemed much clearer. He started to try and identify some of the celestial bodies when a celestial body of a different kind interrupted his view.

Katarina was bent over him; a small towel was around her neck and a toothbrush was in her hand.

"What are you doing here?" she asked.

"Getting comfortable. Mike has a girl in the room so I am going to sleep here."

"No you are not. You are coming to bed with me and Kirsten."

Billy sat bolt upright and then paused. It must be a misunderstanding, a mistranslation. Maybe they had an extra bed in their room. Katarina extended a hand towards him and pulled him to his feet and led the way, holding tight to Billy's hand as if she was afraid he would make a run for it. Billy let her lead the way back to her room. He had already decided that there must be an extra mattress in the room which he could use although it was unlikely there would be sheets and blankets for it.

When Katrina pushed open the door Billy stopped dead in his tracks. Unlike the room, he shared with Mike which was completely bare of detail, in the short time since their arrival the two girls had made a real attempt to make the place look homely. There were a couple of candles burning on a table and there were silk scarfs hung artfully to give the place a very Middle Eastern look. But it was the bed that drew Billy's attention.

The standard Kibbutz bed was a single-sized metal frame measuring two metres in length and about eighty centimetres in width, with a single foam mattress placed on top. There were two of these in his own room. The girls had been creative here too. The

two frames had been pushed together and the legs secured with straps so there was one large double bed in middle of the room.
"Wow." It was the only word Billy would trust himself with.
"You like?" Kirsten, the other Swedish girl asked. She had the same sing-song accent as her roommate, and the same blonde hair, blue eyes and fantastic figure as Katarina. Now that she was back in her room Kirsten had also taken the liberty of removing her shorts so she was standing by the bed wearing only a loose vest top and a pair of white knickers.
Katarina had to pull Billy bodily into the room. He had stopped dead in his tracks in the doorway.
"We want the door closed to stop the flying bugs." She stated, as if trying to explain away her actions.
"Of course," Billy stuttered, still not fully trusting his voice.
With the door shut Katarina hung up her towel and then unzipped her shorts and stepped out of them.
The two girls moved to either side of the bed and sat down.
Billy stood frozen on the spot with indecision. He didn't want to presume anything and was waiting for an invitation. He didn't have to wait long.
"Are you okay to sleep in the middle?" Katarina leaned over and patted the bed, indicating where Billy was expected to sleep.
"Er yeah, er sure."
What happened next was something that Billy had only dreamed of in his wildest wettest dreams. The two Swedish girls both stripped off their vest tops and naked to the waist slid under the sheets.
Billy followed suit losing his t-shirt before crawling up the middle of the bed and scrambling to get under the covers as well.
"No no no." The two girls held down the sheets.
'So', Billy thought, 'They expect me to sleep on top of the covers'.
That was to be expected he thought.
"You take off shorts before you get under the covers."
Billy reached for the fastening of his shorts and stopped dead.
"We might have a problem there."
Billy's last act before heading off to join the party had been to pull on a pair of Bermuda style board shorts with the sown in nylon lining. This lining made the wearing of underpants uncomfortable so Billy had gone without.
"Problem what problem?"

Katarina was resting her head on her hand and looking up at Billy who was now kneeling in the middle of the bed..
"Well to put it bluntly I only have these shorts on, no underwear, no boxers, you understand."
"So where is the problem? Are you shy? You want us to blow out the candles?"
"Well as long as you understand." Billy had never been shy, but at the same time he didn't want to assume anything and risk upsetting his two gorgeous hosts.
Kirsten laughed and said something to her friend in Swedish which Billy obviously didn't understand.
Katarina replied and then turned to Billy.
"Kirsten has told me off for teasing you and said we should be kind to you."
She looked over at her friend and said one word in Swedish.
Kirsten nodded and the two girls both reached under the covers only for their hands to appear moments later holding their underwear.
Now there were two totally naked Swedish beauties under the covers. Billy accepted defeat, peeled off his shorts and joined them under the sheets.
This was going to be a long night and Billy was conscious of the effort he was having to exert to avoid becoming aroused. This effort doubled as the three got comfortable in the bed and naked skin started to make contact with naked skin.
The candles were extinguished and they all lay there in the dark.
"Well goodnight" he said to no one in particular.
"What no goodnight kiss?" Katarina's voice came out of the dark very close to Billy's ear.
He turned his head and their lips met. Billy was unprepared for the force or the passion behind the kiss and it certainly went on for a couple of minutes as their lips darted around each other. Billy eventually broke contact, conscious of the effect the kiss was having on his manhood, and conscious of the third person in the bed with them. As if to reinforce his feeling a voice spoke behind his head very close to his ear.
"What about me? Do I get a kiss goodnight too?"
Billy turned around and Kirsten pushed herself bodily against him, crushing her breasts to his chest as her lips sought out his lips.

Billy really had to fight to suppress his arousal as the kiss continued for a similar duration.

The whole situation was bizarre for him, bordering on the ridiculous and he thought for a moment that the whole thing was some elaborate hoax and as soon as he tried to make a serious move one or the other girls would point out his foolishness.

But Katarina's hand, that was now gently stroking his stomach was telling him another story and when he broke away from kissing Kirsten and lay on his back both pairs of hands began to stroke his chest before moving down onto the flat of his stomach.

One of Billy's hands was taken and placed on Katarina's body, the other a moment later was placed on Kirsten's. From the angle he was lying at it was impossible to do more than stroke their flanks and upper thighs, although this didn't seem to deter the girls, who were both wriggling into position to demonstrate they wanted a more intimate touch from him. He was not about to shy away from them and suddenly the whole bed dissolved into a whirling maelstrom of writhing limbs, lips and breasts as they all sought to derive as much pleasure from each other as was possible.

In the dark, it was impossible to tell who was who but at some point, one of the girls straddled Billy and slipped his manhood inside her before riding him quickly to a shuddering orgasm, and then being replaced by the other who performed a similar act with the same result. In the midst of all the thrashing sweaty limbs Billy managed his own climax though he was unsure which one of the two was the recipient of his seed until he heard Katarina whisper in the dark.

"And tomorrow you finish with Kirsten."

Billy took a moment to try and decide whether she meant their threesome was to be a one night only affair or whether her words had a more literal meaning. He was still trying to figure this out as the three of them fell asleep in an untidy mass of exhausted bodies.

\#

The strangest thing about waking up naked in bed with these two women was the total lack of embarrassment shown by either of them about events of the previous evening. It was almost as if nothing had happened, but at the same time it was clear that something had.

When Billy opened his eyes, Kirsten was already out of bed and busying herself making coffee, which she brought back to bed and they all sat there under the sheets, drinking coffee, and talking about their expectations for the day ahead and indeed in the longer term, where they ultimately wanted to be put to work.

Billy felt slightly uncomfortable sitting there, naked between two lovely girls and some of his discomfort must have showed on his face. The girls were both happy chattering away when almost together they both stopped talking and turned towards Billy.

"Are you alright Billy. You are very quiet this morning."

Billy nodded his head dumbly, his mouth full at that precise moment with coffee.

"What happened last night? This has made you happy?"

Billy who had swallowed his coffee by now managed to get out a quick 'yes' before Katarina continued speaking.

"We don't do this all the time, but last night was our first night here so we made a promise on the plane we would stay together the first night. When I told Kirsten that I wanted you she said she would have you too so we could be together the first night you see?"

Billy did see. He was still having flashbacks to the contorting pleasure seeking bodies of the previous night and these visions were causing him intense discomfort as he tried to disguise his growing arousal. There was no hiding it from the two girls.

Kirsten noticed it first and pointed it out with a string of excited Swedish which like all their previous exchanges, went straight over Billy's head. Katrina replied in the same language and Billy's half-finished coffee cup was taken away from him. He was about to complain when it suddenly dawned on him what was about to happen. The girls had set aside their mugs as well and were getting ready for a little morning action.

A while later when they were all sat together with fresh cups of coffee and big satisfied smiles on their faces the conversation returned to their expectations for the day ahead.

During the party the previous evening several of the established Volunteers had been offering advice to the newcomers on the potentials and the pitfalls of the various jobs on offer to the Volunteers as well as offering their own speculation over where the "newbies" were likely to end up being placed.

This assessment was based, in part, on what was going on in the Agricultural lifecycle of the Kibbutz. At harvest times, there was a higher demand for workers in the fields or the orchards. At other times, more emphasis was placed on other areas. There was also a "macho" culture attached to certain jobs. A long day out with the irrigation team was considered to be a job only for real tough guys, or tough girls, the Kibbutz culture didn't seem to discriminate when it came to gender, whereas the inside jobs were considered to be for people of a more delicate nature.

The two Swedes had both set their hearts on working with the young children and had already made their wishes known to the Volunteer leader, although he had remained noncommittal on their eventual work placement.

With the coffee finished Billy felt it was time to make himself scarce and return to his own room. At the very least he hoped that things might be concluded between Mike and his partner, so he could at least get access to his clothes and toilet bag so he could shower and change.

He climbed out of bed and hunted around for his shirt and shorts. He was naked but after last night he felt he had no secrets to hide from the two girls who sat watching him from under the covers. He located both items and slipped into his shorts and pulled the shirt over his head. He slid his feet into his flip-flops and then went over to Katarina and kissed her goodbye. Kirsten let out a little whimper of distress so he went around to her side of the bed and did the same to her and then took his leave.

The block outside the Swedish girls' room was deserted, there was not another volunteer anywhere to be seen. Billy was pleased that there were no prying eyes to watch him leaving and therefore no chance of difficult or embarrassing questions being asked later on. He found his way back to his room without meeting a soul. Obviously, those volunteers scheduled for work would be long gone and the new arrivals, no doubt, sleeping off the after-effects of last night welcome party.

Outside the door of his room he paused and pressed his ear to the door. There were no sounds from inside, so he risked a glance through the window. In the gloom within, he could make out the figure of Mike asleep in his bed and he appeared to be alone. Billy paused and then pushed the door open.

The metal door was heavy and let out an audible squeak as it swung open. It was not excessive but loud enough to cause Mike to stir from his slumber. He rolled over and opened one eye. Seeing Billy standing in the middle of the room he sat up bolt upright.
"Billy, I am so sorry. I don't know what came over me last night."
"Did she come over you or the other way around?" Billy grinned and got a wide grin in return. "At least tell me you know her name."
"Of course. And as a gentleman I will not discuss my private life. Not even with my best friend."
"Well you are no fun." Billy sat on the edge of his unmade, and as yet unslept in, bed.
"No seriously mate. I feel really bad about shutting you out of your own room. Just where did you sleep. I came looking for you about 6 am but you were nowhere to be found."
Billy gave a knowing smile. "I was taken care of, thanks very much."
"By one of the Swedish girls."
"In a manner of speaking."
"You dog."
If only you knew the half of it, Billy thought to himself.
He, like his friend was reluctant to fill in all the gory details. Some things were best left unsaid. They had never been very much for gossiping about the more intimate details of their lives.
Billy started to sort through his luggage, looking for towels, soap and shower gel and a fresh set of clothes for the day ahead. The temperature outside was already starting to rise as he headed off for the shower block.
The area of Tel Boker set aside for Volunteers lay separate from the rest of the Kibbutz and consisted of several blocks of prefabricated concrete rooms laid out in rows of five. There were eight blocks arranged in two groups of four and each group was serviced by a communal shower block. The volunteer blocks were not segregated by sex and it seemed to Billy that the same went for the showers.
As he was arriving there were two girls leaving and although he was alone in the shower block while he undressed he had barely managed to work up a lather with the shower gel before he was joined by another young lady. She seemed to be cool about the mixed nature of the shower and disrobed and jumped under the

water, so Billy remained calm and continued with his ablutions, trying not to pay any attention to the other bather. He just felt that it was rude to stare.

He did have a private chuckle to himself at the thought of some of the more conservative English girls discovering they had to share their shower time with guys. He could not imagine that being too well received. But then after a short reconsideration and in order to be fair he revised his opinion. He was English and he saw nothing wrong with mixed showers, so why should anyone else. It was all part of the Kibbutz experience.

He did not make too much of a show about his nakedness and clad himself in a large towel as soon as he was finished under the shower, using a smaller towel to dry his extremities. His fellow bather didn't seem to be body conscious and although they didn't go so far as to speak she was not in a hurry to cover her body up and was happy to walk around in the changing area, fixing her hair and drying it wearing only a pair of knickers. Billy dressed quickly and then left the block heading back to his rooms. This Kibbutz life was definitely going to be an interesting and eye-opening experience.

\#

When Yossi, the volunteer leader came to collect them all for the start of the sightseeing tour most of the volunteers had managed to pry themselves out of their beds, although one or two of them were still looking a little worse for wear after their first night celebrations and there were a few red faces as people had woken up to the fact that they had made fools of themselves the previous evening. Mike was together with his strawberry blonde. She had approached Mike as soon as he and Billy had joined the group of waiting Volunteers.

Mike, much to Billy's surprise was happy to show affection in public, something he had rarely done at home and after a brief but rather passionate greeting he had introduced her to Billy. Kate had the good grace to flush with a little colour in her cheeks when Mike introduced Billy as his roommate who had to make "alternative arrangements last night."

Billy had moved swiftly to reassure Kate that she could relax, as he had been well taken care of, which solicited another long look from Mike, who then had the good grace to look totally shocked when Katarina and Kirsten arrived and each, in turn, planted a long passionate greeting kiss on Billy's lips.

Mike looked pointedly at both Swedish girls, as if demanding an explanation, as the two of them sat either side of Billy each holding possessively on to one of his arms. Billy simply made a zipping and locking movement in front of his mouth. The message was clear. My lips are sealed. All Mike got was an introduction. Mike shook his head at his friend in total disbelief. He had gone as far as to feel sorry for turning Billy out of the room on their first night and had been worried enough that when Kate had finally decided to return to her own room, he had gone looking for Billy, assuming he would be sleeping out in the open on one of the sofas. Instead it appeared that Billy had been well taken care of, by not one, but two stunning Swedish girls. He definitely had to revise his opinion of his friend given his apparent success with the opposite sex in the last week or so. Billy had never seemed to be much of a ladies' man but clearly the decision to travel had changed all that.

Yossi was minus his clipboard today and merely did a brief head count before leading them off in the direction of the Kibbutz administration buildings where they were treated to a tour of the Kitchen and Dining Room before sitting down to eat a Brunch breakfast.

The buffet, set up on a long table was a foretaste of the food that they could expect to be served every day. There was a prevalence for healthy foods like salads, yoghurts and cream cheese, eggs, both fried and boiled were also available. It was strange for Billy to watch people piling their plates with salad for breakfast but he looked at his own plate with a pair of fried eggs and two pieces of bread on it and re-considered, quickly returning to the buffet line and adding a couple of scoops of the mixed salad of cucumber and tomato to his plate.

Yossi pointed out the tables that were set aside for Volunteers, although he did add that they were free to sit anywhere in the Dining Room. The tables could sit eight so Billy, Mike, Kate, Katrina and Kirsten almost filled a single table by themselves. The last three places were taken by two English guys and a girl who seemed to have travelled together from home.

Billy was trying to figure out the dynamic of this small group. Were two of them a couple and the other just a friend, or were

things more complicated? He guessed that would take some time to figure out but the three were friendly enough and everyone was excited to be getting to know new people. The strangest thing about this assembled group was that they all spoke English when talking together. What struck Billy as really strange was that the Swedish girls even began to speak English when talking to each other. Billy made mental note to ask the girls about this later.
After brunch, they were taken to the car park behind the dining room where they were met by a thirty-ton truck and driver, waiting to take them on their tour. The truck itself was painted battleship grey, although at some time in its past it had probably been a more military green as there were places where another colour paint was visible. It had clearly started life as a military vehicle used to carry troops or supplies around. It had wooden sides and metal struts supporting a canvas roof.
At the rear there was a short ladder welded on to allow people to climb up and into the back. Billy waited his turn in the queue and then followed Mike, Kate and the two Swedes up the ladder. Inside the truck smelt of a mixture of wet canvas, dust and diesel oil. Billy took a place on one side between Kirsten and Katarina. Billy guessed the wooden benches in the back of the truck would not be easy on the bones as they traversed the dirt tracks around the settlement and he was right. No amount of clinging on could prevent them from being bounced around like the contents of a washing machine. Some of the impacts were bone-jarringly heavy and once they had left the access road that ran from the Kibbutz gate to the administration block and Dining Hall they were riding mainly on dirt or sand tracks.
The first port of call was the Refet or Dairy and waiting to give them the sightseeing tour were Billy's two friends Stig and Dingo. They split the group into two and took the different groups off in opposite directions. Mike and Billy were with Dingo and he took them first inside the main block which held the milking parlour and storage tank. The milking parlour was not in use so it was strangely silent except for the occasional drip of water from a leaking hosepipe or off the drying milking machines.
They went down into the operational area where they were shown how the machines worked and how to put a machine on a cow. After that it was back into the sunshine and a trip around the calves' area where they kept the younger claves in small stalls and

pens. A quick trip up to feeding area where all the meals were prepared for the cattle and the tractors and trailers were in the process of making the afternoon food. As they stood on the edge of the area they were able to watch the precision dance between the two vehicles involved in the process, the smaller yellow JCB tractor that scooped up the food in a huge bucket before dumping the correct amount in the feed trailer, pulled by a much larger green John Deere.

After this they wandered back through the cow pens and got back in the truck. There were several of the Volunteers who expressed their distaste at the general smell of the place and showed doubt about being able to work there, but someone was quick to point out there was little likelihood of any of the new volunteers being rostered to work in the Refet.

The next stop on the tour was only a short drive from the Refet. This was one of the most important places on the Kibbutz.

Being on the edge of the desert, there was very little rainfall during the main growing season so all the crops had to be irrigated and the Irrigation Yard was the centre of this operation.

There were two main types of irrigation employed by the Kibbutz. There were the upright sprinklers that cast a spray of water in a large arc over the crops. These were used with crops like cereals. The other sort was the drip lines which were laid along the rows of crops and targeted the roots of the growing plants with a more focused and controlled stream of water. These were used on larger plants or bushes like Maize and Cotton or in some cases in the Orchards.

The long steel pipes for the sprinkler systems were laid out on huge cast iron frames and a special trailer was driven underneath and the frames could then be lifted and driven out to the fields. The black plastic drip lines were stored on what looked like huge cotton reels. These could be attached to a specialist winch that was mounted on the back of a tractor and the lines could then be run out or wound in as needed.

The boss of the Irrigation team was there to give them a general introduction and pep-talk on the work done by his team and he went a long way to stress the importance of his team and their work in the general success of the agricultural part of the Kibbutz economy. He was also looking for more hands to join the team as they faced a particularly busy period in their working year.

The pep-talk obviously worked as there were several of the volunteers who seemed keen to join the team in Irrigation as they drove away from the yard and onto their next stop which was the polar opposite of the agricultural side of the Kibbutz.

A few years before some clever heads in the Kibbutz management team had seen that there was money to be made by moving the Kibbutz away from an agricultural only economy and had looked into investing in some form of industry. Tel Boker had chosen plastics as their field of industry, more specifically manufacture of sheet plastics.

With the research and development phases completed the factory had just switched over to full production and it was difficult to hear yourself think inside the main production hall where the enormous machines were running. At the one end the raw plastic, in the form of plastic beads, was being poured into huge hoppers. These beads were then heated to melting point and the molten plastic was poured out in a long line where it was then sent through heated rollers and flattened out into sheets. The eventual thickness of the sheets at the end of the process was what defined their end usage. The thicker, heavy-duty plastic sheeting would be used to line reservoirs and swimming pools whereas much thinner examples could be used to provide roofs and walls to greenhouses. The boffins in the labs had also done research into which colours worked best as greenhouses and which colours reduced the evaporation of water in reservoirs and swimming pools. When it came to water it was all about collecting and saving as much of the precious resource as possible.

At the end of the production line a gigantic machine rolled the sheet plastic onto huge spindles that were then taken off and transported by fork-lift to the warehouse area to await shipping. The whole place was noisy and the heat inside the production hall was unbearable. Given that the outside temperature was climbing towards the mid-thirties, to be in this manmade hell would truly be a punishment.

Unfortunately, it was for precisely this reason that Volunteers made up a large slice of the workforce and the volunteers that Billy noticed were definitely not a happy bunch.

Yossi was quick to point out that attachment to the factory crew would only be a temporary one and that Volunteers could expect to be reassigned to other teams after only a few weeks unless of course, by some weird coincidence they enjoyed the work, in which case they would be welcome to stay as long as they liked. Billy was shaking his head in disbelief. Could anyone actually choose to work in these conditions rather than be forced into it. He was still shaking his head when they left the deafening noise of the factory complex. Back aboard the truck and heading for the next destination, there was a general hum of conversation among the newcomers. As a group the volunteers had clearly been shocked at the possibility of having to work in such awful conditions and were debating among themselves what they could do to get out of it. The general consensus of opinion was that by offering to work in one of the other areas or expressing a desire to do so might prevent them being condemned to the factory for a month.

Billy and Mike were both debating applying to work on the Irrigation team as then at least they would be working outside and not confined to the biblical fiery furnace of the factory. Their next destination was the complete opposite. They arrived in the middle of the Avocado orchards. This was a real hive of activity as they were right in the middle of the harvest. The picking machines, like mini cranes, zipped around in and out of the rows of trees, depositing the picked fruits in large plastic crates.

The man in charge of the Avocado orchards was an ancient looking fellow who appeared to have been carved out of wood from one of the trees he tended with such love and care. Burnt dark by the sun, his face was creased into heavy lines by decades of exposure to the elements. Yossi introduced him as an original "Sabra", one of those people who had been born before Israel was really Israel when the British Government had been in charge and the area was known as the British Mandate of Palestine.

Jacob stepped in as Yossi was about to embark on a full account of his heroics in the various wars that had defined the Israeli state since its inception.

"Enough already," he growled, his voice matched his appearance, rich and dark. "There will be time for all of that later."

Yossi, who clearly respected the older man deferred to him and stood back to one side.

"Right," Jacob took centre stage in front of the assembled newcomers. "A fair few of you will be joining me tomorrow morning as this is the principal focus for the Kibbutz at the moment. We have just started the harvest and this will probably take us a week or more to finish, even with the extra hands. I will of course be here to help you and explain the job to you so I look forward to seeing you tomorrow." His short speech finished he nodded to Yossi and disappeared back among his trees.

Billy noticed there were a couple of Volunteers driving around on the picking machines and they all seemed to be reasonably happy in their work.

The truck had turned around and was pointing back the way they had come so they all piled back on board and headed for their next destination.

Their route took them down by the border fence and Yossi stopped long enough to climb in the back and explain the setup.

The fence was two metres high with coiled razor wire along the top edge. Between the fence and the border road there was an area of ploughed sand.

"Is that a minefield?" one of the volunteers asked, half seriously, half as a joke.

"No it's not a minefield, but the Army come by every day and plough the sand."

"Why?" another asked.

"So that they can see footprints in the sand if someone manages to cross over the fence."

"Does that happen often?" another voice asked.

"Not as often as it used to. But we do still get the occasional incursion."

The use of that word elicited a few alarmed looks from the Volunteers and Billy felt a small quiver of fear in his left leg.

"But," Yossi continued, "hopefully the Army get to them before they get anywhere near the Kibbutz."

The cautionary tale on security had the desired effect on the assembled group and they were subdued as they continued on their journey.

It was only later in the afternoon when they were all called together with the rest of the Volunteers that Yossi's tale of imminent death at the hands of terrorists was exposed for what it really was, a scare tactic.

According to the established Volunteers who were on hand, there had been two incursions in the last year. On one occasion, it had been a young man who had been trying to get to an optician to buy some new eye-glasses. He had been intercepted on his way back. On the other, the guy had walked into the arms of an army Patrol who had promptly taken him to the nearest checkpoint and sent him back across the border. He had been trying to go shopping for food and supplies, in the supermarket in the nearby town. Neither had posed the remotest threat to the local communities.

One of the older volunteers had pointed over to the far side of the open area where a door was leaning drunkenly against the end of one of the blocks. It was the same size, shape and colour as the heavy steel doors for each of the rooms on the block with the exception that there were three large holes punched right through the metal skin from front to back, the ends on the inner side peeled back to sharp points and revealing the silver of the metal under the paint.

"If you ask Yossi or any of the others they will tell you that those holes were caused by bullets fired by a terrorist. The reality is that it was a Dutch volunteer who got drunk one night. He was pissed off that his girlfriend had left him and was with another volunteer. He took matters into his own hands and attacked their door with a short length of metal pipe"

Billy took a moment to examine the damage. The holes were about the right size to have been made by a pipe, but then he had no idea what devastation or damage a bullet might wreak.

Billy looked over at Mike who was stood a few feet away also examining the damaged door.

"So it looks like we have to worry more about drunk Dutchmen than Terrorists."

"Only if you steal their girlfriends Billy boy."

The reason all of the new Volunteers had been called together was that Yossi was due to arrive to hand out the job assignments for the following morning.

Some of the established volunteers were present because, as the current incumbents of the jobs in the dining room and dishwasher, the arrival of new blood was their only hope of escape from the drudgery and the chance to move on to new work assignments.

They were therefore as excited as the newcomers to discover what those new assignments would be.

During the rest of the trip which had taken in the Orange orchards, the Greenhouses which were just a little bit hotter than the factory, if that was possible, and the Cotton Fields, Billy had not seen anything that really inspired him so he had, like Mike, put in a request to work in the Irrigation team. Now they were both eagerly awaiting their fate along with all the other new volunteers.

Mike and Billy were both lucky, they had been picked to join the Irrigation team, although they felt a little less fortunate when they were told to be ready at the assembly point for collection at 05:30.

"That's the middle of the night." Billy grumbled under his breath. Then looked anxiously around to see if anyone had heard him. His comment had gone totally unnoticed in the general hubbub that had broken out after Yossi had finished his announcements. There were more than a few of the Volunteers, both established and new who were unhappy with where their names had ended up. And voices were raised in protest against their collective fates.

Yossi, for his part, had not stuck around to listen to their moans. He had made a hasty exit almost as soon as the last name was out of his mouth.

"Good man management skills there." One disgruntled volunteer commented.

"Fuck it, let's get drunk." Another of the disillusioned one's added. This seemed to be a vote winner and they all headed back to the party area and someone cranked up the stereo and put on some music. Others handed out the beers and other drinks. It was a well-oiled machine grinding into action as it had done the night before and would do again every night that there were volunteers who wanted to party.

Billy and Mike took a short break when the Kibbutz shop opened for the evening session. This was their first of many ventures into the General Store that served the needs of the Kibbutz.

There were larger stores in the nearby town, Supermarkets, other shops, bars and restaurants, offering all the other services that one would equate with a small city.

The shop on the Kibbutz was tailored to the more immediate needs of the local residents. There were basically two aisles with shelves on both sides so there was a flow around the shop.

The merchandise was in keeping with what people living in a place where their main dietary requirements, their three square-meals a day were catered for. There was a heavy emphasis on those extra items that could not be provided by the Kibbutz. There was a large section for sweets, biscuits and cakes. There was a freezer cabinet well stocked with ice cream and more exotic items like frozen gateaux.

There was a section for toiletries and personal grooming although Billy noticed the aftershave collection was all items that had been fashionable decades ago in the UK and most of the boxes looked old and dusty.

The largest section of the store was devoted to soft drinks and the place seemed to do a roaring trade in large bottles of Coke and other related beverages, which the members seem to be buying in bulk.

Next to the soft drink section was a much smaller area selling alcohol. Israeli's as a nation were not big consumers of alcohol and this was reflected in both the limited selection and the quantities in stock. This area of the shop proved popular with the volunteers and there was a long queue of them collecting crates of beer or bottles of the stronger spirits, exotic looking bottles with equally exotic looking labels.

When Billy and Mike made it to the front of the queue they had a split second to review their options before the press from behind them pushed them further on. Billy made a snap decision and grabbed the one bottle from the shelf with a label he could almost read. He assumed Wodka was just a fancy way of saying Vodka, or at least that was what he hoped. Mike grabbed a bottle as well. At least they could both suffer together.

Before he had got around to reading out the work assignments list Yossi had issued all the new volunteers with their shop cards. These blue slips had their name and an amount of money in shekels scribbled on the top. Billy and Mike were clutching their cards in their hands now.

They had only ventured over there initially to collect their free cigarettes, toilet paper and aerogrammes, but in addition to the Wodka they also came away with three crates of the local beer. They both felt they should make a contribution to the party drinks situation and it was a contribution that was gratefully received. They placed one of the crates in the hands of their hosts to be placed in the fridge and took the other two back to their room.

They had to return the trolley they had borrowed to transport their purchases back to the room and when they returned to the party it was in full swing. Billy sought out Katarina and found her with the other Swedish volunteers.

All of the four new girls had been rostered to join the Avocado harvest and were scheduled for pick up at 05:30 like Billy so they were all, sensibly, being a little careful about what they were drinking. The same could not be said for the English who were chucking the stuff away like there was no tomorrow. Billy was already beginning to see why Yossi had been so hostile from the start. If this was an example of the way the Brits behaved then it was clear to see why there was general dislike for them among the Kibbutz members.

Billy was not claiming to be a saint, far from it, but he didn't really want to risk a full day out in the hot sun with a monster hangover so he was a little restrained over his alcohol consumption. Coupled to this he was not sure what would happen later with Katarina. She spent most of the time with her fellow countrymen and women and Billy was not sure if the previous night had been a one-off. He was not getting the same loving vibe that he had experienced the previous night and it left him slightly puzzled.

He watched Katarina from the over the top of his glass, following her every movement and then tried to look away every time she looked in his direction. It was childish, playground stuff but it worked because after about an hour she detached herself from her group and crossed to where Billy was sitting. She perched on the arm of the sofa next to Billy and leaned over him. Billy tried very hard not to stare down the front of her t-shirt which gaped open. She placed a hand on each of his shoulders.

"Hello handsome, have you missed me?"

With those words all the doubts Billy had been having evaporated.

"Oh I have been trying to imagine life without you." Billy replied with a sly grin.

"Oh yeah." Katarina removed her hands and crossed her arms across her chest, her face was a stern mask. "And how did that make you feel?"

Billy pulled a sad face, "Miserable".

"Good," the smile returned to her lips and more importantly to her eyes. She bent her head and kissed Billy passionately. When the kiss finished, she pulled her head back slightly and whispered under her breath.

"Kirsten is sleeping with the other girls tonight so it is just you and me."

Billy gave a wicked smile. He had been happy for the three of them to repeat the previous night's exercise but if he was truthful he felt more comfortable in a one on one situation.
"Just tell me when you want to leave and I will be right behind you."
"How about now? I am so horny."
Billy polished off his drink in one gulp.
"Lead on princess."
.

CHAPTER SEVEN

Katarina's alarm clock bleating pulled Billy from his slumber. It was electronic and it was annoyingly loud. Billy rolled over on his side and buried his head under the blankets.
"Time to get up," Katrina planted her foot in the middle of his back and pushed. Billy rolled over and out of the bed impacting on the stone floor.
"Ouch." He sat up and rubbed his elbow where it had struck the cold marble floor.
Katrina was sat up in bed the blankets pooled in a heap at her waist. She stretched languidly like a cat her arms way above her head tightening her breasts into two firm and glorious mounds of delight. The cool air had got to her nipples which stood out like two ripe cherries.
Billy banished any lustful thoughts as he reached for his shorts and pulled them on. He had to get back to his room and pull on some work clothes, try and find a cup of tea or something else warm to drink and he had only half an hour before pick up. He leaned across the bed and gave Katrina a passionate lingering kiss.
"Good luck with work today." He offered over his shoulder as he made for the door.
He pushed open the door to his own room without pausing and created a veritable storm of movement in the bed as naked limbs were hastily concealed under inadequate blankets. He had obviously interrupted more than a good morning kiss.
"Sorry guys but I need to get some work clothes." He offered and moved over to his locker and opened the door.
He risked a glance across at where Mike's bed was and was greeted by a lovely sight of a pair of satin smooth, white female buttocks peeking out from under the blankets.

He refocused his attention on finding a pair of blue shorts and a work shirt and used the cover of the locker door to perform a quick change. He tossed his casual shorts and t-shirt from the previous evening in a pile on his bed then pulled out his work boots. These were tan in colour, made of canvas with a rubber sole. He pulled them on his feet and then glanced over at Mike's bed. The buttocks were still on show and Mike was making no sign of moving any time soon.

"We have twenty minutes till the truck leaves for the fields, you had better make it fast." Billy said with a degree of humour in his voice and he left the room.

At the end of the block there were a group of volunteers congregated around a kettle and as Billy approached his nostrils were assaulted by the smell of fresh brewed coffee. Somebody put a glass of the thick black liquid in his hand and Billy took a long sniff of the strong aroma.

"That will either put lead in your pencil or give you heartburn for a week," one of the other Volunteers offered.

"Right now, I would take either." Billy replied.

"Is there one of those for me." A familiar voice said from just behind him

Mike was stood there in his blue work clothes, his hair wet as if he had just stepped out of a shower.

"My god that was quick." Billy grinned at his mate. "In fact, that must be a new world record."

"World record for what?" one of the other volunteers asked

"Nothing," Mike said although he did have the good grace to blush a little.

"By the way she's got a nice arse." Billy was not going to let things drop so easily.

"You should not have been looking," Mike whispered under his breath.

"It was a bit difficult it was hanging half out of the bed."

"Well you could have knocked before you barged in on us."

"You are dead right, I could have, but the simple fact is I didn't. I could have been in my bed all night, it is my room too."

Mike looked shocked at the prospect of an audience. "You wouldn't?"

"I might."

Their discussion even conducted in hissed whispers was attracting attention from the other volunteers. Mike was beginning to look worried that his whole personal life was about to become a matter for public debate. He glanced over Billy's shoulders, seeing the assembled crew all listening intently while trying to pretend they weren't interested.

Further discussion was interrupted by the wheezing arrival of the truck to take them off to the fields where the Irrigation crew were assembling for the day's work.

\#

Billy was on his last legs. He was physically finished, exhausted and ready to give up. Even at this early hour the sun seemed to beat down relentlessly, reflecting back off the hot sand. What was more worrying for Billy was that he had stopped sweating an hour ago. He was no medical man but even he knew that when the body stopped sweating you were getting perilously close to dehydration. The dull thump in his temples was a further sign that there was trouble on the way. He had taken breaks with all the others when they were offered and had drank water, like all the others, but he was still struggling now. He felt nauseous and faint.

The work they were doing was relentless. A tractor and trailer arrived at one end of the field and then moved slowly down the field dropping the long metal pipes off the side. Behind them a crew would move in and connect the pipes together. It was a non-stop process and as they neared the end of the field so another trailer filled with more pipes would arrive and manoeuvre into position.

Then, after a few moments pause they would be off again in the opposite direction. In Billy's mind the only thing missing was the heavily built man with the bald head and the loincloth wielding a whip. He was certainly able to hear the drumbeat pounding to keep them all in time, until he realised the beat was in his head and was in fact the sound of his own heartbeat.

What made things worse was that Mike did not seem to be suffering anywhere near as badly as Billy was. If anything, Mike seemed to be getting stronger as each row passed. He was certainly managing to keep pace with the others, which Billy was not. Billy had never considered Mike to be a fitness freak. He was not the sporty type. Like everyone else they had both played sport at school, but this sporting life had ceased for both of them the day they left school. The only difference between the two was that Mike travelled everywhere at home by bicycle whereas Billy took the bus or walked. Could that really be the difference between them? It certainly seemed to be.

Billy knew that at the end of this particular row there would be another short water and rest break and so he focused all his energies on making it to the end of the row and the waiting water container.

Billy bent down and grabbed the free end of the next pipe section drawing it towards the length of pipe that he had been building and he married the two ends together, flicking the clasp that sealed the two ends together. He straightened up again, moving to the left where the next section of pipe was lying. He reached across the pipe to grab the end and the whole world tipped on its access, there was a rushing wind roaring in his ears. His first thought was there was an earthquake and as if to confirm his fear, as he watched, in slow motion, the ground at his feet rose up towards him, slamming into his face and the whole world went black.

Seen from another angle it was a totally different story.

Mike had looked over to check on Billy's progress and as he watched he saw Billy reach for the next pipe section before he pitched forward, face down in the dirt.

He dropped the section of pipe he was holding and ran over to his friend, grabbed him by the shoulder and turned him over onto his back. Most of the others when they eventually noticed what had happened all stood there laughing.

Mike was angry and yelled at them to come and help as he half carried, half dragged Billy's unconscious body to the end of the field and into the shade offered by one of the Irrigation teams vehicles. He lay Billy gently on the sand and then went to retrieve one of the water containers. He screwed the big lid off the top and splashed a large amount of the still cold water on his face. This helped to revive his friend a little. Billy shook his head and although his eyes remained closed he began to mumble incoherently.

The team boss seeing that the situation was maybe a little more serious than he had first thought, barked at the rest of the team to carry on working while he came over to assess the situation.

He knelt down beside Mike and began to examine Billy. He checked the temperature of his forehead and the back of his neck and tutted. He lifted one of Billy's eyelids and tutted again. He stood up and reached in the back of the truck and pulled out a length of cotton rag that stank of diesel. He took the water container from Mike and soaked the rag in cold water.
"Put this on the back of his neck."
"Is it bad?" Mike asked as he applied the cold compress.
"It's not good. He has dehydrated. Was he drinking last night?"
"No more than anyone else. In fact, he hardly drank anything."
"I don't believe you. You volunteers always drink too much and then wonder why you get sick in the sun." He stalked off shaking his head in disgust and yelling at the rest of the team to pick up the pace.
Mike didn't want to argue with someone who probably had years of experience working in hot conditions but he was not happy that Billy was unable to defend himself and if he was honest with himself he had not been watching Billy all night. Billy had not appeared to be drunk unlike so many of the other volunteers who were present at the party.
The cold cloth was obviously working its magic because Billy began to stir a little and mumble, if still a little incoherently.
"Come on Billy boy," Mike spoke gently to his friend. "Open your eyes and look at me."
His voice did the trick and Billy's eyes popped open.
"What is that awful smell?" Billy turned his head from side to side. Mike pulled the rag out from behind Billy's head and wafted it in front of his nose.
Billy's face screwed up with distaste. "That's terrible."
"Sorry mate, it was all that was available."
Billy struggled a little and sat up, obviously still a little dizzy and disorientated. Mike put a hand behind his friend's back to support him and offered him the water container.
"The boss man thinks you are dehydrated because you had a skin full last night."
"Well the boss man can go fuck himself. I wasn't pissed last night, not even close. You can ask Katarina."
"I don't think I want to open an enquiry about your abilities in the sack."
"I didn't mean that, she will be able to testify I was sober."

"To be honest I don't think it matters about individuals. We all get tarred with the same brush, which isn't fair."
"Well from what I have seen so far, they are not far wrong."
"Sad, but true." Mike seemed genuinely upset.
They were interrupted by the arrival of their fellow workers who had completed another row of pipes and were now going to have a short water break.
They all flopped down in the shade of the big truck and began to pass the water containers around and light up cigarettes. The air was quickly filled with voices and thick tobacco smoke.
The gang boss came over to where Billy and Mike were sat.
"I need you both back on the gang for the next round, is that going to be a problem?"
Mike looked at Billy who had regained some of his colour but still looked out of it.
"I am OK but I am not sure about Billy."
"I'll be all right mate."
As if to reinforce his statement Billy got to his feet using the side of the truck for support and stood there swaying slightly.
"Woah." He made a grab for the door handle to steady himself.
"Still a bit dizzy?"
"Yeah a bit."
"Well I don't think you are up to it Billy and I don't want to have to haul your sorry ass halfway up the field if you go down again."
The gang boss had been watching Billy and carefully assessing his capability. He obviously reached a decision because he reached inside the cab and pulled out the mic for the shortwave radio. A brief but terse conversation took place in Hebrew, and at the end he tossed the mic back on the front seat. He turned to the two friends.
"You," he pointed to Mike, "You are back on the team. You," he pointed to Billy, "You wait here. Someone will come and collect you. You are no use to me."
With that dismissal he moved away, bullying the rest of the workforce in a mixture of Hebrew and English and driving them back into the sunshine and another run down the field.
"Looks like I will be taken to the corner of the field and shot."
Billy grinned at Mike.
"Just look after yourself mate. I will see you later."

Mike bounded off like an over exuberant puppy to take his place on the line and waited for the signal to go. Billy sat back down and waited for his ride.

As he waited the black dog of depression stalked his thoughts. He had felt certain he was fit enough to take on this type of work. As for the accusation levelled by the field boss that he had drunk too much alcohol the previous evening, Billy had the feeling that this might haunt him for the rest of his stay. He knew that this kind of label had a habit of sticking around. All he wanted right now was to get back on the job, but even he had to admit he was not physically up to it right now, and somehow, he doubted they would give him a second chance at least not today, if ever.

As Billy waited the team in the field completed another row and took a break at the far end of the field. He had managed to stand up and move around a bit without wobbling and without using the truck for support. Well at least he would be able to walk to the jeep when his lift arrived and not have to crawl or stagger. It was getting even hotter out of the shade of the big truck and as the sun climbed higher in the sky, the shadow cast by the vehicle was getting progressively smaller.

When the jeep sent to collect him bobbled into view from around the stand of Eucalyptus trees, Billy was unhappy to see that Yossi, the volunteer leader, was behind the wheel. He guessed that given the views already expressed by Yossi, he was in for another lecture on volunteers and their drinking habits.

Instead it was completely the opposite and in fact much worse as it turned out. Yossi sat in stony silence all the way back to the Kibbutz and only spoke as Billy was getting out of the jeep beside the Volunteer quarters.

"Get some rest. I will come and talk to you later." Then he drove away in a cloud of dust.

That parting shot was a bullet in the heart and the harsh words were still ringing in Billy's ears as he made his way back to the room.

Back in the room he grabbed a towel and shower gel and took off for the shower block.

A short while later, showered and changed out of the blue work clothes and back in his own clothes he made his way slowly back towards the room. A quick glance at the time told him it was just before eleven and so he had nothing to do for an hour until the dining room opened for the lunch sitting.

As he approached the rooms deep in thought he came past the communal area.

"What's up Billy? You are back early." A voice spoke from one of the armchairs. Billy turned towards the sound of the voice.

The two guys from the airport trip, Stig and Dingo were sitting there with feet up, drinks and cigarettes in hand.

"Oh hi guys, yeah I didn't quite make the grade on the Irrigation team." Billy went on to tell them of his humiliating fainting episode and the aftermath. The two lads sat in silence until Billy had finished his tale.

"Oh that explains why Yossi was by here an hour ago asking about you."

"What was he asking about?" Billy looked up, concerned at the news.

"He wanted to know what you had been up to last night. If you had been partying."

"What did you tell him?"

"Not much we could tell him. We weren't here until later, we were milking again, and by that time you had disappeared for the night with your Swedish lovely."

"I would just relax about it. Did he say anything to you on the way back from the fields?"

"Not a word and somehow that was worse." Billy tried to keep the despair out of his voice.

"My advice to you is to go and find yourself a clean glass and come and join us." Stig produced a bottle filled with a milky liquid from beside the sofa.

"What's that?"

"Breakfast" said Dingo.

"The breakfast of champions." Stig corrected his brother. "Arac and water." This was for Billy's benefit.

Billy found a glass and rinsed out the dirt and other crap at the tap that was fixed to the wall on the end of the block, tipping the water onto the sand, and re-joined the two brothers. Dingo poured him a glass of the liquid and Billy took a sniff and then a trial sip. It smelt and tasted of aniseed. He had tried the drink before. At some point during the first night festivities Billy like all the other new volunteers had been conned into trying the drink.

Each 'newbie' who chose to take part, was singled out in turn and made to stand in the centre of the circle.

They were then dressed in the 'floater regalia'. An inverted plant pot with a lit candle was placed on the head and a belt with an outrageously large leather phallus was strapped around the waist. The victim was then handed a glass containing the Arac spirit, floating on a couple of inches of Orange squash. The idea was that the drink was consumed in one long swallow, and if there was any doubt in the victim's mind the surrounding audience chanting "down in one" in unison, assured them of what was expected. Billy remembered that he had acquitted himself during the task and although the harsh spirit had brought tears to his eyes he had managed to keep the contents in his stomach. This was more than could be said of everyone who took the challenge.

Some choked halfway through, others ejected the fluid out of their noses and in one or two cases regurgitated the whole lot a short time after completion. Billy's only memory was the sour taste it left in his mouth for a long while afterwards and the aniseed burps that had continued for most of the night. This stuff, however tasted different and Billy said so.

"Oh, you probably drank the cheap stuff that they sell in the Kibbutz shop. This is slightly more upmarket. This is Elite."

Billy settled down on one of the sofas and took another sip.

"So don't you guys have work today?"

"Yeah, we have to milk this afternoon. We were on the night milk again last night."

"We swapped shifts with two of the members who wanted to go a-courting on another Kibbutz last night."

"Been a lot of that recently."

"First sign that spring is in the air."

"Er, Dingo, its nearly Summer."

"You know what I mean."

"And anyway I meant night milks not horny members."

The banter between the two was non-stop so Billy just sat back and listened. It helped that some of it was actually funny and therefore took Billy's mind off his own problems. This went on for a while but eventually the two turned their attentions to Billy, albeit indirectly at first.

"Dr Dingo, do you think the anaesthetic has taken effect?"

"Yes Dr Stig, the patient looks suitably relaxed."

"Then maybe we should begin the procedure."
Dingo reached under the sofa and produced a crudely fashioned homemade machete.
"Where shall we make the first incision?"
Billy had the good grace to look a little worried as Dingo waved the heavy iron blade around his head.
"I made this myself over in the garage and it is razor sharp." As if to demonstrate he ran his thumb down the blade and small drop of blood sprang from the pad. He sucked his thumb for a moment to staunch the flow.
"Put it away before you take someone's eye out. You know Yossi has warned you about swinging your chopper in public."
Stig poured himself another glass of Arac and water and waved the bottle in Billy's direction. He in turn was beginning to feel the warm buzz from the alcohol, so he readily accepted a refill.
"I don't get this Yossi guy. He seems to hate the English, they all seem to hate the English and yet you two seem to get on really well with him."
"Do you want us to let you into our little secret?"
Billy nodded.
"We're not English."
"Yes you are. I guess you are both from somewhere in or around London by your accents. You said you were Londoners when we first met."
"Well that is where you would be wrong. We are, as far as everyone here is concerned, not English, but Irish."
"You don't sound Irish at all, you even sound like Londoners."
"We're London Irish. At least that's what we told them when we arrived."
"And they believed you?"
"Sadly yes, they did, although they did point out the accent in the same way you did".
"And we gave them the same answer."
"But are you Irish?"
"By a gnat's whisker we are. One of our grandmothers was Irish, or at least her father was."
"And that was enough to convince them?"
"We didn't even have to draw them a family tree, they just accepted our word."
"And this worked?"

"Been getting away with murder ever since." The two high-fived each other.

"And that includes turning up for work pissed."

The two brothers recoiled in mock horror.

"The boy doth cast vicious brickbats at us." Dingo said adopting a mocking Shakespearian tone of voice.

"We are not pissed, we are just getting suitably prepared for a little milking room rodeo."

"But none of this is helping you is it." Stig was back to a serious demeanour.

"I just don't know what to do next. I guess I failed the test in the fields."

"You aren't the first new volunteer to have problems with the heat, and you won't be the last."

"Yeah," Dingo agreed with his brother. "It just might take you a bit longer to get used to the heat and find your feet."

"So you guys seem to know a bit about this. What would you suggest."

"Take a job indoors for a couple of weeks, but try and spend some of the afternoon, the early part is best when it is still hot, outside. Start by walking about a bit and then maybe after a while try running, or some other exercise. Sometimes there is a pickup football game on the basketball courts by the pool in the afternoon. All that will help you build up your stamina and then apply again and have another go. But only when you feel ready."

"And remember, no one will think any less of you if you work indoors and not out with the macho lot in the fields."

"Just as long as you turn up on time and do the job they ask of you then you will have no problem with Yossi or any of the other members here."

"Talking of not being late for work, brother Dingo, it's time for you and me to collect our stuff and head for the Refet."

"You get the towels and soap and I will get the boogie box and don't forget the Arac from the fridge."

"You are allowed to drink at work?"

"Not allowed, but we do."

"We drink all the time. Catch you later Billy."

The two headed off and Billy looked at his watch and noticed it was time for Lunch so he headed off in the direction of the Dining Room although with all the Arac he had consumed the path ahead looked like too much of an uphill struggle so halfway there he turned around and headed for the room. He collapsed on the bed and was asleep almost as soon as his head hit the pillow.

CHAPTER EIGHT

Billy woke up with a sore head to find Mike was crashing around their shared space. He was stood with his hand raised and the door of his metal locker was still reverberating from the force he had just employed to slam it shut.
Billy rolled over and looked up bleary eyed at his friend.
"What time is it?" He mumbled. His mouth felt dry as a desert and his tongue was stuck to the roof of his mouth.
"Oh, you are awake," Mike's surprised voice barely concealed his sarcasm.
Billy struggled upright. His head was pounding like the bass drum in a marching band.
"Don't get up on my account. You just lie there in a drunken heap all afternoon."
Mike was so clearly pissed off at Billy and Billy could guess why. Mike had clearly finished his shift, had lunch and then returned to the room to find his friend passed out from an overdose of Arac at lunchtime. Billy could smell the spirit seeping out of his pores where he was sweating in the heat of the room. Suddenly he was afraid.
"Did Yossi come by yet?"
"Not since I have been back, although I did go and take a shower." Mike seemed to notice his friend's concern and he even seemed to be enjoying it.
"Come on man, be fair."
"Be fair? You pass out from dehydration not three hours ago, get brought back here before the end of the shift and promptly get shit-faced and you tell me to be fair."
This made Billy mad.
"Is that what you are pissed at? I came back here and there were a couple of volunteers having a drink. I joined them and when they

went off to work I realised I was a bit more pissed than I thought I was so I came to lie down."
"And that makes it all better? It was someone else's fault? Come on Billy boy, this is the big wide world now. You gotta grow up and start owning your own problems."
While he had been speaking Mike had been gathering his stuff together and he stood now with a towel over his shoulder and a bottle of suntan cream in his hand.
"I am going to the pool for a swim. I will see you later." He turned around and left the room.
"Well go on then, you self-righteous prick, fuck off to the pool with the goodie-goodies."
Billy snarled at the iron door as it closed behind Mike. He bent over and picked up his work boot from the floor and hurled it at the blue metal. It struck the door with a deep resonating boom.
Exhausted from the effort, seething with anger and in pain from the marching band in his head Billy collapsed back on the pillow and closed his eyes.
He must have drifted off to sleep again because the next thing he was aware of was a pair of warm soft lips brushing his cheek with a kiss.
He opened one eye and saw a pair of soft lips and a wrinkled, slightly sunburnt nose and then the delicious golden locks and blue eyes of Katarina starring down at him.
"You stink."
"Pease don't you start. I just fell out with Mike about it."
"Just fell out with Mike? He has been with us all at the pool for an hour or more."
"Oh damn I must have dozed off again."
"Mike told me you were passed out in your bed. That's why I came to find you."
Billy looked closer and saw that Katarina's hair was still a little damp and she was only wearing a vest top and a bikini. He reached out to her to pull her down into the bed beside him and she slapped his hands away.
"Not until you have taken a shower you smell of booze."
Billy pushed himself up on one elbow and discovered the extra sleep had sent the marching band packing and his head was gradually returning to normal.
"Seriously?" Billy sat up fully.

"Seriously what?" Katarina looked puzzled.
"All I need to do is take a shower?"
"Maybe, it would be a big help."
Billy bounded out of bed and grabbed his towel and washbag off the table.
"Be right back. Don't move an inch."
He almost ran all the way to the shower block and threw himself under the nearest shower head, turning the tap as he stood there, and then screamed as a stream of ice cold water cascaded down his back.
As he stood there shivering under the freezing water he realised that the steady stream of volunteers returning from work had depleted the supply of hot water and the boilers had not managed to reheat the water yet.
By the time, he had rinsed off the soap his teeth were chattering and even a vigorous rub down with a towel and redressing did little to help. He walked out into the afternoon sun and stood there hoping the heat would soak into his bones as he strolled back to his room.
He pushed open his door and saw straight away that the bed was empty and the room was deserted. He tossed his toilet bag on the table and then went back outside to hang. his towel over the washing line to dry in the sun.
He couldn't hide his disappointment that Katarina had not waited for him and he went back inside the room and dug around in his bag for his book about Israel. He went to the communal area and grabbed a cold tin of coke out of the fridge and returned to his room where he pulled the pillows and his sleeping bag up against the wall, popped the ring pull on the tin and took a long swig before settling back to read.
The section of the guide book he was reading was about the Old City district of Jerusalem and he was engrossed in a section about the walks around the ancient walls when the door burst open. Billy had enough time to register blond hair, wet and a large blue towel being tossed to one side, before he was overwhelmed by Katarina's naked body. She was panting slightly, probably from the run back from the shower block.
"I am fucking freezing. Do something."
Billy engulfed her in his arms and kissed her.
"Not helping much. Fuck me hard."

Billy didn't need a second invitation and he whipped his shorts off and complied with her request willingly and with great gusto.
Afterwards when they lay there with their heartbeats and breathing slowly returning to normal Katarina buried her face in Billy's neck and let out a satisfied moan.
"Now I am warm again. Fuck that water was cold."
"Tell me about it." Billy grinned to himself.
"I just did." Katarina looked up at Billy, a slightly confused look on her face.
Billy realised it was another classic case of misunderstood communication.
"Ah OK. Sorry it's a turn of phrase. I guess it really means I agree with you. Probably at some point there was a "You don't have to" before the "tell me about it". But I guess that just got lost somewhere back in time."
"English is a stupid language." Katarina pronounced
"Tell me about it." Billy grinned and they both burst out laughing.
After a few moments of silence Katarina stroked Billy's chest lovingly.
"Do you want to talk about this morning? What happened out in the fields?"
Billy stiffened momentarily as if he was offended then he relaxed and thought 'what the hell.'
"I don't know, it was hard work but all of sudden I am facedown, kissing the dirt. I passed out and then had to be carried off the field by Mike."
"I know he told me part of the story earlier, but said I had to ask you about the details."
"What exactly did the smug bastard say?" Billy couldn't keep the anger out of his voice.
"Calm down Billy, he was not talking about you behind your back. I thought you two were friends."
"So did I." Billy said gloomily.
He was unhappy with the way he had been treated earlier by Mike. He couldn't see what he had done wrong and it distressed him that they had fallen out in such spectacular fashion and after such a short time, but he couldn't get over the fact that he thought Mike was being uptight for all the wrong reasons.
He knew that deep down he would have to apologise to him later and that was giving him an internal crisis of conscience. Billy

thought nothing of apologising for anything if he had done something wrong but right now he was failing to see any error in his actions.

"I would love to stay like this for the rest of my days but I have a sneaking suspicion that people are going to start coming back from the pool soon so I guess we had better get some clothes on."

His prediction was right. No sooner had they both redressed than they heard the tell-tale sound of people returning from their afternoon by the pool. It was not long until the door opened and Mike came into the room.

"Hi Katarina, I see you found the prodigal son." Mike nodded in Billy's direction.

"I had better leave you two alone." She stood up and moved to the door.

"No kiss?" Billy asked. She crossed the room again and gave Billy a kiss. Then went out the door closing it behind her.

"She is something special Billy."

"Yeah I know. I am a lucky guy."

"So don't fuck it up."

"Don't fucking start again. I know I fucked up."

"I kn." Mike stopped himself in mid sentence. He didn't want another fight and Billy's admission of fault had taken him a bit by surprise.

"But I don't need you telling everyone who wants to listen what a dickhead I am."

Now it was Mike's turn to lose his cool.

"Do you really think that's what I have been doing."

"Katarina told me you were telling everyone about my face-plant out in the field this morning. I bet that got a few laughs."

"I never mentioned it to a soul. I only told Katarina because I felt she had a right to know and she was asking where you were."

Billy was still seething with anger and now so was Mike. The two starred daggers at each other across the room. It lasted for about twenty seconds and then they both burst out laughing.

"I can't stay mad at you, you're a dopey fool. As a punishment, you will go to the fridge and get us two beers."

Billy stood up and wiped the tears from his eyes and gave Mike a mock salute.

"Right away mon Kapitan."

He left the room, returning a few moments later with two ice cold bottles of Goldstar. He passed one to Mike and then sat back down on his bed.

"Listen Bill, I don't want to make a big thing about this but after you left the boss of the Irrigation said some pretty unpleasant things about volunteers who drink too much."

"Well I wasn't pissed last night."

"I know that mate, but then I came back to the room and the door was unlocked and you were lying there passed out on the bed. It didn't really go anyway to proving your innocence."

"I just learnt not to trust Stig and Dingo when they are making the drinks."

"My point is that anyone could have walked in and seen you like that and drawn the wrong conclusion."

"I know. I won't let it happen again."

"So what do you think Yossi will say? What did he say to you earlier?"

"Nothing. We drove the whole way in stony silence. Apparently, he was asking questions before he drove out to collect me."

"Really?"

"Yeah really." Billy told Mike about his earlier conversation with the two brothers and what Yossi had asked them.

"So they were able to confirm you were not up half the night drinking."

"Yeah it looks that way."

This piece of news seemed to cheer Mike up.

"We will just have to see what he says. Did he tell you when he would come by?"

"No we didn't make any arrangement but according to Dingo he usually does his rounds before supper. I guess we can expect a visit sometime soon."

They were not disappointed and true to predicted form Yossi turned up an hour later. The two friends had made two more trips to the fridge and were halfway through their third bottle of Goldstar when the door opened and Yossi was stood in the doorway.

Billy noticed that he had not even bothered to knock first. He did not come all the way into the room but stood just inside the doorway, leaning against the metal locker that was stood against the wall beside the door. He still had his sunglasses on so it was

difficult in the gloom to see his eyes and Billy found this slightly unnerving. He didn't know what Yossi was looking at or more importantly he could tell nothing about his mood.
Yossi started by addressing Mike.
"Well done today. It can be tough for the first few days. It's hard work out in the fields. You will sleep well tonight, even without the drink." Yossi cracked a smile. This seemed to evaporate as he turned his attention to Billy and his expression became harder.
"Now Billy, what are we going to do with you? The only thing in your favour is that I know you were not up all-night drinking. That would have put you in serious hot water. But even I have to accept that not everyone is cut out for hard physical labour."
The last few words stung Billy like a slap to the face.
"But we have jobs for everyone here in the Kibbutz so tomorrow morning at seven you can report to the kitchen and try your hand in the dishwasher. Enjoy your evening." He turned on his heels and left the room.
Billy was quiet but Mike could see his friend was unhappy. He decided to try and put a positive spin on the news of Billy's new work assignment.
"Well it could have been worse."
"Yeah. How?"
"It could have been the factory."
"That is only just below the dishwasher on the list of shit jobs."
"Well it might not be for ever. I am sure in time something else will come along. Maybe you just need to get acclimatised a bit."
"Yeah that's what Stig and Dingo said earlier. They said there is sometimes a pick-up football game up by the pool in the afternoons."
"Yeah, they were having a kick around when I left the pool earlier."
"Well I might give it a go tomorrow."
"Just take it easy on the lunchtime drinking if you want to play footie."
"Hey." Billy slung a work boot in Mike's direction but it went wildly off target and landed harmlessly on the floor.
"You need to work on your aim buddy." Mike grinned. Billy was about to launch the second boot when there was a loud bang on the door.
"Enter." Mike yelled.

Katarina and Kirsten came in the door and behind them Billy could see there were a few others who were grouped together on the veranda.

"Any one for a trip to the Dining Room?"

Billy was on his feet in an instance.

"I am starving I missed lunch."

"Ah, poor baby." Katarina caressed his cheek in a motherly way.

"That was your own fault Billy-boy." Mike said from behind him

"Can we change the record please now." Billy fired back over his shoulder.

They all headed off in the direction of the communal dining room which was packed and buzzing at this time of the evening.

The food wasn't up to much but as Billy really was starving he managed to polish off three bowls of the murky looking soup and numerous slices of bread and butter all washed down with several cups of tea.

There was an awkward moment when another volunteer approached Billy from behind and placed his arms around his neck in a friendly hug. Billy shrugged off the unwelcome advance but not before the stranger had a chance to say his piece.

"Thanks man. You really are a life saver."

Billy looked up into the face of a fellow volunteer. One he had never clapped eyes on before. Not wishing to be seen as ungrateful for the attention Billy offered a muted acknowledgement and the stranger went on his way.

Billy looked around the other volunteers at the table hoping for some form of explanation.

"He has been in the dishwasher for the last four weeks and it was driving him mental." One of the others at the table offered by way of an explanation.

Billy just about managed a wan smile in reply.

"It seems that news of your fate has been made public." Mike said.

"Let's hope I get plenty of sympathy in the form of free drinks later on." Billy tried to see a positive in his work assignment for the following morning, but news that he might be consigned to the dishwasher for the next month was not particularly encouraging.

He finished his meal in silence and then joined the flood of volunteers returning to Volunteer Central where the stereo was already blasting out some party tunes, the fire was alight and happy smiling faces, some already flushed with drink, showed Billy that at least for tonight everything was as it should be in the world. Billy took a seat on one of the sofas and accepted a beer and focused on the challenge that he would face in the morning.

CHAPTER Nine

When the alarm clock rang for the second time that morning Billy tried his best to ignore it but Katarina, who had left the room an hour earlier after the first alarm had moved the clock from its position on the night stand over to a table on the other side of the room. Billy was forced, by the incessant beeping, to get out of bed and cross the room to silence it.
Her trick worked and now that Billy was out from under the covers and upright the cool morning air began to chill his naked body. He reached for his shorts and pulled them on, followed by his shirt, pushed his feet into his flip-flops and headed out. He locked the door to Katarina's room and placed the key on top of the doorframe. It was pointless security as everyone knew this was where the key was hidden, indeed all the volunteers, almost without exception did precisely the same thing.
Billy dragged his feet as he walked the short distance to his own room and then changed into his work clothes and headed for the dining room.
There was a marked lack of a spring in his step as he crossed the Kibbutz. Anyone watching might have thought he was a condemned man on his way to the gallows.
Despite the fact that he had been given a later start time Billy had still avoided getting completely paralytic the previous evening, although as he walked, he cast his mind back to the two brothers, Stig and Dingo and how they had disappeared off for work the previous afternoon already drunk. He wondered if this might be a better option and decided to see how his first day at work progressed before he made any rash decisions.
As he entered the Dining Room he caught sight of the team of Volunteers who were on duty there. They were all sat at one of the tables set aside for the volunteers enjoying a warm drink and a

cigarette before embarking on their various morning tasks. Billy had no real idea what these duties were but the presence of various mops, buckets and other cleaning materials nearby indicated that a degree of cleaning was probably a major part of their working day. They didn't seem to be in any hurry to start working so Billy decided he would join them and he made himself a cup of tea and took a free seat at the table. More than one or two of the people sat at the table were clearly suffering the after effects of the previous evening. One of the guys was sat with his head on his arms and looked like he had fallen asleep.

The conversation was muted and as Billy looked at the faces around the table he realised that he hadn't met any of these volunteers before. It was as if they came from an alternative group.

"Are you the new king of the dishwasher?" a slightly plump girl with red hair and a welsh accent asked him.

"Yeah that's me."

Billy replied with absolutely zero enthusiasm.

"Well you had better get your skates on and report for duty. If Shlomit has to come and find you then you will be in hot water."

This was obviously considered the height of humour amongst the assembled group because Billy heard giggles from more than one of them.

"Hot water, dishwasher, I see where you are going with this." He replied sarcastically.

He left his cup where it was on the table and pushed himself to his feet. This was going to be a nightmare of a day.

He went through the opening in the wall to where the big shiny aluminium shape of the dishwashing machine stood. Right now, it was silent and all he could hear was a tell-tale dripping of water from somewhere inside. The plastic trays used for stacking the plates, cups and glasses and the baskets for cutlery were all piled up over to one side ready to be hauled up on to the conveyor belt and then fed into the maw of the machine.

The air was thick with the cloying smell of bleach, disinfectant and industrial soap.

He walked around the dishwasher and on into the kitchen beyond. The contrast between Kitchen and Dining Room was sharp. Here things were really buzzing as the assembled staff worked feverishly to prepare breakfast and make preparations for meals to be served later in the day.

At large tables over to one side there was a team preparing vegetables and salad, slicing and dicing various items and piling them into deep plastic trays. On the other side at the hot station there was mass production of fried eggs taking place under the watchful spatulas of two Israelis. Several large cauldrons were already steaming away and Billy could only hazard a guess at what they contained.

Billy looked around and quickly spotted the central figure, the queen bee in this hive of activity. Stood in the middle of the Kitchen like a battlefield general marshalling her troops, barking orders to left and right was the diminutive figure of the Kitchen manager.

Short in stature, rotund in form with her dark hair scraped back from her face and imprisoned under a white hygiene cap, the white apron taught across her ample chest, Shlomit was in the process of berating two hapless volunteers who were obviously not meeting her exacting standards.

The large carving knife in her hand was being used like a conductor's baton to demonstrate to the two the exact size the cucumber pieces should be, before they were placed in the serving dishes. Several pieces were selected at random from the tray and then tossed violently in the garbage, rejected for being too large.

Billy waited patiently in the doorway while the scolding ran its natural course and when Shlomit seemed satisfied she had made her point and the two were suitably chastised he stepped forward. Her eyes zeroed in on his movement, like a predator seeing its prey emerging from cover.

"Are you the new dishwasher?" She barked across the intervening space.

"Er yeah, I guess so." Billy's eyes remained fixed on the business end of the large knife that was now pointing in his direction.

She turned her head towards the grill station and barked a name that sounded like "Ezra" followed by an unintelligible stream of words that must have been Hebrew. What was said and whether it was complimentary or otherwise Billy didn't know. The effect was that one of the people at the grill detached himself and came over to where Billy was standing.

He took Billy back into the dishwasher area and handed him a plastic apron and a pair of yellow industrial rubber gloves. He then went through a brief demonstration of how the equipment worked, how the trays were to be loaded into the machine and then how to stack the washed and dried crockery after it was finished. Billy nodded on several occasions just to demonstrate he was paying attention and five minutes later he was alone with his new responsibilities.

He looked around and moved a couple of the trollies to where he felt they would be better placed for stacking the clean plates and glasses and then he waited.

Of course, he expected there would be busy periods around the two main mealtimes but outside of that the flow of dirty cups and glasses was light and Billy didn't feel unduly stressed as he reached the end of his shift and prepared to shut the machine down for the last time.

He went out to check if there were any tables that had been missed and if there were any plates, cups or cutlery to run through on the last run.

By this time it was nearly two in the afternoon and the dining room was largely deserted. A few of the volunteers were pushing mops and brooms around in a half-hearted fashion but there was nothing else for Billy to do. He went back to his station and removed his apron and gloves, hanging them up on the hook provided and went through to the Kitchen to say goodbye.

The last of the Kitchen staff were finishing up their cleaning tasks and Billy looked around for Shlomit. She was nowhere to be seen but Billy noticed Ezra was lurking over by one of the fridges and chatting with one of the Volunteers girls. He had his arm up against the wall and it looked suspiciously like he was preventing her from getting away from him. She for her part was smiling nervously at him, while casting an occasional frightened glance at the large arm obstructing her escape. Billy approached quietly until he was right behind the pair.

"Ezra, I am all finished." Billy said his mouth right next to Ezra's ear. Ezra jumped and turned to see who was behind him and for a moment took his eye off the Volunteer girl, who seeing her chance to escape, slid under his arm and tried to get away. Ezra caught her movement in his peripheral vision and tried to impede her departure. Billy reached out and grabbed Ezra's arm giving the girl the valuable seconds she needed to make her break for freedom. Annoyed the Israeli shook his arm free and turned his anger on Billy.

"You are not even close to finishing. Here look in there." He pointed across from where he was standing. Billy followed the outstretched hand and saw two trollies piled high with pots, pans, serving dishes and plastic buckets.
"This all needs cleaning as well."
Billy approached the untidy pile and took a closer look. By the food waste dried into some of the trays, this pile had been accumulating here since breakfast time. Billy kept his cool, despite seething inside. He wheeled the trollies into the dishwasher area and set about cleaning the pots and pans. Some of the more encrusted utensils needed a good soak in the sink before they could pass through the dishwasher and come out clean so it was after three before Billy stacked the last of them on the trolley and wheeled it back into the Kitchen.
He tossed the plastic apron and rubber gloves on the floor and left the quiet of the now completely deserted Kitchen and went in search of a shower and a clean set of clothes.
As he walked down towards the Volunteer rooms he reflected on his day. It had not been too stressful. Clearly, he would have to keep an eye on the back kitchen and work the pots and other cooking equipment into the general flow of the day and he knew catching them while they were still fresh would speed up the cleaning process but overall, he felt it had gone well.
Mike was already back in the room, showered and changed when Billy walked in. They had exchanged a few words at Lunchtime when Mike had arrived with the rest of his crew for their lunchbreak but as Billy had already eaten and was in one of his peak busy times their exchange had been brief.
Now Mike wanted the full story of Billy's first day, chapter and verse.
"Let me take a shower first and grab a beer." Billy pleaded. Mike concurred and even offered to collect the Beers while Billy showered. Fifteen minutes later they were both sat down outside their room with a couple of cold beers.
"No swimming pool today?" Billy asked
"Pool's closed, no lifeguard. They say he is sick but the rumour is he is still hungover."
"Oh great, another stick to beat the Volunteers with."
Mike nodded. "Anyway, Billy boy tell me about your first day in hell."

Billy went through the high points and low points of his day and then had to repeat himself almost word for word when Katarina turned up and asked him the same question.

#

By the end of the week Billy had made the Dishwasher his domain. He had mastered the idiosyncrasies of the machinery and was able to change all the chemicals and fix any minor problems as they occurred. He had realised that instead of taking a break to grab a coffee and a chat with the dining room crew he could use that time to check on the kitchen and grab any dirty pots. This meant that come the end of the day when the Kitchen staff were finishing up so was Billy.
On his second morning Billy received a visitor shortly after starting work. The female volunteer who Billy had helped escape from Ezra's lecherous attention arrived in the dishwasher with a pile of dirty oven trays and an offer to cook him a "special" breakfast as a way of saying thank you. This simple unintentional act on Billy's part had elevated him to hero status among the other female volunteers on the Kitchen crew who had all, at one time or another, suffered from Ezra's unwanted attention. This new spirit of cooperation made Billy's life much easier as at least the Volunteers would bring trays and pots to him rather than him having to go on a hunt for them.
The only black cloud, if there was one, was that he had clearly made an enemy of Ezra and as he seemed to be Shlomit's right hand man this could have proved disastrous in the same way that Billy's bad relationship with Hollingsworth had, if it was not for one huge difference. Nobody liked Ezra and more to the point after Billy had showed he could be stood up to with impunity, no one else was scared of him anymore. Furthermore, it appeared that every female who had ever had the opportunity to work in the Kitchen had come in for his unwelcome attention. So, as the relationship between Billy and Ezra deteriorated so Billy's personal stock rose with the rest of the volunteer staff in the Kitchen and Dining room.
It was therefore, with a high degree of confidence that Billy approached his first Shabbat meal as the main Dishwasher. For the extra shift and the extra work generated by feeding the whole

Kibbutz at one sitting, Billy was assigned two extra helpers. These were both actual Members of the Kibbutz and Billy assumed they would, having lived in the place for years, know more about the job than he did. Nothing could have been further from the truth and the two constantly looked to Billy for guidance and for him to take the lead and set the pace and the tasks. This was an unusual feeling for Billy but he tried not to let it go to his head. The three of them proved to be a good team and they were finished well in time for everyone to depart and enjoy the Shabbat with their families and friends. For Billy, this meant the first Friday Night Disco.

#

It is said among Volunteers that no one ever forgets their first Friday Night disco, although it is also said a fair few don't remember the event too clearly. It might be that the sheer hedonism from what is outwardly a very conservative society strikes a chord or it could be that the majority of these events take place in some form of converted bomb shelter so the descent into the steaming depths of smoke, noise, writhing semi-naked bodies, deafening music, and free-flowing alcohol just sear themselves into the very centre of your soul. Whatever the reason, Billy's first experience was up there with the best.
The shelter was right at the centre of the Kibbutz adjacent to the Dining Room and had probably originally been constructed to house a fair number of people as it was spacious.
The walls had been painted white and there was a bar area and a DJ booth at opposite ends of the main room. In each of the four corners there were large speakers mounted to the walls and from the ceiling an array of spotlights, also controlled from the booth were sequenced to the music.
By the time Billy arrived with Katrina, Mike and Kirsten the place was already alive. The level of the music prevented any real form of conversation apart from the right up close and yell in the ear variety but Billy managed to get some idea of what everyone wanted to drink only to discover that as "newbies" they all had to undergo the initiation ceremony which involved drinking a large glass of punch which was stored in a large plastic rubbish bin behind the bar. The contents of this mixture were known only to the makers and as Billy touched the glass to his lips and the first

waft of alcohol assaulted his nostrils Billy guessed it was going to be eye-wateringly strong. He was not wrong, but he did manage to swallow the complete contents of the glass and unlike some of his fellow volunteers also manage to avoid throwing the whole lot back up again a few moments later. The bar staff were obviously use to this happening as one of them was stood waiting with a plastic bucket in case this occurred.

Billy actually quite liked the taste of the punch so while his friends switched to beer or vodka he stayed on the punch and suffered badly later on as a result of that rash decision.

At one point there was a technical problem with the sound which made conversation possible. Billy happened to be standing by the bar at that moment and asked the two Volunteers serving drinks what was the point of the object stood in the corner. In the half-light, it looked like a door with some straps attached to it.

"Is that some torture device? Looks like you could use it for waterboarding someone." Billy half joked.

"That's known locally as the failures taxi." One of them replied. "How we get the passed-out volunteers back to volunteer central at the end of the night."

"And the occasional young member." The other chipped in.

Further conversation was drowned out as, technical problems solved, the music resumed. Billy collected the drinks from the bar and returned to where his friends were. Looking back at that evening later, through the unspeakable pain of a major hangover, incidentally the worst hangover Billy could ever remember, he could not remember the exact point that he lost control.

Recalling the events of that first Friday Night disco was not a very difficult task. There were, naturally, no end of people more than happy to regale him with their own recollections of his behaviour, but after they had taken such pride in doing so, separating what was actually a real memory from what was someone else's did prove difficult.

Taking all of the information on board Billy was later able to construct a pretty accurate picture of events, even if some of them were a complete blank for him.

With some concentration Billy was able to remember his conversation with the Bar staff and returning to his friends with the drinks but after that things began to become a little hazy. This was where other people's memories began to fill in the blanks. At some point, Billy had taken to the dance floor, initially with Katarina as his dance partner but as the beat of the music had combined with the alcohol coursing through his veins everyone on the dance floor had become fair game for his attention.

Dirty dancing, grinding, intimate clutches, male or female it made no difference to Billy, he was in a world of his own making. This fevered burst of energy lasted for the best part of an hour until, according to bystanders Billy suddenly went rigid, mid samba and then keeled over landing with a thump, face down on the floor. Several people helped to pick him up and remove his comatose body to a safe place at the side of the room where he was abandoned on one of the side benches. Katarina, who had lost her patience with her errant boyfriend earlier and taken herself off to bed was alerted to his condition but apparently in a sudden burst of cold Nordic fury, had told the messenger to piss off. Mike had also departed with his girlfriend so it fell to a couple of Good Samaritans to place Billy on the door, strap him in and deliver him to one of the sofas in Volunteer central to sleep it all off and this was where Billy came to in the first light of the new day, disorientated, dehydrated and feeling generally very sorry for himself.

Billy had suffered his first, and by no means his last, Arac Attack. The punch he had been guzzling all evening was a mixture of several bottles of the cheap spirit and several bottles of cheap vodka, diluted with fruit juice to cover the taste of the alcohol, the final sting in the tail of this Friday night concoction were two bottles of ninety-five percent proof alcohol. This particular spirit was actually not sold in the alcohol section of the Supermarkets but had a more fitting place in the section which sold bleach and other cleaning materials. Drunk neat it probably could have killed you, as a mixer in a punch it just rendered the drinker insensible, as Billy could certainly testify.

Repairing the damage, he had done to his relationship with Katarina took considerably longer than it did to recover from his hangover and that took him most of Saturday.

Apparently dirty dancing with other women was bad enough but dancing intimately with men was a definite no-no in the lexicon of Scandinavian social behaviour and Billy was therefore on the receiving end of a very Nordic cold shoulder when he dropped by to see Katarina that afternoon.

If the hangover was making him still feel rotten the complete rejection by Katarina made him feel worse. He wasn't really up to facing either so he retreated to his bed and sulked for the rest of the afternoon, drinking tin after tin of cold coke.

\#

It took several days and the intervention of a one of Billy's kitchen allies to get back in Katrina's good graces. Billy, for his part, was prepared to show he had learnt his lesson and he was a living example of abstemiousness. This was no mean feat in an environment where drinking heavily was such a way of life.
In the end, and Billy only found this out a few weeks later, it was the actions of one of Billy's co-workers in the Kitchen that swung things in his favour. This particular young lady had been paying an inordinate amount of attention to the young man in the dishwasher and when it became clear to her that Billy still only had eyes for Katarina she took the bold step of seeking out the young Swede and asking her outright to put Billy out of his misery so that he could finally move on and maybe get something going with her instead.
The realisation that there were others interested in Billy and that some of them were circling like sharks in the water, was enough to convince Katarina that she should end the enforced separation and take Billy back. This had always been her intention from the start, it had just been fun watching him suffer, so it had gone on a little longer than originally planned. Also, Katarina had been secretly enjoying the extra effort that Billy had been making in his attempts to win back her affections. But with the threat of losing him to another, Katarina finally decided to call a halt and welcome him back into her arms.
Billy, largely unaware of the machinations going on behind his back, was simply focusing on his job in the dishwasher and trying to avoid drinking too much in the evenings but the absence of Katarina in his life was making him increasingly more depressed. After the first few times he had tried to talk to her or made a fuss of her, and been cruelly rebuffed he had given up trying and now apart from the odd attempt to be nice to her if she passed close by, he merely sat in silence at most of the volunteer gatherings and

watched her as she moved about between her friends and fellow workers from the orchards, seemingly without a care in the world. Being ignored by Katarina had become the status quo for Billy, so much so that when she did eventually relent and come to speak to him he almost missed it.

She was stood in front of him with a hand outstretched as Billy suddenly realised what was happening.

"I am not going to repeat myself for a third-time Billy Randell, let's go for a walk. I need to talk to you."

Billy noticed the hand first then the face and body and voice associated with it, took the hand and stood up.

He had tuned back in to catch the "I need to talk to you," part of the sentence.

"So let's talk." Billy said.

"Not here. Let's take a walk."

Billy felt certain that this was to be his final dismissal so he was pleased it would not be taking place in front of everyone. He reluctantly followed Katarina as she left the fire ring and headed off into the dark. Part of him wanted final closure in order for him to be able to move on, but if he was honest with himself he had to admit that he was still totally besotted by Katarina.

They walked for a short distance in silence until they were far enough away not to be overheard by the others, then Katarina stopped.

Billy waited patiently for the axe to fall. All the fight had left him. He was miserable and depressed and he just wanted an end to the uncertainty. He knew that inside he would be devastated and there would be a period of personal mourning and regret for his own stupidity but he had learnt from his mistakes and he knew that if he could find love again with another person he would work harder to make it work. and definitely keep an eye on what he drank.

"Billy," she began, "this is stupid. I can't go on like this. I love you." Billy listened hard. He was waiting for the 'but'. It never came.

"Ah, oh, really?" Billy stammered.

"At this point, you are supposed to say something like 'I Love you too'." Katarina was standing her arms by her side, a look of mild irritation on her face.

Billy didn't trust his voice so he reached out and put his arms on Katarina's shoulders and pulled her towards him. She came willingly into his arms and he kissed her, long and slowly.
They didn't bother returning to the party. Instead they went straight to Katarina's room.
Afterwards Billy lay back in her bed. Everyone was right. Make up sex was great.

CHAPTER TEN

Billy climbed the ladder and took up his position. From atop this platform he had a clear view of the whole pool area. He adjusted his cap and then put on his sunglasses. Around his neck on a cord was a steel whistle, the type favoured by football referees. The white t-shirt he was wearing had the word 'Lifeguard' stencilled on the back in big red letters, in both Hebrew and English.
For the past two months Billy had occupied this chair every day, except Saturdays, keeping a watchful eye over the patrons of Tel Boker's swimming pool.
Being appointed as lifeguard for the swimming pool, one of the most prized jobs for the volunteers had been more by chance than anything else.
Billy had settled down to life in the dishwasher and like any job he had ever had before, had tried to make the best of it, despite his ongoing feud with Ezra, which had showed no signs of abating. Having the support of the other Kitchen volunteers had helped him a little but he made the job his own through his own sheer bloody-mindedness. He had even managed to elicit tacit praise from his boss in the Kitchen and everyone was quick to point out that Shlomit offering any sort of praise was a rarer than rocking horse shit.
Other volunteers asked him if he had considered working other places but life in the dishwasher suited Billy. Once he had the rhythm of the job he was able to finish in good time, get back to the room, shower and change and be into his second beer before either Mike or Katarina made it back from work tired and sweaty after their shifts in the fields or the orchards. After the Avocado harvest had finished Katarina was one of the lucky ones who got to carry on working with Jacob in the orchards. She had never made it to the Children's house but she seemed happy with her job.

Billy's job itself was pretty mindless for the most part but again that suited Billy as it meant he could focus his thoughts on other things, one of which was his desire to learn a smattering of the local language. He had recruited one of the young Israeli soldiers to teach him a little and in the afternoons when everyone was resting he would seek out his teacher and they would spend an hour or more learning words and phrases in Hebrew. In return Billy was teaching his host English.

In the solitude of the dishwasher with the machine running to cover his mistakes and his notes protected from moisture by a plastic wallet and stuck on the side of the machine, Billy would practice speaking the language out loud.

On the odd occasion, he was caught by one of the members they would smile and correct his pronunciation but as the weeks went on those corrections became less frequent and instead they would pay compliments to him on his command of their language or if he had just asked a question they would smile and answer it in their own language. Therefore, as time went by the Members began to realise that Billy was becoming skilled in the language and they stopped speaking English to him and started to speak Hebrew instead.

It was through this improved communication and overhearing discussions about life in the Kibbutz that Billy was presented with his chance to escape the Dishwasher.

One afternoon at the end of the lunch shift two of the Members approached the dishwasher deep in conversation. In the midst of their conversation, the subject was another member who was due to depart imminently to serve his month on reserve duty with the army, Billy heard a word repeated several times that he didn't recognise. Curious he interrupted and asked politely what the word actually meant.

One of the members paused for a moment and said he knew the word in German, and from there the three of them worked out the English word was Forklift truck.

It appeared that Avram who was the forklift driver at the factory was about to depart for a month and there was no one qualified to take his place.

Billy in a sudden lapse of judgement blurted out that he had a licence to drive a forklift. The two members, one still clutching the piece of cutlery he had used in their translation exercise, both looked at Billy with mounting disbelief. Could this volunteer really mean the difference between them having to halt production for the month they were missing their driver. There were no shortage of members willing to take over the driver's seat in the factory but secretly both of them knew there would be accidents and a general drop in production with one of these amateurs in the proverbial hot seat. It would be cheaper in the long run to close down the factory and cease production rather than pay for the damage and repairs that would be necessary with an amateur forklift driver. Was the solution to their problem really standing in front of them wearing a plastic apron and a pair of rather fetching yellow marigolds?

In typical Israeli style they said nothing to Billy beyond a friendly farewell, but they were both deep in hurried whispered conversation as they left the dishwasher.

It took a moment for it to dawn on Billy that his days in the dishwasher might be numbered and not for the first time in his life Billy regretted his inability to keep his mouth shut.

He had not even managed to finish his first beer of the afternoon before Yossi came a calling.

The taciturn Volunteer leader looked uncomfortable as he entered Billy's room. Clearly, he did not like asking volunteers for favours but under the circumstances and under pressure from the other members he had been left with no alternative.

"A little bird tells me you might be able to help us out of a crisis."

Billy, who had time to reconsider the rashness of his earlier pronouncement was ready for the question and reluctant to leave the safety and comfort of the dishwasher for the unknown.

"I don't know." He said, not committing himself one way or the other.

"Do you have a forklift permit or not?"

"I do, but then so does Mike"

"Mike is already assigned to work out in the Irrigation. He is not available. Do you have the papers with you?"

"I might have."

This evasion was beginning to annoy Yossi and it showed on his face. He folded his arms across his body clutching his hands under them to stop them shaking with anger. He looked like he was about to do Billy some physical harm. His voice however remained measured even if there was a slight strain in it.

"Billy, if you have the correct papers and you are prepared to help us out with this for the next month then I can guarantee you can have the pick of any job, anywhere on the Kibbutz."
"Really?" That gave Billy pause for thought. One month driving a forklift, a job he could do with his eyes shut and in return his pick of any job in the Kibbutz. It was certainly worth considering.
Billy stood up and went to his cupboard. In a pocket of his rucksack he had a plastic folder with all his personal papers in it. He and Mike had decided to bring everything, including driving licences and truck licences, with them when they left England. They did not know where they might end up and to have proof might mean the difference between getting a job and not getting one.
He fished out the truck licence and handed it to Yossi.
"It's in English," he apologised.
Yossi clicked his tongue to demonstrate this would not be a problem as he took the document and studied it.
Satisfied that it was genuine he passed the document back to Billy.
"Look I hate to beg for anything from a volunteer but…"
"If I can have a pick of any job", Billy interrupted, "then congratulations you have got yourself a forklift driver."
Yossi smiled.
Afterwards Billy tried very hard to remember a time when he had actually seen Yossi smile before and despite thinking long and hard he couldn't.
Later that afternoon, with only two days to go until his departure, Avram came and found Billy and gave him instructions for the following day.
For their first shift together Avram took the driving seat but on the second day it was Billy's turn. There were three main jobs for the forklift driver.
The first was to lift the heavy sacks containing the raw plastic in bead form, up to the hopper where the loaders could open the sacks and pour the beads in. The second was at the other end of the process when the heavy rolls of plastic had been placed on pallets. These pallets needed to be taken into the storage area to await dispatch. The third task was to take those same pallets out and load them onto the waiting delivery trucks.
There were several things Billy was warned to watch out for. The first was the low ceiling in parts of the factory. The roof was held

up with steel girders and these were low enough that the forklift truck could not drive around with the forks fully extended. This meant that after lifting the sacks of raw plastic up to the hopper, the truck had to reverse a few feet and lower the forks before driving away. The same applied for loading pallets onto the top shelves in the storage area. As Billy drove around the factory a quick glance up showed him where previous drivers had failed to observe this simple rule as in places the roof girders were twisted, dented and scraped clean of paint as a result of past impacts. Billy was no expert but even he knew enough to realise that loads would have been lost from these impacts and most likely the truck itself damaged or rendered unserviceable by most of them. Either of these two scenarios would have also brought production to a halt.

After Avram's departure for the army Billy was finally alone and in charge and he settled quickly into his new role.

The month flew by and suddenly Billy was in his last week as temporary forklift driver. Yossi sought him out at the factory to ask him if he had any thoughts about where he wanted to work next. Billy had to ask for another day to consider his decision. In light of their new cooperative relationship Yossi agreed willingly. Billy found this new spirit of collaboration a little strange after the open hostility that had been prevalent when he had first joined Tel Boker. He didn't want to jeopardise it by discussing it with anyone so he just kept it to himself. He did, in quieter moments, wonder what had brought about this paradigm shift in their relationship, whether it was the length of time he had been a volunteer, the fact that he had taken time to learn the language or was it simply that he had been willing to help the Kibbutz out when they had been facing a dilemma. Despite their new relationship Yossi was adamant that he needed Billy's decision soon. Billy had promised to give Yossi an answer.

Billy hadn't really thought anymore about what he wanted to do next. He had discussed the subject with Mike at some length but they hadn't arrived at any sensible solution. By now with several months on the Kibbutz behind them, they had both had a chance to learn about most of the jobs on offer but Billy couldn't think of anything he really wanted to do. He had even considered asking to return to the dishwasher.

With just one more day to go the new job sort of fell into Billy's lap. He had been settling down for a quiet read when the room door had flown open and Mike had stalked in. He was clearly furious and threw his towel at the wall in frustration. Billy looked up over the cover of his book.
"Pool shut again?"
"Yes, that piece of useless shit lifeguard is drunk again and not turned up for work. Yossi has said it's his last chance. He is getting kicked off tonight."
This got Billy's attention. He sat up and put the book down.
"Yossi is really going to chuck Steve off?"
"That's what he said."
"I'll believe it when I see it."
"I think there is too much pressure from the members now. Remember they are effected every time the pool is closed."
This was not strictly true. The rules were different for members. If a responsible adult could be found then the pool could open for the members and their children. In this case life went on for them but the volunteers were excluded if no lifeguard was on duty.
What was true was that in the afternoon, when most of the adults were either at work or resting after their shifts then it was often difficult to find someone willing to step in. This was part of the reason there was a lifeguard in the first place.
Aside from this Billy was still doubtful that Steve's removal would actually occur. In all the time, they had been on the Kibbutz no one had been removed. A few volunteers sensing the end was nigh had left under their own steam and Yossi had made a point of telling everyone they had jumped only hours before they were pushed but an actual expulsion was something new.
It was not until teatime that they received confirmation that it had actually happened.
In the quiet of the afternoon Yossi had arrived in the volunteer block and told Steve to pack his stuff. The lad had then been driven to the end of the road and left at the bus stop. There had been no fuss, no public walk of shame, in fact only two volunteers had witnessed the whole event.
According to them Steve had begged, in tears, to be given another chance but in the end, Yossi had ignored these pleas and the two had driven away in Yossi's jeep.

Now as they sat at the supper table the subject switched to who would replace Steve on the lifeguard's chair.
It was considered one of the cushiest jobs on the volunteer roster. Just sitting in the sun all day was hardly challenging work. One of the longer serving volunteers did point out that there were other things that needed taking care of, from time to time, like cleaning and maintenance work and that at the end of the season the pool needed to be drained and scrubbed clean by hand.
Mike, who was sitting next to Billy suddenly dug his friend in the ribs.
"How about it Billy? You could be the new lifeguard."
Others sitting close by, who knew Billy's spell at the factory was coming to an end agreed. When Yossi came by the table a little later Billy offered his services as the new lifeguard. Yossi looked Billy up and down as if considering him.
"You did say any job." Billy reminded him
"OK Billy, I will drop the keys to the pool off with you later on."
There was various whoops and back slapping's of congratulation and Billy was officially the new lifeguard at Tel Boker pool.

#

Now two months on and several things had changed for Billy. He was no longer together with Katarina but their separation this time was not because of any drunken antics on Billy's behalf. This time they had separated as friends when Katarina's stay on the Kibbutz came to an end and she left to return home to Sweden to continue her University education.
They had an emotional last few days together and exchanged addresses and made promises to write to each other. This feverish exchange of letters and cards had lasted for another month and then fizzled out.
Following Katarina's departure Billy had not been alone for long. After a few days, he got together with the young lady from the Kitchen who was still carrying a torch for him after his intervention with Ezra. Their affair was short lived as Billy, in his new role as lifeguard, found he suddenly became the centre of attention for many of the women on the Kibbutz. His position atop the lifeguard station also gave him a great view of all the women who came to the pool in the afternoon to sunbathe and swim.

Sitting there, Billy could, from behind his sunglasses, check out all of them as they passed by his chair or lay on the grass on either side of him.

And Billy's conquests were not confined to just volunteer girls. In the last two months, he had been together with three volunteers, two young female Israeli soldiers and one of the young members from the Kibbutz.

Each of these different groups had provided their own challenges. The volunteers were probably the easiest group of the three as relationships among the volunteers went largely unnoticed and unchallenged, unless they went sour and impacted on the involved volunteers work life. If any disagreements or break-ups could be handled in an adult fashion then there was little interference from the Kibbutz authorities.

Billy's relationship with Katarina, the first non-English girl he had dated, had piqued his interest for foreign women and as the current volunteer group was such an international mix he was able to satisfy his curiosity. His first girlfriend after the Kitchen girl, Andrea, who was from the UK, had been a rather willowy dark German girl called Candice. She was almost boyish with her short dark hair and her slight build. She was very forthright in her attitude to the relationship and what she expected from Billy in return and this almost Teutonic efficiency, even in bed was a little hard for Billy to handle. They broke up after a week but remained friends. His next girlfriend was Emma who was from Australia, a much smaller, bubbly blonde with a gorgeous honey-like tan. She was great fun to be around and could drink most of the lads under the table.

They separated only because Emma and her travel companion decided to leave the Kibbutz to travel around Israel and Egypt and she never returned to Tel Boker. Billy did get a postcard a few months later to say that they had quit the Middle East and were now both living in a shared flat in Earls Court in London and if Billy made it back to the UK to drop by and look her up. Billy placed the card in the back of his Israel book with all the other addresses he had collected, just in case.

After Emma's departure, he had started a short but very passionate affair with one of the Young Israeli soldiers.

This particular group were mostly city kids who had decided to split their national service between active duty with front line units and time served in a farming community, like a Kibbutz. Most of these groups of youngsters came from the same towns, and some of them had grown up together and attended the same schools. This made breaking into the group especially difficult. Each girl had a dozen 'older' brothers looking out for her wellbeing. It was quite intimidating. What was even more scary was the other girls.

Billy was totally unprepared for the visiting delegation of 'older sisters' who arrived at his door on a Saturday morning. The reason for their visit became clear as they entered the room asking what his intentions with their roommate were.

The fourth girl in this group, a pretty raven-haired firebrand from Tel Aviv called Rachel, had spent several hours the previous evening chatting to Billy and they even had the occasional dance together and despite the fact they had both returned to their respective rooms after the party this was still excuse enough for the visiting inquisition.

In this particular case, the three friends thought they were looking out for Rachel's best interests. Unfortunately, she didn't see their intervention in quite the same light. After an hour of intensive questioning the three departed and obviously went to report their findings. Clearly their conclusions were not particularly well received. The young lady in question presented herself at Billy's room door less than fifteen minutes later wishing to apologise for her friends' actions.

Billy was magnanimous enough to dismiss the whole affair but it seemed that this was not enough to satisfy Rachel. She wanted to show Billy just how much remorse she felt, and he was not about to stop her.

Later on when they finally made it to the Dining Room for a bite to eat, Rachel was immediately kidnapped by her friends and peers and taken away for questioning.

Later that evening Billy received another visit from the young lady who had apparently managed to give her captors the slip. She stood in the open doorway, not certain if she was still welcome to enter after the earlier incident.

She asked if they could talk and Billy asked her to come in and make herself comfortable. Rachel took her time explaining what her friends had concluded about him and how they felt that a relationship between the two of them was far from appropriate for her.

Billy took the criticism manfully, although deep down he was hurt that people could assume the worst about him without really knowing him, or certainly after only an hour-long interrogation. At the end of her speech Billy asked her what she thought about the whole thing and she said she wished her friends had not intervened but now that they had she had to respect their opinion. Billy sensed that this might be the end of their brief affair, and he asked that question with a degree of trepidation. In the short time, they had known each other he had grown quite fond of Rachel. He eventually summoned up the courage to put the question into words.

"Does that mean we are breaking up?"

She listened to his question and then sat on his bed with the flickering candle light shining in her glossy rich hair. She didn't say anything for several minutes as if she was having an internal argument with herself. Eventually she reached a verdict, smiled sweetly at Billy and said.

"Yes." Looking downwards she couldn't meet his eye, "But not until tomorrow morning." She looked up and gave Billy a lascivious smile.

When he awoke in the morning in a tangle of bedsheets there was an empty space beside him. Rachel had sneaked out at some point during the night.

This stop and start performance carried on for some considerable time with late night visits from Rachel when her friends' backs were turned, or they were otherwise occupied. It was a little strange for Billy to be ignored totally and indeed even avoided when they met in public but then visited with such passion in the dark of the night. Not that he ever objected.

Eventually the pressure of all the sneaking around proved too much and Rachel called an end to their clandestine affair.

The fact that Rachel had been ignoring him in public and he therefore appeared to be unattached actually worked in his favour. In a close-knit community like a Kibbutz where everyone knows each other's business, it is very difficult to keep secrets and everyone knows who is dating who and who is sleeping with whom. Trying to start a new relationship in those circumstances where there was still a whiff of attachment to a previous partner was therefore next to impossible.

Of course, as soon as the coast was clear then it was once again game on. With Billy and Rachel proving the exception to the rule and keeping their affair secret and even appearing publicly to dislike each other the interested females were already circling again even before Rachel had called time on the relationship. Billy's next girlfriend was Danish. Susanna had the most startlingly bright platinum blonde hair and deep azure blue eyes. Her teeth, the product of the Danish free dental care system, were perfectly straight and dazzlingly white and she smiled frequently. She had arrived on the Kibbutz with a small group of fellow Danes and they had all been assigned to two adjacent rooms, four girls in one room and three guys in the other. These two rooms were on the same block as Billy and Mike's room although these days Mike was not very often in residence. He had been bold enough to ride the storm of criticism and unspoken threats and to start a relationship with a young member who had her own room in another part of the Kibbutz and Mike slept up there most nights. This was useful for Billy as it meant he had the room to himself. By now Billy, was approaching the end of his sixth month on the Kibbutz and was among one of the longest serving volunteers. Only the eternal Refet workers, Stig and Dingo had been volunteers for longer, although they had only recently returned after a short stint away on a Refet Moshav where they had been paid squillions of shekels to do what they had been doing on Tel Boker for a year for next to nothing. They had spent some of their pay check on a week-long holiday to Sinai and had returned, rested, tanned, and ready to party again.

Billy had gratefully handed back the responsibility of being the Father figure among the volunteers to them almost as soon as their backpacks and guitars had hit the floor in their room.

But Billy, as the third in line to the title was also frequently consulted about all things to do with volunteers and the seven new Danes being neighbours always called on him first if they had any questions.

Like most volunteers Billy was a collector. As Volunteers left, their personal items and things they had scavenged were up for grabs. After one group left, a garden swing set was abandoned and Billy with a little help, managed to get it moved to the open ground adjacent to his room.

In the afternoons and early evenings, he was often to be found gently swinging, drinking a beer and enjoying some music or a good book.
From this vantage point he could see the whole length of the block and he became quite used to the sight of his Danish neighbours, topless, both boys and girls wandering around. The girls, often only wearing their knickers. He tried not to stare too much but this proved almost impossible the first-time Susanne came down the block wearing only a pair of startlingly white Sloggies and sat down beside him on the swing.
Billy, ever the genial host, asked if she would like a beer and when she accepted he retrieved a cold one from the fridge.
Another advantage of their long service on the Kibbutz had been the acquisition of their own fridge. The volunteers had communal fridges on all of the blocks and one large fridge in the party area, but over the months and years a few had managed to secure "personal" fridges and like all other items of room decor, when Volunteers left these were passed around among the remaining volunteers. The fridge had been one such item. It meant that Billy and Mike when he occasionally came down to slum it in Volunteer central had access to cold drinks in their own room and in the height of the summer this was an added bonus. Also, it meant that they could be proper hosts and pass out beers to their guests and this was what Billy was doing now. He handed the chilled bottle to the semi-naked Danish girl who was sitting on his swing-set.
It was a blisteringly hot Saturday afternoon and what happened next could only be described as mildly pornographic as Susanne used the cold glass bottle to cool down parts of her body. Billy was struggling to control himself and his manhood in his board shorts, but he clearly failed as Susanne starring wantonly at his crotch asked if he was turned on by her near nakedness.
Billy knowing that lying was out of the question as his arousal was becoming more obvious by the minute just blurted out a strangled 'Yes'.
"Well what are you waiting for?" Susanne winked.
Billy, who was not sure if the whole thing was an elaborate wind up just sat there with a stupid grin on his face. Susanne was clearly serious about the offer.
"Are you going to fuck me or just sit there? I have not had sex for two months."

Billy was on his feet in seconds, beer and book forgotten as the two of them rushed into Billy's room slamming the door behind them.

Susanne proved almost as adventurous as Katarina and it was only later as they lay in bed that Billy discovered that the Danes, despite all their claims, were more like their German neighbours than their Swedish ones.

As they lay there in each-other's arms Susanne suddenly went rigid and sat up.

She poked Billy hard in the shoulder with a finger, hard enough for it to leave a mark.

"When are you going to ask me if I am on the birth pill?"

"What?" Billy was stunned

"Before you came inside me. Did you not think to ask?"

"Well, are you?"

"Yes but that is not the point. You should have asked."

She hunted around in the bedclothes and found her underwear, got out of bed and slipped them on. She collected her now warm beer bottle from the table and left the room without another word.

"Bye." Billy mumbled at the closed door.

He had the feeling that this might be the last he would see of Susanne. She had scratched her itch and now she would move on. He did think about seeking her out later and apologising to her for his behaviour, but it proved unnecessary. Susanne came to his room later that afternoon to ask if he was coming to the Dining room and she clung to his arm all the way there. She had obviously forgiven him for his lapse of manners and now considered they were an item.

This time it was Mike who was indirectly instrumental in the break up with Susanne. Mike's relationship with Yara, his young member, had hit the buffers quite spectacularly when she had suggested that her and Mike should become engaged. Whilst Mike was not totally against the idea in principal, he had not considered the wider picture and when he was summoned to a meeting of the Kibbutz council and asked how he felt about becoming a candidate Member and leaving the Kibbutz to study on an Ulpan course with a view to converting to Judaism, he panicked and called time on the relationship. Whilst he felt he truly loved the young lady there were limits to what he was prepared to endure and adult circumcision was not on his list.

With Mike and Yara breaking up Mike effectively moved back into the room and this put an end to Billy and Susanne's cosy little arrangement.
The end of the private sleeping arrangements put their sex life on hold and without the sex Billy found he had little in common with Susanne and they just drifted apart.
He then had a drunken one-night-stand with Mike's ex, Yara and was riddled with guilt for about a week as Mike was still besotted with her, but when it became clear that Yara was not going to pursue him and consequently Mike would never find out the guilt eased a little.

#

Billy, sat atop his lifeguard perch was therefore at this point in time blissfully single and so he felt free to ogle the available talent. Clad in bikinis or swimsuits, some wet from their recent dip in the pool, some so brief that they left little or nothing to the imagination Billy was like a kid in a candy shop and a blow of his whistle and a yelled reprimand in either English or Hebrew and suddenly all eyes were on him.
The rules of the pool were quite simple. Like most pools there were basic safety rules like no running or no horseplay, but unlike most public pools there were no rules about consumption of food and drink except the obvious one, no glass. This was generally only a problem with new volunteers who wanted to bring beer in bottles to the pool in the afternoons, but this ceased when the Kibbutz shop started to stock beer in cans. The only other rule concerned Volunteers and intoxication. One or two beers were ok but any more and the Kibbutz authorities threatened to step in and ban all alcohol.
This, of course, put Billy in an awkward position. He was there to enforce the rules, even if he didn't agree with them. This was particularly the case with water melons. In an attempt to smuggle strong spirits into the pool area some bright sparks came up with the idea of slicing the top off a melon and pouring the contents of a bottle of Vodka or Arac inside. The result, when chilled in a fridge was a very alcoholic snack. This was OK on the face of it, if the volunteers didn't get too pissed. The problem came when the young Kibbutz kids, seeing watermelon slices being eaten, came

and asked if they could have a slice. To refuse went against the whole spirit of communal living but to hand over a slice and watch a kid suffer was also totally unacceptable. The Volunteers saw sense, thankfully, and stopped the practice in its tracks.

So, Billy had to tread a tightrope between offending his fellow volunteers and ending up in hot water with the Kibbutz authorities. He preferred those days when all he had to do was blow his whistle and tell the occasional over exuberant kid to stop running.

Although that in itself could also present problems when it came to the older kids, particularly the teenagers. Some of them were just finding their feet and their voices in the world. His predecessor had been lax with them, wanting to be "one of the lads", and had given them plenty of latitude over their behaviour. Billy was not so understanding and this led to conflicts. He was a pretty laid-back person but when the teenage lads started to horse around and their behaviour was beginning to upset other visitors to the pool he had to step in and stop them. This in turn resulted in a very public argument with Billy and a group of the teenage lads yelling at each other across a group of sun loungers. Billy knew that as the adult he had to call a halt to these proceedings so he stopped shouting and in a quiet voice simply pulled rank. He was in charge of the pool and if the kids didn't do what he said then they were all welcome to leave. With that parting message Billy had simply turned around and walked away. What he heard next made Billy stop dead in his tracks.

One of the lads, the defacto leader of the group made a side comment to one of the others. Whether he had temporarily forgotten that Billy spoke his language or whether he realised this and made the comment on purpose knowing that it would offend, Billy was not sure but for him it was the final straw.

"The trouble with these volunteers is that they quickly forget who the masters are and who are the slaves in this arrangement."

Billy didn't turn back to challenge the comment he just kept walking all the way down to the end of the pool area and entered the room where the pump and filtration equipment was. In one corner of the room was a small cubbyhole with a telephone. He picked up the receiver and dialled an internal number from memory. Yossi answered the phone and Billy recounted the substance of his recent exchange with the youngsters.

At the other end of the phone Billy heard Yossi swear loudly in Hebrew. He was poolside five minutes later where he rounded up the young lads and frogmarched them out of the pool complex. The ring leader returned to the pool the next afternoon chastened and apologetic. Clearly the whole group had been given a stern lecture on their responsibilities as hosts and what was expected of them in terms of behaviour.

This was an isolated and never repeated incident but the afternoons in general could be stressful and Billy had to be ever vigilant. Therefore the best time of day for Billy was the mornings when the majority of the Kibbutz were either working or at school and he could get a few of the more mundane maintenance tasks finished. As well as the cleaning of equipment and the pool area there was the upkeep of the flowerbeds and lawns which for some reason were his responsibility rather than the team who kept the rest of the Kibbutz gardens in top condition.

During this time, he was largely on his own although occasionally a Member or two, on a day free from work would come by for a swim or to just lie in the sun by the pool.

This was how Billy came to meet Daphna. She was a writer, living on the Kibbutz with her husband. He had been born and raised on Tel Boker and was one of a select group of members who worked outside of the Kibbutz. He was a manager at a local orange juice pressing plant so he left early every morning in his company car and returned at some time during the afternoon or early evening. For a writer, she did not seem to do much writing; not from where Billy was standing. She always seemed to be wandering around the Kibbutz or sunning herself by the pool.

They had never spoken together but were on a nodding acquaintance. Whenever she came into the pool area she would nod a greeting and smile at Billy.

Then suddenly one day, out of the blue, she spoke to him. It might have helped that Billy was working in one of the flowerbeds a few feet from where she was lying on her sun lounger, but it was still a surprise for Billy when it happened.

"Do you enjoy your life in the Kibbutz?" The question was in English so Billy felt he should respond in the same language.

"Yes I do. I enjoy it very much. Do you?"

"Not really." The answer seemed to shock Daphna as much as it surprised Billy. She covered her mouth with her hand. Then winked conspiratorially at Billy.
"I guess that is a little off message. It's the truth that dare not speak its name."
"I always thought that was love." Billy responded.
Daphna looked puzzled for a moment so Billy explained.
"I thought the phrase was 'the love that dare not speak its name.' It's Oscar Wilde or at least associated with him. I believe it is a quote from a poem."
Realisation dawned in Daphna's eyes.
"Yes. You are right. It's a euphemism for homosexuality."
Now it was Billy's turn to look confused.
"I don't see…"
Daphna cut him off. "I guess it was a bad choice of phrase. At least with someone who has studied 19th century poets." She smiled at Billy again.
"I wouldn't go that far, but I do read a lot."
Billy had pushed himself up off his knees and moved closer to where Daphna was lying. She had to shade her eyes to look up at him despite wearing sunglasses.
"But you seem to be a cut above the usual. I have never found anyone who has even heard of Oscar Wide. Not among the volunteers at least."
"I am sure there are one or two who might have heard of him."
"This place is a literary wasteland. Hence my earlier comment, which I would appreciate you keeping to yourself."
Billy made his usual zipping and locking movement with his hand in front of his mouth.
"Can you sit with me a while?" Daphna indicated the lounger beside hers.
Billy cast a quick glance around and as there was no one else in the vicinity, he plonked himself down.
"I can sit with you for a while."
"Good then I can explain."
Having found a willing ear, Daphna started to pour out her heart. She started by explaining that as a writer she needed the company of other literary minds, and she had largely surrendered this when she had moved with her husband back here to the Kibbutz. These people tended to congregate in the major cities, like Tel Aviv and

Jerusalem although there were other pockets of writers on Mount Carmel near Haifa and in the largely Orthodox enclave of Safed. Therefore, coupled with her sense of professional isolation, was an element of personal isolation. A distance between her and her husband and her husband's friends.

Whilst the conversation remained on writer's colonies and the fact that here on the Kibbutz the height of polite conver-sation was usually about crops and yields, Billy remained comfortable, but when the conversation turned to more personal matters Billy started to squirm a little.

Daphna, feeling she had finally found someone she could trust was determined to unload all her personal baggage.

When she touched on the more delicate subject of her intimate relationship with her husband Billy started to blush. Daphna noticing his colour started to laugh, then stopped herself.

"I am sorry," she said, "I didn't intend to embarrass you. I thought you might understand my position. My husband is probably fucking his secretary as we speak."

Billy didn't know what to say. He guessed that Daphna was probably only in her thirties and lying there in her bikini she had a glorious body. He wondered why someone would neglect such a superb looking woman.

"I don't know what to say." Billy did know what to say. He had just thought it, but he still felt embarrassed to give voice to his feelings.

"You don't have to say anything I can see it in your eyes, but please no pity."

Billy shook his head.

Daphna seeing, she had Billy's agreement then proceeded to pour out all her personal worries, including all the occasions she had sat at home waiting for her husband to return from work, the phone calls, late in the evening, the excuses, problems at the factory that needed his attention, breakdowns in production, staff troubles. They all added to her suspicions.

Billy felt very uncomfortable sitting there listening to Daphna pouring out her heart about her husband's alleged infidelities or at least her suspicions. Daphna however, was nothing if she was not sensitive to her surroundings. She sensed Billy's growing discomfort so she stopped in mid-sentence.

"Is this too much information?"

"No. It's fine." Billy lied. For once in his short life Billy wished he had the nerve to speak the truth, because what followed was much worse.
Daphna then embarked on an almost clinical dissection of her current sex life, or in some cases, lack of one.
Billy got the distinct impression that Daphna was clearly highly frustrated by the status quo in the bedroom and was almost pathological in her need for some kind of release.
Billy decided that at this point enough was enough. He made a move to stand up.
"I should really get on with my weeding. It will be lunchtime soon and then the hoards will descend and I will have to go back on duty."
Daphna was very apologetic.
"I am so sorry for bending your ear."
"It's OK, glad I could help."
"Well you certainly are a good listener."
"You are welcome. Anytime."
"Really?"
"Yes really."
"You are so sweet."
Billy had the good grace to blush at the compliment, coming as it did from an older and more mature woman.
Billy got up to walk away and Daphna reached for her voluminous handbag and pulled out a packet of cigarettes and lit one. She lay back on the sun lounger and stretched out like a languid cat. Billy took one last look at her superb body and turned back to his chores.
About a half hour later Daphna rose from her sunbed, collected her stuff and with a wave across the pool at Billy, slipped away. Billy watched her backside as she walked away. Her husband really was a fool if he was not attending to her needs.
The afternoon at the pool was uneventful and Billy locked up and headed back to Volunteer central for a shower and a well-earned beer.
He didn't go back to the room but headed straight for the shower block. He had everything he needed with him in his small backpack including a fresh set of clothes.
It was just after five when he pushed open the door to the room to be greeted by a cloud of flying clothes.

Mike was in the process of sorting through every stitch of clothing he possessed and t-shirts, shirts, vest tops and other garments were being picked up, sniff tested and rejected.
Billy stood in the doorway observing the maelstrom and trying to decide if it was safe to cross the room to the refrigerator and liberate a cold Goldstar.
He decided to err on the side of caution and remain where he was.
"Mike, what's up man?"
Mike stopped dead, a white shirt clutched in his hands only mere inches from his face. He turned to see Billy leaning nonchalantly on the door frame.
"Is none of this clothing clean?"
"I don't know mate. It's your stuff."
This indicated a clear difference between the two of them and their respective upbringings. Billy had, from a very early age, realised that if he wanted clean clothes to wear then it was his responsibility to put them in a bag and take them to the local laundromat. Mike, on the other hand, had grown up with the luxury of a laundry basket in the bathroom where dirty clothes were placed and then magically returned a few days later, freshly washed, ironed and folded.
Mike had not quite accepted the fact that the bottom of his cupboard was not a magical laundry basket like the one at home. In the time that they had been on the Kibbutz it had always fallen to Billy to suggest that they bag some of their clothes and take them to the Kibbutz laundry.
While Mike had been together with Yara this responsibility had largely disappeared and when Mike had moved back in he had returned with most of his clothes clean and folded. Now it appeared that it was time to make a trip to the laundry.
"Anyway," Billy continued, "What's the sudden need to find something clean to wear."
"Yara has asked me out on a date tonight."
With the cessation of the violent storm of flying clothing Billy felt safe enough to enter the room. He moved over to the fridge and extracted two beers and popped the lids off. He handed one to Mike.
"So you two are getting back together again?"
"I hope so."

Secretly so did Billy. Mike had been very difficult to live with since the break-up of his relationship with the lovely Yara. He had definitely not been able to move on since they split up despite countless approaches from single female volunteers.

Mike sat on the edge of his bed atop the pile of discarded garments and took a long pull on his beer.

"She has asked me to go with her to another Kibbutz tonight. She has sorted out a car and she needed a driver."

"So you are a glorified chauffeur." The words were out before Billy could stop himself.

Mike stiffened and he flashed an angry look at Billy. The way he reacted proved to Billy that this thought had also crossed his friend's mind.

"Fuck off Billy. I don't want to talk about it. Anyway, it's not gonna happen unless I can find a clean shirt. Have you got anything I can borrow?"

Billy ignored his friends curse. In some way, he had deserved it. Instead he waved his beer bottle in the direction of his own cupboard.

"Knock yourself out mate. What's mine is yours. Just leave it as you found it. I don't want to have to pick up all my clothes from the floor after you have gone." He grinned as Mike stood up and opened Billy's cupboard.

Inside there was a pile of neatly folded t-shirts and Mike started to sort through them looking for something suitable.

He found a plain blue t-shirt and pulled it out.

"This will do. Can I borrow it?"

"Sure, no problem."

Mike was holding the t-shirt in one hand and the pile of discards in the other. He went to replace the discards in the wardrobe being careful not to drop them. His attention was drawn to the t-shirt that lay on the top of the pile still on the shelf.

He placed the discards pile to one side and pulled out this other shirt and held it up so it unfolded showing the design on the front of the shirt.

The t-shirt was for the band the Cure.

"Is this John's missing shirt?"

Billy looked up at the shirt hanging from Mike's hand.

"It might be."

"Where did you find it? He looked everywhere for this shirt. He accused virtually everyone on the Kibbutz of stealing it. Did you?"
"Nah, of course not."
"So where did you get it?"
"I found it."
"Where?"
"In the guts of one of the washing machines:"
"You what?"
"Yeah, Yossi came by the pool one day and asked if I could give him a hand. One of the women in the Laundry had managed to drop her wedding ring inside the machine and Yossi needed a pair of extra hands to help him move the machine out so they could get the back off it. When we unscrewed the back, we found all sorts of stuff in there along with the ring. Mostly socks and underwear but also one or two t-shirts and that was one of them. And the woman was so grateful we had retrieved her wedding ring she offered to wash and iron it for me. She has ironed most of my t-shirts ever since."
"Well at least we got to the bottom of John's lost t-shirt. You gonna write and tell him?"
"No way. Let him complain about it for a while longer,"
"The way he reacted he will probably still be moaning about this thirty years from now."
Mike carefully folded and replaced the t-shirt in the cupboard, straightened the rest of the pile and closed the door.
Mike's hot date meant that by eight o clock Billy was able to settle down on the swing outside his room with a glass of Arac and water and relax. Off in the distance he could hear the happy voices of the volunteers around the fire and the beat of the music told him that a party was developing. He weighed up the prospects of wandering over there but he was quite comfortable where he was right now. There was a bottle of Arac and water already mixed and within his reach. The gentle movement of the swing was comforting and he could hear the music, muted slightly by the distance. He knew that a new group of volunteers had arrived earlier in the day so he felt that he should at least show his face and welcome them, but that could wait until a bit later. The party would, if it ran true to form, probably go on until the early hours.
"Hi Billy. Can I join you?"
Billy looked up the glass halfway to his mouth.

Daphna was stood there in the dark beside the frame of his swing, one hand resting on the metal upright. She was clad in a pair of very short denim shorts and a wispy gossamer off the shoulder blouse with a plunging neckline. Her hair was brushed and caught up in a clip and she was wearing subtle but effective makeup. Billy wondered if the make-over was for his benefit or whether she had a party to attend later. He chose the latter of the two options but swung his feet around and invited her to sit down.

She perched on the edge of the swing her feet on the floor and her body half-turned toward him.

"You did say I was welcome anytime."

Billy cast a hurried look around him to see if there was anyone else in earshot. The coast was clear.

"I did." Billy admitted.

Although he had not expected Daphna to take him up on the offer and certainly not to come and visit him here in the Volunteer quarters. Whilst it was not unheard of for some of the Younger members and the kids to come and spend their evenings among the volunteers, older members and particularly married older members would normally not be seen dead hanging around with volunteers. This was behaviour that would be frowned on at best and would be the subject of gossip and possible censure at worst. It was just not done.

But here she was sitting next to him on the swing. What could Billy do?

He took a large swig from his glass of Arac hoping the fiery spirit burning its way down his throat would give him some help. It didn't. It just made his eyes water a bit. When he regained the ability to speak he turned to her.

"So how are you doing this evening?" It was such an insipid question that Billy squirmed inside.

"I am fine, thank you Billy. I was just passing and thought I would drop by and take you up on your offer."

Billy knew she was lying. None of the Members had any reason to be 'just passing' the Volunteers quarters. They had been built in a separate, isolated part of the Kibbutz to expressly prevent that necessity. Members venturing down here were mostly looking for drunk volunteers who had failed to turn up for work, so most of them were only here during the hours of daylight. Knowing therefore, that Daphna had made the trip down here specifically to visit him, made him even more wary.

Their conversation had been so easy earlier in the day when they had been in the sunshine in the public setting of the Kibbutz pool. Now it was guarded and measured as if they were both afraid of how their words might be interpreted. Billy was certainly weighing up every word he said and taking frequent sips from his drink. Billy noticed his glass was empty and was about to reach for the bottle to refill his glass when he remembered his manners.

"Would you like something to drink? I have beer, cola, or something stronger." He nodded at the Arac bottle.

"A beer would be nice. If it's cold."

"One cold beer coming up." He jumped up from the swing and crossed to the room. The light from the adjacent street light provided enough illumination for Billy to cross the room and open the fridge. The light inside the fridge meant he could see the row of Goldstar bottles lined up on the top shelf. He reached for one of them and straightened up pushing the fridge door closed with his knee. The light in the fridge went out and Billy found himself in darkness.

Daphna had followed him into the room and closed the door behind her cutting out the light from outside.

Billy could sense rather than see her in the dark as his eyes struggled to adapt to the sudden darkness. He was stood paralysed for a moment, with the unopened bottle in his hand.

He felt her hand reach out and touch his shoulder. He shivered despite the heat in the room. Daphna's hand moved from his shoulder to his cheek and then down to cup his chin, stroking upwards to the point. Billy stood stock still.

The hand continued down the side of his jaw and then around under his hair to the back of his neck, pulling him slightly forward. She turned her head to the side and moved closer to him. The kiss was inevitable but when it came it shocked Billy by its intensity and desire. It was if she was trying to suck the soul out of him, empty him of every last trace of breath.

Billy took a moment before he reacted. One hand was still holding the beer bottle but he slid the other hand up between them and placed it on her shoulder. He pushed gently, hoping to free himself but Daphna clung to his neck tightly.

Billy felt her tongue, now snaking into his mouth and her breathing through her mouth was becoming more passionate and ragged. Billy had to break this off, now. He pushed a little harder and Daphna sensing the movement, removed her hand from his neck and took a step back. Her breathing was still shallow, her face, even in the semi-dark looked flushed, but there was a troubled look in her eyes.

"What's wrong?" She was the first to find a voice.

"Nothing. Everything." Billy stammered feeling for the first time in a long time like a naughty schoolboy.

"What if someone walks in. Not everyone knocks first down here."

"Are you worried about the scandal? Surely I have more to lose than you do?" Daphna was smiling broadly now.

"I don't care about the scandal, not from my side."

"So you care about me?"

"Of course I...." Billy stopped himself from blurting out the rest of the sentence. Right now, he was confused he didn't really know what he cared about. He did feel sorry for Daphna and the obviously shit life she was having to endure, but he really didn't want to get embroiled in a Kibbutz wide scandal that might result in two members getting divorced. That was definitely not in Billy's playbook.

"Were you about to say that you care for me?"

Billy looked at Daphna and now his eyes had become accustomed to the gloom he could see there was a real earnest look on her face. What Billy said next really mattered to her.

He knew he needed to think very carefully before he replied to her question. He remembered the bottle in his hand, so he popped the lid off and handed it to her, hoping to buy himself a little more time. She accepted the bottle and put it to her lips and took several long swallows, then wiped her mouth with the back of her hand.

"I am waiting for your answer. Do you really care for me?"

"Yes I do." Billy wanted to clarify that statement but he was stuck for words. Daphna on the other hand took the words at face value and moved back in close to Billy.

"So what is the problem?" Billy could smell the faint aroma of beer on her breath but this was overpowered by the strong fragrance of her perfume and the smell of apple shampoo from her hair.

This time, the kiss when it came was less frantic and more tender and Billy felt Daphna's arms snaking around his neck again. He felt himself responding to her kiss and he placed his hands on her waist. Billy broke away again, but this time more reluctantly than before.

"The problem is you are married."

"My husband is fucking his secretary." Somehow the word "fucking" spoken in the half-light in this room had a more devastating effect on Billy, than when it had been used earlier in the day at the pool, in broad daylight.

The word wormed itself into Billy's mind and helped conjure up unwelcome images of Daphna and him writhing passionately on his bed. He tried to dispel the image and failed.

"So what are you suggesting. Revenge?"

It was Daphna's turn to pause and think. She knew in that moment what it would mean if she said that she was just out for Revenge. Put in that context it would be tantamount to admitting that this was all Billy meant to her and she knew this was not the case. It was true that she did feel slighted by her husband and she would love to extract some form of revenge, but she was not about to involve Billy in this kind of ungodly mess

"No Billy, I am not looking for revenge. What my husband does is up to him. This is more about me doing things for myself. I need to get my own life back. I am being suffocated intellectually by this place and the people. That's why I came here tonight to try and start to breathe again. Will you help me?"

Billy was still unsure of what involvement with this woman would mean for him. He was really struggling with his conscience. She was a married woman, but she was clearly not being treated well by her husband, or at least this was what she claimed.

Daphna had moved away from him now and sat down on the edge of the bed. She patted the bed beside her.

"Is this one yours?"

Billy nodded his head and then realised she might not be able to see him in the dark.

"Yes." He said.

Daphna placed her half-finished beer bottle on the floor and then patted the bed beside her.

"Come and sit beside me."

Billy felt like his feet were welded to the floor, but slowly, one step at a time he crossed the floor and sat down on the bed.
"There, that's better." Daphna placed a hand on Billy's knee, just at the point where the fabric of his shorts ran out. The feeling of her warm, soft hand on his skin awoke those familiar feelings of lust in his core. He fought against them but quickly lost the battle as Daphna's hand started to move up his leg under the fabric. Billy was conscious of Daphna's naked thigh pressed against his other leg and he let his hand drop down to the stroke the soft, tanned skin. Her leg was warm and as he brushed his fingers upwards he felt a shiver wrack her body. At the same time, a small moan escaped from her lips.
Billy was conscious of the passage of Daphna's hand even though he was focusing more on what his own fingertips were doing. As he passed the mid-point on her thigh he let his fingers slip lower in between her thighs and he was rewarded as he felt her legs open and her body arch towards his.
Daphna's free hand was plucking at the buttons of her shorts and as she released the buttons she suddenly stood up and shook herself, allowing the shorts to slide down to her ankles and she stepped out of them.
She turned to Billy and straddled his legs sitting down heavily on his thighs and then pushing him with both hands on his chest. Billy was not struggling in anyway and he lay back on the bed, enabling Daphna to wiggle seductively up until she was straddling his crotch. Billy reached for her hips and realised with a shock, that Daphna was naked from the waist down.
She had left her house at the other end of the Kibbutz without underwear. She had obviously planned for this to happen all along. He felt the heat from her body as she ground herself onto his manhood.
She tugged and Billy helped and his shorts were off too and with a free hand she guided him inside her.
Her orgasm, when it came was quick and brutal and afterwards she collapsed onto Billy's chest, panting.
After a moment's respite, she pulled Billy over on top of her and clinging on to his buttocks rode him to another climax allowing Billy to reach orgasm too.
They lay there in the dark for many minutes afterwards until Billy had a sudden panic attack.

"The door is not locked. Anyone could come in here and find us."
Fear of discovery broke the spell for both of them and they struggled to quickly make themselves presentable again.
Billy lit one or two of the candles so they did not appear to be hiding in the dark and then went to retrieve his glass and the Arac bottle from outside.
When he came back in Daphna was once again sat demurely on the edge of the bed sipping from the beer bottle.
The room smelt of sex so Billy left the door open to allow some of the cool evening air inside.
He perched on the edge of Mike's bed, hoping that if anyone walked in they would not realise what had just happened here.
Daphna, however, was prepared to let Billy off the hook.
Finishing the last of her beer in two quick gulps she stood up.
"I had better go before anyone discovers me here and starts asking difficult questions."
"OK. It is probably for the best."
Daphna paused by the door.
"My husband is starting his reserve duty next week so he will be away during the week. Come to my house and we can do this thing properly. See you at the pool."
With that she walked out. Billy took a large mouthful of Arac and swallowed it. He stood up slowly and picking up his bottle he crossed the room to his bed, the scene of the crime and sat down.
He could not believe what had just happened, but the ache in his groin and the vague smell of sex wafting into his nostrils was confirmation that what had just happened had really happened, even if he couldn't quite believe it.
At some point, in a daze, he must have crossed the room and closed the door before returning to his bed and lying down.
Reality came crashing back to him as the room door burst open, crashing back on its hinges.
Billy sat bolt upright. His first thought was Daphna's husband had come armed with an Uzi to extract some kind of revenge, but it was Mike who strode into the room, clearly in a foul temper.
"The fucking b-i-t-c-h." he cursed. He strode across the room and punched the wall. Hard. Hard enough for his fist to leave an impression deep in the cheap plaster board. It hurt his hand and he sucked on his knuckle as a wave of pain shot through his damaged hand and up his arm.

The pain quickly brought him to his senses and he turned to the fridge looking for something to ease his smarting hand. He pulled one of the frozen water bottles out of the ice box and then sat down on his bed.

"She fucking took me for a ride, the little slut. I thought this trip was all about us getting back together. But no. Sweet fucking Jesus no. All I was tonight was a fucking glorified taxi driver, a fucking pimp. She has got the hots for some pimply youth on Tel Shomer and I am expected to deliver her into his arms and probably his bed."

Mike was wretched with anger and cast the water bottle aside and went over and prepared himself a drink.

"You want one?" He held the bottle up for Billy who still sat bolt upright in his bed. Billy nodded and Mike did the honours and presented the drink to Billy. He didn't bother to resume his seat but simply offed the first glass and poured himself a second, which went the way of the first.

"You're very quiet tonight. Not even an 'I told you so'?"

Billy was sipping his drink slowly as his heart rate which had gone from normal to light speed when the door burst open was slowly getting back to normal.

Mike, despite his own anger and anguish detected there was something troubling his friend.

"What's up? What happened while I was away playing the cuckold?"

"N,n,nothing." Billy stammered. Billy had looked up alarmed at Mike's choice of words. He was instantly presented with an image of Daphna's husband wearing the horns and waving an Uzi in his direction a look of murderous intent on his face. He shook his head trying to dispel the image.

"It doesn't seem like nothing to me. Normally you would be heaping scorn on me for being a fool and you sit here like a mute at a music festival. Come on Billy spill the beans."

Billy took another sip from his glass and then took a deep breath.

"OK I will tell you, but you have got to keep this strictly between you and me. You must promise me not to tell a soul."

"Wow. That sounds serious. What did you do, kill someone?"

"Worse. I had sex with Daphna, you know the member, the writer."

Mike was clearly struggling to put a face to the name, but then realization and shock arrived together on his face.

"You mean that Daphna, who is always sunning herself at the pool?"

"Yes her."

"Fuck me Billy. Have you seen her husband? He is a fucking bull of a man."

"It's not her husband I am worried about. It's everyone else. I doubt the Kibbutz authorities would look too favourably on a Volunteer having an affair with a married member."

Mike hadn't considered the problem from that angle but he quickly saw the problem for what it was or what it could develop into.

"Shit. What are you going to do about it?"

"I don't know. She wants me to visit her next week while her husband is away."

"Are you going to?"

"To tell you the truth I have no idea what I am going to do. Right now, I just want to get some sleep and I will worry about the rest of it in the morning."

Mike went back over to the table by the fridge and collected one of the half empty Arac bottles from there. He pulled a bottle of cold water out of the fridge and mixed the two together. After a shake, he held up the resulting cloudy mixture for inspection.

"No work tomorrow, I stupidly booked a day off hoping to spend it with Yara, so I am going to go out and see if there are any volunteers who want to keep me company while I get rat-faced drunk."

Mike picked up the bottle and left the room closing the door behind him.

Billy slid back down the bed and tried to get comfortable again but sleep would not come a second time. After a half hour of tossing and turning he threw back the covers and got up.

Pulling on some shorts and a t-shirt, he mixed his own bottle of Arac and water and went in search of his friend and a party so he could also take his mind off his troubles.

CHAPTER ELEVEN

"My god this Vodka tastes like aftershave. Haven't we got any of the Stoly left?"
The upper class, cut glass tone, slightly slurred by Alcohol drifted over to Billy as he strode towards the end of the block.
He knew what he would see as he rounded the corner. His swing would be there, moved again, whilst he had been at work.
This was the second time in four days he had returned to find the swing missing from its place outside his room, and he had just about enough.
The thieves had arrived on the Kibbutz just five days ago. Four English lads, all friends, all from some Public school in the middle of Berkshire. All upper-class twats in Billy's opinion. Billy had never been one to look at life in terms of a class war. If he was honest with himself and measured life in that way then he would have to admit that he was from the working class. That fact was indisputable. In the same way, Mike would probably be considered upper-middle class, and he and Billy got along fine. But Billy did not get along with these four newcomers.
On their first full day on the Kibbutz, their acclimatisation day they had wandered around the volunteer quarters nicking anything that was not nailed down. Now outside their room they had accumulated a sofa, two armchairs and worst of all Billy's treasured swing. And Billy wanted his swing back. He had already taken an hour off work the previous day to come down and move it back and then when he arrived back at the room this afternoon it had gone again and Billy had no doubt where it had been moved to.
He came around the corner and saw the four of them relaxing outside the room. One of the guys was sprawled full length on the sofa, one in each of the armchairs and the last was lying on the

swing. All of them were dressed similarly in tan chino shorts, Turnbull and Asser blue poplin shirts and brown docksiders. It was like they had all become so used to wearing a school uniform that they found it impossible to dress differently even after leaving the school regime.

"Look out pleb at three o clock." One of them had spotted Billy. The others all turned around to give him their full attention.

Billy stopped a few feet away and placed his hands on his hips.

"I want the swing back." Billy was careful not to use the word "my" in the sentence.

"Look we have already been through this. We are on a Kibbutz and on a Kibbutz, everything is shared. So how can you say it's yours?"

"I didn't say it was mine. I said I wanted it back." Billy corrected him.

"Well good luck trying to take it. Angus has chained it up to the post now so it looks like we are going to be hanging onto it for a while."

Billy followed their eyes and saw that a piece of shiny new chain was looped around one of the uprights and the other end looped around the concrete post that supported the roof of the veranda. The chain was secured with a heavy padlock.

"Now be a good chap and fuck off."

Billy stood for a moment and considered his options. There were four of them and only one of him so the odds were not in his favour if it came to blows. Two of the group were stocky, muscled chaps. The other two less so. Their leader and the main speaker was tall and rangy. The fourth was short and had weasel like features. Billy reckoned that if he could disable one of the large lads then he might have a chance to win but failure to knock down one of the big lads and he might be in for the beating of his life. Billy stood his ground as he waited for his chance.

"Are you still here? I thought I told you to fuck off."

Billy folded his arms across his chest and fixed the leader with a steely glare.

He spoke slowly and forced his voice to remain calm, despite the fact he could feel the adrenalin starting to pump through his system.

"Can I just confirm that you are not going to unlock this chain and carry this swing back to where you found it."

The weasel faced guy stood up from his armchair and turned to face Billy.

"Are you deaf as well as stupid? Seb just told you to fuck off, so be a good boy and fuck off."

Billy measured the distance to weasel face. He was within striking range but Billy did not want to waste the element of surprise on one of the weaker ones. He wanted his first strike to be one of the larger lads. He needed to provoke them into attacking him, but how could he achieve his ends?

Billy stood there with defiance showing on his face. These four were obviously used to getting their way and having their orders followed by those whom they considered to be from lower on the class ladder and Billy's refusal to budge was starting to have the desired effect. They were unable to ignore him so they needed to remove him.

Billy's upper body had changed in the last six months. The countless days working in the sun had thickened his arms and strengthened his upper body. His forearms were thicker too. His biceps stood out from under his crop-sleeved t-shirt. This obvious physical strength was enough to dissuade weasel face from attacking him, which was good and Billy doubted Sebastian the leader would get his hands dirty so it would be one of the other two who would be called upon to physically remove him. Just as he hoped for.

"If there is one thing I hate more than a pleb, it's a pleb that doesn't know his place and you just don't understand your place in the order of things."

Billy ignored the taunts. He was looking for action and he was ready for it. He was not a naturally violent person but he knew that for some people this was the only lesson they understood.

"Now I am going to count to three and if you have not removed yourself I am going to ask Angus here to fuck you up. Angus please stand up." Sebastian was obvious bored of this little game and wanted things brought to a swift conclusion so he could go back to moaning about the quality of the local Vodka.

Angus obeyed his friend and stood. Billy fixed his attention on his opponent. He was a good head taller than Billy, well built across the shoulders with heavy forearms hanging from the rolled sleeves of his light blue shirt. Billy noticed that the lad's thighs stretched the legs of the shorts. He was going to be strong but maybe, Billy hoped, not too agile on his feet.

"Angus here," Sebastian waved a hand in his general direction, "was a prop forward for the First fifteen."

"I don't care if he was wide receiver for the Miami fucking Dolphins." Billy shot back.

Sebastian tipped his head forward and peered over the top of his Ray-Ban sunglasses.

"Angus, do him."

The former Rugby player exploded into action. Billy took a step backwards as Angus rounded the arm chair and came towards him, his fists bunched tight and his arms swinging apelike.

He roared as he opened his arms wide, hoping to enfold Billy in a crushing hold.

Billy timed his strike to perfection. Whipping his arm back at the elbow he put all his force into his right wrist and planted his fist squarely on Angus's nose which emitted a sickening crack as it broke. Angus let out a howl of pain as his hands shot to protect his face and a spray of bright red blood stained the front of his blue shirt. He was hurt, but he was still on his feet. Billy addressed that fact next.

The punch to the face had slowed his target down enough for Billy to take aim and he let fly with a foot to the targets groin, connecting with his testicles with another sickening crunch. The scream that followed and the spray of blood told Billy he had found his target and Angus collapsed on the floor weeping in pain. As Angus had made his move the other three had all stood in anticipation, hoping to get a good view of Billy getting a beating. Instead they were positioned well to see their companion as he collapsed into the dirt. But they were also well placed to come to his aid and all three moved as one. The fourth member of the group was also clearly a former Rugby player judging by his build and he made a grab for Billy's arm. Sebastian was in front of Billy trying to distract his attention while weasel face danced around behind the two, yelling obscenities and screaming like a little girl. The ruckus quickly drew attention and while Billy fought bravely to defend himself other Volunteers were drawn to the scene of the fight.

Most stood by as silent spectators, a couple however, yelled at the tops of their voices, baying like wolves.

Billy guessed he was in trouble as the other rugby player had managed to get a firm grip on his left arm near the shoulder preventing Billy from moving. While he struggled to free himself from the grip, Sebastian moved in from the right and aimed a couple of punches at Billy's face and upper body. Billy twisted and turned to avoid the blows but one or two of them connected.

Billy felt like he was being dragged to the ground and he saw that the bigger opponent on his left was trying to do just that. Once he was on the ground they would be able to kick the life out of him. Billy could feel the lad's weight bearing him downwards and he felt his knees start to buckle with the force.

Suddenly the weight on his shoulder disappeared and Billy who had been focusing on Sebastian fists glanced round to see the rugby player sailing backwards and crashing into one of the arm chairs before rolling onto the floor.

A split second later and Sebastian was sprawling in the dirt beside his companion and the now weeping figure of Angus. The last man standing was weasel face who seemed oblivious to the fact that the fight was largely over and was still capering about like a madman throwing imaginary punches in the air and yelling obscenities.

Billy looked around to see the source of his salvation.

On his left was Dingo and, on his right stood Stig. Both of them were barefoot and wearing only their undershorts, their long hair, unruly at the best of times, was matted with sweat from where they had both been dragged from their afternoon slumbers.

Dingo had placed a firm grip on Billy's shoulder and Billy was not sure whether it was to help him to stay on his feet or to restrain him from taking any further action. He decided to lower his fists and see what happened.

He looked at his fallen enemies. Sebastian had struggled into a sitting position and was holding his jaw. A line of blood trickled from the corner of his mouth. Angus was still curled up in a foetal position clutching his damaged groin and weeping like an infant. The other rugby player had recovered enough to regain his feet and was looking to the others for guidance, whilst surveying the two newcomers and assessing his chances now the odds had tipped against him. Weasel face now realised that the fight was over and his side had lost spectacularly, so he stood mute and surveyed the carnage. He was also the first to find his tongue.

"You fucking animals. Someone call the Police I want to report an assault." This last was directed in the general direction of the crowd of assembled volunteers.
"I suggest you shut the fuck up before I give you a right royal kicking." Stig said
"Then I'll have you too. My father is a top London barrister. I will have you in court."
"London is about two and a half thousand miles away so good luck with that."
"I will ring the British Embassy." He was not giving up.
"Be my guest I am sure they would love to learn how you four pricks picked a fight with one person and lost."
"I will complain to the Kibbutz authorities." He was now getting closer to home. I have witnesses."
"And who do you think they will believe? You four Johnny come lately's who arrived five minutes ago or the two of us who have been respected volunteers for the past eighteen months?"
"I suggest you just help your friends to get sat down and cleaned up while we sort this mess out."
"Neither of us like being woken up in the middle of our siesta."
"Have you calmed down?" This last was Dingo speaking to Billy
Billy nodded and Dingo released his grip on his shoulder.
"Go get us a couple of glasses of Arac would you?"
Billy nodded and headed off in the direction of his room, returning a few moments later with a bottle of Arac and water and three glasses. While he was away the four newcomers had been picked up from the floor and were now sitting on the sofa's and armchairs. Dingo and Stig had taken up places on the swing facing them.
Billy did the honours and handed over the drinks. He stood to one side. He didn't feel it would be right to sit down on the swing. That would be too proprietorial. He remained standing and sipped on his drink.
Dingo and Stig took time to taste their drinks and light cigarettes.
"Right you four are new here so maybe we need to go through a few rules of the Kibbutz. Rules that maybe Yossi didn't feel the need to mention to you when you arrived.
Rule Number One is no fighting. Rule Number Two concerns ownership of possessions like this swing." Dingo patted the cushion he was sitting on.

"This swing belongs to Billy as he was gifted it by the volunteer that had it before him when that volunteer chose to leave. This swing, therefore belongs to Billy until such time as he leaves the Kibbutz or choses to gift it to someone else. Are we clear about that?"

Sebastian having recovered a little from the blow to the jaw had also recovered some of his former cockiness.

"It looks like the swing is staying here. We have chained it to the post and thrown away the key." He had a self-satisfied grin on his face and seeing this change his other three friends recovered some of their former swagger and attitude.

"So the little pleb can have his swing back if he is prepared to go and grovel in the long grass over there and find the key to the lock."

Dingo was unmoved by the petulant outburst. He looked long and hard at Sebastian before asking.

"Are you sure you have thrown away the key?"

"Yes." Sebastian folded his arms across his chest in what looked to be a final show of defiance.

"Stig, go get the bolt cutters from the jeep."

Stig got up and wandered off. A few moments later he was back with a huge pair of bolt cutters. Sebastian's jaw dropped. He clearly thought that Dingo had been calling his bluff.

Stig didn't even pause for a moment but took the bolt cutters and made short work of the chain. He tossed the mangled chain into the space between the swing and the other seats and took his place back on the swing.

"We use them out in the fields on some of the fence wires." Dingo offered to the assembled group by way of explanation.

With the swing released it was merely a question of picking up it by the legs and carrying it the short distance back to its place outside Billy's room.

On the way Billy asked the two brothers about their swift intervention and the devastating martial arts moves that they had used.

"It's called Krav Maga and it is taught to the soldiers in the Israeli Army. We have had one or two friends who have passed through here who gave us a few lessons. Don't like using it except where necessary and trust me if we had not intervened you would have received a real kicking."

"I don't like bullies." Added Stig.
"And particularly upper-class bullies." Agreed Dingo. "You had better watch yourself around that lot from now on I can't guarantee they won't seek some sort of revenge."
"I'll be careful and thanks for your help."

#

Mike returned a little later after Billy had discovered the punch he had delivered and one he had received to the side of his head had left him with swollen knuckles and a blackening eye. He was therefore, lying on the swing with an ice bag on his cheek and his hand wrapped in a wet towel. He had taken one of the frozen bottles of water out of the freezer box and smashed it into small lumps and placed them in a plastic bag. The wet towel he kept damp and cool by applying more cold water from a melting bottle by his feet.
"What the fuck Billy. Have you been in the wars?"
"Slight disagreement over ownership of the swing."
"Not those public-school pricks again?"
"The very same. But Stig and Dingo turned up and put some Ninja moves on them and then persuaded them to see the error of their ways. How was the football game?"
"We won in the end but it was a close match. I am sure the other side had a couple of ringers on the team."
"Some people just have to win at any cost."
"Ain't that the truth. Well I'm off for a quick shower and then I think a bite to eat. Are you coming with me?"
"Not to the shower if you don't mind." Billy's grin was sure sign that he was not feeling sorry for himself and the buzz from the Arac had started to kick in. He had been hoping that the numbing effect would help because tonight he was supposed to be visiting Daphna at her home. He was still not sure if he was prepared to go through with it.

CHAPTER TWELVE

In the dark Billy caught sight of the digital clock. The red numbers clearly visible across the room. It was just a little before four in the morning and he knew it was time for him to be heading back to his room. If he left it any later he could risk running into other members who were on their way to work and it might be very difficult to explain his presence in this part of the Kibbutz at this time of the morning.
Daphna was still sleeping so Billy slid carefully out of the bed and found his clothes. He dressed quickly and then bent over the still sleeping woman and kissed her gently on the forehead. She stirred briefly but only to turn over and fall asleep again. This was the last night they could spend together as her husband was returning home this weekend to spend the weekend on Tel Boker. He would have liked to say a proper goodbye but time was running out. He slipped out of the house and paused in the shadow of the porch, listening for any indication that anyone else was around. Hearing only silence he left the safety of the porch.
This was now the sixth night in a row, that he had visited Daphna and so far, he had managed to avoid meeting anyone on his way back from her place to the Volunteer quarters.
He always took a different circuitous route home, crossing and re-crossing the Kibbutz in the hope that if he came face to face with anyone then his point of origin would not be immediately clear to the person he met.
On this particular morning, he made an extra-long detour forcing him to enter the volunteer quarters from the opposite side to his room.
Entering Volunteer central without interception was always a relief. He knew that in this area of rooms he could come across volunteers who had either just woken up, were still awake from the

previous night's debauchery or like him were returning to their rooms after a night of passion. The only difference was that most of them had not just spent the night in the arms of a married female member. He was therefore not too concerned about meeting volunteers.
He started to walk along the veranda in front of the first group of rooms. There were voices coming from the end of the block.
It was where Angus, Sebastian and the other two had their room. It looked like they were still up as they were sitting around on the sofa's and armchairs still dressed in their own clothes rather than the Kibbutz blue work clothes.
Another clue came from their conversation which was audible from a long way off and would therefore be intrusive to anyone trying to sleep in any of the surrounding rooms. Listening to the inane ramblings indicated that the four were clearly intoxicated and this was reinforced by their occasional, false hysterical laughter.
Billy was secretly pleased that his room was far enough away that they would not be a problem for him as long as he could pass them without attracting their attention. In the state they were in, there was a probability that things would turn nasty very quickly and he was not in the mood for another fight.
Since their earlier confrontation, the four English lads had been keeping a low profile. They seemed reluctant to participate in everyday volunteer life, and were never present at the evening gatherings with the other volunteers. Instead a rumour went around that they were spending most of their nights off the kibbutz in a nearby town, where there were pubs and a nightclub, often returning by taxi to the Kibbutz in the early hours of the morning. They had not made any friends among their fellow volunteers preferring it seemed, their own company. Their elitist attitude had alienated them.
They complained about everything from the standard of the accommodation to the quality of the food and drink, whilst boasting freely to anyone prepared to listen about the superb meals they had eaten in nearby restaurants and the money they had spent keeping their liquor cabinet stocked with the best quality spirits. This apparent bottomless money-pit and their general attitude was the complete antithesis to Volunteer life.

Their Champagne Charlie lifestyle also impacted on their work and they were frequently absent, often using pathetic excuses to justify their absenteeism. If one was honest they only saw the work as an obstruction to what would otherwise be an rather excellent holiday. As Billy got closer to where the four of them were sat he caught a whiff of something more exotic. Clearly their euphoria was not caused by the grape or the grain but by hash. A quick glance over and Billy saw that there were two spliffs doing the rounds and a third and fourth lying ready rolled on the table between them along with what looked like a large plastic supermarket carrier bag overflowing with weed.

Billy was not naïve and he knew that there were places in the nearby town where all sorts of drugs could be bought relatively cheap. Hash or weed was brought over from Gaza or distributed by the Bedouins who grew it out in the desert. But what he did know was that there was a zero-tolerance policy to drug usage on the Kibbutz.

This was one of the red lines that the Members drew. It was always being drummed into the Volunteers about their hedonistic lifestyles and how they were a danger to the youngsters growing up in the Kibbutz and Billy had sat and listened on numerous occasions whilst the lecture was delivered to each successive new wave of volunteers about what was acceptable and unacceptable to the members. Drugs, in all their forms, were a definite no.

Billy knew that if word got out that there were volunteers using drugs then the whole trust system between the members and the volunteers would be in danger of collapsing. To a large extent, the members tolerated the debauchery of the volunteers because they were safe in the knowledge that the substances abused were legal. If they caught even a whiff of illegal substances then this could be a game changer.

Billy walked quickly past without acknowledging the four and thankfully they seemed oblivious to his presence.

Billy made it back to his room and crawled into bed but as tired as he was he could not fall asleep. He was troubled by what he had seen and knew that he needed to discuss this with someone. It was not a secret he wanted to keep to himself.

At moments of uncertainty like this he knew exactly who he should talk to so as soon as it was light enough he went in search of Stig and Dingo.

As the two longest serving volunteers they probably had come across this problem before and would know how it was dealt with in the past.

He finally located the two of them at work in the Refet where they had just completed the morning milking session and were in the process of cleaning the milking parlour.

He came across Dingo first. He was in the main parlour filling the large sinks with the water and acid needed to cleanse the pipes and collecting jars used during the milking process. As soon as the word 'hash' was mentioned Dingo pulled Billy roughly by the shoulder out into the yard at the back where Stig was using a high-powered pressure washer to clean all the cow dung from the floor and walls.

Billy explained to the two brothers what he had seen and smelt a couple of hours before and asked them what he should do.

Both were unhesitating and unanimous in their response.

"You have to report this to Yossi." Stig said.

Dingo nodded in agreement.

"If you have any suspicions of drug use then report it to him. It's up to him to deal with it. It's what he gets paid to do." He added "Only one thing, you have to be one hundred percent sure of your suspicions because things will most likely get ugly."

"Yeah the Police will probably end up getting involved so don't get involved yourself."

Billy looked at the two of them. They were both clearly unhappy at the prospect of drugs making their way into the Volunteer quarters.

"Well I saw a large carrier bag stuffed with weed, sitting on a table. Would that be enough evidence?"

The two brothers agreed that a large amount of weed was probably enough evidence.

"When is a good time to tell him?"

"As soon as possible. He will probably be in the Dining Room in a while he normally joins us for Breakfast."

"Have you had breakfast Billy?"

Billy shook his head.

"Better come to the Dining Room with us. We just need to finish here and then we will head over there."

Ten minutes later the three volunteers joined the rest of the crew from the Dairy and headed over to the Dining Room for breakfast. All the other members and volunteers had eaten earlier but there was always a special breakfast laid on for the Refet staff. The excuse given was that they had certain tasks to complete before they could eat but the truth was no one else wanted to sit in the room with the overpowering smell of cow shit and sour milk that emanated from them all like a cloying cloud.

Billy had shared many breakfasts with them as his job at the pool started later so he could always sneak a lie-in and then join the Refet team for breakfast at the later time. The smell didn't bother him but he often caught sight of the other volunteers who worked in the Dining Room wrinkling their noses or just giving the whole Refet crew a wide berth.

Yossi failed to appear by the time they had finished eating and it was by pure chance that Billy ran into him outside the Dining room later that day as he was on his way to work.

Billy was at the rear of the Kitchen where there was loading dock and he was filling one of the large water containers from the special tap that produced ice cold water.

He spotted Yossi across the yard and he jumped down to intercept him before he climbed into his jeep and drove away. He was already half in the cab when Billy called out to him. He climbed out and leant on the front wheel arch.

"Yossi I think there is a problem."

"I don't have a problem Billy, you do. I am not the one fucking a married woman."

Billy was poleaxed by Yossi's comment and the shock was visible on his face.

"How did you…?"

"It's not just me. Half the Kibbutz knows about it."

"Oh shit? How?"

"A Kibbutz is a small place, in this heat people sleep with their windows open and Daphna Aaronovitch is a noisy woman in her more passionate moments. And don't you think people will talk if that passion happens while her husband is away on reserve with the army? All night and every night? People begin to ask questions. And then to cap it all she has been walking around most days with a stupid grin on her face."

"Oh fuck. Does her husband know?"

"Fortunately for you and Mrs Aaronovitch, old Dov is not the most liked or most respected person on the Kibbutz. Like anywhere there are factions and cliques and despite being a child of one of

the founders he has not won many friends among the members. But a word of warning the Members council will not allow things to continue for much longer. It sends out the wrong message."
Billy had recovered a little of his composure.
"Well thanks for the heads up. Anyway, that was not the problem I came to tell you about. We have a drug problem among a group of the volunteers".
Now it was Yossi's turn to look alarmed.
"Tell me." His voice took on an urgency Billy had never encountered before.
Billy told him all that he had observed earlier that day, naming names and places. At the end, Yossi was silent for a while as he took in all the information.
"Well I guess the best way to deal with this is to call in the Police and get them to search the rooms. They have special sniffer dogs that can find drugs. Do you think it is isolated among just that small group you mentioned?"
"I don't know. The amount they had in their possession might mean they are going to pass some of it on to others."
"All right leave it with me." Yossi looked at his watch. "You should be opening the pool in ten minutes."
"I was just on my way up there now."
"You want a lift?"
"Yeah. Just let me get my stuff."
Billy grabbed his bag and the water container and heaved them into the back and then climbed into the front beside Yossi.
As they drove out from the Kitchen yard neither of them noticed the two figures emerge from behind the dumpster where they had been skiving off and having a quiet smoke.

\#

The raid came in the dark hours before dawn. Most of the volunteers were asleep in their rooms which was exactly what the Police wanted. Any drugs found in a room with a volunteer present would be considered to be the property of said volunteer or one of their roommates.
They deployed silently, the dogs being held in reserve until the holding teams were in position. A couple of officers were deployed to the rear of the blocks to ensure no one was able to escape or

dump anything out of the windows and likewise a couple of officers were deployed adjacent to the showers and toilets to ensure no evidence could be flushed away.

Once all the officers were in position the dogs were brought up to the first block of rooms. This dog unit had summoned from central Police headquarters in Tel Aviv and were most often found at work in the cargo areas at Ben Gurion Airport. Today they had left their kennels early and made the hour-long drive down to Tel Boker. It was a day trip for both dogs and owners and despite being professionally trained the dogs could sense the difference and were excitable.

The three dogs, two were Border Collies and one was a Labrador arrived with their owners outside the first row of rooms.

This was the block that Yossi had indicated was the home of the main suspects and although the dogs would make a thorough sweep of the whole area it was felt that this should be their starting point as this was where the main suspicion fell.

When the go order was given over the radio the various Police teams moved in. Their first task was to remove the volunteers from their rooms and isolate them from their possessions. This would give the dogs and their handlers unfettered access to both the rooms and their contents.

The first phase of the exercise went off without any real problems. Some of the volunteers swore at the Police, mostly because of the rude awakening, but the Police had been trained to deal with this so they remained calm and professional as the volunteers were ordered to get dressed and move outside onto the verandas.

Once they had been lined up outside they were escorted by two officers away to an area where they could be held until the search teams had completed the sweep.

The dog teams had been given no prior information about where their potential targets were situated, but it was clear from the outset that the room inhabited by the four English lads had got the dog assigned to it rather excited. This particular dog, one of the border collies, was crossing and re-crossing the floor and barking. This behaviour was an indication of the presence of illegal drugs but the physical search by the Police turned up nothing, not so much as a spent roach. Drugs had probably been present at some point in the recent past but there was no evidence of anything to be found now.

The place was therefore declared clean and the dogs continued their search. Room after room was searched and the dogs, although their occasional positive responses indicated there might have been drugs at certain places in the past, turned up nothing of interest. Yossi, as the key witness and the person who had called in the police in the first place was kept informed of their progress and was surprised when the search of the room occupied by Sebastian and his friends turned up as clean.

Standing with the officer in charge of the raid he asked if one of the dogs could make a sweep around to the rear of the volunteer blocks in case, by some miracle, or forewarning, the drugs had been spirited away and buried there. The officer spoke briefly into his radio and one of the dogs peeled away and began to quarter the area of ground behind the volunteer blocks.

Yossi didn't like to made a fool of. And right now, he was feeling very foolish. He knew that if the raid drew a blank then he would be in for some merciless teasing from the other members. He had taken the precaution of informing the Members Council of his decision to call in the Police before he had gone ahead and contacted the local Police Superintendent.

The number of rooms remaining unsearched was slowly dwindling and still there had been only vague indications of the possible past presence of narcotics.

As Yossi and the Police captain watched, the dog teams moved onto the last block. Yossi was in a pit of despair as he knew all of the residents of the remaining rooms and they were, in his opinion, the least likely to be involved in illegal narcotics.

The dogs started to search the final block, one room after another and, after a quick initial search of each room the dogs drew a blank and moved swiftly on to the next until there was only one remaining.

The occupants of this last block were stood in a loose group off to one side as the Police team entered the final room. After a split second inside one of the dogs started to bark furiously. Yossi turned to the Police captain looking for an explanation.

"We have got a hit." The Police captain said with a look of satisfaction on his face. As if to confirm his statement an officer emerged a moment later holding aloft a carrier bag. The sniffer dog was dancing around his handler's legs excitedly and barking and wagging his tail. The handler restrained the dog and offered it one of the special treats reserved for a job well done.

"Looks like we have found the drugs."

The Police captain said stating obviously, what was clear to Yossi, even if he was having difficulty believing his own eyes.

The Police captain went over towards his men. He motioned Yossi to accompany him.

"I need you to point out the volunteers who live in this room."

It was a bit of a pointless statement as they were only two volunteers remaining. The others had all hastened to distance themselves from these two as soon as the dog had begun to bark, they were now loitering in doorways, in small groups, anxiously awaiting the end of the search and keen to witness any possible arrests.

The two remaining volunteers had witnessed the recovery of the carrier bag and one, in particular, was vehemently denying any knowledge of it or its contents, to the two uniformed officers who were standing ready to restrain them. The officers had so far not made any move to do this. Clearly, they were waiting for orders from their Captain. When the Captain and Yossi approached, the volunteer directed his attention and his complaints to the volunteer leader maybe hoping for a more compassionate hearing.

"Come on Yossi, you know me. These aren't mine. For Christ sake, I was the one who alerted you to the presence of drugs in the first place. Why would I do this if I was the one hiding them in my room. It doesn't make any sense."

On the face of it Yossi had to agree with Billy, it didn't make sense, but then seen from his point of view he had to act as the whole thing had happened in front of witnesses and officers of the law.

"Billy, the drugs were found in your room." He turned to the officer who made the discovery and confirmed his discovery.

"The bag was hidden in your luggage."

"Someone put it there. It must have been last night while we were asleep. We both had a little too much to drink last night and passed out. Yossi come on man you know exactly who these drugs belong to. I told you."

Mike had remained silent on the matter until now. Now he spoke up.

"Yossi, you know there has been no love lost between those tossers and Billy."
"I know the full story of what has happened between them but this does not change the simple fact the drugs were found in your room and you are therefore responsible and right now you are both in a whole heap of trouble."
The Captain nodded to the two nearby Police officers who extracted two sets of handcuffs from their service belts and expertly and quickly cuffed the two friends.
They were taken to separate Police cars to await removal to the Police station. With the operation finished the Police officers started to withdraw back to their vehicles. The dogs were given a chance to let off a little steam with their owners before the long trip back to their kennels in Tel Aviv.
There was a definite air of anti-climax as Billy and Mike made the walk of shame through the volunteer block and up to the car park, although there were some grumblings of disbelief among certain of the volunteers that these two were in possession of narcotics and one or two yelled encouragement and support to the two friends.
As they came past the first block Billy caught sight of the four English lads, the true owners of the drugs. They were stood in a line, a distinct look of triumph on their faces. Sebastian and Tobias both extended their hands and then made the thumbs down gesture made by Roman emperors to signify the death of the vanquished in the arena. Billy seethed with anger but was restrained from making any move by the firm hand of the Policeman on his shoulder.
Mike remained annoyingly silent during the whole walk up to the waiting Police vans. Billy would not blame him if his friend chose to disown him but he had said nothing except to confirm that the rucksack where the drugs were discovered was not his and did in fact belong to Billy.
Right now, Billy could have done with some kind words of encouragement from his friend but none were forthcoming. The two were placed in separate vehicles to wait.
After a half hour of waiting Billy saw Yossi and the Police Captain coming towards them. His arms, still restrained by the cuffs were starting to ache and he was fidgeting around trying to ease some of the pain in his elbows, without any luck. He just wanted to get out of the car and into a police cell and await his fate.

He was not sure what the future held for him. In the past, there had been talk of volunteers caught with drugs being simply charged, issued with a hefty fine, which most of them couldn't pay and then being deported from the country on the first available flight home. He didn't think he would end up doing time in an Israeli jail, but at the same time a return to the UK was not something Billy relished. He had heard, second hand, through a letter that Mike's parents had sent, that his mother had been visited by Delchie Matthews and some of his crew once it had become clear that Billy had not purchased a delivery van and was not about to honour their business agreement.

Billy's mum had told Delchie that Billy had left the country to which Matthews had said it was just as well and probably for the best if he never returned. Admittedly this information was several months old but Billy had a sneaking suspicion that Delchie Matthews would not have changed his mind in the intervening months and a return home was tantamount to a death sentence. So, at this point a long stay in an Israeli prison looked more appealing than deportation and a certain painful and messy death.

This was the only news he had received from home since his arrival. He had not written a single letter home, preferring to keep his whereabouts a secret from his mother. If she didn't know where he was then she couldn't tell anyone where he was and no one would come looking for him. Mike's parents had, at first, pleaded with their son to force Billy to contact his mother but after their initial appeals had been ignored both Mike and eventually his parents had given up.

Billy, now sat in the Police van awaiting his fate, considered the supreme effort it must have taken for his mother to have sought out Mike's parents and appealed to them for help. Although Mike and Billy had been friends all these years the two families had never formed any bond worth mentioning. Personally, he felt rotten about keeping his mother in the dark but deep down he knew that it was for her own safety. If Delchie Matthews had even the slightest hint that Billy's mum knew where he was then he would be likely to try and force that information out of her and that could only be bad for her. No in all truth it was better that Susie Randell remained in the dark about her son's whereabouts.

The Police captain came up to the patrol car where Billy was sat and spoke briefly to the officer who had been leaning against the front wing and smoking a cigarette. The cigarette had been dropped and the man had stood almost to attention as his superior approached. After a brief exchange the rear door was opened and Billy was pulled roughly out.

He was then frogmarched, behind the Captain, to the Kibbutz administration block and escorted into a meeting room.

Sparsely furnished, with little more than a table and four plastic chairs the room was already occupied by Yossi and another man Billy recognized as the Kibbutz secretary. He was the man elected by the members to act as their leader. His well-built muscular form pointed to an early life of hard labour in the fields and although most of the time nowadays he drove a desk, he was no stranger to the controls of one of the tractors or other big farming machines. His face, dominated like most of the older members by a huge dark beard, was otherwise kindly and he had piercing green eyes that twinkled when he was amused. They were not shining now. His face unsmiling was set like stone in a serious frown. Billy looked at Yossi for some support but saw no encouragement in the volunteer leaders countenance either. This was not going to be an exchange of pleasantries Billy suspected.

The police captain released the cuffs from Billy wrists and Billy rubbed them furiously trying to restore some of the circulation to his numb arms.

"Sit down Billy." Yossi indicated one of the chairs opposite him. Billy sat.

"Right well this is an unfortunate position we find ourselves in this morning. Narcotics were discovered in your room after a thorough search and you have been held by the Police. Please note that at this point you have not been arrested or charged with any offence."

Billy nodded that he understood.

"And really, we would like things to remain that way." This was from the Secretary. He continued on. "It will not be good for the Kibbutz or our reputation if this is taken any further by the Police and results in some form of prosecution."

Billy couldn't believe his ears.

"So, you believe me? I was set up. Yossi, you know who is guilty here."

"Silence." The Kibbutz secretary thundered "I am not interested in who is to blame. Drug possession and use among our volunteers is unacceptable and an example has to be made."

Yossi looked angry now. Billy was not sure whether the anger was directed at him or at someone else. He decided to follow the secretary's advice and keep his mouth shut.

"Whilst we can avoid any scandal with the police we cannot allow you to remain a volunteer on this settlement. Your contract of employment with this kibbutz is therefore terminated henceforth and you are to be expelled from the Kibbutz by the end of the day. The same goes for your roommate. He will be informed in a few moments."

"Now wait a minute. This has nothing to do with Mike. He really is innocent." Billy turned to the Police captain for support here. "The drugs were discovered in my luggage, am I right?" The captain nodded his head once.

"Then it stands to reason that they are mine and I should take the fall. Mike had no knowledge and nothing to do with it."

The Secretary looked at Yossi for confirmation. The volunteer leader nodded his head.

"Very well. Mike will not be expelled, but his behaviour will be put under review. Any further misdemeanours and he will be expelled."

With the judgement delivered the secretary stood up and his huge bulk filled the small space as he edged out from behind the table and exited the room. Yossi stood up and shook hands with the Police captain who also turned on his heels and left the room leaving Yossi and Billy alone.

"That was very courageous of you. Taking the fall and preventing Mike from getting kicked off."

"Come on Yossi, now we are alone at least you can admit the drugs aren't mine and I was framed."

"What I think, feel or know is irrelevant right now. The drugs were discovered where they were discovered. How they got there and who they actually belonged to is of no concern to me. Right now, I need you to go to your room and pack your stuff. In two hours' time, I will come by and then drive you to the end of the road and drop you by the bus stop. I am sorry this has ended like this."

Despite his brusque and business-like attitude Billy did detect a small shred of regret in Yossi's voice.

"The other thing I have to tell you is that later this morning I will be phoning all the major agencies that recruit volunteers, both for Kibbutzim and for Moshavim. I will be giving them your details and asking them to add you to the blacklist. This will mean that no Kibbutz in Israel will sign you on as a volunteer. Without a place as a volunteer your visa will not be renewed and after your current visa expires, if you are caught, you will be expelled from the country. My advice to you is to take a bus to Tel Aviv, go to one of the bucket shops on Ben Yehuda street and buy a plane ticket home. If you do this then there will be no further action taken. Stay in the country and you run the risk of getting into more trouble. The Police Captain wanted to throw the book at you and your name will definitely remain on their computer records for several years to come. Do yourself a favour and go home. Like I said earlier, I am sorry it had to end like this."

As Billy walked back alone through the Kibbutz he wondered if Yossi was really sorry that he was leaving. After their conversation the previous day about his involvement with Daphna he wondered whether his imminent departure from the settlement presented a solution to more than one potential problem.

True to his word Yossi was waiting outside Billy's room two hours later. Billy had packed all his stuff back in his bags and they were stood by the door. Mike had taken the morning off work and the two friends had spoken about what had happened although neither of them discussed exactly what Billy intended to do next.

Returning home to face the wrath of Delchie Matthews was not even mentioned as an option by either party.

When Yossi arrived, Mike came out and asked to accompany Billy to the bus stop. Yossi had no objection so the three of them climbed into the Jeep and drove out to the main road.

The bus stop for the Tel Aviv bus and all other buses heading north was on the far side of the road from the Kibbutz approach road. Yossi parked his jeep at the side of the road and Billy and Mike got out. He didn't want to intrude on the friends' farewell so he remained in the cab.

Mike and Billy crossed the road and Billy placed his rucksack in the shelter. He had his smaller pack loaded with some water and a few snacks. According to the timetable the next bus to Tel Aviv was due any minute.

"Let's not make this more difficult than it has to be. Just drive away and we will see each other when you get back to England."
"Are you going home?"

"No I won't be going home. There is a small matter of the money I owe Delchie Matthews."

"Where will you go?"

"Probably I will lose myself in London, but as soon as I am settled I will get in touch."

"Do that."

The two shared a brief hug then Mike re-crossed the road, climbed into the Jeep and drove off in the direction of the Kibbutz.

As soon as the Jeep was out of sight Billy picked up his rucksack and slung it over his shoulder and crossed the road. There was another bus stop on this side. From here the buses headed south. Billy had no intention of heading home to England. He had other ideas.

CHAPTER Thirteen

Even this late in the afternoon the air was hot and dry. A sharp contrast to the air-conditioned interior of the bus. Billy emerged into the heat and choking diesel fumes of the Eilat bus station. He collected his rucksack from the open luggage area in the belly of the bus and shouldered it. His smaller knapsack was hanging from his left hand as he followed the rest of the passengers across the concrete towards the bus station entrance. His fellow passengers were a mixture of Israeli tourists and people who either lived in the city or had other business there.
The difference was easy to spot. The holiday makers were in family groups with large suitcases on wheels, the others were individuals with little or no luggage.
Billy seemed to have been the only non-Israeli on the bus. When the bus had left the southern city of Beersheba there had been several volunteers on board but they had all disembarked at settlements along the way. The last group of three had stopped the bus close to a Kibbutz that lay a few kilometres north of Eilat.
It seemed however that this time of day was a bit of a 'rush-hour' for arrivals in Eilat as several buses had either just arrived or pulled up in the moments following the arrival of Billy's bus.
The area around the ticket booths and concession stands was crowded with people either arriving or departing and in among the confusion there were a whole bunch of other people.
Distinguishable by their slightly scruffy appearance, even for volunteers, their hair in a variety of outlandish styles and cuts from dreadlocks to Hare-Krishna skin heads, punk spikes and plain old long hippy hair, their clothes were also an eclectic mix of denim, tie die and worn out volunteer blue, footwear seemed to be sandals or flip-flops but there were a few who seemed to have shunned any

form of shoes and were walking about barefoot. This group were moving around and through the arriving crowds handing out flyers. One spied Billy and came towards him.

"Welcome to Eilat. Are you looking for somewhere to stay?"

A small paper folder was thrust into Billy's hand.

"Er thanks." Billy said, glancing down at the cover.

The yellow piece of paper was a crude imprint, almost no more than a photo copy and the front cover had a half moon crudely drawn in biro and the word "Bedouin Moon Hostel" and an address underneath.

Billy had been reading up about Eilat in his Israel book during the journey down. He had learnt a little bit about the city and its history and the current state of affairs. He knew that there were a few hotels popular with Israeli tourists and also a large number of Hostels that were much cheaper offering very basic board and lodgings. For those too hard up to afford either there were always the beach camps, although these did come with several warnings about the dangers of sleeping rough.

Billy had made a quick check of his finances on the way here. He still had over half of Delchie's money safely stowed away in a UK bank, and he had quite a bit of cash both in local currency and in dollars and sterling. He had contemplated checking into a hotel for a few days to give him a chance to settle in, although he knew that would eat into his available funds more quickly, so maybe a hostel would be a better alternative.

By the time he had reached the street outside the bus station he had collected five more of the advertising flyers for hostels and two for bars that were situated in the old part of the city.

He decided it was time to go and sit down, drink a beer and decide where he was going to stay for the night.

Across the road from the Bus Station was a parade of shops and a couple of cafes so he navigated his way across the busy road and sat down at the first table.

He pushed his rucksack under the table to prevent anyone falling over it and perused the drinks menu.

Billy sensed a presence beside the table and looked up expecting to see a waiter. Instead he saw another one of the flyer distributers. This one was female and quite young. She had bleached blonde hair, maybe sun bleached but it could equally have been from a bottle, shaved on one side and long flowing curls on the other. Her

eyes were a startlingly deep blue, her nose pierced with a ring. She wore a tie-died vest top and what looked like a pair of kibbutz work shorts. On her feet, she had some simple leather sandals. She was clearly used to the outdoor life as the parts of her body normally exposed to the sun were a deep dark brown.
"Are you looking for somewhere to stay tonight?"
In her hand, she was clutching a whole bunch of the hostel flyers. These were red and Billy hadn't been handed any red flyers.
"Yes, I am still considering my options." Billy waved his hand at the pile of flyers he had already received which were sat on the table beside the menu card like a deck of cards in a colourful game of patience.
"Well this is a great hostel, very friendly."
She held up the brochure for Billy to see the cover.
"A good price and very friendly staff and guests. Close to the centre too."
"OK that sounds interesting." He reached out a hand to take one of the flyers.
"No touts at the tables." A voice roared from behind Billy and the girl beside him shied away. Billy looked over his shoulder to see a man in an apron bearing down on them waving his fist in a menacing manner.
Billy reacted quickly.
"Sit down." He said to the girl who seemed so startled by Billy's reaction that she complied automatically without even thinking.
As the proprietor arrived at the table he made a move to lay a hand on the girl.
"Are you here to take our order?"
The man's hand hovered over the girls shoulder uncertain how to proceed. He was now faced with what looked like two paying guests and a quick glance around at the terrace filled with mostly empty tables told even a casual onlooker that he could not afford to piss off even one paying guest.
He turned away and yelled at a waitress who came from inside the cafe strapping on her money belt and reaching for her order pad. The proprietor said something to the waitress as he passed but Billy was unable to catch the exchange.
He looked across at his guest.
"What would you like to drink?"
"Are you serious?" There was a look of disbelief in her eyes.

"Like a heart attack." Billy grinned. "Anyway, you were in the middle of your sales pitch when you were so rudely interrupted. If it takes buying you a drink to allow you to finish then it will be a small price to pay."

The girl, still hardly believing her ears turned to the waitress and ordered a large draft beer. Billy told her to make it two. She turned and walked back to the Bar to prepare their drinks.

"Now, where were we before we were so rudely interrupted?" Billy looked across the table at his new-found friend.

"I was telling you about what a great place the Peace Hostel was. But to be honest with you I am only trying to sell it to you because I get a discount on my room for every new guest I bring in. If you hand this flyer to the manager he will give me a reduction on my rent."

Billy examined the flyer and saw that there was the word 'Blossom' written in pen on the back cover.

"Is that you? Blossom?"

"Yes that's me."

"Hello Blossom, my name is Billy. I suppose if we are going to have a drink together we might as well get acquainted."

"Nice to meet you Billy. Are you a volunteer?"

"Ex-volunteer to be precise. I parted company with my Kibbutz this morning."

"Oh dear. There are quite a few of us ex-volunteers here in Eilat."

"I figured that might be the case."

"May I ask what got you the boot?"

"A misunderstanding." Billy didn't want to go into more details as the whole thing had left him feeling raw.

"Oh, a misunderstanding. That is the predominant reason why most of us are here."

When Billy took a moment to analyse that comment he realised that it sounded like the convicted criminals in jail all claiming they were innocent. Except in his particular case he actually was innocent.

"Are you an ex-volunteer too?"

"Yes, I was on Kibbutz Tel Shomer for a couple of months but I have been here in Eilat all summer."

"God it's a small world. I was on the Kibbutz next door to Tel Shomer at Tel Boker."

A quick listing of Volunteers they had both known proved that they had no mutual friends among the Volunteers of either settlement, although Blossom had heard of Stig and Dingo, but purely by reputation rather than any personal friendship.
Their drinks arrived and with them a demand for payment. Billy coughed up the cash and the waitress made change and walked away, leaving the bill on its tray.
"Blimey do they think I was going to do a runner without paying?"
"Exactly. They have learnt from bitter experience." She smiled. Billy thought she had a sweet smile and he said as much. The compliment elicited another dazzling smile of thanks.
The beers were cold and very refreshing and at the end of the first one Billy asked first and then ordered them both a second.
The sun was beginning to set when they left the cafe and made their way down into the old city and to the green metal door that was the entrance to the Peace Hostel.
Beyond the door the place lived up to its name. After passing down a short corridor the room opened up beyond him into a wider atrium, open to the sky. The walls were decked with hanging plants that grew up from floor level, vines, and flowering plants cascaded in waves of colour, their scents mingling in the warm afternoon air. There were plastic tables and chairs and the occasional wooden bench arranged in groups around the room and Billy could hear the sound of water tumbling into a basin somewhere among the greenery. The whole place was a peaceful, sweet smelling, cool oasis after the harsh heat of the afternoon street. He stood in the doorway, exhaled then inhaled the heady perfume
The manager, or owner was sitting at one of the tables with a large mug of coffee and an overfilled ashtray in front of him. He appeared to be chain smoking whilst doing business with his customers. Billy joined the line waiting to check in for the night. Blossom, after reminding Billy to mention her name, had disappeared off into the back of the hostel.
When it was Billy's turn he remembered to mention Blossom's name and noticed as the manager who introduced himself as Yoram, made a note on a piece of paper beside his ashtray.
Sitting across the table Billy noticed that the man was well built and like most Israelis of a certain age had a thick beard and curly hair although both hair and beard were now frosted by touches of

grey. Billy estimated the man was probably in his late forties or early fifties and his English, although good grammatically, was heavily accented.

He laid out the terms, conditions and rules for the hostel. The rules were few in number but the red lines were no drugs and if you are returning to the hostel after eleven then keep the noise to a minimum. Other than that, it seemed that guests were pretty much free to do as they pleased which suited Billy. He handed over the cash for five nights and was given a receipt and key to a locker and then shown to his room.

The room was a very basic square box with a stone floor and three sets of bunkbeds and six metal locker cupboards, in groups of two. A door at the far end of the room opened into a bathroom with a toilet, sink and a shower. The room was clean as was the bathroom, although the later did smell faintly of pine disinfectant. Two of the lower bunks were occupied with sleeping forms so Billy slung his rucksack on the empty third lower bunk and then returned to the courtyard.

On the way down, with Blossom, they had agreed that as a return favour for the two beers she would show him around the city and she was waiting for him when he arrived back in the courtyard.

"I booked in for five nights. Does that mean you get discount for all five nights?"

"I hope so. Well are we ready to go?"

"Yes let's go and see what the fleshpots of Eilat have to offer us tonight."

They set off to explore the city together.

As they wandered around the centre of the town, only a short hop from the front door of the hostel, as Blossom had rightly promised, Billy noticed that most of the cafes and bars were largely empty with only a small number of hard core patrons sitting nursing drinks this early in the evening.

"Most of these places don't come alive until later. Most of the patrons are sleeping at the moment."

Billy thought back to the two sleeping forms in his room in the hostel.

"Most people seem to work, sleep, get up and party all night then go to work."

"So it's not very different from Kibbutz life."

"Most of the people I know here in Eilat were, at one time or another, volunteers. Most of them were, like us, expelled and found their way here. A few of them just rocked up here for a party and never left."

And as they circled the whole of downtown it seemed that Blossom knew plenty of people. She was forever stopping to chat to this person or that, making loose arrangements to meet up for a drink or a chat at some point either later that evening or on another day.

They did stop at a few of the bars to have a beer but Blossom wouldn't let them settle anywhere. She seemed to have an ultimate destination in mind so eventually Billy challenged her on it and she revealed it.

"There is only really one cool place to go and drink here in Eilat. That's the Underground."

Eventually they arrived at their destination and Blossom made a beeline for a particular table and group of people.

She took a moment to introduce Billy around and while Billy went to get drinks for them she sorted out a place for them both to sit. Billy had ordered a large pitcher of Goldstar Beer and was amazed at how quickly it disappeared. It seemed that everyone around the table had a crushing thirst and that he was the only person with the financial wherewithal to satisfy that thirst, but being new to the group and wanting to quickly make friends he was not in any position to complain too much and again he felt it was a small price to pay for acceptance.

In the early hours of the morning he made his slightly tipsy way back to the hostel. He was grateful of Blossoms company because at that time of the night and after their tour around the centre of the city and given the amount of alcohol they had consumed, he was not sure he would have found his way back to the front door of the Peace Hostel under his own steam.

#

The next morning Billy awoke when the owner banged on the door of his room. A quick look at his watch told him that it was nearly eleven and he remembered from the previous evening that all residents were expected to vacate their rooms from eleven until three in the afternoon so that the rooms could be cleaned and prepared for new guests. Billy crawled out of bed and pulled on a pair of shorts before packing his knapsack with items he might need throughout the day. His rucksack he left on his bunk. It was the best way of securing the space for the coming night, and deterring any newcomer from taking his place.

With his bag packed he ventured out into the courtyard. There was nobody about at this time of the day. He assumed that any of the residents who were working were long gone and any who were on holiday had already headed off to the beach. This was what Billy had decided to do but first he made a detour via the bakery to grab something to eat and a cup of coffee.

With a couple of fresh baked croissants in a paper bag and a large milky coffee Billy made his way down towards the beach. Even on a work day there were still plenty of people on the beach, either relaxing on towels or on the plastic beach loungers. Billy spread out his large beach towel and settled down. He had discovered an abandoned paperback novel, one he had never read, in the room at the hostel so he pulled this out of his backpack and as he opened the paper bag and bit into the first croissant he turned to page one. Pausing only briefly to remove his shirt and apply some suntan cream Billy read page after page of the novel taking a short break to find a concession stand that would sell him a large cold bottle of water and something to eat.

At regular intervals along the boardwalk there were small Falafel stands selling Israel's favourite handy snack. These deep-fried chickpea balls were served in a pita bread pocket with large helpings of salad. Billy had first tried these snacks while on a trip to Jerusalem and he knew that each stall owner was fiercely proud of their product, their special sauces and salads. He hadn't devised any particular system in selecting which of the stands to approach and had merely started with the one nearest the entrance to the beach. But as he gazed along the line of stalls he could see that a full study might take several days.

He took the snack and the water back to the beach and settled back down with his book.

He was about halfway through the afternoon and the same through the novel when Blossom found him.

They had made a loose agreement before parting ways the previous evening that she would come and find him on the beach when she was through with her job dishing out flyers at the bus station.

Billy was surprised but secretly pleased that she had turned up. He had expected her to latch on to another newcomer like she had with him yesterday but she had either been unlucky in that respect or maybe, just maybe, her friendship with Billy counted more.
The time on his own, and when he looked up from the printed page to rest his eyes, had given him time to assess his position. He knew that the money he had with him would not last forever and Eilat as a place was not the cheapest, but right now he was not worried and provided he did not get saddled with buying all the drinks every night his money would probably last him a couple of weeks. There would be plenty of time to worry about looking for work in the interim and as Billy saw it, every drink he purchased now was a favour he might be able to reclaim at some time in the future.
Blossom announced her arrival by standing directly between Billy and the sun, her shadow looming over him forcing him to look up and shade his eyes.
"Hello you, have you finished work for the day?"
"Yes. Shove over and make room."
Billy scooted over on the towel and right in front of him at his eye level, Blossom wriggled out of her shorts. She was wearing a very small pair of bikini briefs, but they left little to the imagination. She sat down on the towel and then reached into her handbag and extracted an equally flimsy bikini top.
Billy was ready to give her the elbow room necessary while she negotiated donning the top part of her bikini whilst not removing her vest top, a trick he had always admired in women. But experience had taught him that proximity could result in injury from flying elbows. Blossom was a little more straight forward. She whipped off her vest top and sat there bare breasted while she figured out what was top and bottom of the microscopic piece of material. Billy tried not to stare.
She turned her back to Billy.
"Could you do me up?"
Billy gathered the strings and tied them into a neat bow.
"There you go."
"Thank you." She gave him a radiant smile. "What are you reading?"
Billy showed her the cover of the novel. "I found it abandoned in the room."

"I don't think I have read it. Can I borrow it when you are finished?"
"Sure, I won't spoil it for you by telling you the end."
"I'd appreciate that."
Blossoms arrival on the beach was the precursor for a much larger invasion as the other ex-volunteers from the previous evening arrived back from their jobs or from wherever they had spent the daylight hours until now.
Some of them made a beeline for the surf to wash away the sweat of the day and to cool off.
Slowly the size of the encampment around Billy and Blossom expanded outwards. Some of the volunteers arrived with bottles of Arac and Vodka, others arrived with cases of cold cans of beer. One or two of the more practical souls had arrived with bags of pita bread and dips. In a very leisurely fashion a bit of an impromptu beach picnic broke out. Everyone was there to share what they had. At some point, Billy and Blossom departed and made their way to the local supermarket where besides two cases of cold beer they also picked up some fruit, some bread and several large bags of corn chips.
By the time they got back, the sun was starting to set and the other beach goers were starting to pack up and head off back to their hotels or apartments.
The volunteer party, on the other hand was just getting started. A couple of people had produced guitars and were playing some old Irish folk songs, the rest of the group were all talking, laughing, telling jokes or teasing each other.
"Is it always like this?" Billy asked as they returned to their towel, which despite the general crush had remained unoccupied in the middle of the group.
"Not always like this, but it does happen. People here live hand to mouth. You work, make some money and then enjoy the money."
Billy thought long and hard about the implications of such a way of life. He was still thinking through this concept a while later when things started to wind up, and folk drifted off back to hostels or to other places where they slept. Some hardy souls were heading on to the Underground so Billy and Blossom tagged along but only stayed for a couple of beers before heading back to their hostel and an early night.

#

Due to hitting his bunk earlier than normal, Billy found he was awake much earlier on the second morning and was able to join the majority of the residents in the courtyard for breakfast.
The buffet was laid out along one wall and as Billy walked along with his paper plate he could pick from a range of cream cheese's, fresh vegetables, fruit, yoghurts and the ever-present pita bread. There was tea, coffee and water in various thermos jugs at the end of the table. Billy loaded his plate up and then joined the table where Blossom was in conversation with three other residents, two girls and guy.
Billy offered them a hasty good morning and then took his place. The conversation was about the various tasks that needed to be done around the hostel that morning. It appeared that the two girls were employed as chamber maids and cleaners while the guy was, like Blossom, a part of the marketing team, although he did seem to have some other role around the place as a general handyman if the tool belt slung on the table was anything to judge by.
He was introduced as Ian and his laid back laconic accent marked him as Australian, even before you took his tall, well-muscled frame in a cut off t-shirt and board shorts into account. His blonde hair was a little on the long side and had the annoying habit of flopping over his eyes. He was therefore forever sweeping his hair back with a free hand.
Sat next to him was Trudi. She was German, dark haired, brown eyes but with an open smiling face. She spoke passable English but with a very heavy accent, making it sometimes difficult to figure out exactly what she was saying without paying particular attention to her, which suited her Teutonic nature perfectly.
The last of the three was Linda who was from the northern part of the UK. She was a very intense looking person who gazed myopically from behind a pair of tortoiseshell glasses. Her mousy brown hair was cut short in a bob and her fair complexion meant that even a small kiss from the sun resulted in sunburn and peeling on an alarming scale. She was squat and a little overweight but sweet natured. Billy was surprised to learn that Linda and Ian were an item given their wildly different statures and natures.
Inevitably once the subject of the day's chores had been exhausted the four of them turned on Billy and his plans for the day.

THE EILAT TRAP

He had decided he was going to catch a bus up the coast and visit the Undersea Observatory. He had read about the place in his book and it sounded like the perfect way to while away a morning. He promised Blossom that he would be back on the North Beach by mid-afternoon and arranged to meet her there.

Their breakfast conversation was cut short by Yoram who came over to the table to enquire when his workforce could be expected to actually do some work.

Billy, left alone at his table made short work of the rest of his breakfast and then packed his backpack for the day before heading up to the bus station.

He waved at Blossom who was in mid sales pitch with a couple of recently arrived backpackers and boarded the waiting bus heading down to Coral Beach and the Observatory.

Outside the Observatory there were several tourist buses parked and there were two or three tourist groups milling around like lost sheep in the area near the ticket office. Each group was distinguishable by the different brightly coloured 'tembel' hats bearing the logo of the organisation leading the tour.

Billy had first come across these hats on a trip to Jerusalem where they were in abundance among the tourist class. As a way of finding and remaining with your particular group in the tight confines of the streets of the Old City they were ideal but they served an additional purpose for the observant volunteer. Most of these tours came with a paid guide and provided one could find a group where the guide spoke English it was possible to attach yourself loosely to the group and receive a free tour with an experienced guide.

These hats did however come with a downside. They acted as a beacon, attracting the attention of every crook, thief and pickpocket while advertising the presence of foreigners to any other unscrupulous individuals who made a living ripping off tourists.

Billy bought a ticket and attached himself to a group of Americans whose tour guide was, judging by his accent, an Israeli, but who was giving his commentary in English. With a group of nearly fifty tourists of mixed age it was possible, if you were subtle, to float on the fringes of the group. Never appearing to be part of the group but being close enough to benefit from the pearls of wisdom from their paid guide.

When the official tour was finished and the coach party departed for their next destination, Billy took his time to revisit some of the highlights of the Aquarium at a more leisurely pace.
He was under no time pressure and was not being herded around by some angry red-faced guide in a bush cap brandishing an umbrella or a handwritten sign on a stick.
When he was finished, he caught the next local bus heading back to the city centre and disembarked by the Airport. He walked down and around to the beach and ended up close to where he had spent the previous afternoon.
Again, it was mid-afternoon when people started to arrive, spread out towels and blankets and begin to relax after the day's work. Billy recognised most of the faces that arrived, there were one or two newcomers but the majority were people he had met either here the day before or later on at the Underground.
It was already late in the afternoon by the time Blossom arrived and she did not immediately approach Billy when she arrived. Instead she spent a long time talking to a new face that Billy hadn't seen before and judging by the body language between the two, things were progressing nicely for both of them. This just happened to coincide with a shift in the group dynamics which left Billy largely abandoned on his own with no one to talk to.
With no distraction, Billy found he was staring at Blossom and hoping that she would come and rescue him from his loneliness but she was definitely more wrapped up in her new friend and oblivious to Billy's situation.
Billy felt the first flower of jealousy growing deep in his guts. He shook his head trying to dispel the feelings. He tried being rational about things. The two of them had only met for the first time less than 48 hours ago and in all the time they had been together Blossom had shown no interest in Billy as more than a friend. She had been generous enough to invite Billy along when things were happening, she had even acted as a guide on that first evening, but at no point had she shown even the slightest interest in Billy in any romantic way. So why should Billy now think that there was anything romantic linking them and that Blossom was not free to flirt with whoever she chose.
Try as he might, Billy could not conquer the gnawing feeling of rejection.

In his mind, he started to add up all the money he had spent so far on this group. It was not that he begrudged them the money per-se, but more that in return for his investment he would have expected a little more attention, more friendship.

As he sat there he wondered what would happen if he stood up and left the group and disappeared off alone. Would anyone even miss him? He decided to put his theory to the test and he stood up suddenly and collected his stuff together and shouldering his backpack over one arm left the group. No one, not one single soul offered any comment or question.

Billy was furious as he stalked away up the beach, kicking out at the sand with his bare feet.

Back on the boardwalk he turned his face towards the town and the nearest supermarket. He was on a form of remote control but he knew ultimately what his next destination was going to be. He was booking a one-way ticket to Oblivion.

If he had paused for one moment to consider the environment he was in, the people he was surrounded by, the city itself, then maybe he might have put on the brakes. The simple fact was Billy didn't look back, he didn't waste a single second on any form of consideration. He went to the nearest supermarket and bought a litre bottle of Elite Arac and two litre bottles of water. The first bottle of water he tipped half out on the sidewalk then topped it off with Arac in a fifty-fifty mixture. This he began to swig at as the made his way through the centre of town. He wanted to get away from people so he headed in the opposite direction from the beach, walking up towards the top of the town. This was mainly a residential area with flats, apartments and even some houses.

He was moving fast now and soon found himself beyond the last of the houses and out into the edge of the desert. There were several sand tracks that led away from the backs of the houses and as the sun had now set the desert was darkening and cooling at almost the same pace. As he walked along the track he collected scraps of wood. Some were the remains of pallets used, most probably, to transport building materials during the construction of the nearby homes, others were bits of dry brush and remains of garden rubbish dumped here by unscrupulous contractors.

Billy didn't care he collected the makings of a small fire and when he had enough he found a spot on the side of a large sand dune and built one.

Once the wood had caught he settled back and focused on his Arac and water. He had not eaten properly since lunchtime so it didn't take long before the spirit began to bite and Billy felt the familiar but in today's case welcome woozy feeling that signified approaching drunkenness.
If Billy had been a drug addict he might have seen the warning signs. Back in the kibbutz they had often drunk Arac and water but in much reduced concentrations. Now he was drinking half and half, the drug addicts equivalent of almost pure product. The effect was almost immediate and devastating. One minute, Billy was coherent and starring into the flames of the small fire, the next he had slumped over to one side unconscious, the remains of the bottle of Arac and water pouring out onto the crotch of his shorts soaking them through.

#

When he awoke several hours later in the depths of the night it was the damp feeling in his crotch that led Billy to believe he had lost control of his bladder. The plastic bottle, now all but empty, had rolled away to one side. The fire was almost out and the overwhelming darkness made it difficult for him to see.
He felt around for his backpack. He remembered it had been at his side when he passed out. His hand made contact with nothing, only empty space and sand. In the dark, he widened his search sweeping his hands in ever wider circles, both to left and right but made contact with only the empty plastic bottle, which he, in his frustration, picked up and tossed away. He reached in the pocket of his shorts and found the lighter he had used to start the fire. He flicked the roller and a short flame shot out the top, casting a yellow glow on his surroundings. He looked around him hurriedly and saw no sign of his pack. He stood up and began a feverish search, looking further afield in every direction. The backpack was nowhere to be seen.
He sank down on the sand. Slowly the awful truth dawned on him. He had been robbed. The backpack was gone. While he was unconscious someone had chanced on his lifeless body and stolen his pack. He checked the back pocket of his shorts. His wallet was still there, but the pack had contained his other documents, like his passport, driving licence and his bank cards.

When he had arrived in the hostel on the first night he had been warned about leaving valuables in the hostel. He was advised to carry or keep all his documents with him at all times. Apparently from time to time the hostel had fallen victim to outbreaks of theft. Documents were a particular favourite.

A valid UK passport could sell on the black market for as much as two thousand pounds and UK driving licences as they contained no identifying photo were also worth something, particularly as part of a stolen identity.

In the light of this advice, Billy had made a habit of carrying everything with him in his backpack, the backpack that was now missing. The only exception had been the notes and coins in local currency which he had kept in his pockets. The rest of his money, in UK currency and US Dollars, had been in his backpack and that like his passport was now gone. He had not been stupid enough to bring all of the money he borrowed from Delchie in cash. A substantial part had been deposited in a bank back home, but without his bank cards that money was also out of reach.

Billy felt like screaming and crying at the same time but knew that neither would solve his current predicament. More importantly for him at this moment in time was the first signs of dehydration beginning to set in. He knew he had to get back to civilisation and get some water on board or he would be in real trouble. He set off back in the direction of the street lights.

As he walked he scanned the path on both sides in the vain hope that the thieves may have searched his backpack, found his cash and then cast the rest aside as being too much of a hassle to dispose of.

He did not have the time or the energy to do a full and thorough search of every bush and rock pile. This was just a superficial sweep as he struggled through the deeply rutted sand.

On his way out, the previous evening Billy hadn't noticed the deep ruts caused by the Jeeps and other off-road vehicles that made regular use of these tracks, but now as his mind was maybe more focused on the effort involved he noticed them.

As his anger at the theft began to evaporate it was replaced by a sense of shame. His own stupidity had brought this on himself. He felt he had been used and then rejected by his new friends and had sought in some petty way to punish them by removing his financial support. In the end the only one who got punished was Billy. He really had no one else to blame but himself.

Coupled to the shame was embarrassment. He knew that he would have to keep what had happened out here secret or risk being teased mercilessly. Such a fundamental error of judgement and over something so petty as jealousy would invite ridicule on a whole new level. Also, if he admitted what had happened then he might be forced to reveal his true feelings for certain people and this was also a place he was not prepared to visit. All in all, it was best if the whole incident remained secret.

As if God or a higher power was in agreement with him as Billy came around the corner and arrived back at the first row of houses he spotted his backpack lying abandoned, and empty by the side of the track. He picked it up and turned it upside down. Everything had been emptied from it. His wallet with his bank cards, the plastic folder that contained his foreign currency, in pounds and dollars, his passport and all the other personal papers that he had been carrying in it.

He shouldered the empty pack and struck out down through the town heading in the direction of the main drag and the all-night gas station where he knew he could pick up a cold bottle of water.

CHAPTER fourteen

Billy arrived back in front of the hostel just as the first souls were leaving to start their working day. This first wave of departees were those employed in the hotels and cafes who had start times before seven. They had jobs as hotel chamber maids, kitchen porters, dishwashers or cleaners. They were all reasonably respectably dressed in a variety of uniforms.

Hot on their heels although fewer in number were those heading in the direction of the Wall. This single stretch of masonry opposite the Peace Cafe, another favourite bar with the Volunteer community in Eilat, was the pick-up point for casual day workers. These few were an altogether more feral looking bunch. Wearing a mixture of castoff Kibbutz work clothes and casual wear from their own small wardrobes and all sporting the ever-present heavy work boots they emerged blinking myopically into the strengthening sunlight, some hungover, some still clearly drunk from the previous night's excesses. The half-dozen individuals moved as a single organic unit off down the road in the direction of the Peace Cafe.

By now Billy had been lurking outside the front door of the hostel for a good half-hour. He was summoning up the courage to go inside and face the music. His own personal level of shame at his actions the previous night and his feeling of stupidity over the outcome of those actions were at an all-time high.

Outwardly there were no physical signs of the incident, he was not injured in anyway. In that respect things could have been so much worse, but in his head, Billy was convinced that someone would read the signs in his face and his secret would be exposed and the scorn and ridicule he so justly deserved would be heaped upon him.

In any event, he knew he could not loiter in the street for ever so he summoned up the last of his courage and pushed open the door of the hostel and went inside.

In the courtyard everything was pretty much normal. There were a few individuals loitering over the breakfast buffet and a couple of people sitting around in groups discussing their activities for the coming day. Guide books and maps were spread out on tables in front of the tourists and there was the odd copy of the Jerusalem Post being read by others. Cigarettes were alight and coffee was being consumed. There was a general hum of contented business in this peaceful oasis.

No one seemed to pay Billy any attention as he strolled over to the buffet and grabbed a paper plate. He began to load food onto the plate and grabbed a cup and filled it from the hot water urn before dunking a teabag in it and ladling in a couple of teaspoons of sugar.

He wandered over to one of the empty tables and sat down.

A couple of people he recognised nodded at him as they passed through the courtyard but no one stopped to say anything to him, leaving Billy to doubt if his absence had even been noticed. He felt the familiar pangs of rejection start to build up inside him.

Retribution for his selfish actions of the previous evening, when it came, was swift and devastatingly painful.

A rabbit punch, delivered to his right kidney with pinpoint accuracy caused him to rear up. The punch, like the sword prick from the executioner in Chop-Chop Square, caused his back to arch with the combination of shock and pain. Unlike the executioner the next blow was not a sword strike to the neck, but a balled fist to the side of his head that left his ears ringing and his eyes watering.

"Where the fuck did you get to last night."

Billy turned his head slowly, wiping away the tears to see Blossom stood over him with her hands firmly placed on her hips. The twin blows to his body seemed to have had no effect on her at all.

Billy's ears, on the other hand were still ringing.

Through the tears he took in Blossoms face. She was furious but at the same time there was concern behind the anger and if Billy was not totally mistaken an exhausted look on her face, as if she had slept badly. This was confirmed a moment later.

"I didn't sleep a wink last night I was sat up all night waiting for you to come home."
Billy did his best to look sheepish and contrite.
"I got lost." It sounded lame as the words came out of his mouth but it was the best that his bruised brain could come up with.
Blossom had straddled the bench and was facing Billy.
"You just took off from the beach without a word and then when you didn't show up later or stop by the Underground I began to worry. Where did you go?"
"I went out to the desert. It looked like you were wrapped up with your new boyfriend."
"Him? What the guy on the beach? That's Patrick. He and I arrived here in Eilat on the same day. He has been south into Sinai and just arrived back at the bus station yesterday afternoon. We had masses to catch up on. You could have just come over and said hello and I would have introduced you."
Billy was hurt that he had misread the signs so badly but at the same time he was angry so he let his mouth run away with him.
"It looked like I would have been the gooseberry in that conversation."
As Billy watched a look of realisation crossed Blossom's face, and then she began to laugh.
"Oh my god Billy, no. You don't think? Us two? Oh, please."
The stream of words interspersed as they were with hysterical laughter were like successive strikes with a stiletto blade to Billy's heart.
If he needed confirmation of what he meant to Blossom he now had it. It was a devastating blow to his confidence and given the already low self-esteem he felt after the incident the previous night it was all he could manage to stand up from the table and walk away without bursting into tears. He made straight for his room, without a backward look, and curled up on his bunk.
He must have fallen asleep at some point as he was fast asleep when Trudi came into the room to tell him that he had to vacate the room as she was going to clean it. Billy struggled upright and hunted around in the general detritus on his bed for his towel. He found the offending article under the bed and went into the bathroom to take a quick shower. He came back into the room a few moments later after a freezing cold shower to find the German

girl waiting patiently with a bucket of cleaning materials and a mop.
She had clearly made short work of the dormitory and was now waiting to clean the bathroom. Billy, who was shivering a little from the after effects of the cold water stood to one side so she could gain access. As soon as the door was closed Billy stripped off his towel and shimmied into a pair of shorts. He was hunting under the bed for his flip flops when he heard the bathroom door open. Trudi was stood in the doorway leaning on her mop.
"You know Billy, you are an idiot. You really upset Blossom this morning."
"And you don't think she upset me this morning? She boxed my ears and then laughed in my face."
"I would probably have done the same or worse." The Germanic lilt to her voice made the threat sound even more sinister than it probably was.
"But I don't care about you. I care about Blossom. She is my friend."
"And I don't count for anything around here. A lesson I am coming to learn through bitter experience. Now if you will excuse me I have an appointment with a towel on a beach."
Billy had collected his things while the exchange was taking place and he now left the room in high dudgeon.
Billy was furious and his anger burned slowly and long after he had arrived at the beach and spread out his towel.
He had made a detour via the supermarket and collected some supplies for the day, noticing that the amount of money he had left in local currency was dwindling fast. He stuffed the remaining notes and coins back in his pocket vowing to do a full accounting later on. Right now, he had one intention and the first step in his plan was to mix up a bottle of Arac and water although he was careful to ensure that the strength of the mixture was a little more moderate than it had been the previous evening.
Unfortunately, the result was the same as before even if it took slightly longer to get there and instead of total blackout Billy just felt his senses slowly slipping away from him. As always the first sense to go was his self-control.
By the time other people came to join him on the beach Billy was really a long way past caring and had become a nasty and abusive drunk, which did little to endear him to others. By the time

Blossom arrived there was a large circle of towels and blankets laid out but all were a fair distance away from where Billy was sat on his own towel, prattling insanely to anyone he felt was listening to him, which given the stream of bile and nonsense that was pouring from his lips was in fact nobody.
As he spied Blossom weaving her way across the crowded beach Billy's voice raised in volume by a couple more notches earning him angry looks from those nearest to him as he interrupted their conversations.
"Here she comes. Make way for the Queen Bee, the most important person in her small world." Billy pursed his lips and blew a mock trumpet fanfare which tailed off into a loud raspberry before he collapsed theatrically in a fit of giggles.
Blossom pretended she hadn't heard him and squatted down beside his towel.
"Hello Billy."
Billy looked up at her and then pantomimed looking confused as if someone had spoken to him and he couldn't quite identify the origin of the voice.
"What? Did someone say something to me? Am I worthy of notice at last?"
Blossom waited patiently for Billy to finish his tirade.
"Have we been drinking again?"
"Yes." As if to emphasise the point Billy pulled out the almost empty bottle of Arac and water and took a big gulp, then wiped his mouth with the back of his hand.
Blossom said nothing in response so Billy continued.
"Can't share with you, it's the last of my booze and I can't afford any more. Bit short of money so I probably won't see you again."
"What do you mean?" Blossom was slightly offended by what Billy was suggesting.
"Well once the money runs out then so do you." Billy gave a half-drunk grin at his bon-mot.
Blossom was clearly not in the least impressed with Billy or the direction this conversation was heading in.
She simply turned her back on Billy and talked to one of the other people nearby.
Billy merely took this rejection as further evidence that he had been right all along and began a solo tirade at Blossom's back which proceeded to catalogue every fault that Billy could think of.

He continued for about five minutes until Phil the Australian Janitor from the hostel, clearly exasperated by Billy's childish and hurtful antics intervened. He hauled Billy up by the arm of his t-shirt and pushed him out of the circle of towels. Someone had the presence to collect Billy's towel and pack from the sand and owner, pack and towel were propelled a long way down the beach, with clear instructions not to return.

As Billy stalked away he failed to notice the tears streaming down Blossoms cheeks or the sobs that were wracking her whole body.

\#

By the time he returned to the hostel later, it was clear that news of his tirade at the beach had spread. As he walked through the leafy atrium eyes followed him but none of them were smiling. There was no warm welcome from any of the residents, familiar or newcomers alike. It was like the walk of shame. Billy for the most part was oblivious to the stares and frosty reception, he was still steaming drunk. He nodded at a few faces he recognised in the group but was past caring if he received a response. He simply made a beeline for his bunk and crashed out.

The next morning it was a very different story as the full impact of his behaviour the previous afternoon came crashing through his senses. When he arrived in the dining area for breakfast it was clear that Billy had been well and truly ostracised. No one would make eye contact with him and none of the residents or staff would even give him the time of day. Billy cut a very lonely and forlorn figure as he sat alone at a table and munched his way through his breakfast. In his solitude, he had time to reflect on and to regret his actions and words.

He had clearly underestimated the way things worked here in Eilat. Things were however, about to get much worse.

Billy had nearly finished his breakfast and while eating he had resolved to at least attempt to make amends with Blossom, at the very least he wanted to apologise for his actions. He was surprised that he had not seen her arrive for breakfast and he looked up expectantly at each new arrival.

He didn't notice Yoram, the hostel manager, until he was stood over Billy's table.

"I need a word with you." The voice was flat, neutral, giving no sign of intent.

Billy looked up searching the bearded face for some indication of which side of the argument the Israeli was on. He hoped that the man's business sense would prevent him from taking sides in the quarrel but he knew that as an employee here Blossom had some entitlement to his protection.

"I need your bed back."

Billy looked down and saw that Yoram was holding a handful of bank notes in his hand.

"I made a mistake in the booking and the hostel is full from tonight."

He slapped the cash down on the table in front of Billy and turned and walked away.

Billy scraped the money towards him and thumbed through the pile. It was all there. Billy didn't believe for one moment that the place was full. There had been empty beds on each of the nights he had stayed here and for the place to suddenly fill up in the middle of the week was unusual. He took the news as what it was, further evidence that the place was closing ranks against him.

He was truly shocked at the influence this young lady had brought to bear but he knew he could do little to counter it. He finished his breakfast and returned to his room to pack his stuff. He didn't bother waiting around to say goodbye to anyone. He didn't feel it would be appropriate. So as soon as his bags were repacked he shouldered his rucksack and left the room, passing through the courtyard and out into the street.

While he had been packing his stuff, he had come across the flyers he had collected on his arrival from the bus station so his first job was to set about finding somewhere else to stay. He consulted the first flyer and figured out from the hand drawn map on the cover that it was only a couple of streets away so he turned his feet in that direction and set off at a brisk trot. Billy was convinced that he would find another hostel to stay in and could start again.

After the third place had turned him down claiming there were no vacancies, Billy was beginning to see a pattern emerging.

He had always assumed that Israelis would be shrewd businessmen and let the head rule the heart but clearly here in Eilat there was another set of rules.

By mid-morning he was still no nearer finding a place to stay for the night and he was running out of options fast, so he resolved to return to the bus station and hope to confront Blossom and appeal to her directly to get this stupid ban lifted.

He made his way across town to the city bus station and walked onto the concourse. He scanned the crowds and picked out the characters who were there handing out flyers to arriving travellers. Blossom was not among that crowd. Instead he spied the German girl, Trudi, so he approached her instead.

When she saw him making his way through the crowd she stood still and folded her arms across her chest, placing the stack of flyers she was carrying out of reach, under her arm.

Despite the fact her presence at the bus station made a liar out of her boss. If she was looking for guests for tonight then the hostel was clearly not as full as Yoram had claimed, Billy decided to give her a pass on this and ask her about Blossom's whereabouts.

Before he could open his mouth to speak, Trudi spoke to him.

"What do you want?" The tone was aggressive and unfriendly.

"Where is Blossom? I need to speak to her."

"She don't want to speak to you. She is working as chambermaid today. We swap jobs."

"Look I just need to talk to her, to apologise."

"It's too late for that now. Damage is done. Now go away."

Trudi turned her back on Billy and stalked off into the crowd.

Billy was left watching her departing back. Well at least he knew where he could find Blossom, so he went over the road to the cafe where their friendship had all started and had some lunch.

At one point, he looked across the road and saw that Trudi was standing together with some of the other leaflet pushers and as he watched she pointed him out before saying something to all of them. Obviously, she was marking him out to the competition, just to be on the safe side. This annoyed Billy as he felt what had started out as a minor disagreement between two people was being blown up into an international incident.

At the same time, he found that old stubborn determination rearing up. If the intention was to run him out of town then they were going to find that they had picked a fight they would not win.

Billy knew that if he could just get to speak to Blossom and maybe have the chance to apologise then this whole thing would probably go away in a couple of days, once news of their reconciliation got around.

At least the cafe owners were a little thicker skinned and would take his money, even if the hostel owners wouldn't. That was some consolation for him. At least he wouldn't starve.

He finished off the last of his sandwich and his beer, left a small tip for the waitress and set off towards the Peace Hostel.

The door was closed and when Billy tried to open it he found it was bolted from the inside.

Billy leaned his face against the cool green metal and listened for sounds of movement from within. There was nothing but an eerie silence from the other side of the door, no sounds of voices, people working or music playing carried to where Billy was stood. He took a step away from the door and clenched a fist. He pounded on the door three times. The hollow metal skin set off an ominous booming that must have reverberated around the interior space and carried to the furthest corners of the building.

Billy hammered again three times on the door and then stood back. He knew that whoever was in the building would have got the message and it was now a question of waiting to see who answered the call. He didn't think for one moment that Blossom would come to the door but he hoped that it would not be the owner Yoram.

In the event as he stood there he heard the clunk as the bolts were drawn back and the door was opened.

Through the crack of the slightly opened door appeared Ian's head. Billy could not see past the face into the darkness but he sensed there were other parties in the hallway behind Ian.

"Oh it's you. What do you want?" The Australian's accent was thick and flat. He was clearly not intimidated by Billy's presence, but sounded bored that he had to act as gatekeeper.

"Is Blossom there? Can I speak to her?"

"She doesn't have anything more to say to you." Ian began.

"It's alright Ian. I can speak to him."

Billy saw a female hand grab the edge of the door and it was opened fully. Blossom stepped through the gap and took half a step into the street.

Billy took a step back to give her room on the sidewalk and to reassure her that he posed no physical threat to her. Billy could see her shoulders were raised and her arms were crossed in front of her, both sure signs of a defensive stance.

"What do you want Billy?"
"To talk to you. I think we need to end this silliness."
Billy was aware of the looming figure of Ian standing framed in the doorway, watching his every move and hanging on his every word.
"And what silliness are we talking about?"
"My stupidity. I was drunk and hurt and I said some things I regret saying."
"Do you regret them because you are sorry or are you just saying this to clear your conscience?"
Billy considered his answer before replying. He knew his next sentence would be crucial.
"I regret them because they upset you."
Billy saw the first sign of a smile play across Blossoms lips and behind her eyes. He had made the right choice. As he watched her posture changed and the arms came down to her sides and her shoulders dropped noticeably.
"And you don't deserve to be upset. You did nothing wrong."
This time the smile was even more obvious.
Billy studied her face looking for signs that she was going to forgive him. For the first time, he noticed that she had her hair caught up in a bandana. Clearly Blossom had felt that her new role as a chambermaid required the requisite headgear.
"And you look drop-dead gorgeous rocking the Axel Rose headgear."
As Billy watched Blossom's face seemed to melt and crease up and tears sprang from her eyes. She let a moan like a wounded animal, turned on her heels and cuffing the tears from her eyes, pushed her way past Ian in the doorway.
The Australian, sensing that his presence as a bodyguard was no longer required had taken his eyes off the couple and he was startled as Blossom pushed past him.
Registering the upset on her face as she passed him but unsure over what had caused it, Ian assumed the worst. His features hardened and he delivered a stinging rebuke.
"You fucking cunt. You couldn't let it lie."
The door slammed shut in Billy's face and as he stood there he heard the bolts clang back into place. Billy stood there on the sidewalk stunned by the turn of events. What the hell had just happened?

Billy waited ten minutes for the door to open again and for Blossom to emerge but it remained resolutely closed. In the end Billy began to feel stupid so he wandered off in the direction of the beach.

\#

He knew that to set up camp in the regular place would be to invite hostility from the cabal that formed the core of Blossom's friends so instead Billy took himself further along the beach until he was a safe distance from the place he expected the others to assemble. This brought him closer to the fringes of the tent city that spread out from the edge of the beach and sprawled out into the scrubland beyond the sand and pebbles.
At this end of the beach the clientele was different. Their clothing was more ragged and their appearance was more dishevelled. Hair was even more unkempt, unwashed and un-brushed. Facially they looked more haggard, underfed and lacking in sleep. The whole mood was more downbeat and the overwhelming smell of hash smoke was thick in the air.
The atmosphere was tense and almost threatening, with an air of suspicion and mistrust. It was almost as if a small spark could ignite scenes of mayhem and violence. Billy was no stranger to such situations, any public house in his home town on a Friday night could be just as bad but maybe the months away from home had affected Billy's ability to deal with such things because he certainly didn't feel comfortable surrounded by tension like this anymore.
Billy settled down keeping his bags close to hand. He opened his small pack and pulled out a can of beer and popped the ring pull. He took a long swig instantly feeling a dozen pair of eyes watching his every move. He knew he would stand out as a newcomer, his clothes were too clean and he looked too well fed to be one of them. He drank the first beer slowly anticipating at any moment that someone would approach him, no one did. He was certain that he was being watched, observed from a distance but nobody came closer to investigate. By the time he was onto his third can of beer he could almost hear the smacking of lips in the background. There was plenty of movement among the crowd but they all seemed to

be avoiding the area of beach where Billy was sitting as if they were waiting for something or someone.

Billy was beginning to get jittery. He was starting to regret his rash decision to come this far down the beach. Clearly, he was the centre of attention and he was fine with that but he knew it would be dark in a couple of hours and then anything could happen. His mind began to play tricks conjuring up various nightmare scenarios where some ominous "King Rat" figure emerged from the tent city behind him demanding some form of tribute to join his happy band of reprobates, whilst his loyal followers formed a smirking ring of sycophants around him.

The approach when it came took him completely by surprise. A petite waif-like creature appeared beside him and squatted down in the sand.

"Hi there, how're you doing?"

Billy took a moment before answering. Her hair was cut short in a pixie-bob at the front but was shaved close at the back. Her clothes, a purple vest top and matching Bedouin pants were ragged but clean. Her feet were shoeless and her wrists and ankles were adorned with the woven friendship bracelets in a multitude of colours. Her only jewellery was a very subtle nose stud and a single toe ring. As she tucked one of her bangs behind her ear in a gesture of childish innocence Billy saw she also had several rings in her pierced ears.

"Er hello, thanks I am doing fine."

"You don't look fine, sitting here all alone with all your expensive gear around you. Why aren't you checking into a hostel and mixing with the other tourist volunteers down the other end of the beach."

"It's a long story." Billy said with a slight sour tone in his voice. He didn't really want to tell the story to a complete stranger.

"Well if you have another one of those tins of Maccabee in your pack I have the time to listen."

Billy extracted a tin and passed it across to the girl, who went from squatting on her haunches to sitting down on the beach. She then pulled the ring on the can and took a large mouthful from the can.

"So come on Billy tell me your story."

"Wait. What? How do you know my name?" Billy was confused and his face and voice both showed it.

"Oh come on, it's the talk of every bar and hostel from here to Taba and back. And there is not much that happens in Eilat that we don't get to hear about."

"So you know my story and yet still you took my beer?"

"I know their version of the story. The beer is payment for hearing your side of the story."

It was fuzzy logic but Billy accepted it and began to recount his version of the events of the past few days. He decided to be brutally honest and not to try and paint himself in any particularly favourable light, even admitting to his stupidity in going off alone and getting mugged and having his money and passport stolen. It was a very cathartic and cleansing experience. At the end, he looked up at the girl, who had remained silent throughout, just occasionally taking a sip from her beer, and saw in her eyes a real sense of understanding.

She smiled at him and took the last of the beer from the can into her mouth, swallowed, and then crushed the empty can in the middle to show it was empty before setting it to one side.

"Do you want my opinion?" She asked.

"Is it going to cost me another tin of beer?" Billy looked at the empty can, languishing on the hot sand.

"I wouldn't say no. My name's Melanie by the way, but most people call me Mel."

They shook hands formally before Billy reached in his pack and handed another tin over. Melanie popped the ring and took another mouthful of beer. Billy did the same and waited for the verdict.

"It's simple," she said after a moment's pause, "that girl is in love with you."

Billy choked on his beer and spluttered for a second.

"No way."

"Yes way. It's absolutely clear from her actions."

"I think her actions show her true feelings."

"I don't think what has happened to you is as a result of her actions. I think it is more a case that you have fallen victim to a few over-protective friends. Friends who think they have her best interests at heart but actually are just making matters worse."

Billy was shaking his head throughout the whole speech at the end he just looked over and said.

"To be honest I can't see it."

"That's because you are not looking at it from a women's point of view."
"But what about the whole scene outside the hostel when I tried to apologise? That only seemed to make matters worse."
"That's is exactly what convinced me that she has feelings for you."
"She has a bloody funny way of showing them." Billy was half smiling as he spoke and the humour came through in his tone. This caused Melanie to smile back at him and Billy realised that under the grime and rough appearance she was actually quite attractive. In addition, the position she had adopted, sitting leaning slightly forward and at an angle to Billy, he was getting a generous glimpse of side-boob where her vest top was gaping open. He looked and then looked away again instantly. Mel, if she noticed him staring, didn't seem to care.
"Ah Billy boy, there are better men than you who have burned with frustration trying to understand the ways of women."
The use of that form of address brought back memories of the only other person who called him by that name and for the first time in several days Billy wondered how Mike was getting along.
"Penny for your thoughts?"
Billy looked up.
"I was just thinking about my mate, Mike. He used to always call me Billy-boy."
"And where is this Mike now?"
"He is back on the Kibbutz. I got kicked off, but I took the blame so Mike was able to stay."
"So you are a true friend. Not many people would have taken the blame for a friend."
"In actual fact we were both innocent, but as I was responsible for the whole thing I took the rap. It was the right thing to do. Besides, Mike was the one who wanted to come to Israel in the first place, and work on a Kibbutz, I was just along for the ride."
"And now that train has hit the buffers so to speak."
"It looks that way."
"And you are running short of money, you got robbed and then turned on by the people you thought were your friends?"
"You make me sound like I should be standing on the end of the pier with a rock tied around my neck."

"Wouldn't work. The water is too shallow." Mel grinned at him.
"Anyway, cheer up it's not all bad. You still have your health and you can always work and earn some money."
"Are you talking about the Wall?"
"The very same. Slave labour in the blossoming black economy."
"I have heard about it. Do you know how it works?"
"In theory, but not in practice." Mel grinned at her own obscure joke.
Billy picked up on the grin. "Explain yourself or there will be no more beer."
"Oooh please sir, don't be mean sir?"
"You sound like a Victorian courtesan when you say it like that."
"A Victorian what?"
"Courtesan, a hooker."
"Charming. I can see why Blossom went off you if that is your best chat-up line."
"I haven't even started on the best lines yet. Now are you going to tell me what you meant?"
"It's simple really, I have never had to work the Wall."
"Lucky you. Are you sure you are not a hooker?" It was Billy's turn to grin.
His reward for his cheek, was an empty beer can which was aimed at his head. It missed.
"So why have you never worked the Wall?"
"Because I am getting an allowance from my dear old Dad back home in England, regular as clockwork, first day of the month, deposited into my Israeli bank account."
"So why am I, a person of now severely depleted means the one who is supplying the beer?"
"It's simple. You are paying for my sparkling company and in return I am delivering valuable information?"
"Paying for your company? You know what that makes you?"
"Will you quit with the hooker jokes. They are wearing a bit thin now." Mel was still smiling and she continued with a smile still in her voice. "When we have finished your beer, we will go to the supermarket and buy some more and it will be my treat."
Billy looked her up and down, studying every aspect of the woman sat beside him. He so dearly wanted to believe that she was telling the truth but when he compared Mel to the other people he had met here in Eilat so far, she did not display any outward sign of having

more than a handful of shekels to her name and certainly not enough money to supply the next frame of Maccabee.
Melanie caught sight of him appraising her one more time.
"Are you staring at my boobs?" She self-consciously adjusted her position and rearranged her clothing in an attempt to cover herself up.
Billy's face reddened with embarrassment. He had been admiring Mel's body, not openly leering at it but just casting the occasional appreciative glance in her direction.
"No." He stammered lamely.
"Coz that will cost you another beer."
Guiltily Billy handed over another cold can, conscious that this was the last but one in his pack.
"You had better come good on your promise. These are the last of my beers."
"Oh I am good for it." Melanie popped the ring on her latest can and took a swig. "But I get the feeling that money is something of an issue for you."
"Well the thieves made off with most of my cash and my bank cards, so the only money I have is a few dozen shekels."
Mel considered this for a moment.
"Have you got anything to sell? A camera? A stereo? A Walkman?"
"I have a stereo and a camera, why?"
"Because we can sell both of those for you and that will give you a bit of cash to carry you over until you can get a job off the Wall."
"And you just happen to know where I can get a really good price." Billy couldn't keep the note of suspicion out of his voice.
"It just so happens I do." Mel had either missed the tone in Billy's voice or had chosen to ignore it. "Also, if you don't sell them someone around here will probably steal them and sell them for you. At least this way you get to keep and spend the money."
Billy considered her offer for a few moments. The stereo, he knew, required electricity to run and out here on the beach power outlets were not available. Batteries, the alternative, were a luxury he could ill afford. Likewise, the camera needed film, another luxury outside of his current financial purview. He had used all the films he had brought with him from home and the spent film canisters were safe in a pocket of his rucksack awaiting development. What Melanie was suggesting therefore made sense to him and the

prospect of losing these two valuable items to theft was not something he wanted to happen. He therefore agreed to sell the items.

"Can we sell them this afternoon?"

"As soon as you want to. The buyer has a stall up in the centre of town. He is the one that will give you the best price."

"Well what are we waiting for." Billy scrambled to his feet. He did not totally forget his manners and offered his hand to help Melanie up. She took his hand.

Billy noticed that the skin of her hand was warm and soft under his fingers.

"Wow," Melanie sounded impressed, "A real gentleman. I can see why the ladies fall for you." She grinned impishly at him.

Billy huffed at her teasing and bent down to pick up his rucksack, swinging it over one shoulder.

"You could probably get a good price for this too." Melanie tapped the frame of the rucksack. "It looks almost new".

"And what would I keep my stuff in?"

"Down here you don't need much. A few extra clothes, a sleeping bag, that's about all. You could probably keep all you need in that day pack of yours. And it is much easier to carry that around with you than lug that huge rucksack everywhere and there is nowhere safe to leave it here."

Billy could see the sense in her observation and he gave it due consideration as they walked across the beach and back into the centre of town.

As they strolled along Billy's curiosity got the better of him.

"Why do you live like this, particularly if you have money?"

"Because I want to. I grew up in the lap of luxury. Big house with two cars in the drive. Private school education. Pony club gymkhanas at the weekends. Holidays to the South of France. You get the picture."

Billy did get the picture. With the exception of the Private education and the Ponies it sounded very much like Mike's childhood.

"I know what you mean." Billy added. "I have a friend who would understand you perfectly."

"And where is this friend now?"

"He is back on Tel Boker, the Kibbutz, it's Mike, the guy I told you about."

"So Mike has chucked it all in as well. You see living like that can become very suffocating. Out here I am free to do what I want."
"But you still take the money."
"What do you mean by that?" For the first time, Billy heard genuine annoyance in Mel's voice.
"Well Daddy still sends out the money and you are happy to spend it. So, you are not really free."
Mollified by his explanation Mel calmed down a little. As Billy watched her shoulders, which had tensed up as she had spoken, slowly relaxed.
"I am a hell of a lot freer here than I was at home."
"And your parents are happy with you being a beach bum."
"They don't know I am here. They think I am still happily picking Apples on a Kibbutz in the Galilee. I call them once a week from a payphone to let them know what has been happening and they are happy."
"But what about mail, letters, birthday cards and the like."
"A friend back on the Kibbutz sends them to me Post Restante here in Eilat. But my family are not great letter writers. They are more into instant communication and they are happy that I call them collect."
"So you are an ex-volunteer. Did you get kicked off?"
"Yeah."
"What for?"
"Threatening a member with a Kitchen knife."
Billy whistled with mock shock at her action.
"Not the smartest thing to do." He added with a smile.
"There is a bit more to it than just that. But it hurts to talk about it."
Billy stopped in his tracks.
"You don't have to tell me anything that will make you uncomfortable."
"Ah Billy to be sure you're a nice man." Mel said with a thick southern Irish accent.
"And you do a lousy impression of an Irishman."
Mel stuck out her tongue.
"Ah what the hell, I might as well get it off my chest."
Billy raised an eyebrow and was rewarded with another fist to his bicep.
"You men are all the same. Only one thing on your mind. Which brings me neatly to what happened. I got involved with a married

Member, he was separated from his wife but that didn't seem to matter. The other Members were not happy about it as they seemed to think I was going to bewitch this guy and then take him back to England with me. I finished the relationship and broke the guys heart when I told him."

Mel looked at Billy to see if he was taking her seriously. Billy trying to avoid another punch on the arm and keen to hear the full story, maintained a straight face.

"Anyway, after we broke up the word got around that I was an easy lay, not sure where the rumour started but I have my suspicions, and one of the other guys decided to try his luck."

"And you weren't having any of it?"

Mel nodded her head.

"This guy was a creep anyway. He had hands everywhere, especially all over the female volunteers. One day he touched more than he should have."

"And you waved a knife under his nose. Good for you. We had a guy like that in the kitchen at our place."

"There's probably one on every Kibbutz."

"Well I stood up to the one on Tel Boker and after that no one took him seriously."

"You didn't threaten him at knife point."

"No, I was not that crazy, but you could have used a knife to cut the atmosphere in the kitchen afterwards. It was tough."

Mel nodded her understanding and took him by the arm just above the elbow.

"Anyway, after word of the knife incident got out the Volunteer leader came by my room and asked me to pack my things. They were not stupid enough to kick me off for the knife incident, I could have really made a stink about that. Instead they citied the affair as the reason they were asking me to leave."

"Well that sucks. I wonder how many women were treated the same way? You are the second person I have heard about who got involved with an Israeli and got kicked off."

"I bet the women in the kitchen were grateful for your intervention." Mel said, changing the subject.

"In so many ways." Billy grinned lecherously and was rewarded with another thump on the bicep, but there was little power behind the fist. It was more like a friendly pat. Mel didn't let go of his arm so the two of them carried on walking towards the centre of the town.

Billy had to admit to himself he was a little cautious about his new friend's apparent willingness to help and he kept a tight hand and a close eye on his possessions as they walked towards the centre of the city. But his suspicions proved groundless as Mel kept her word and led him straight to the market and introduced him to a merchant who had a stall in the centre of the pedestrian area of the city. His stall sold all manner of electronic goods, digital alarm clocks, personal stereos, Walkman's, Cameras. There were even a couple of fridges and a few TV sets. Not everything was in original packaging but most things looked to be in good condition. The owner made Billy an offer for both his camera and the stereo which Billy thought was reasonable. He was on the point of accepting when Mel intervened. She pushed the price up by another two hundred shekels. Billy, seeing the look of disbelief on the stall owners face and fearing he was about to lose out was going to intervene and accept the original offer. As he opened his mouth to speak the owner's face split into a wide grin and he mumbled something about how he 'nearly got away with it'.

He offered his hand to Billy to seal the deal and then started to count out the notes onto the top of a nearby cardboard box. They watched carefully as the notes were laid down and then picked up and handed to Billy. He in turn handed over the two items and then pocketed the cash. They said their farewells and then walked off into the crowd.

They made it around the corner before Billy swept Mel into a crushing embrace.

"Thank you, Thank you. How did you know that he would go that high?"

Billy had been working out that the price he had just been paid was exceedingly close to the price he had paid for the two items the day he had purchased them and he had been using both items since that day.

"Second hand electrical goods have a good resale value in Israel. The new stuff is extremely expensive so there is a seller's market here. I just estimated the price to buy the two items new and took a little bit off for the fact that they have been used. It's really as simple as that."

Billy knew that he would have settled for the lower price so he was grateful for Mel for her intervention and he intended to show his gratitude.

"How about I buy us both dinner?"

"I never say no to a good meal."

"Where do you want to eat?"

"Well we could go to the Hard Rock Cafe."

"Really?" Billy tried to hide his disbelief. He was familiar with the concept. The franchise had opened an establishment in London in the seventies and was famed for its collection of rock and roll memorabilia. Billy had visited the London location on a couple of occasions but the interior of the Hard Rock Cafe, Eilat, bore absolutely no resemblance to its London sister. The owners had created a space with all the feel of a traditional English pub.

The walls were white with faux Elizabethan wooden beams. The furniture was dark wood with plank tables and a mixture of plastic and wooden chairs. The menu on offer was more akin to a British transport cafe with a heavy emphasis on fried foods, but Billy was not fussy so he ordered a double sausage, egg, chips and baked beans and then settled back with a pint. Mel had ordered something similar and as they waited for their food to arrive Billy looked around the place. The décor consisted mainly of garlands of plastic flags representing most of the nations of the western world, although there seemed to be a predominance of union jacks.

One wag in an attempt to tip his hat to the original concept of the franchise had hung a ukulele on the wall by a piece of string. Scrawled on the body in black marker pen were the words "with love and peace Jimi". The idea of the great Hendrix playing a ukulele brought a smile to Billy's face.

The clientele like all of these types of establishments throughout Israel was a mixture of young westerners, mostly current or ex-volunteers and a smattering of young men and women from the local Israeli youth. For the most part, the two groups seemed to get along although there were occasional flashpoints when the males from one group made an unwelcome approach to the females of the other tribe.

This early in the evening the place was only half full so they didn't have to wait long for their food, and when it turned up it was surprisingly good and when Billy made a comment, Mel told him that the cook was an Englishman and that they imported most of their ingredients from the UK. Billy nodded his head in understanding. That was why he was convinced that the two sausages lying on his plates looked and smelt like prime Walls pork chipolatas. With this knowledge Billy took a moment to study the menu scrawled on a blackboard behind the bar. Mentally he listed the other meals he would have to come back and sample. The bangers and mash was the meal at the top of his list, although the cheeseburger and fries came in a close second. Right now, with the cash from the sale of his camera and stereo burning a hole in his pocket he was looking forward to a few more days of eating and drinking well.

When they had cleared their plates, wiping up the remnants of their eggs and beans with slices of buttered bread, the two of them sat back to finish their drinks.

Mel lit a cigarette offering the pack to Billy who shook his head.
"So now I have some money but it's not going to last forever so let's talk about this "Wall", what can you tell me about it?"
"It's made of stone," Mel began
"Ha ha ha, very funny. I think I could have worked that out for myself. I am more interested in how the thing works."
"It doesn't work, it's a wall." Mel pulled a silly face.
Billy chose to ignore her latest attempt at humour. Mel, realizing he was a tough audience, gave up her attempt at comedy and instead adopted a serious manner.
"Basically, in the morning, anyone who wants to work turns up and waits by the wall. If there are jobs to be done then people come by and hire you. You agree a rate for the day in advance and then you get taken away to wherever they want you to work. It's mostly unskilled labourer work, building sites, gardening, stuff like that. At the end of the day the boss comes back and pays you."
"Sounds a bit dodgy. What if the guy refuses to pay you or doesn't come back?"
"Then he won't be hiring anybody the next day. Word travels fast and if someone was cheating people then his name and face would get around and no one would work for him ever again. Having said that if you try to cheat them by not doing the job properly then your name will end up on a blacklist and none of the bosses will hire you. That makes it a two-way street."
"So each worker is responsible for negotiating the rate for the day."

"Yeah, pretty much. The lads will be able to give you a better idea of what the going rates are. I couldn't help you there."
"I know, you don't have to work coz Daddy sends you money every month." There was no trace of malice in Billy's voice. "Are you going to tell them you have left the Kibbutz?"
"I might have to eventually. They keep threatening to come and visit me."
"And that would be the end of the adventure?"
"Yeah pretty much so. I can't see my dad financing me in this kind of lifestyle."
"So, what would you do? Go home?"
"I don't know. A couple of the lads are talking about going further maybe across Asia and then down to Oz and New Zealand."
"Wow that would be a real adventure."
"Yeah," Mel nodded her head, "And a bloody expensive one at that. Which is why I am not holding my breath."
"What do you mean?" Billy looked confused.
"Come on Billy you're a sensible guy. Time to face facts. Down here it's a hand to mouth existence for most of us. We earn the money, we spend the money. We don't save anything. Some of the people down here don't have two shekels to rub together. How would they afford a trip even over the border to Egypt, let alone any further afield? Some of them can't even afford the bus fare out of here. They work, they eat and drink and when the money runs out they work some more. It's a vicious circle. It's the Eilat Trap, Billy" She mimicked holding a microphone up to her voice, "and you've been caught." Mel dissolved into fits of giggles at her own joke.
Billy looked over at her across the table.
"Thank you, Bob Geldof." The musical reference had not escaped his notice.
"Is that what this is? The Eilat Trap."
"It's what we call it locally. And you will be caught if you stick around for a few more days."
There was no trace of bitterness in Mel's voice. She was simply stating the facts as she saw them. Billy thought about the balance of Delchie's money sitting safely in his bank back in England. With that money, he could embark on a great adventure to the mystic East, but right now without his bank cards he had no way to

access that money, so as Mel had just pointed out he was trapped here.
"Ah well as long as we are trapped here we might as well enjoy ourselves. Fancy another drink?"
Mel nodded so Billy went up to the bar.
Several hours and many drinks later the two of them made their unsteady way back to the beach. Mel was giggly drunk and having difficulty walking so she was leaning heavily on Billy.
He led the way back to where they had started their journey earlier in the afternoon and even in the dark it was easy to see the beach was now deserted. There were occasional voices from behind them in the dunes.
They collapsed on the sand together. Under their legs Billy could feel the ground was still warm as the sand slowly surrendered the last of the days heat.
Mel was lying flat on her back starring up at the stars so Billy lay down alongside her, their heads almost touching.
"Where are you sleeping tonight Mel? Do you have a campsite?"
Billy had no idea where Mel usually slept. He had brought them back here to the approximate area where they had started from, hoping the he was at least close to where Mel normally slept. Mel was unresponsive so Billy took matters into his own hands. He rolled out his under mat and then his sleeping bag, which he unzipped and opened to make a cover for both of them. Mel had shifted her body onto the mat as soon as Billy had laid it out. He placed a sweatshirt over his rucksack to make it a comfortable pillow and then settled back pulling the sleeping bag over the two of them. Mel shifted closer to him under the covers, using the rucksack as a pillow for her head. Billy lay on his back gazing up at the heavens. He felt Mel shift a little making herself comfortable and pressing herself even closer to him, her arm snaking out and around his chest. He felt her lips brush the bottom of his chin and he smelt the beer on her breath.
"Goodnight Billy. Sweet dreams."
A moment later Billy heard the first long intake of breath as Mel fell into a deep sleep.

CHAPTER fifteen

Sweet dreams were not something Billy enjoyed that night. It was the first time he had slept outdoors and not been surrounded by a large group of other volunteers and watched over by a couple of guys carrying Uzi's. That coupled with his recent brush with the thieves the other night had left him doubly anxious. Every little sound or movement brought him instantly wide awake.
There was plenty of through traffic both coming and going along the beach throughout the night as people made their way to or from the campsite. Some of them were noisy, clearly drunk or otherwise intoxicated, whilst others appeared out of the dark like silent shadows.
As a result, Billy slept fitfully, only finally succumbing to a deep sleep just as the first light of dawn was kissing the tops of the mountains on the Jordanian side of the border.
He woke an hour or so later when the first light of the sun hit the beach. He sat upright, rubbing the sleep from his eyes. Mel only half awake turned over and buried her head deep under the flap of the sleeping bag, trying desperately to cling to the fringes of sleep. She was clearly not ready to face the day.
Billy tucked the loose end of the bag around Mel's sleeping body and searched around him for the bottle of water. In the night, it had rolled a foot or two away from their sleeping place and Billy reached out with his foot and hooked it in. He unscrewed the top and took a long swig. The night air had cooled the water down so it was sweet and refreshing. He put the bottle to one side and began to watch the proceedings around him.
Even at this hour of the day the beach was a hive of activity, although it started out slowly. The first thing Billy noticed was the scattered piles of what looked like rags around this part of the beach, but as the light intensified Billy made out the huddled

sleeping forms of other volunteers, some in sleeping bags, others under colourful blankets. They resembled corpses strewn across the dunes in the aftermath of some seaborne invasion, covered up to hide their awful injuries. The only signs of life the occasional twitch or movement of a body part here and there as someone tossed or turned in their sleep.

Into this landscape of carnage ventured the people of the city of Eilat, the natives and residents. They came in two distinct groups, the Lycra clad fitness fanatics who used the firm sand just above the tideline as a running track. Rainbow clad and with headphones in their ears they jogged to the rhythm of their lives, some at high intensity speed, others at a more relaxed pace. They jogged past heading East and as he watched and waited, they returned in the opposite direction, some of them blowing hard from their exertions.

At a more sedate pace came the dog walkers, although the dogs seemed to be even more energetic than the runners. Those who were free of their leads were roaming far and wide across the sand with a few even venturing close to investigate the sleeping corpses. One particularly brave animal even came close to Billy, although when he offered his hand to the dog to sniff the animal stopped dead in its tracks, turned on its heels and beat a hasty retreat back to its owner.

Over to his right in the direction of the main part of the beach Billy noticed a group of older people clad in dressing gowns were assembling. As he watched they disrobed and formed an orderly group. Billy had seen these people before, not this exact group but one similar, on the beach in Tel Aviv. These were the elderly population who assembled in the early morning to do some exercise. In its form, it looked like a cross between Yoga and Tai Chi. All of the participants were clad in identical black swimming costumes and their collective forms and movement were like some early morning ballet for the over sixties. Billy had the good grace to stop starring when they started to bend at the waist and touch their toes. That was just not a sight he could endure at this time of the morning.

Amongst the general comings and goings of people Billy noticed a fair few of his fellow beach dwellers. Most were heading into town and Billy guessed they were heading off for work. Some of them even made use of the public showers on the beach to get cleaned up and he noticed one or two even redressing into uniforms before they left the beach. The majority though were dressed in the same eclectic mixture of t-shirts, shirts and shorts, a fair proportion of which were the ever-present Kibbutz blue, although some seemed to be wearing castoff army clothing in either green, tan or light sandy colours. Some had managed to retain their canvas work boots while others wore sandals or flip-flops. Those dressed in uniforms were heading for their jobs, the rest, Billy guessed, were heading for the Wall.

This group included one or two of the corpses from the dunes who, as if some internal alarm clock rang, suddenly emerged from under their covers, collected their bedding and their other personal items and headed off in the direction of the Peace Cafe. Breakfast for those individuals was a mouthful of whatever they had been drinking the night before and a bummed cigarette. Real food would have to wait until later when they had some money.

#

As Billy sat there and watched proceedings unfold around him he took a moment to consider his own position. Under the sleeping bag Mel had shifted position slightly and the firm round of her buttocks was now pressed tight up against his thigh, a not altogether unpleasant feeling. He considered his 'new-found' friend. According to her she was funded by her family back home and during the previous evening she had reached in her pocket a couple of times to pay for a round of drinks. This had made Billy strangely grateful. He was still a little wary of the fake friendship factor that seemed to exist here in Eilat. People could be overwhelmingly friendly if you had your hand in your pocket or they suspected you had money for drinks and smokes, and Mel knew exactly how much money Billy had, almost down to the last shekel as she had stood with him while the tradesman had counted out the money for his stereo and camera. Given that knowledge she was bound to stick around whilst there were free meals and free drinks on offer. But Billy knew his money would not last for more than a few days and he wondered if their friendship would.

Billy was not by nature a cynical person but events of the past week had opened his eyes to the grim realities of life here among the underclass in Eilat. Billy knew what it was like to be poor. He had grown up in poverty, never having two coins to rub together, always reliant on Mike to put his hand in his pocket to buy the drinks or pay for the movie tickets but at least he had possessed a sense of guilt. He had genuinely felt guilty when Mike was always the one to pay, even though Mike had never once raised it as an issue. And to top it all Billy knew that when he had money he would pay his own way, which somehow made a difference. Here in Eilat there didn't seem to be the same sense of sharing. In this place, it seemed to be every man or woman for themselves, take as much as you could and more fool the mugs who paid up.

As he sat there going over all this in his mind Billy resolved that he too would have to toughen up his approach or he was in danger of going under.

It was ironic that as he reached this decision in his head he felt Mel stir beside him. She turned over slowly and her arm snaked across his torso under the sleeping bag. She used this arm to push herself upright and her head emerged from under the flap of the bag.

She gazed myopically about her trying to focus through eyes that were almost totally shut. She looked like a new-born baby rat and Billy had to stifle a laugh with his fist.

The sweat had caused her bang to become plastered to one side of her face and the other cheek bore heavy marks where she had been sleeping on his rucksack.

She pushed the hair off her face and looked up at Billy.

"Good morning sleeping beauty." He smiled at her.

"Don't look at me. I look a sight and I hate cheerful people first thing in the morning."

"Well it's lucky that it's almost lunchtime." Billy teased.

"Stop it. Now. What time is it?"

Billy consulted his battered wristwatch.

He had been so proud of this watch when his mother had presented it to him on his thirteenth birthday. Now a decade later it was battered and worn out. The face was scratched and cracked in two places, but it still kept remarkably good time.

"Well according to Mr Timex, it is ten minutes to nine. Why have you got somewhere you need to be?"

Mel had now worked herself into a proper seated position.

"No, nowhere special. It's just that the place I go to eat breakfast stops serving at nine-thirty, so if we are going to catch breakfast we need to get our skates on."

Mel disappeared under the sleeping bag and immediately emerged again.

"Did you redress me last night?"

"Do what?" Billy was confused.

"Simple question did you put my knickers and trousers back on after we fucked last night."

"Sorry to disappoint you but we didn't."

"You mean we didn't fuck last night?"

"Nope."

"Damn that was very vivid dream then."

"Was I good?"

"What?" It was Mel's turn to be confused.

"In your dream, did I push the right buttons?" Billy grinned.

Mel had the good grace to blush, but then she punched Billy in the bicep.

"Ow. Would you cut that out? That's the last time I share my sleeping bag with you."

Billy had rolled away after the blow on the arm and he now stood up from the sand.

Mel pushed the sleeping bag aside and Billy bent down to gather it up and fold it.

"I have to pee." Mel announced and made a beeline for the long grass at the top of the beach.

Billy carried on packing up his stuff, thinking he needed a leak too but he would try and hold on until he could use a proper toilet. He knew that in the future he might have to go in nature but while he was able to hold on and use a toilet he would do so.

Having packed his stuff Billy sat on his pack and waited for Mel to return. He was just beginning to think that she had done a runner and was feeling for the cash in his pocket, convinced that somehow, she had managed to worm her hand in there while he slept and relieve him of his money. He patted the pocket and it felt like the bulk of it was still all there. He was about to pull it out and count it when Mel suddenly appeared from out of the dunes. She waved at Billy indicating that he should join her, so he shouldered his rucksack and headed up the beach.

The two of them set off in the direction of the town. Mel took a moment to explain their destination.

"We are heading to a place in town called Marcellos. At night it is a pizza restaurant and takeaway but before they open the next day they want to get rid of any food they have not sold the previous evening so they open the kitchen early and serve all the leftovers as breakfast to us. It's an invitation only affair and I just happen to have secured you an invitation. And best of all it's free."

Billy was a little wary of eating leftover food scraps, particularly if the food had been hanging around in the desert heat for a while, but he had to acknowledge that a free meal was a free meal and while he hoped he would not be reduced to scavenging in bins in the near future, he had to accept that money would be tight in the near future so economies would have to be made.

As it turned out the food was excellent. As well as the pizza restaurant, the owner also ran a nearby falafel stand and used the kitchen at the restaurant to prepare and store all the food. As a result of this there was a huge metal container full of salad, left over from the previous day. As this was made fresh every day, the leftovers were available as part of the breakfast buffet. The pizza takeaway also had a house speciality of pizzas made on top of pitta bread so there was always a large plastic bag of leftover pitta for the hungry guests.

Billy walked away an hour or more later feeling very full. He had visions of a lazy morning on the beach again but Mel had other ideas.

"We need to get rid of that bloody rucksack. You will get fed up carting it around very soon, and while it is in pristine condition you will get a good price for it."

"But what about all my stuff? Where will I put it?" Billy had become quite attached to the rucksack in the short time it had been in his possession and he could not really face parting company with it.

"What stuff are we talking about here?"

"Well, all my clothes for starters."

"How much clothing can you actually wear?"

Billy considered the question for a few moments but he could see the wisdom behind Mel's argument.

He had a huge stock of t-shirts and shorts and he could only wear one pair at a time. If he made provision for a change of clothes then he would still only need a maximum of three t-shirts, not the fourteen he was currently carrying around.

Together they found a corner away from the main pedestrian flow and started to unpack.

Billy laid his stuff out carefully, evaluating each item and then deciding if it was to go on the 'keep' or the 'chuck' pile.
At the end of the process, there was a huge imbalance between the two piles with the 'keep' pile being by far the smaller of the two. He could see that all of the items in the smaller pile would fit quite nicely into his smaller day-pack. This pack also had the requisite straps to attach his sleeping back and carry-mat.
Mel disappeared off and a short time later returned carrying a huge black plastic bin liner. They loaded all the unwanted clothes into the bin liner and then together carried everything back to the market square where they managed to get a very reasonable price for the rucksack. The owner of the stall also threw in a small belt pouch for free. Billy strapped this around his waist as they walked back in the direction of the beach.
"What do we do with all this lot?" Billy held aloft the bin liner containing all his unwanted clothes. "Sling it in the nearest bin?"
"No way." Mel shook her head violently. "I know some people who will be very happy to pick their way through the contents of that bag, although I have to warn you it's a little weird for the first few days when you see a complete stranger wearing one of your t-shirts."
"There, obviously speaks the voice of experience." Billy said with a wry grin on his face.
Back at the beach Mel made her way into the camp and for the first time Billy wandered through the place that would become his home for the foreseeable future.
In amongst the sand hills at the top of the beach a tent city had sprung up. Not everyone was lucky enough to have a tent so dispersed among the brightly coloured canvas there were a fair few bedrolls and mats, blankets and even the odd tarpaulin. Some lay flat on the floor others were strung up on poles or the branches of sturdier bushes. In amongst the bedrolls and tents were scattered rings of stones that from the evidence of ash and half burnt wood served as fire-pits for cooking. Even at this time of day there were bodies around. From what Billy saw several of the residents were still recovering from the previous night's entertainment.
A few were recumbent in sleeping bags or dozing under awnings. Some merely sat in narcotic or alcohol induced silence their eyes glazed over and fixed somewhere in the middle distance. One group sat in a loose circle a number of joints circulating amongst

them. The overpowering odour of the locally grown Bedouin hashish was thick enough to coat the back of throats and leave eyes watering. Billy felt himself growing sleepy and dizzy at the same time.

As Billy gazed around him at the scene he was reminded of paintings and prints he had seen of field hospitals from the Napoleonic wars where men, exhausted, wounded, shell shocked and dying after battle sat in huddled groups waiting to discover their fate or praying for a quick death to relieve them of their suffering. Where drugs were absent, the medication of choice seemed to be alcohol and bottles of all shapes and sizes were being passed around among the residents, and a fair few empties were scattered across the open space or if there was a deposit reclaimable on the glass had been stacked in loose piles.

This seemed like a small sign of some organisation amongst the predominant chaos.

As they passed through the general disorder of the camp Billy's eyes flicked from left to right, studying faces, looking for some reaction, some fleeting guilty acknowledgement. Eyes that met his, widened in recognition and then looked hurriedly away. He could not help feeling that his mugger might be lurking somewhere among the camp inhabitants and that even if Billy was unable to identify them maybe they would react when they recognised him. No one even gave Billy a second glance.

Their arrival went largely unnoticed and certainly unremarked. Folk around here seemed to accept the ebb and flow of humanity or were too out of it to really care.

Mel led them over to where a large green tarp had been stretched out between two acacia thorn bushes, the corners tied with thick plastic bailing twine. The trailing edge was held down with several large rocks. Under this primitive lean-to were several ratty looking blankets and a loose pile of bedding that might have been sleeping bags or just simple nylon eiderdowns.

Mel ducked under the tarp and pushed some of the bedding to one side. She patted the blanket beside her.

"You can put your stuff in here. I guess Dusty won't be coming back anytime soon."

"Who is Dusty?"

"He was here for a few weeks but he disappeared a few days ago and no one has seen him since."

"And that doesn't bother you?"

"Not really. People come and go all the time. Some of them suddenly get lucky and disappear off. Others reach rock-bottom and send out an SOS to the folks back home. None of them ever come back and say goodbye. Probably too ashamed to face us and admit their defeat."

'Or victory.' Billy thought to himself, but he kept that thought to himself as he placed his now meagre possessions in the space provided.

Mel was taking a moment to change her clothes and instructed Billy to look the other way while she shimmied her way out of her clothes and changed into some fresh ones.

"So, you don't think this Dusty fellow will be coming back?" Billy said over his shoulder.

Mel's answer was muffled by the folds of the t-shirt she was pulling over her head at the time but sounded negative.

"So what happens to his stuff?"

Mel's head appeared through the neck hole.

"Why is there anything there you fancy? You can help yourself."

Billy poked the pile with a finger delicately. There were a couple of threadbare and sun-bleached t-shirts and a pair of blue work shorts. The bedding was as had appeared from outside the shelter, a nylon eiderdown and as Billy shoved it aside he caught a whiff of a vague animal smell from the bedding. No, he decided there was nothing there he wanted and he said as much.

"Well we can gather it all together and stick it outside. If anyone needs anything they can help themselves."

Mel, now redressed began to do just that, gathering all the clothes into a pile and then bundling the whole lot together with the bedding and then tossed the whole pile outside onto the sand. It landed beside the black bin-liner containing the bulk of Billy's clothes.

Mel finished up with her stuff and tossed her small pack into the shadows at the back.

"Don't you worry about that getting stolen?"

"No one touches my shit. I have nothing worth stealing in there and you should be the same."

Billy did a mental inventory of the contents of his pack and decided that, indeed, there was nothing worth stealing in there, unless someone was desperate for a clean t-shirt or pair of faded and threadbare boxer shorts.

The undeveloped films in their plastic containers had no value to anyone but Billy took a moment to secure them in a tightly wrapped plastic bag which he placed in the very bottom of his pack. Used films were worthless to anyone but the memories they contained meant a lot to Billy. With that sorted he abandoned his pack at the rear of the shelter, collected the bin-liner of clothes and then followed Mel as she set off deeper into the heart of the campsite.

The dealing out of the clothes and Dusty's meagre possessions had caused a minor stir in the life of the camp but when it was over, nearly all of Billy's gear had been claimed by new owners and even some of Dusty's stuff had found new homes. There was only a meagre pile of rags remaining in the open space at the centre of the camp.

The majority of the scavengers had returned to their prior occupations leaving Mel and Billy to gather up the last of the scattered possessions and put them in a pile.

It seemed that life in the camp consisted of brief periods of manic interaction followed by long periods of lethargic inaction.

Mel caught Billy glancing at his watch.

"Is it lunchtime?" She asked hopefully.

"Near enough."

"Well let's go and grab a beer at the Peace Cafe and we can start your education."

"Yes Miss." Billy put on his best eager schoolboy voice and was rewarded with another playful punch to the bicep.

\#

Mel, despite the fact she was not an active participant in the practice, seemed to know an awful lot about the rules and rituals for working the Wall, and these she imparted to Billy while they sat in the shade outside the Peace Cafe and enjoyed a couple of beers. By lunchtime the Wall was largely deserted.

Most of the activity involving hiring took place first thing in the morning with prospective employers arriving with offers of employment and potential employees lined up patiently waiting to hear what was available. Usually the deals were struck quickly and people went off about their business.

Occasionally throughout the day a stray person would drift by hoping to snag a body for a specific task but on those rare cases there were either the unlucky ones who had not made the morning cut who were loitering in the area or patrons idling away their free time in the Peace Cafe who could be roped in to help out.

Mel didn't paint a particularly flattering picture of the work that was on offer, although she did clarify her words by saying that this was just feedback she had been given by other people. The list of jobs available seemed to cover the complete spectrum of unskilled manual work and from what Billy could gather the pay was also suitably grim, barely enough to maintain a subsistence, hand-to-mouth life style. Being placed in the black economy there was no tax of any form to pay but this meant that the wages could be kept artificially low and no one seemed to complain.

By mid-afternoon the first of the casual workers were beginning to trickle back and Billy observed at first hand why the Peace Cafe did nothing to discourage the daily practice of the Wall. The vast majority of the returning workers after many hours in the hot sun made straight for the service windows inside the cafe and ordered themselves a large beer or two to slake their thirst.

After that was taken care of they would often stick around chewing the fat with the others, griping about the shit conditions they had endured that day and how hard this or that person had made them work. As the trickle of workers arriving turned into a flood the bar area became crowded and Billy estimated a fair slice of the establishments profits were made straight from the hard-earned cash of these casual workers. Cash that had barely had time to settle in their pockets.

As the sun slipped behind the hills and the mountains on the Jordanian side of the border took on their rich red hue, people started to drift off. Some went in search of food, others went looking for dealers to satisfy their particular addictions.

Mel and Billy had both been drinking steadily since lunchtime and Billy was certainly feeling a little he worse for it, so he was happy when Mel suggested they venture into town with one of the groups who were going in search of food.

The evening meal, unlike the breakfast, was not made up of kitchen scraps and leftovers although Billy did witness another side of life on the underside of Eilat.

The restaurant or establishment chosen for the evening meal was somehow broadcast by word of mouth out to all those interested and then people would start to arrive. People would order up plates of food and these would arrive on the tables that the group had occupied. The food was then consumed communally with everyone using their hands. Usually the meals were served with baskets of pitta which was used to mop up any sauces or to fold in some of the hot meats. It was all in all a very relaxed way of eating and, much to Billy's surprise, no one seemed to leave the table hungry and on that first night Billy left the table stuffed again, much as he had after breakfast earlier in the day.

'Well I am not going to die of starvation here.' Billy thought to himself as a large group of them made their way back to the beach camp.

The camp itself had come alive by the time they arrived back. Several fires were burning brightly and could be seen from a long way off. Bodies could be seen moving in the firelight, dancers wilding gyrating to music still inaudible from this distance.

Billy slowly became aware of the undertones of percussion. This was the sound of hands and short pieces of wood being drummed rhythmically on a variety of containers from plastic waste bins and water containers to empty olive oil cans.

Over the top of this tribal rhythm, voices were raised in chant and as a counterpoint as they got closer was the melody being played on guitars. The music was relentless driving the dancers into a whirling, spinning, stamping ecstasy.

Each musical piece lasted an age and at the end the dancers collapsed to the floor. There was brief pause while breath was gathered and the musicians took on some liquid refreshment then the first of the drummers would start with a new beat and the other musicians would join in.

After a few moments respite the dancers would leap to their feet and recommence the dance. It was primitive and tribal and somehow at one with the setting, the firelight and the darkened beach.

As they moved through the camp Billy noticed couples were making out in the shadows, blissfully unaware of the audience observing their public passion and uncaring of their intimacy being on display to passers-by. Not surprisingly the main fuel of the passion and the hedonistic music was alcohol which was being passed freely among the participants but interspersed with the circulating bottles Billy detected the odd whiff of hash smoke. Somehow in the more liberal setting of the beach camp the presence of the illegal drugs didn't bother Billy as much as it had done on the Kibbutz. In some silly way, it seemed appropriate to the setting.

In the firelight crazed faces mad with drink or drugs took on demonic features as the intensity of the drumming music rose to a fever pitch. Clothing was discarded and naked bodies, bathed in sweat glistened and entwined in parodies of the love act, all illuminated by the dancing flames.

Billy and Mel had a grandstand seat outside their shelter and they sat together with the two other residents, passing a bottle of Arac and water back and forth amongst them.

The other two, an English couple, who seemed more interested in each other than the dancers eventually left for the quiet and darkness of the dunes leaving Mel and Billy to sit close and finish the bottle between them.

Billy was still wary of his surroundings and the memory of his recent episode was still fresh in his mind and to cap it all he was still not sure if he could trust his new-found friends. Therefore, Billy only drank sparingly, but it was still enough to give him a buzz and to relax him enough to embrace sleep when it came.

He slept deeply, maybe as a result of the Arac or more likely because of the sleepless night he had endured the night before. When he woke up he rolled over on his sleeping mat instantly becoming aware of an overwhelming smell of human piss filling his nostrils with its sharp ammonia tang. He sat bolt upright as an overwhelming sense of disgrace washed over him. As reasoned thought cut through the shame he began to see things more clearly. He had never been so drunk in his life that he had wet the bed and by his recollection last night was not even close to the drunkest he had ever been. Why, therefore now would he have pissed himself. He began to feel the cover of the sleeping bag. It was bone dry. This meant that the smell was not emanating from his bedding, but it was definitely coming from his end of the lean-to. He patted the floor around his bed-space, still unable to locate the source of the smell.

By gradual process of elimination and use of fingertips and nose he was eventually able to isolate the source. The last third of his sleeping bag, that part that lay closest to the entrance of the shelter was spattered with urine stains and this and the mat underneath were in fact the source.

It seemed that what had happened was that at some point during the night someone passing by had chosen to relieve themselves outside the tent or against the outer wall and in doing so had splashed urine over the lower part of Billy's sleeping place.

Billy knew that the coming heat of the day would only make the smell worse so he got out of his sleeping bag and removed mat and bag from the shelter. He was just finishing up when Mel walked over. She had a towel wrapped around her upper body and just a small pair of panties maintaining her modesty. Her hair was still wet and straggly, fresh from her recent shower. She noticed Billy struggling with his bedding.

"What's the matter Billy?"

"Someone pissed on my sleeping bag in the night. The whole place stinks of it."

"Oh that's not good. We need to get your bedding rinsed out as soon as. Let me get some clothes on and I can show you where you can get fresh water."

She bent down and pulled over her bag. She sorted through her clothes and selected a pair of shorts and a clean vest top.

She shimmied her way into the shorts and then stood up and whipped off her towel. Billy got a brief flash of pert breasts and rosy nipples before Mel pulled her vest top over her head and covered them up.

She met his gaze frankly almost challenging him to say something. Billy just looked away quickly, blushing slightly.

Dressed, Mel now led Billy and his pile of reeking bedding up through part of the camp until they arrived close by a service road. Here by the roadside Billy saw two of the standpipes used to supply water to places that needed irrigation. These pipes had been scattered throughout the Kibbutz, both in the fields and also in the Kibbutz itself.

The ground between these two pipes was muddy and soft denoting that they were in regular use, even if they were not connected to any active irrigation system.

Mel went and stood in the space between the two taps.

"Listen very carefully you want to make sure you get this right. On my left with the green tap handle this is the pipe that gives out clean fresh water. On my right with the red tap is the one that pumps out sewage for irrigating the flower beds. If you are washing you do not want to get these two mixed up."

She turned on the green tap and together they rinsed out Billy's sleeping bag and washed off the sleeping mat. They carried the two items back through the camp and then spread them out on the roof of the shelter to dry in the sun.

After that particular exercise and working in close proximity to the freshly showered Mel, Billy was made aware of his own odour. He had not had a shower or bathed for several days now and he felt this was not a problem he could address by excessive use of roll-on deodorant and a change of t-shirt.

Billy nodded at the drying items on the roof.

"Now these are clean, what can I do about myself?"

"Ah well the personal hygiene options for us camp dwellers are a little limited. First option is a return to the stutzers, but the water is a tadge cold at this time of the morning. The other options are the showers on the beach, very popular at this time of the day and not segregated, so try not to stare." Mel grinned at her own joke. "The final option is to take a dip in the sea although that is refreshing you need to rinse the saltwater off in the shower afterwards."

"Might as well just take a shower and be done with it." Billy grabbed his towel and his soap from his backpack.

"Well get a move on we have to leave for Marcellos very soon or all the food will be gone."

Billy doubted that assertion but he did not hang around in the shower for long.

Billy stripped to his boxers and stood under the stream. The water was not cold but more lukewarm in temperature. Billy used the hand soap to work up a lather and then stood under the flow to rinse off. There were a couple of other people in the shower, two guys and two girls and like Billy they were in various stages of undress. Billy took Mel's advice and avoided making any eye contact with them. Once he had rinsed off the suds and rinsed his hair Billy towelled himself down, redressed in a clean pair of shorts and t-shirt and made his way back through the camp to the shelter.

Mel was sitting outside the shelter waiting for him and the two of them set off together to Marcellos for breakfast.

The place was filled with those who Billy now guessed were the usual suspects. It was the same faces he had seen the previous day, with a few exceptions and those newcomers were clearly no strangers to the group. Those faces missing were most likely the ones who having run short of funds were trying their luck today on the Wall. Returning later, they would in turn be the ones who, being flush with cash, would furnish the others with food and drink tonight. It seemed like a well organised and harmonious arrangement where, as long as everyone was prepared to pull their weight and to contribute, there should be no reason for dissent.

Of course, there were arguments. You could never add alcohol to the mix without there being the occasional flair up; that feeling that a person had taken a bigger share of the pizza than they were entitled to, or taking one too many puffs on a joint. But, for the main part these occasional arguments although some became quite heated and violent were resolved quickly without serious injury as the warring factions were quickly separated and given time to cool down. It was in no one's interest for these conflicts to escalate into major incidents as this would only result in the Police being summoned and most of the inhabitants of the camp were happy to lead their lives below the Police radar.

CHAPTER sixteen

Life continued in much the same way for the next week or so but as Billy watched, the funds from the sale of his stuff slowly dwindled away. He had tried to be careful with his money but life was not cheap in Eilat, even living in the beach camp.
He had set himself a goal that when his personal funds dipped below one hundred shekels he would venture out to the Wall and try to get some work. He made the same pledge for when his fortune hit fifty shekels.
In the end he sat one evening and counted up his money and knew that even with all the small change his personal wealth was under ten shekels. The next morning, he would, without doubt, be joining the crew on the Wall. He didn't make any special preparations for this event. Like exactly before his first day at work in the Kibbutz, he spent the evening drinking with the rest of the camp crew and finally rolled into bed in the middle of the night. He was convinced he would be awake at first light. So far since joining the camp he had. He was woken up first thing, most days, by the general noise and commotion of the people moving around the camp, so why would tomorrow be any different?
When he finally woke up Billy was disconcerted to see that the sun was already high in the sky. He checked his watch and it was a little before eight. He rolled out of his sleeping bag, laced his boots, grabbed his belt pack and took off at a run in the direction of the Peace Cafe. He arrived, a little out of breath and joined the bodies sitting on the Wall. He recognised a few of the faces or was at least on a nodding acquaintance with some of them. As he took his place so the first pair of those faces stood up and wandered away. In turn, one after another, others began to follow suit. Bit by bit the numbers dwindled down until there were only a handful of people left. Billy didn't recognise any of them but they looked a

pretty desperate bunch, looking for the most part as if they had nowhere to go and nothing to do except sit here and wait for work. One of them sidled over to Billy.
"Got a smoke?"
"No sorry I don't."
"Got any booze?"
"Nope not with me:"
"Got any dope?"
"No I haven't"
"Got any money?"
"Would I be here if I had money?"
Billy was getting a little fed up at the abruptness of the questions.
"Well I guess you are fucked as well. If you aren't here by six then you won't get no work. So, I guess you will go hungry tonight."
Billy didn't think he would starve but he was certainly conscious that he had only a few shekels left.
"Yeah." Billy tried to sound downbeat about his prospects. "I guess I will starve."
His tormenter satisfied with his ability to crush another soul gave Billy a wolfish grin and returned to his friends, who had obviously collectively decided they were going to move on elsewhere.
Billy was left alone on the Wall. He wondered whether he should stick around in case one of the bosses came by looking for additional hands. There could be no harm in waiting another half an hour, just to be sure.
He made himself comfortable in a patch of shade offered by the plastic awning that covered the terrace outside the Peace Cafe and waited. He was still sitting there patiently when Mel strolled over.
"I heard you leave this morning and judging by the hour I figured you might still be here. Come on let's go and get breakfast."
"So I won't be starving today after all." Billy said with a smile.
"What are you talking about?"
"Just something someone said to me a short while ago. He tried to pump me for drugs, fags, booze and money and when I said I had none of them he said I would starve then."
"Why would I let you starve?"
"You probably wouldn't, but I can see what he was getting at, and I can't expect you to support me forever."

"I am glad you realise that as I wouldn't do that. Can't afford to keep you. Not even if you were my 'boyfriend'." Mel arched her eyebrow in Billy's direction

Billy looked up sharply as the "b" word escaped Mel's lips and noticed her raised eyebrow.

"Is that such a strange concept?" Billy said with a tone of mock indignation.

"Well no." Billy's question had taken her by surprise. She decided to laugh it off. "Anyway, you seem to be already spoken for. Surely you haven't forgotten lovely Blossom already?"

"I think it is probably the other way around. She has already given me up for dead."

"I wouldn't be so sure about that." Mel gave him a knowing look. Billy squirmed under that know it all gaze.

"Are you still convinced that girl is carrying a torch for me?"

"What a wonderfully old-fashioned turn of phrase"

"What would you prefer me to say, something sexist like 'Has she still got the hots for me?" Billy reply sounded slightly tart. He didn't mean it to sound so harsh. Mel just seemed to let it drift over her head.

"Oh Billy, she is probably still crying herself to sleep at night about losing you." Mel's tongue in cheek comment brought Billy down to earth. He grinned across at Mel.

"You know, sometimes I wish I had your optimism. But I think I am over her, completely"

"Come on let's go and eat. I am starving." Billy pushed himself off the wall and started to walk away. Mel linked her arm through Billy's and they walked away together.

As Mel matched Billy's stride she thought about the exchange. Billy was a good-looking lad and if he had lost interest in this Blossom woman, or she in him, then he was available.

Mel had no doubt that Billy would eventually get work from the Wall and she had enough cash to keep them both happy until that happened.

She clasped his upper arm tighter and considered the prospect of the two of them together. It brought a wide smile to her face. This small change to her facial expression must have had an effect on her whole body because Billy, walking beside sensed something and stopped dead in his tracks.

"Are you laughing at me?" Billy got totally the wrong end of the stick.
It was Mel's turn to look embarrassed. "No, I am not laughing at you." She stammered but she could not wipe the smile from her face but she tried to hide her face under her arm and turned away walking quickly up the road. Billy moved to follow her and caught her hand. Mel's hand felt small, warm and dry in his but at the same time the way she entwined her fingers through his made his heart skip a beat. Mel feeling the strength in Billy's hand felt the same way. She walked a couple of inches taller as they made their way to Marcellos.

#

Billy made it on time the next morning but once again he waited in vain for someone to come and offer him work. He took his place on the Wall among the others and watched as the various bosses arrived on foot or in pick-up trucks. They were a widely diverse group of individuals, from men dressed in work clothes and overalls to others dressed casually in denim or in more formal clothing like suit trousers and open necked shirts.
He realised early on that most of these employers were regular visitors as they seemed to only be looking for certain people or groups, asking for them by name. Billy really couldn't blame them for wanting to use the same faces. If the job required explanation then having to explain to a totally new person everyday was a waste of time and energy, but it was frustrating to watch these people roll up and just collect people without even bothering to look at who else was available. The same went for the workers. Occasionally an employer would hold up a number of fingers showing he had need for extra help and leave it to the worker to pick his own crew. Again, the person restricted their choice to people that they knew and would pick their crew from among their friends.
The one advantage Billy did gain from that first day was an insight into the types of jobs that people were being hired for and more importantly the rates that were being paid. He overheard more than one exchange as he sat patiently waiting his turn to be approached, but again he waited in vain.
So, although, in the end, he was once again unlucky and remained

still seated on the wall when Mel swung by later on, he felt that the exercise had not been a complete waste of time.

There was also an interesting development that took place later in the day. After a day on the beach with Mel they had returned to the Peace Cafe in the late afternoon to have a drink. It was about the time that the majority of the workers were returning from the day's work. One group of five lads who had disappeared that morning in the back of a pick-up truck returned from their employment and if their dusty and slightly sun-burnt appearance was anything to judge by, they had spent the day working outside on some kind of construction site.. They arrived in a noisy group demanding jugs of beer to quench their thirsts. One of the crew knew Mel and came over to say hello. When he was introduced to the group he took a moment to look at Billy.

"You were on the wall this morning weren't you?" He had a broad Liverpool accent.

Billy who had just taken a mouthful of beer nodded.

"Any luck?"

Billy still with beer in his mouth shook his head.

"He doesn't say much, does he?" The bloke laughed at his own joke.

Billy who had now swallowed his beer opened his mouth to speak but was cut off.

"Well if you are serious and you can put in a good day's work then come by in the morning and I might be able to put you on the team. But be here early."

Billy stammered his thanks as the guy got up and walked away. Mel seemed pleased that Billy had at least the vague promise of work the following day.

"Do you know that guy?" Billy asked.

"Vaguely. He has been around here for six months or so. He's a bit of nutter when he's drunk."

"Aren't all scousers?" One of the others in the group asked. Billy looked up at the comment. It was one of the group he only knew vaguely, but from his accent he hailed from the London area.

"I think he has a particularly colourful past which he told us about in some detail one evening around the fire."

"Does he have a name?" Billy asked.

"Not sure. I think everyone calls him Scouser." There were several nods of agreement among the group.

"That's original," said Billy with a wry smile.

"Never trust a scouser, they're all thieves and scallys." This was the Londoner again.

"Ah come on Mick, that's a bit of stereotyping, do you just hate Liverpudlians or is it all northerners?"

"I don't discriminate. They are all heathens north of Watford Gap." Mick was smiling now so no one took him seriously.

Mel still felt that a forfeit should be paid and sent Mick to the bar for the next round.

Billy looked over at where Scouser had joined his mates and the beer was starting to flow. With his dark permed hair and his small pencil moustache he did look like the stereotypical scouse lad from central casting. All that was missing was the dayglow shell suit and the pimped-out trainers. Instead he was dressed like most of the others in the bar, in cast off or cut off volunteer blue, which showed off his muscles, his tan and his tattoos.

\#

The next morning Scouser was there with his usual crew. Billy nodded a greeting as he walked past but received no acknowledgement in return. Fearing that the offer from the previous evening had been forgotten he found a free space on the wall and plonked himself down. He had been hopeful that this morning he would get his big chance and had rashly spent all but the last few of his shekels the night before. Now there was mostly fluff, a couple of copper coins and two phone tokens rattling in his pocket.

He knew that Mel would always be there with a handout but he didn't want to always be waiting for her to reach for her money belt. Their relationship had still not got off the ground, they were still circling each other like a couple of wary animals, both afraid, apparently, of making the first move.

Billy got the impression that Mel thought he was still hung up on Blossom and Billy seemed unable to persuade her otherwise. He was deep in his misery when the guy sitting next to him thumped him on the arm. Billy turned on him with a flash of anger to realise the guy was pointing over at Scouser and his crew who were already aboard the pick-up. Scouser was waving madly in his direction indicating for Billy to join them.

Billy pushed off the wall and sprinted the short distance before vaulting over the tailboard and landing heavily in the truck bed. Someone banged on the roof and the vehicle lurched away, quickly picking up speed.

Willing hands helped Billy into an upright position and he wedged his back against the side wall leaning against the wheel arch for support as the pick-up went into the first bend. As they sped off into the rising sun Billy was introduced to the rest of the crew, a mixture of names and monikers that went in one ear and out the other. He knew that in a couple of days, if he lasted that long, he would get to know them but on that first day the only name that stuck was Scousers, mostly because he was sat in the centre of the truck and did most of the talking.

Nominally he was the team boss, and he took his orders direct from their employer. He also handled all the money and paid out the workers at the end of the day. He maintained that he enjoyed this privileged position as he was the only one who spoke Hebrew. Billy was about to mention that he also spoke the language, but at the last minute he decided to keep that fact to himself until he had seen a little bit more of the setup. He didn't want to tread on anyone's toes on the first day, particularly Scouser's as he was the guy who seemed to be calling the shots and he had just given Billy his first break.

Scouser explained, mostly for Billy's benefit, that they were working as a team on a site just outside Eilat where some new homes were being built. Most of the work was unskilled manual labour, fetching and carrying, digging ditches and other hard graft. Billy looked closely at his fellow passengers and noticed that most of them had hard callouses on their hands from long days wielding a pick or a shovel. Billy's own hands were hard enough but he knew that by the end of the day he would probably be exhausted and may have a few weeping blisters on his hands. He had not worked hard for a couple of weeks and it would take some time to get back into the swing of things.

Billy put that particular concern to the back of his mind as the pickup was slowing down and the others knowing they were approaching their destination were getting ready to disembark. They gathered in a circle with Scouser and his Israeli counterpart in the centre. The man was not introduced or given a name and he delivered a rapid stream of instructions to Scouser about the tasks

for the day. Billy stood there pretending he didn't understand a word of the exchange where actually he was absorbing every word. At least his Hebrew had not faded with lack of use. He hoped his muscles and stamina had fared as well.
After the briefing, the Israeli disappeared off to the site office and Scouser dealt out the tasks to them. Billy was the last to be assigned a task and Scouser led him over to where there was a huge pile of sand and a waiting shovel and a wheelbarrow.
"Right Billy, your task for the day is to shift this pile of sand all the way over there beyond that last house. The delivery truck dumped it in the wrong place."
Billy looked at the huge pile of sand and the distance he had to travel. Well that was him set for the day. He grabbed the shovel and made a start. After two solid hours and countless trips with the barrow he didn't seem to have made any impression on the pile. He was sweating freely his shirtless upper body streaked with sand, grit, dust and grime. His shoulder muscles were howling for a break and the palms of his hands were red raw. He was relieved when Scouser came by and told him to make his way over to the open-sided shelter where there was breakfast waiting for them. This was a very straight forward meal of boiled eggs, salad and pita bread but as well as the food, Billy was grateful for the respite. When the meal was finished they passed around a coffee pot that had been sitting on a fire just outside the shelter. The thick coffee was like treacle but Billy knew the raw caffeine hit would help give him a boost. One of the others produced a bottle from out of his pack and passed it around. People were tipping a generous measure into their tin cups.
Billy caught a glimpse of the label, it was a locally produced Israeli dark rum. Billy wasn't sure he was up to drinking and working in the hot sun but he was wary of alienating his fellow workers. In order to avoid any problem, he showed his hands palms upwards so everyone could see the mess the shovel had made of them.
"Mind if I use my tot as an antiseptic?"
The owner of the bottle nodded his head. "Go right ahead."
Billy remembered he had once heard a story about floggings in the British armed forces where the man after he had been punished was given a pint of rum with half poured down his throat to numb

the pain and the other half poured on his back to help sterilise the wounds.

In this case Billy didn't have a pint merely a shot so he used it all on his wounded hands.

It stung like hell and brought tears to his eyes, but slowly the palms began to feel better.

All too soon the break was over and they all returned to their various tasks. Billy, having had a brief rest was keen to get going again and attacked the sand pile like a maniac with the result that when Scouser came by again to tell him it was lunchtime Billy had finally made what looked like a visible dent in the huge pile. It was certainly enough to earn a favourable comment from Scouser.

"Wow Billy, slow down, you will make us all look bad."

"I doubt it."

"Well come on man it's lunchtime. A whole half hour to relax."

The break was again welcome although Billy had got more into the swing of things and somehow found his second wind. He was just hoping that an extended break would not give his muscles chance to cramp up.

There was queue to use the water tap so Billy took the time to do some stretching exercises, which gained him some funny looks from the rest of the crew. Billy took his turn at the tap, using the water to rinse the dirt from his hands and forearms before ducking his head under the stream and letting the ice-cold water run down his neck and under his shirt. He stood up and shook his head and followed the others to the shelter.

At some point during the morning someone had placed a large pot on the fire and this was now bubbling away nicely. Billy stared inside and saw the contents was a mixture of vegetables and pulses with a thick rich tomato sauce. The pot was lifted off the fire and placed in the middle of the shelter on an open patch of sand. They all gathered around the pot sitting or lounging on blankets and old foam mattresses.

The large flat breads were passed around and everyone tore of chunks which they used to dip in the food and eat. Tea was served in small glasses, fragrant with the large handful of fresh mint leaves that had been placed in the teapot at the last minute while it was still in the flames and boiling, left to infuse for a few minutes, while the tea cooled down, before being removed. The atmosphere was all very relaxing and the conversation matched the mood.

Inevitably as the newcomer to the group Billy was asked to tell his story. They all let him talk for a few minutes uninterrupted until he got to the part where he was expelled from the Kibbutz. At that point Scouser interrupted him.

"What for?"

"I beg your pardon?" Billy looked puzzled.

"What were you kicked off for?"

"Possession of Drugs." Billy was about to explain that the drugs weren't actually his and were in fact planted in his luggage by the real owners, when he noticed the overwhelming admiring looks and nods of approval passing between his workmates, so he decided he would leave that small detail out.

At this point the rest of them thought it was only fair to offer their own reasons for expulsion as to a man they had all be removed from their respective Kibbutzim for some form of misdemeanour, however small and mundane. No one, it seemed, had arrived in Eilat with the express wish of working in the black economy, well at least no one in the shelter was admitting to it.

The rest of the crew were expelled for a range of different offences ranging from drunkenness, to laziness, fighting or fucking the wrong person. It was an all too familiar story to Billy's ears, he had heard it retold, or variations of it, by nearly everyone he had met so far in Eilat.

Scouser was the only one who had not volunteered his reason. Later when Billy replayed the events in his mind he wondered whether Scouser had left his story to last for dramatic effect or whether maybe he was ashamed of what had happened and was reluctant to tell the story. Nevertheless, in short sentences the full story was revealed.

It had happened that Scouser had been working out in the fields on his Kibbutz when he had stopped his tractor to take a leak. As he was standing there he happened to glance down and to one side and spotted something lying in the long grass and tangle of weeds that grew wherever the Kibbutz had one of their standpipes for irrigation. He bent down for a closer look and discovered a pistol lying in amongst the weeds.

He picked it up and stuffed the weapon into the waistband of his trousers, climbed back on the tractor and continued on his way. By his own admission in a later, private conversation about the incident, with Billy, he couldn't remember why he didn't drive straight to the Administration building and hand over the weapon, instead choosing to return to his room and conceal the weapon among his personal belongings.

Being a teenage lad from one of the rougher areas of Liverpool he was familiar with guns and although he had never owned or carried one in his life he knew enough about them to make sure the weapon was unloaded and safe before he put it away.

He didn't tell anyone about his discovery, waiting to see if there were any comments made by the members or others about a missing weapon. No one made any mention. This made Scouser wonder where the weapon had come from and who had lost it.

Like everyone who had spent any time in Israel he was familiar with the presence of lethal weapons in everyday life. From the casually carried pistol in a holster at the waist, the Uzi nonchalantly slung over one shoulder like some deadly handbag or the more obvious long guns carried by the young soldiers in and out of uniform, the magazine fixed to the side with a heavy rubber band but ready for use in a moment should the need arise, these sights were a common enough occurrence that they had eventually lost their fascination after a few weeks even for the most ardent opponent of firearms.

Everyone carried if they were required to do so, but at the same time kept careful eye on their personal weapons. As young recruits, issued with their first personal weapon, every new soldier was made aware of the rules governing those weapons. Loss of a personal weapon was a serious offence and under the code of Military Justice, if a recruit could not prove he had lost his weapon, which would be totally impossible to prove, then it was assumed that he had sold said weapon to an enemy of the state and was therefore guilty of a treasonous act and sentenced to a long spell in military prison.

Recruits were encouraged therefore, to never let their weapons out of their sight. This first lesson stayed with most of the Israelis throughout their lives so for a weapon to have been mislaid and for no one to have made any mention of it was unusual to say the least. But if no one was going to come forward to claim it then Scouser felt it was reasonable for him to hang onto it and that was just what he did.

He kept the weapon secret for several weeks but then one drunken night during a disagreement with another volunteer he pulled the gun out of the wardrobe, still unloaded, and waved it in his antagonist's face. Confronted by a gun the aggressor had immediately backed down, backed away and fled the scene, but the damage had been done. You cannot produce a firearm, loaded or otherwise in a room full of drunken volunteers and not expect word of the incident to get to the wrong ears. And this was exactly what happened. The next day Scouser was challenged, his room was searched and the weapon and ammunition discovered. His fate was sealed when the Volunteer leader emerged from Scouser's room carrying the pistol and the clip of ammo.

It was at this point in the story that Billy sensed a new level of bitterness in Scouser's voice.

"The bastards waited there while I packed all my stuff and then took me out to the main road and dumped me."

It was only later when Billy had returned to his sand pile that he got his answer. Scouser was making his rounds in the afternoon checking on everyone's progress. He was also carrying a large water container and encouraging his team to take a short break and drink some water.

While Billy was taking a long swig of water Scouser asked him straight out.

"So, do you still do drugs?"

Billy swallowed and shook his head.

"Can I be honest with you? I never did drugs in the first place. The drugs belonged to someone else and the Volunteer leader, who I thought was my friend knew as much. Unfortunately, as the Police had got involved I had to take the fall."

"I knew it. I didn't think you were a stoner."

"I'm not, can't stand the stuff. Messed up too many of my friends and family when I was a kid."

"A bit like my childhood and guns. Too many young lives cut short by bullets and violence."

"Yeah it always seems to be the young that are the victims."

Scouser nodded his agreement. Although they came from different ends of the country it was clear that they both had similar experiences growing up, and that their Kibbutz dreams had been brought to an abrupt halt in the same fashion.

"And the worse thing," Scouser said retrieving the water container and screwing back the lid, "was that I really felt a part of the Kibbutz. I had been there over a year, worked hard, learnt the language and I was friends with loads of the Members, got invited to their homes, their parties, but in the end, none of them spoke up for me. I called up one good friend when I got here and she told me the story circulated after I left, was that I had broken in to some members house and stolen some money and the gun. But I found the gun lying there by the standpipe in the middle of a field, and I never took no money."

It was obvious to Billy that this aspect of the incident bothered Scouser much more than the actual fact that he had been expelled from the Kibbutz. In some way, it called into question a fundamental facet of his character and how he, in turn, diverged from the popular misconception that all scousers were thieving, drug addled, scallies.

Billy found he could empathise more with Scouser because it seemed that like him, the lad hadn't really broken any rules, he had maybe been naive to hang onto the gun instead of handing it in to the proper authorities, but his treatment like Billy's was still unfair, particularly given that both of them seemed to have contributed to the life of the Kibbutz and taken those extra steps to embrace their new lives and try and integrate into society. Of course, at this point Billy was still not ready to reveal his ability to speak the language. That piece of information he would keep to himself for the time being.

Scouser suddenly snapped out of his reverie, realising that the two of them stood idle, Billy leaning on the handle of his shovel, could be misconstrued by their gang boss.

"Here Billy you better get a move on. I need the rest of this sand moved by the end of the day."

Billy gazed forlornly at the huge pile in front of him. It was true that it had shrunk in size considerably from this morning but there were still some back breaking hours of work ahead of him. He grasped the shovel and bent his back to the task as Scouser went off to do whatever he had to do.

Billy surprised himself. After his chat with Scouser he got back into the swing of things, found fresh reserves of strength he didn't know he had, and slowly the sand pile shrunk in size. By the time the sun was setting towards the mountains in the west he was scraping the last of the sand together and depositing it into the wheelbarrow. He ran the last load over to the site of the new pile and dumped it out, bounced the barrow on its wheel to expel the

last traces of the sand, threw in the shovel which landed with a loud and satisfying clang and headed back to the main gate.
He appeared to have finished his task just in time as the rest of the gang were assembling outside the portacabin that served as the site office. Through the open door, Billy could see Scouser was in deep conversation with the gang boss. As they concluded their business and shook hands Billy saw an envelope pass between the two which Scouser folded and stuffed in the back pocket of his shorts. Billy guessed that it contained their payment for the days endeavours and he was not disappointed.
While the site foreman, who was also the driver of the pickup that would deliver them back to the Peace Cafe, went about his daily ritual of shutting and locking all the containers that contained the tools and equipment used on the site, Scouser gathered them all in a loose circle and dished out the money.
This was where Billy got his final shock of the day.
Outside the Peace Cafe earlier that day he had been offered fifty shekels for a day's work. This sounded quite a reasonable rate and given that he had absolutely no money he was not about to haggle about it and had accepted the offer. Now, at the other end of the day he was presented with forty shekels. When he asked about the missing ten he was told that this was a hiring tax paid to Scouser as the gang boss. It was payable for every day worked in the first week after which it dropped to five shekels a day until the end of the first month. After that if he is still on the crew he would be on full pay.
Billy knew he was in no position, financially, or otherwise, to argue with the rules but it did leave a slight sour taste in his mouth. He kept his own council for now but one of the others must have read something in Billy's facial expression because he was quick to point out that Billy was free to leave at any time and seek work elsewhere. Billy was, on the whole, happy with working with Scouser and so he said as much. Scouser obviously felt the same way as he smiled at Billy and offered an encouraging. "You done good today Billy."
They all piled into the back of the pickup and drove back to Eilat. When the truck pulled up outside the Peace Cafe, Billy saw Mel was waiting for him on the steps with a big smile on her face. Billy jumped out of the back almost before they had come to a halt and swept Mel up in his arms, spinning her around, before putting her

back on her feet and doing a slightly crazy samba-like dance with her and waving his arms above his head.

"You look happy."

"I got paid, I have money."

Scouser dug him in the ribs as he walked past into the bar area.

"Come on Billy the first round is on me."

Billy and Mel linked arms and followed the tall figure into the bar. When they all had their drinks, they found a spare table and all the crew sat down together. The first mouthful of beer tasted so sweet to Billy, washing away completely the dust and the heat of the day in one delicious golden torrent.

The second beer, bought by one of the other team members, joined the first as Billy sat there in amongst his new-found friends, relaxed and with an overwhelming feeling that at last, he had arrived. On top of this feeling of accomplishment Billy also felt a strong wave of tiredness sweep over him. He tried to stifle a yawn but it somehow escaped between his fingers.

Mel, who was sitting by his side on the bench seat, talking across the table to one of the others girls who had joined them, suddenly turned to Billy and smiled.

"Oh someone's a tired little bunny. You know you are going to be in all sorts of pain in the morning."

Billy hadn't really thought about it but he had to agree with her. He had put his body through a severe test today and pushed his muscles further than they had been pushed in a very long time. Billy could only nod as another yawn overwhelmed him. At the same time, he was conscious of the strong sense of camaraderie among the team and he didn't want that feeling to end, At the very least he didn't want to be the one to break up the party. He was aware that he was in danger of falling asleep where he sat and knew that to do that would open him to some merciless teasing from the rest of the lads.

He finished his beer and then stood up, offering to get the next round of drinks in. He went to the bar and ordered and then returned with the drinks on the tray. As he handed the cold frosted glass to Scouser he casually dropped the question.

"Will it be same time tomorrow?"

Scouser looked up at him weighing up his answer. He was waiting to see what Billy's reaction would be to the pause. Would he see desperation or indifference in his face? Billy guessed what was going on and tried to keep his facial expression neutral. For the most part, it worked.

Scouser cracked a smile.

"If you are here at 6 then you are on the team. Amiram wants a full team tomorrow."

"I will be here at six."

Mel stood up, finishing off the last of her beer as she did.

"Hey you don't have to leave the party. I am just going back to the shelter to sleep."

"It's OK I want to come with you." Mel placed her empty glass on the table.

Said like that across the table and in full earshot of everyone within a five-yard radius it was tantamount to a declaration of love and elicited an appropriate response from the rest of the group.

Billy and Mel left the Peace Cafe with the jeers and cheers of their friends ringing in their ears.

Back at the shelter they made their preparations for bedding down for the night. The camp was its usual lively self with plenty of noise and people moving freely between the shelters attracted like moths to the numerous fires that were alight. But their little corner of the camp was shrouded in darkness. The nearest fire was several metres away and although the occasional person passed their shelter, in the dark, it was for the most part quiet.

Billy had washed the worst of the dust and grime from his body at one of the beach showers and then used a plastic mug of water to clean his teeth spitting the minty froth into the undergrowth. With fresh clothes and fresh breath, he slid into his sleeping bag and then watched as Mel went through her nightly routine.

Even in the dark he caught a brief flash of bare legs as she dropped her trousers and then the moonlight caught her slender body in profile as she turned around and dropped down to slide into her own sleeping bag.

Once inside the bag she shuffled over to where Billy was lying, propped up, using his back pack covered with a sweatshirt as a pillow. She snuggled under his arm resting her head on his chest. Billy bent his head forward and kissed her hair.

"I don't think I have thanked you for the help you have given me so far."

Mel looked up at Billy.

"We should celebrate your new-found good fortune."

"How?"

"Well as everyone is now convinced we are shagging we might as well do it." Mel's hand snaked inside the sleeping bag and pulled up his t-shirt. She began to nuzzle his chest, planting small kisses there.

This was not quite the way Billy would have put it but he had to admit he was very fond of Mel and she was very sexy. He might have preferred to be the one to make the first move but under the circumstances it was Mel who had expressed the doubts about Billy and his relationship with Blossom so maybe it was better that the first move came from her. And as her hand went lower into his sleeping bag he found himself responding to her touch.

\#

Mel had turned on her side at some time in the night as the first thing that Billy noticed on waking was the firm curve of her warm bare buttocks pressed tightly against his thigh. Neither of them had redressed after sex and so both were still nude under the sleeping bag. They had pulled one over them as a cover, the second sleeping bag, Billy's, was open underneath them. Billy sat up slowly trying to maintain a modicum of decency for both of them as he searched for his shorts and t-shirt. His watch told him it was time for him to get up if he wanted to make it to the Wall on time. Mel mumbled something in her sleep as she turned over again. Billy slid out from the bed, replacing the covers and tucking them in well to cover her nakedness.

He pulled on his boots and grabbed his day pack and headed off up the beach to the Peace Cafe.

Scouser and two of the others were already there all looking like they had not made it to bed or if they had it had only a brief flirtation with the sandman. Billy was expecting a ribbing for disappearing so early and he was not disappointed. By the time Scouser and the other two had finished taking the piss about weak and feeble Southerners, the rest of the crew had arrived and they were all in the truck and on their way to the site.

The day on the site was another long, hot, back-breaking eight-hour shift with only the short respites of meal and water breaks. Billy felt the teasing he had to endure throughout the day was worth it as he watched his fellow crewmen struggling following their largely sleepless night. After the final water break of the day Billy realised he would have to tone down his exuberance and energy or make the others look bad. He did not want to cast them in a bad light as he genuinely wanted to remain part of this crew and he needed the work.

When they finally packed up their tools and climbed into the pickup for the journey back there was an exhausted silence among them all and back at the Peace Cafe they had one single drink before most of them disappeared off for some real sleep. Billy, still with money in his pocket and starving hungry went back to camp to find Mel, to shower and clean up before heading into the centre to find somewhere to eat.

The rest of the week continued in the same vein with work, mostly manual and heavy in nature as the site was prepared for the arrival of the cement mixers that would pour the concrete used to form the walls.

After his initial baptism as a spade man Billy was moved on to the team that was building the wooden cases that formed the moulds for the walls. In this process frames were erected and covered in sheets of plywood with voids, like the doorways and windows pre-cut and shaped in them. The flexibility of this process allowed for smooth arches and circular windows to be created.

When all the moulds had been built the team had a few days off while the concrete mixers arrived on site and got the majority of the pouring completed.

In those few days Billy managed to pick up a couple of days work elsewhere. It appeared that the gang bosses communicated with each other and that Billy's efforts on the building site had not gone unnoticed.

The first morning he was not required for the building site he approached the Wall with some trepidation. He knew that after the pouring was completed they would be back on the site to finish dismantling the moulds but until then he was at a loose end. He felt as he sat there among the rest of the workers that he was back at square one waiting for someone to pick him out. He did not have to wait very long. A large man with a florid face and a breathy whisper of a voice came and stood in front of him.

"Did you work for Amiram?"

"Yes I did." Billy stood up not out of any respect but out of need to get closer to hear what the man was saying.

"I have a small vineyard of grapes that need to be picked. Do you have any experience with grapes?"

Billy said yes automatically. He didn't know whether the three days he had spent picking grapes on a holiday in France at the age of fourteen would count as "experience" but he was willing to give anything a shot. All he could really remember about the process was that they were expected to taste a grape from each bunch before they cut it from the vine and after the first morning feeling sick to the stomach and from then on only tasting grapes when he thought someone was watching. That trip to the Gironde had been more memorable for his nightly fumbling's with the lovely Nathalie, the daughter of the owner of the guest house where they were staying, who taught him so much about love, not least being what it really meant to "French Kiss."

Beside the lingual ministrations of the beautiful Nathalie details of the rest of the holiday faded into insignificance.

Mention of money brought Billy back to present day Israel and the Wall in Eilat. The hand extended to seal the deal had the consistency and body of an oily limp fish. Billy shook it and then surreptitiously wiped his hand on his shorts as he followed the figure back to his ride. From the back, his new master appeared scruffy. His trousers, which may have in the past been part of a suit were now wrinkled, worn and shiny at the backs of the knees and stained in several places, as was the shirt, that might have, in its heyday, been clean crisp white cotton, but was now a sad off-shade of grey. A kippah was attached to thin greasy hair by a yellow gold hair slide.

The Subaru pickup that ferried them out to the vineyard was as wheezy and asthmatic as its owner, with probably only a slightly longer life expectancy than the former.

Once behind the wheel the driver had taken two long puffs on a blue inhaler but this seemed to have little or no effect on his breathing and as they drove along the highway out of Eilat Billy had to concentrate hard to pick up the few words that were exchanged.

The smallholder was explaining that he kept two small plots of land in the desert settlement, one with Mango trees and the other for a small vineyard.

Apparently, the Mango orchard had been due to start producing fruit this season but production had been set back a year by an over-zealous worker who had been set the task of pruning the young trees and had cut off most of the fruit bearing growth. With that single action the decision had been made to fire the volunteer and to instead use only occasional day labourers like Billy when the need arose. Billy offered a silent prayer of thanks to the Deadly Mango Mangler and wondered where the poor lad was now.

They were only about a half hour from the city limits when they took a right turn off the main highway and bounced their way along a desert track coming in a short time to the gates of small desert community. The gate, like so many of these isolated communities was guarded by a couple of soldiers in their green IDF uniforms and they obviously recognised the driver or the vehicle because they made no attempt to stop the Subaru or inspect the passengers.

Driving through the centre of the settlement was interesting for Billy. Here he could see the site he had been working on as recently as yesterday, as it would look after ten years of continual habitation. In the site office, there were photographs and architect's illustrations of the finished products with neatly trimmed lawns and tidy herbaceous borders, clean lines and brilliant white walls glistening in the sunlight.

The reality could not have been further from those "artists" impressions. The walls, after several years enduring sand laden desert winds had taken on an ochre quality. The lawns were far from the lush green of the mock ups being more faded grey, with patches of desert sand poking through in places. The clean concrete lines of the houses had been "developed" with temporary structures built from wood, corrugated tin and plastic sheeting, the yards filled with broken down and rusting machinery parts. The whole place had the tired air of a junkyard fallen on hard times. It was clear that the focus on this particular settlement was clearly not on the aesthetics but more on functionality.

Each property stood on its own plot of land with areas for cultivation situated to the rear of each of the houses. Each individual owner chose what they planted. There were some who had invested in green houses and were growing flowers or tomatoes, others had chosen to turn the whole acreage over to citrus fruits or vegetables.

There were only about two dozen houses in all and their destination was the last house on the sand track.

The Subaru wheezed to a stop outside the house and Billy was taken past the house, shown briefly where he could come and fetch drinking water. The single cold tap was mounted on the wall of a concrete box-like structure. The metal door was hanging open and Billy glanced inside. There were two spaces inside. One was a small square room with a raised concrete platform with a single foam mattress placed in the middle. The other was just a cubicle with a hole in the floor. The smell of rancid shit coming from that room left Billy in no doubt that this was some form of toilet. The presence of a rusted and worn out showerhead mounted halfway up the wall pointed to the room actually being a bathroom, although Billy could not imagine wanting to spend too long under a shower with that smell filling his nostrils, it really was appalling.

Overall Billy was shocked by the primitive conditions and that this was apparently the living quarters for the volunteers who had worked for this farmer. It made the worst rooms on Tel Boker look like the Hilton.

Billy shook his head and followed his employer. They emerged at the back of the house and before them lay the familiar serried ranks of grapevines. Beyond the vineyard stood the mango trees again in lines each one apparently linked to the other by its own dark plastic umbilical cord which fed it the water and nutrients it required to survive in the harsh desert environment.

There was a flatbed trailer parked at the end of the first row of vines and on the back, was a stack of blue plastic crates and a pile of unmade cardboard boxes.

After hearing the story of the Great Mango Massacre in some detail, Billy did not expect to be left alone and he was not disappointed. He was taken to the trailer showed the plastic crates and the clippers and then taken to the top of the first row of vines. As he stood and watched he was shown how to pluck and eat a grape, a task he could probably have managed on his own, until he realised that unlike before when the entire grape harvest had been intended to be used for wine production in the local chateau, these grapes were for eating. The farmer pointed out that the harvest was aimed at four target markets. The first, the export market was for only the best quality of grapes, but they needed to still be slightly sour, not totally ripe in order for them to reach their peak when they arrived at their destination, which might be on another continent.

The second crop was for the domestic market. These were grapes which had reached their peak of ripeness and the bunches retained their good form and shape. The third crop was for shipping to the markets in Gaza and the Occupied Territories. The fourth crop, which basically consisted of everything else, ripe, unripe, and overripe was earmarked for "Industry". Billy pondered that word for a while, wondering exactly which industry the farmer was talking about. Eventually he gave up and had to ask.
"Winemaking," was the simple answer. Billy thought back to the loving care shown by the crews at the French vineyard where the best grapes were taken for the wine production and even though he had just turned fourteen, he was allowed to sample some of the finished product there.
Comparing the vineyard wine to the awful wine he had so far come across since arriving in Israel he could now understand the huge difference in quality given the source and quality of the grapes used in the production process.
It was almost lunchtime before Billy was finally trusted to harvest some of the grapes alone, and even then, the farmer seemed to be loitering anxiously by the trailer every time Billy returned with a full crate of produce. He seemed to feel the need to act as Quality Control and pack the harvested grapes into the various boxes for the different markets. Billy found this lack of trust annoying at first but after a while he began to see things from the other viewpoint. This was the guys livelihood they were dealing with. He had every right to be cautious.
Billy was still undecided about his new employer as they approached lunchtime. He didn't know what to expect from him. He guessed that there would be no communal pot of food like they had enjoyed on the building site but having left the Wall that morning, without a single morsel of food, he was hoping to be offered some form of sustenance. He was sadly disappointed. When the farmer finally called a break for lunch he simply turned on his heels and disappeared inside his house, firmly shutting the door behind him, leaving Billy standing alone in the driveway. Billy having had nothing to eat since the previous evening could feel his stomach grumbling in complaint. Stranded like this in the middle of the desert, even having money in his pocket was of no benefit. He did contemplate banging on the door and asking if he could buy some food but decided instead to take a walk around and

explore his surroundings. He hadn't noticed a communal shop as they had driven through the settlement earlier in the day but it might be that such a place existed hidden away in some corner of the site.

With his farmer occupying what was the last plot before the perimeter fence and the open desert beyond, there was only one direction for Billy to head in and that was back up into the heart of the settlement. He could have made his way along the dirt track that sliced its way through the houses but he had already seen the whole place from that perspective on his way in, so, instead he stuck close to the perimeter fence and walked along the backs of the individual dwellings. This gave him a much better idea of what each of the individual smallholders utilized their land for.

If the view from the roadway on the journey in had revealed a settlement beset with a general air of shabbiness, the view from this side was little improved and only tempered to some degree by the presence of well-tended fields of living, growing crops and orchards heavy with ripening fruit. Where not actively in use for cultivation the land was dry, dusty or overgrown and choked with weeds and scrub grass.

But what became clear to Billy very quickly was that the sandy desert soil could with the simple addition of water become a fertile medium for raising robust crops. Everywhere he looked he could see the evidence of this small miracle. Some places were still in the middle of the process where an open patch of sand had either just been cleared and was being irrigated, small seedlings had been planted in neat rows between wooden stakes and trailing wires or in one or two cases where the plants had grown up among the wires and there were the first signs of the ripening fruit visible through the green foliage.

On the plot, directly next-door to where Billy was working the tomatoes were already ripe and judging by the fruits Billy could see, would need picking very soon.

Billy was wondering whether he could approach the owner and offer his services. It might mean another couple of days work after he had finished with the grape harvest. He was about to cut up between the rows of tomatoes in search of the farmer when a small wiry man emerged from the opposite direction. He was obviously as startled by Billy as Billy was by him.

The two stopped abruptly in their tracks each one eyeing the other warily. Billy studied the newcomer. He was small in stature with a dark, weathered face tanned to the consistency of old leather by the sun. He sported a flourishing dark bushy moustache and his red and white head covering or Keffiyeh marked him as an Arab. This far south he was unlikely to be a Palestinian and more likely, Billy thought, to be Bedouin. Billy knew next to no Arabic except for the traditional greeting and how to say thank you. He tried the greeting first and was greeted in return with a gleaming smile and a response. The Bedouin having studied Billy decided to be forthright.

"I have no English."

"Hebrew?" Billy offered in that language and was rewarded by a furious head nodding and another smile.

Although Billy had kept his ability with the Hebrew language a secret for the most part since his arrival in Eilat, he felt safe revealing himself to this older Bedouin and who knew what valuable information he might gain from him.

The Bedouin in turn welcomed someone he could talk with who was not in a position of control over him.

Billy noticed that the Bedouin had a handful of fresh picked tomatoes in his hands. The Bedouin noticed Billy looking hungrily at them.

"Have you had lunch?" he asked.

Billy shook his head. "No food."

The Bedouin smiled at him. "Come and eat with us we have plenty of food."

He turned around and headed back among the row of ripening tomatoes. Billy followed the man, feeling and hearing his stomach rumble with anticipation. It was not far to where the Bedouin had set up their camp. Billy smelt the cooking food before he saw the fire.

The fire was small in size and there was a single pot nestling in the edge of the coals, a tantalising, single wisp of steam curling upwards like the smoke from a cigar. On the other side of the fire an upturned metal pan was being used to bake the traditional flat bread. A woman in full black, her face and head covered was tending to the bread.

The Bedouin whose name was Suleiman introduced his wife Fatimah to Billy. Billy made no move to shake hands, knowing that would be too familiar a gesture so he placed his hand over his heart and bowed his head in greeting.

Suleiman was busy explaining who Billy was as he handed over the tomatoes to his wife. She in turn made short work of them, slicing them into small pieces before scrapping the contents of the chopping board into the stew pot and giving the whole thing a stir with a wooden spoon. Suleiman had indicated a place on a blanket where Billy could sit down and as he watched the final preparations for the meal, the old Bedouin handed him a glass of mint tea. It was hot and overpoweringly sweet but remarkably refreshing.

In no time at all the pot was hauled out of the fire and placed on the ground where they could all reach it, the bread torn up and placed in an orange plastic bowl to one side.

They ate in silence, Billy savouring every mouthful. In the pot was a mixture of tomatoes, aubergines and potatoes and some herbs and spices.

It was hot on the tongue from the fire but also had a residual warmth from the spices. Every time he emptied his tea glass it was refilled from the kettle by either Suleiman or his wife. Billy was able to eat his fill without problem and when they had all had sufficient Fatimah set about the task of clearing up. The remaining contents of the pot were emptied into a plastic Tupperware container and the pot was washed out.

The remaining bread was folded into a tea towel and container and bread packet were placed in a leather shoulder bag. While this was being done Billy and Suleiman sat on their blankets and chatted together. Suleiman was relaxed puffing on a cigarette as he talked. Suleiman, true to Billy's estimations, was a goldmine of information on the settlement. He told Billy about his own farmer, whose name was Eli. He ran a successful real estate business from an office in downtown Eilat, selling mostly holiday apartments and condominiums to wealthy clients from Israel's major cities.

Billy hearing this took a moment to glance up at the house that sat on this particular plot. He noticed something he had not seen before. This property of all of them he had taken notice of seemed to be a cut above the rest. There was no overgrown yard or tumbledown, ramshackle structures. This house was all tidy gardens and clean lines. It was sharp contrast to the property next door.

Suleiman was also able to enlighten Billy about the man he was working for. First, he told him his name, only his family name, because the two had never been introduced and the family name was all he had ever heard Eli use when referring to him. Weismann was, according to Eli, not a very nice person. He was mean, greedy and resentful. His greed had most likely led to his resentment because in the past he had been one of the senior officials at the local desert desalination plant and had been fired after there was an investigation into corruption.

The loss of this salary had left Weismann entirely reliant on the revenue he could generate from his small holding and this had turned him into a penny-pinching miser. Though he did not go as far as to say it, he hinted heavily that Billy should watch his step as Weismann would look for any excuse to escape paying him.

Billy checked his watch and saw he still had fifteen minutes before he needed to be back at work. He wanted to use the time usefully. "So my friend," he turned to Suleiman, "tell me about life as a Bedouin in the Negev."

Suleiman had seen Billy look at his watch so he looked Billy straight in the eye.

"We don't have enough time today to do the subject justice but if you are here tomorrow come and eat with us again and we can make a start."

Billy took the hint and stood up. He thanked both the Bedouin profusely for their hospitality and then picked his way back through the tomato rows until he was back on the Weismann plot. He was sitting on the back of the trailer waiting when Weismann appeared.

\#

The rest of the afternoon passed uneventfully and at the end they drove back downtown in silence. Billy didn't feel there was any bad feeling between them, they had both attended to their allotted tasks and although no praise had been forthcoming Billy had not expected any. It was not that anything between them had changed it was just there was nothing for them to say. Outside the Peace Cafe Billy sat while Weismann counted out his money. It was a slow process as he only had small bills. All the time that he was laying the bills down on the central console Billy was waiting to be

asked about the following day. He didn't think he had performed badly and there was definitely at the very least another day of work at the vineyard, maybe two. Weismann remained silent as he handed over the money and it was not until Billy reached for the door handle that he suddenly spoke.
"Are you interested in work tomorrow?"
Billy stopped his hand pressed down on the handle, the door already half open, his body was half turned ready to climb out. He was surprised by the sudden question and collapsed backwards into the seat.
"I thought you would never ask," was on the tip of his tongue. Instead he turned his head toward Weismann.
"Yes that would be great. The same time as this morning?"
Weismann simply nodded his head.
Billy swung the door fully open and climbed out onto the pavement. He shut the door and the Subaru rattled off into the distance.
Billy turned on his heels and went inside the cafe to get a cold glass of beer.
A couple of the regulars were in the bar and once he had collected his drink he went to join them and he was still with them and a little bit the worse for wear when Mel came and found him.

\#

The following morning, he was at the Wall by the time Weismann pulled up in his asthmatic truck. There was no need to go through any formalities. Billy opened the door and climbed in. Weismann bid him a good morning, took his habitual two puffs from his inhaler and put the truck in gear. This morning both truck and driver seemed more congested than normal and there was an occasional misfire from the engine compartment and a wheezing rattle from the driver. Billy sat mute in the passenger seat trying frantically to remember prayers he had not had cause to utter in many a long year.
God was on his side and both vehicle and driver made it to the settlement without either expiring, and Billy set about the days tasks. Today they were mostly focusing on the second crop. This was the grapes that were to be sold into the domestic market.

These needed to be slightly riper but still in good shape and with nicely formed bunches.

As they progressed down the rows with the blue bins he was looking at what was being left behind. He reckoned that if there was a third and fourth crop from this vineyard then he could probably squeeze one more day of work out of Weismann, but that would depend on whether he chose to finish the job off himself, although given the state of the guys asthma and his general sickly appearance Billy doubted if the guy would be physically equal to the task.

Billy didn't slack off and worked hard through the morning. When it was time for lunch Billy went off in search of Suleiman and his wife.

It was not difficult to find them he just followed his nose towards the rich smell of fresh baked bread. The two were sitting in the same shaded area as they had been the previous day, the small fire alight and the bread baking on the upturned metal pan.

Suleiman spotted Billy and got to his feet to greet him, they shook hands and he indicated Billy should take his place.

True to his promise after they had satisfied their initial hunger Suleiman began to tell Billy about life as a Bedouin in Israel. He started with a short history lesson describing how things had changed for his family after the state of Israel had been created and how in the past decades life had dramatically changed for the Bedouin people. He was neither critical nor supportive of the Israeli state merely stating things in an objective manner, offering no personal opinion on the matter.

One thing was clear to Billy and that was that Suleiman respected his Israeli employer and was pleased he had the job here in the settlement.

He asked Billy to tell them a little bit about himself so Billy went through a brief history of his life over the last year or two. He edited out the reason for his expulsion from the Kibbutz, not because he was ashamed to tell the truth but more because he felt there was no relevance in it.

Before they knew it, the break was over and Billy was back at work with the eternally silent Weismann. Billy was correct in his estimation and by the end of the second day they still had at least one more pass to make through the vines to remove the last of the grapes. Weismann said as much as they were driving back towards

Eilat. Unusually for him he seemed to want to talk a little and he asked Billy what he would do after he had finished the work on the following day.
Billy was honest.
"I will be back on the Wall again trying to get some more work."
Weismann nodded his understanding.
"Well if anyone asks me I can tell them where to find you. Are you staying in a hostel in town?"
"No I am sleeping at the camp on the beach. But if you need to get hold of me leave a message at the Peace Cafe and I am sure I will get it."
"I don't think I will have any more work this season but one of the other famers might need a hand and I will certainly recommend you to them."
This praise, from such an unexpected source, was still ringing in Billy's ears as he entered the Peace Cafe and spotted Mel sitting at one of the tables.
She waved to Billy and made the sign for a Beer and pointed to herself. Billy did the honours and presented her with a large cold beer and received a passionate kiss of thanks, before taking his place at the table.
The following morning Weismann was back to his silent uncommunicating old self again so Billy sat in silence all the way from the Peace Cafe out to settlement. He didn't need to be briefed anymore so he set about the days tasks as soon as they arrived.
There was no way that Billy could make the work last more than another day and this much was apparent as they started on the final pass through the vines. Most of what was left was unsuitable for sale as grapes and was therefore consigned to the blue boxes for industry. This was stalks, over-ripe grapes, leaves and all, everything was just cut off and tossed in the box. The smell of the crushed fruit was quite nauseating.
Billy had all but finished the task by lunchtime so he went off in search of Suleiman. He found the old Bedouin talking to another man in smart slacks and crisp white shirt. The neat haircut and the aviator shades led Billy to believe that this was the owner of the next-door property, Eli. He was not wrong and Suleiman waved Billy over so he could introduce him.

Billy approached and Eli turned to face him. The first thing Billy noticed was the open and friendly smile that greeted him. The voice was rich and had the slightest hint of amusement in its tone.
"Hello Billy I have heard a lot of good things about you." A hand was extended in Billy's direction and he took it. The grip was firm and confident. More importantly the palm was dry and warm.
"Hello," Billy felt slightly shy in the tall man's presence.
"I hear you have been helping Weismann the last few days."
"Yes I have just finished his grape harvest."
"So it is your last day here."
"It looks that way."
"Well I might have some work for you."
Billy panicked for a moment, shooting a worried look at his Bedouin friend. He feared that Suleiman and Fatimah would be out of a job. Eli picked up on the fear in Billy's eyes noticed the surreptitious glance.
"No not here on the farm. At some of my sites downtown. Suleiman tells me you worked in the swimming pool on your old Kibbutz."
Billy looked worried again but now for another reason. If Eli knew about the Kibbutz, he might contact Yossi or someone else from the Kibbutz staff for a reference and then the whole drug story would come out.
"I have several condo's in the town which have communal swimming pools. There might be a vacancy for a pool boy coming up soon. If you are interested."
Billy took a moment to gather his thoughts before he spoke.
"I want you to know I would be happy to talk to you about work if a vacancy arises. From what I gather Weismann would be happy to give me a reference if you ask him."
Billy was thinking on his feet and hoping he had avoided the need for Eli to contact Tel Boker. He knew that if anything came of this offer then he would have to come straight out and tell Eli the whole story, more for his own peace of mind than anything else.
"And I gather you are working from the Wall by the Peace Cafe."
"Yes I will be back there tomorrow looking for a new job."
"Well at least I know where I can find you. How long are you planning to stay in Eilat."
Billy thought about his missing Passport and the restrictions that placed on any travel plans.

"For the foreseeable future." Billy smiled inside. It was not a lie as such, more the truth with a huge hole in it.

"Ok Good. Well I must be off now. Nice meeting you Billy."

"Likewise."

Billy stood beside his Bedouin friend as they watched Eli disappear around the side of the house. A moment later he heard the sound of a powerful truck engine starting and that in turn faded into the distance.

"Congratulations Billy." Suleiman smiled at him.

"I haven't got anything yet." Billy was not ready to start celebrating until he had heard a concrete offer.

"You will like working for Eli. He's a very fair boss."

The two new friends went in search of Fatimah and some warm food.

CHAPTER seventeen

The sweat was pouring off Billy's forehead and into his eyes, the salt making them sting. He looked down at his hands, covered in evil smelling slime almost up to his biceps. There was no way he could use either hand to wipe the sweat from his face, not until he had cleaned some of them muck off them.
Billy blinked several times rapidly, hoping this might ease the stinging pain and then tried to shake his head to clear some of the sweat but this just made things worse, if that was possible.
He looked around him at the location. He was in a deep culvert the vicious sun bouncing off the sheer concrete sides turning the whole place into a broiling oven.
Billy bent down for the umpteenth time that day and stuck his arm up another outflow pipe grabbing for the mass of sand and other unsavoury debris that was blocking it and pulling the whole stinking mass free and then shaking the gooey mess off his hands and arms.
Unseasonal and unusually heavy rain had hit Eilat a few days ago. It had been a miserable time in the camp as some shelters had proved unable to withstand the deluge and had collapsed on their inhabitants.
Billy and Mel's own shelter had survived but only just. At one point a large build-up of water had threatened to tear through the thin sheeting but a bit of teamwork from all the inhabitants had forced the water off the roof and saved the shelter.
Other inhabitants in other shelters had not been so lucky and when the rain had finally stopped and the clouds had cleared away to the North the camp had looked like a disaster area. Non-stop sunshine ever since had largely dried out the site and where possible repairs had been made to the shelters and some semblance of order had been restored.

Elsewhere in the city, they had also suffered as a result of the heavy rain. Many drains had been unable to cope with the sheer volume of water and others like the culvert Billy was currently clearing had been backed up with flood water and then choked with sand.

As the water level rose the sand was clogged up in the outflow pipes and these in turn were blocked and backed up. Additionally, the sheer volume of water had caused some of the sewers to overflow and this waste water had made its way into the runoff system. This was why Billy was forced to literally wade through wet sand and shit to clean out these runoff pipes.

The day had started normally with Billy taking his place on the wall and waiting with the others. Since working for Weismann, he had waited every day for Eli to come and offer him work as a pool boy but every morning he was disappointed. Instead he had gone back with Scouser to the site to remove all of the wooden claddings once the concrete walls had been poured and had time to dry.

He had worked other jobs around that building site as well but now the project had reached a point where they needed skilled carpenters and electricians to fit out the houses, neither of which Billy was qualified to do.

Scouser had been upbeat about their prospects of being recalled to the site in a couple of weeks when the houses had been fitted out as there would be work painting the houses both inside and out and plenty of other manual work as the site was cleared up and prepared for the first residents to move in. But in the interim, most of the crew were back looking elsewhere for employment.

A couple had taken off to Sinai for a while in order to renew their visas. A trip across the border into Egypt, even for a few days, and one returned through the Taba border checkpoint with a fresh three-month visa. If you went to the local post office in Eilat and renewed your visa they only gave you a one-month extension and you had to pay for it.

Billy could not join them as he didn't even have a Passport. Instead he went back to the Wall and picked up the next available labouring job.

And then the rains had come and now he was up to his elbows in shit and regretting his decision to get out of his sleeping bag this morning.

The guy who had approached him had told him it would be heavy work and might be a bit smelly but he had handed Billy a spade and bucket. What neither of them had realised was that the spade was too wide to fit inside the outflow pipes and the sand too dense and waterlogged for anything non-metallic to move it. Billy had tried everything he found lying around.

Sticks of varying thickness had all broken into pieces, a piece of heavy plastic pipe had just bent in the middle, even a piece of thin metal that Billy had found had only lasted a short time before bending and then breaking when he tried to straighten it. No there was no alternative he had to bend down and stick his arm up the pipe and scoop the sand out with his hands.

He finished the pipe he was cleaning and straightened up. He glanced over his shoulder towards the start of the culvert and counted the number of outflow pipes he had already cleared and then subtracted it from the total number he had counted at the start of the day.

Good News, he was just over halfway. He reached up and pulled himself out of the culvert and onto the grass verge. Across from where he was sitting was one of the stand pipes used for irrigating the plants in this part of the city. Billy had hung his backpack on it and the spade and bucket were lying uselessly on the grass beside it. He crossed the green and opened the tap washing the muck from off his arms and hands. As soon as one hand was clean, he used it to wipe his forehead and rub his eyes.

With the sludge washed off his arms Billy noticed that some of the horrible smell dissipated, some, but unfortunately not all. He could see he had effluent stains on his clothes and on his legs as well as on his boots.

He reached for his backpack and unzipped it pulling out the large cold bottle of water from inside and taking a long drink. He had brought a filled pitta bread with him to eat for lunch but, if he was honest with himself the smell from the culvert had removed his appetite. He, therefore, resolved to finish the job and then sit and enjoy his sandwich.

He climbed back down into the squidgy mess at the bottom of the channel and continued with his grim task.

He took a further break a little later when he felt that he was starting to get dehydrated from the heat and finished off the rest of the water, but it was already late in the afternoon when he finally stood up from the last of the pipes and scrambled out of the watercourse for, he hoped, the last time. He cleaned himself up as best he could at the water tap and then set off for the walk across town to the Peace Cafe.

This was the arrangement he had made with the guy who had hired him and as he walked he could see why the arrangement had been made this way.

That morning he had been driven across town to the location but he couldn't see anyone in their right mind wanting to share even the shortest of car journeys with him, not the way he smelt right now. He had been given a number to ring when he finished the job and then the guy would come by the Peace Cafe with his money.

As he walked through the centre of Eilat he was aware of the funny looks he was getting from anyone who passed close enough to smell him so he should not have been surprised by the reaction when he walked into the cafe a little later.

The place was half full mostly with the after-work crowd so there was a general level of noise as people regaled each other with stories of their days labours. Like any group there were those with positive stories of the day's small victories and the nay-sayers with their accounts of the day's defeats and disasters.

To have been a casual observer, a fly on the wall might have been amusing, because as Billy made his way through the bar towards the table where Mel and her crowd were sitting, the whole place went silent. Not all at once but conversation slowly petered out in Billy's wake, like he was dragging some sort of bow wave behind him.

Billy, with his eye on the prize, that prize being the first of many thirst quenching beers, was oblivious to the silence expanding behind him and it was only when he presented himself in front of Mel that the truth came out.

"My God Billy," she held her nose, "You stink of shit."

Billy pulled a face. It was not the reception he had been hoping for. Behind him people were beginning to find their voices and adding to the general uproar of complaints.

"I don't smell that bad." Billy said lamely in his own defence. He could see the cool frosted glass of beer that he had been dreaming of for the last couple of hours disappearing like some Holy Grail, hidden again from all but the worthiest of souls.

"Trust me Billy," Mel sounded nasal as she spoke due to the fingers pinching her nose closed. "You smell awful. Go take a bath with your clothes on."

"Can't I just have one beer first."

"No" the collective negative explosion came from multiple sources and hit Billy like a shock wave, knocking him backwards.

He had no alternative so he fled the scene and hurried down to the camp, grabbed some soap and ran for the beach. He went into the sea fully clothed and used the strong soap to wash his clothes as he stood up to his thighs in the water. After washing and rinsing his clothes he undressed and then washed his body with the same soap. He emerged from the waves with only a pair of boxer shorts on and an armful of wet clothes. He wrapped a towel around his waist and walked back to the shelter. The clothes he spread on the roof to dry and he quickly redressed in some dry clothes.

"That's better," Mel greeted him with a smile when he returned to the bar a half hour later, his hair still wet from his bath. She leaned over the table to kiss him on the lips.

"I will have that drink now." She smiled sweetly at him.

He went to the bar and ordered them a couple of beers.

Harriet, a fellow English girl who served behind the Bar looked up at Billy as he approached.

"Hi Billy, what can I get you?"

Billy placed his order. While she was filling the two glasses she looked up.

"Someone came by here this afternoon looking for you. Said they might have a job for you."

"Oh yeah." Billy's ears pricked up at the news.

"Yeah, I think they left a number for you to ring."

Harriet placed the two drinks on the bar top and took Billy's money. When she returned with his change she was holding one of the paper napkins from the dispenser on the bar. Someone had written a number in pen on it.

Billy looked at the number and looked up at Harriet.

"Is that a seven or a nine?"

Harriet looked at the number.

"It's a seven, no wait, it could be a nine."

Billy looked up at her. "Thanks, that is a great help." His voice dripped sarcasm.

Harriet smiled at him with a twinkle in her eyes. "You are welcome." She turned to serve the next customer.

Billy pocketed the napkin and picked up the drinks.

He returned to the table placing the drinks down and taking a seat. "Did you get the message?" Mel asked.

"Yes I did." Billy patted the shirt pocket where the napkin nestled along with the other scrap of paper he had been given that morning. So now he had two phone calls to make.

"Anyone got any phone tokens?" he said to the table at large.

There was a payphone just across the road from the Peace Cafe but in order to use it you needed the special phone tokens, asimonim. Billy asked around the table and people dug in pockets and belt packs. A few rattled onto the table top and Billy scooped them all up. He ambled across the road and waited while the person using the phone finished her call. When she replaced the phone, and stepped aside Billy stepped up. He lifted the hand set. It was still warm from the previous user as he pressed it between his shoulder and ear. He reached for the business card he had been given earlier in the day and laid it down where he could see and read the number. He dropped a couple of tokens in the slot and dialled the number. The phone rang a couple of times and then was answered. The token clicked as it dropped and Billy spoke.

He arranged to meet the guy who owed him money for the today's work in half an hour. He had already been by the site and was satisfied with the work. Billy was pleased that his work had been approved as he had no desire to go back to that site any time soon. When he rang off he dialled the number on the napkin. There was no name written on the napkin but he was hoping that the number belonged to Eli and that there was some good news.

The phone rang several times before it was answered, by a woman. This caught Billy off guard and he stumbled over his words, eventually managing to stammer out his name.

Fortunately the person on the other end was a little more clued in and was able to ask him to hold on while she went and got her husband. She obviously made some comment to him because when he picked up the phone there was trace of humour in his voice.

"Hello Billy, this is Eli. Sorry if my wife fooled you, but she was closest to the phone. I was out in the backyard."

Billy instantly conjured up images of the happy family at home with the wife in the kitchen preparing the salad while her husband

stood tongs raised over the barbecue watching the meat sizzle on the hot coals. It was a million miles from the life Billy was leading right now, and a long way removed from anything he had ever experienced up until now, except those odd weekends over the summer when Mike's parents had held open house parties.
He was grateful that the phone prevented Eli from seeing his red cheeks. He had managed to gather himself together enough to ask what Eli wanted him for.
"Do you remember I mentioned the possibility of coming to work for me."
Billy had thought about nothing else since their earlier conversation but he merely said he remembered. He didn't want to appear over eager or even worse, desperate but the smell of the sewage from today was still fresh in his nostrils, and the prospect of getting a regular job and not having to trust his well-being to the daily vagaries of the Wall were overwhelming him. Despite all this he tried to appear cool.
They arranged to meet the following morning at a cafe in the centre of Eilat at ten. They could discuss the job, the terms and conditions and then take things from there. Billy replaced the phone. He punched the air in elation as he crossed the road back to the bar. A late start meant he could have a few drinks tonight and then sleep late in the morning.
And that was exactly what he did although as he ambled towards the Cafe Razz the next morning the dull throbbing behind his eyes made it clear it was probably not the smartest idea he could have come up with. It was already hot on the streets and he was definitely feeling dehydrated. He walked onto the terrace in front of the cafe and spied Eli sitting over to one side near the back. Eli looked up saw him and waved. Billy went over and the two shook hands before taking their seats. A waiter was hovering near by, waiting to take their orders. Billy ordered a water and a coffee, Eli ordered just a coffee. They made small talk about the weather until their drinks arrived. After the first mouthful of coffee Eli became more focused.
"Okay Billy I mentioned to you that I might be looking for someone to look after the swimming pools in my apartment buildings. Are you still interested?"
Billy was interested but he wanted to find out a little bit more about what was involved before he committed himself. He also

wanted to know what had happened to his predecessor and why they were no longer on the payroll.

But to start off on a positive note Billy indicated that he was interested in hearing more about what was on offer.

Eli launched into a speech he seemed to have delivered many times in the past. He started off with a brief resume of his business and personal achievements over the last decade that culminated with the acquisition of six properties in the Eilat area, all residential blocks, a mixture of longer term leases for a couple of years and short-term holiday leases lasting a couple of weeks. Each property was serviced by a team of cleaners and maintenance crews that included the gardens. Billy's role would be the upkeep of the pools and pool areas.

In that job, he would be expected to visit each of the sites in the morning and ensure that the pool area was clean, the sun loungers were all set up in rows and the parasols were put up. After this was completed he would revisit two of the properties and clean the pools of sand and any organic debris and wash down the patios and adjacent walkways. At the end of the day he would do a closing round to put down any parasols not still in use and do a general tidy up. He would be required to be flexible and be available to attend any of the sites if there was an emergency with the pool or if something needed cleaning up. Billy didn't want to dwell too deeply on what that might entail so he mentally put that to one side. He would cross that bridge when he got there.

"Is there anything I am saying that you are unhappy about?" Eli looked at Billy.

"No it all sounds great." Billy was trying to keep his face non-committal but inside he was jumping for joy. This was the perfect job and if it meant he no longer had to sit on the Wall every day and take whatever shit job was offered him, then he would be one happy boy.

"OK great." Eli reached down the side of the table and picked up a plastic bag that had remained unseen until now.

"I do hope you don't think I was too presumptuous but I was hoping you would agree to my terms so I took the liberty of bringing these along this morning."

He tipped the contents out onto the table. There were several items of clothing all wrapped in individual plastic bags. Billy counted three bags with t-shirts and three with shorts.

Eli placed his hand on the pile.

"I took a guess at your size but I think these will fit you fine. I expect you to wear this uniform when you are on duty. There are three sets and you can use the laundry facilities at the properties to wash your clothes. I do expect my staff to be well turned out."

Billy looked at the shirt in the top packet. He could see it was a turquoise blue in colour and there was a stylised EZ in script on the left breast. Underneath there was the word Apartments in both English and Hebrew.

"Foot wear is optional, either sandals, flip-flops or trainers. You choose. Payday is every Friday, in cash. Do you have enough to tide you over until this Friday or will you need and advance?"

Billy knew he had enough cash to last him until pay day, if he was careful, and he said as much.

"Excellent. Well, in that case all that remains is for you and I to sign the contract."

Eli produced a couple of printed sheets from a document wallet that was lying on the table. He passed a copy over to Billy. Billy scanned the text, it was only a single page in length, pretty standard text. He did a small double take when he saw the figure written in the salary section, it was more than he had expected to be paid so he signed the bottom of the document willingly. Eli signed his name on his copy and then they swapped the contracts over and signed again.

"That's your copy to keep."

Billy folded the paper and put it into his belt pack. Eli had repacked the uniforms into the carrier bag and handed the handles to Billy.

"Right have you got anywhere you need to be this morning?"

Billy had made a loose arrangement to meet Mel on the beach later for lunch but it was a vague agreement and she wouldn't mind if he didn't turn up, so he shook his head.

"OK well then I will take you round and show you the properties and introduce you to some of your new colleagues."

The bill had already been paid so they gathered up their stuff and left the cafe. Outside on the street there was a line of parked cars. At the far end of the line was a blue Subaru pickup. Billy headed towards it.

"Where are you going? This one is mine." Eli was standing beside a very expensive looking white Mercedes saloon with tinted windows. He opened the door and climbed in. Billy went around and got in the passenger seat. The car was cool inside almost as soon as the engine started and the air-conditioning unit kicked in. Air blown through small holes in the leather upholstery cooled the back and legs.

Billy had never ridden in a Mercedes so he sat back in the lap of luxury for what was an all too short journey to the first property. They visited all six properties in turn and Billy met and shook hands with a whole host of people whose names he knew he would have forgotten by the following day.

As they left the last property Eli asked him if there was anywhere he could drop him off.

Billy couldn't resist the temptation and asked to be driven to the Peace Cafe. He was just hoping there was someone who knew him sitting outside when he pulled up in this sweet ride. Sure enough, there were a couple of familiar faces sitting on the terrace when he pulled up and climbed out. The Mercedes purred away into the distance and Billy climbed the steps.

He was met with a stream of banter and abuse which he ignored and he went inside anxious to tell Mel the good news. He looked around the room but there was no sign of her. He went up to the bar and asked if anyone had seen her. The bar staff said they hadn't seen her all morning. Billy went back outside and received another stream of abusive comments which he took on the chin. When they finally gave up he repeated his question.

Two of the patrons said they had seen Mel heading for the beach earlier with a towel and a book and that she was probably still there. Billy left the bar and headed down towards the beach.

When he was asked about it later Billy had no recollection of anything out of the ordinary. He was walking tall for the first time in many months. He had secured a decent job with a decent wage and he had done so on his own back and through his own hard work and effort. He was excited anticipating sharing his latest good fortune with Mel and was oblivious to anything, focused fully on finding his friend and sharing his good news.

The first indication Billy had that something was not right was when the first ambulance sped past him heading at full speed towards the seafront.

CHAPTER eighteen

A second ambulance, a couple of police cars and then two jeeps packed with fully armed soldiers passed him next in quick succession, all heading in the same direction.
About one hundred and fifty metres from the beach he met the first survivors, those who had been close by but not directly involved. They were flocking in the direction of the main city centre in droves, some excited, others with a look of terror in their eyes, but all of them talking at once. They would be the ones who would be dining out on their proximity to the incident for the next few years.
After the initial flood of the survivors came the next group, the walking wounded. They were not necessarily physically injured. Although some were covered in blood it was clearly not their own. Billy fought his way through this crowd with a mounting sense of panic. In the distance, he could see that all of the emergency service vehicles had come to a stop on the beach front and that they were in the process of setting up a cordon of plastic tape effectively sealing off the beach close to where the camp was located. The camp itself was outside the cordon but the tape sealed off the area of the beach just below it.
Inside the taped off area there was a hive of activity as officials in all sorts of uniforms went about their business. Paramedics were tending to the injured before loading people onto gurneys and carrying them away. Soldiers stood vigilantly, weapons raised scanning the crowds looking for further threats. More ambulances arrived on the scene disgorging their crews of orange vested personnel who drifted through the tape and got involved in the operation.
Billy arrived at the taped area and saw there were several people sitting on the ground being tended to by medics. From this close

they looked like they were suffering from a mixture of head traumas or shrapnel wounds to their upper bodies.
Billy grabbed hold of a bystander.
"What happened here?" he demanded a little forcefully.
The man struggled to free his arm from Billy's vice like grip.
"I don't know man, I was asleep at the time. There was like a loud bang and then some shooting. I just got here."
Billy looked over again and what he was seeing began to make sense in some weird way.
The main focus of the operation seemed to be about thirty yards from the edge of the tape. There were a lot of officials standing around what looked like piles of rags left on the beach. Suddenly it dawned on Billy they weren't rags they were people or the remains of them, covered up with whatever was closest to hand. The swooping sensation in Billy's guts caused him to turn sideways and vomit up what little there was in his stomach, much to the annoyance of the onlookers stood close by.
Billy wiped his mouth and mouthed apologies to the complainants. He turned back to look at the scene again. It was sickening to watch but he could not look away. He now knew that some of the bodies lying on the beach had to be people from the camp. The epicentre of the blast was right in the area where they always laid out their towels and blankets.
One by one the injured and wounded were evacuated from the scene and taken away in ambulances with the sirens wailing and the lights flashing. After this stage of the operation was completed a lull descended on the scene and some people started to drift away.
Two of the orange vested officials were approaching the tape heads close together in deep conversation. Billy tried to listen in but only caught the last of their conversation.
"fortunately, most of the dead are ex-volunteers from the beach camp. One of the soldiers who exchanged fire was slightly wounded. The other dead are the two terrorists."
Billy was angered by the first part of the statement and concerned by the second half. A terrorist attack here in Eilat was not good. He wondered how they had got onto the beach in broad daylight. What was most worrying was the confirmation that there had been fatalities and that they included dwellers from the camp.

As he watched the scene they began the horrible task of gathering up the evidence it was then that Billy's heart stopped.
As he watched one of the officials picked up a beach towel soaked in blood. Even in that state Billy could clearly make out the motif on the towel. The character of Ariel from the Disney cartoon, the Little Mermaid with her flowing red hair and her green mermaids tail was unmistakeable even soaked as it was in blood. Billy's heart missed a beat and he felt his legs go weak under him.
He crumpled onto the sand uttering a low moan. The people crowded around him all took a step back as he collapsed. He hugged his knees and rocked back and forth the tears flowing down his cheeks. There was only one person he knew in the whole of the camp that had a towel with that motif on it. He had hung it up a dozen times on the roof of the shelter to dry, he had even teased Mel about it enough. He stood up again, still shaking with grief and forced himself to look over at the scene. Two uniformed officials were bent over gently lifting a body into one of the black body bags. Billy caught sight of a female leg as one of the officials gently eased it into the bag.
Billy took himself away from the crowd and collapsed onto the sand holding his head in his hands as he wept, the tears and snot flowing freely and congealing in the sand between his legs.
He was so overcome with his grief that he lost sight of the body bag containing Mel's remains and when the Black Mortuary Wagon arrived by the tape he was forced to watch as one by one the body bags were wheeled by on a gurney and then loaded into the back. He didn't know which of the five bags contained Mel's earthly remains and that upset him even more.
He was so paralysed with sorrow that he couldn't even summon up the energy to return to the shelter and find something alcoholic to numb the pain. On another level, he knew that returning there to the place where they had slept and made love, where her clothes and bed clothes would still be rich with her perfume would be a hard thing to accomplish, even with his mind dulled by drink.
By now the vast majority of the personnel who had swarmed all over the site had left and there were only a couple of uniformed police officers guarding the tape, preserving the crime scene within. Along with the investigation team and the emergency services most of the crowd that had gathered had also departed. The sun was starting to drop towards the mountains and Billy was

still sat, almost catatonic with shock. He knew he had to do something but he was powerless to move a muscle.

Something moved just behind his shoulder causing him to turn his head and look upwards. A figure was stood over him but the bright light from the setting sun directly behind them made it impossible to distinguish their features. Their whole body was wrapped in a golden halo of light.

"Are you going to sit there all night?" The voice was musical and, in some way, familiar.

"I don't have anywhere to go, I just lost someone close to me."

"Well you could start by getting up off your backside and coming with me." Billy thought for a split second that it was Mel or some spirit presence of her come back to haunt him or maybe take pity on him and give him a chance to say goodbye properly. He didn't believe in all that spirit stuff so he looked for some other explanation.

"Billy, come on stop mucking about. I am thirsty and I need a drink."

Billy leapt to his feet.

"Mel? What are you doing here? I saw you shipped off in a body bag about two hours ago. You are dead."

"Sorry buddy it wasn't me. I just got back to the camp an hour ago. I have been in the city all afternoon."

Billy reached out to touch her arm, still frightened that this was some trick of his grief and that as soon as he made contact with her arm the vision in front of him would dissipate in the breeze. The arm felt solid enough under his hand.

"Ow, let go you great oaf. You are hurting my arm."

Billy apologized and released her arm. Then paused for a second before enfolding her in a bear hug.

"My god I thought I had lost you. I saw your towel all covered in blood and I saw a woman's body being placed in a body bag so I thought it was you."

"Oh shit I forgot I left my towel on the beach. Do you know what happened here?"

Mel pushed away, but Billy still held her at arm's length as if scared to let go of her.

"No, not really. I arrived after the ambulances and the Police were already here. I heard two guys say that there was a terrorist incursion and a stoner from the camp said he heard an explosion and some shots fired."

Mel's face had pulled into a deep frown.

"Shit Billy, terrorists on our beach."

"Yeah killing our people too."

They were both started to walk away from the crime scene tape slowly heading up the beach in the direction of the city lights. Each of them trapped within their own private thoughts.

Billy in his grief had not considered the full implications of what this incident meant and Mel was worried about what a fresh outbreak of violence could mean for her long-term future in this country. She knew that terror attacks were one of her parents red lines.

Determined to get to the bottom of today's incident Mel reached a decision.

"Well I think we should head up to gossip central grab a couple of beers and find out what happened."

Billy roused himself from his personal thoughts.

"Okay. By the way where were you today?"

"I went into town to phone my family."

"But it's not Sunday?"

"Yeah, I know it was my Aunt Prudence's birthday so I had to call the house when she was there so I could wish her Happy Birthday. By the way did you get the job?"

Billy held up the carrier bag containing his uniforms.

"Got the job and you might say got the T-shirt." He grinned.

"So we do have something to celebrate tonight."

Billy thought about his grief which was even now a fading memory, and his overwhelming joy that Mel was alive and unhurt and standing opposite him. The job was very much in third place on his list right now.

"We have plenty to celebrate. And we can raise a glass to Aunt Prudence and thank her for being born on this day and saving your life into the bargain."

Mel stopped dead in her tracks and started to shake. The full enormity of what Billy had just said had just hit her like an express train. If she had not been in the town to ring her family then there would have been every chance that she would have been on her towel on the beach soaking up the sunshine.

Billy had continued on for a few more paces until he realised he was alone. He now turned back and watched as Mel slowly slid down onto the sand in a dead faint.

He rushed over and caught her just before she hit the sand and cradled her head in his arms gently stroking her forehead and kissing her hair.

After a few moments her eyes fluttered open.

Billy smiled at her.

"Hello beautiful are you back with us."

Mel's face creased with tears and she buried her head in Billy's lap. Bill held her there why she sobbed her heart out.

After a while the sobbing stopped and Mel sat up wiping her face on the sleeve of her shirt.

Billy stood up and held out his hand helping Mel to her feet.

"I think I need that drink and it had better be a strong one."

"I think we will not be alone in imbibing strong spirits this evening we have all had a big shock and a lucky escape."

#

As they approached the Peace Cafe it became clear, even from a distance that everything was not as 'peaceful' as it should be.

From up the street it was easy to hear voices were raised in anger, even if it was unclear exactly what they were angry about. Scraps of the argument drifted towards them.

Words like "disrespect for the dead", and "proper time to grieve" were being met with hoots of derision and catcalls.

Billy and Mel both stopped in their tracks.

"That sounds like it's about to kick off."

Mel nodded in agreement.

"The Underground?"

It was not their first choice of watering hole. It was more expensive than the Peace Cafe and catered to a slightly different clientele, but as an alternative it was bearable. They both did an about turn and beat a hasty retreat just as the first sounds of breaking glass and screams erupted behind them.

As they walked through the town there was a generally restrained mood. The city lacked the normal exuberance that Mel and Billy were used to. Most of the cafe's and bars were open but there was a marked lack of people out and about on the streets. The usual hedonistic party feeling was missing. Billy had his own reasons for being quiet. He had not set foot in the Underground since he had left the company at the Peace Hostel under a huge dark cloud. It had of course been the watering hole of choice for Blossom and her friends and frankly the prospect of any form of confrontation with any of the former tenants or staff from the Peace Hostel did not fill him with boundless joy.

Mel did not suspect there was anything wrong, ascribing Billy's silence to his earlier shock. She took hold of his hand and was surprised when Billy took a firmer grip and held onto her tight as if he was frightened she would evaporate into thin air. Billy was holding on to Mel tightly because he wanted to reassure her in the event there was a nasty confrontation with Blossom.

He made a quick scan of the room as they entered but he saw no sign of anybody he even vaguely recognised and he was certain that neither Blossom, Ian or Trudi were among the people drinking quietly in small groups. He kissed Mel's fingers and she smiled at him.

"Do you want a beer or something stronger?"

"I will start with a beer, we can switch to the harder stuff later."

Although the atmosphere in the Underground was subdued at least no one was screaming at each other. Billy got a couple of beers from the bar and they retired to a table out the front of the bar.

Billy was staring mournfully at the few coins in his hand.

"This place is expensive."

Mel patted her money belt. "Remember I just got my allowance the other day."

"Well you can get the drinks in then Miss Moneybags".

Mel pulled a face at him around the glass as she downed the first half of her beer in a couple of gulps.

Billy took a small sip and then put the beer down on the table. He wanted something light to talk about.

"How are the family."

Mel looked up across the table. Billy didn't usually enquire into her family's health and welfare. Then Mel grasped what Billy was trying to do so she decided to open up.

"They are all well, my sister is studying hard for her exams in the summer and getting good grades, there is talk of Oxbridge for her."

Billy made a sound of approval. It was no mean feat to get offered a place at Oxford or Cambridge University.

"The rest of the time I just made up stories, loads of stories about how great life is on the Kibbutz and how I am making lots of friends. It's all total fiction, well apart from the part about you."
"You mentioned me?"
"Well my mum asked if I had met any nice guys."
"And you lied to your mother?"
"I didn't lie."
"Yes you did, you said you had met a nice guy."
"You are a nice guy. I might have made up a few details about you that weren't true."
"Like what?"
"That you were Jewish and your dad was a successful Dentist from Finchley."
"I doubt my dad was ever successful at anything and the only reason he might have been in Finchley was to break into someone's house."
"So I was a little economical with the truth."
"Where I come from that's called lying."
Mel pulled a face and made a circling motion over her head drawing a halo in the air above her own head.
"Anyway, tell me about today. How did it go?"
"It went. Eli was really nice, told me all about the job, showed me around and introduced me to the rest of the crew."
"So you have got a real job then?"
"Sort of."
"You gonna be moving out of the camp and back into a hostel?"
"No, why?"
"Just asking. I thought that might be what you wanted."
"No, I don't, and besides they might still not have forgiven me for what I didn't do. The whole Blossom thing."
Billy cast a nervous and hasty glance around the room, which had slowly begun to fill up with more people, in case mentioning her name had mysteriously conjured her out of thin air. Once again his quick glance revealed no one he recognised.
Billy had told Mel the whole story on the first day they met, more interested in her opinion than anything else so there were no secrets between them there.
"Besides I like the shelter and I like living with you."
"Even if it's dangerous now?"

"We don't know that. Maybe we should see if we can find out a few more details about what happened."

"Let's play detectives." Mel said with a childlike glee in her voice. And they did.

By the time they left the bar later on they had managed, between them to cobble together a passable version of what had happened on the beach earlier that day. Of course, they had to weed out the more incredible versions and disregard some of the ramblings from the drunks but they managed in the end to get to a kernel of truth. According to the more reliable sources a team of two terrorists had come ashore on the beach in a rubber boat. One had been armed with a pistol and had started shooting indiscriminately at sunbathers on the beach. The other was wearing a suicide vest and he had run towards the nearest large group of people which happened to be a group from the camp. The pistol shooter had been shot dead by a passing soldier who, although he was off duty, was carrying his weapon.

The second terrorist, the one with the vest on had also been shot and wounded and had fallen to the ground several metres from a large group of sunbathers. Not dead he had managed to detonate his vest but as he was lying prone on the sand at the time the blast had had a diminished effect and only a couple of unlucky souls who had been standing up at the time, probably trying to flee the scene, were hit by shrapnel.

If he had got any further then the death toll would have been much higher. Unfortunately, one of the fatalities had been the hero soldier who had gone to check on the terrorist with the vest and was standing over him when the bomb went off. The other fatalities had been among the sunbathers and of course the two terrorists both died at the scene.

There were several people still in hospital with serious injuries from burns or shrapnel and several lightly wounded people who had been released after treatment. The local authorities were still not releasing any information about the two terrorists or their nationalities although there was a rumour that the two had paddled the boat across from Sinai in the night and managed to evade both the Israeli and Egyptian patrols. This was a major cause for concern for both sides of the border as it suggested a serious failure of their security systems.

When Billy and Mel made it back to the camp there was a very subdued atmosphere around the place and more than a few empty sleeping places as people had taken fright and gone off in search of safer places to spend the night.
Among those remaining in the camp there was a general air of "lightning doesn't strike twice" fatalism.

#

Eilat as a town bounced back very quickly and after a couple of days, once the tape had been removed, it was difficult to detect that there had been an incident of any sort.
Billy had reported for work the following morning and started his job as a Pool Boy. He was instantly the centre of attention among his co-workers when they discovered that he was a resident of the Camp and that he had been one of the first on the scene of the terror attack on the beach the previous day. There was a general buzz among all of the workers about the safety of the Camp, the beach and indeed of Eilat itself with several people questioning the wisdom of remaining in the city. It was definitely the main subject of conversation in most of the places where the westerners hung out
The first couple of days he was strictly supervised by the site managers at each of the properties. Once they realised that Billy was a good worker and that he knew what he was doing then they took their feet off his neck a little bit and cut him some slack. One interesting development in the first week was Billy finally got to hear about the fate of his predecessor.
He had been taking a break with a couple of co-workers when the subject had come up in conversation. It was almost farcical as the two workers concerned, both members of the cleaning staff, thought that at least Billy would have been warned about the situation that had led to his predecessor's sacking.
So, when they both started obliquely referring to the dilemma and asking what measures Billy had thought to employ to counter the problem, Billy had thought they were making fun of him, giving him some form of hazing ritual so he had played along with them and called their bluff.

He later discovered that his answers were completely inappropriate, but not before there were some red faces in the break room.

The problem, it appeared, was that certain female residents at the apartment complexes had very high libidos and very low morals and despite being married to very rich husbands they seemed to feel that any male member of staff was there for their personal sexual gratification. In some cases, this even extended to their teenage daughters. Apparently, Billy's predecessor had taken the "full-service" part of his job description a little too literally and had been caught once too often in extra-curricular activities, by irate Fathers or Husbands.

Once Billy discovered this he had quickly withdrawn his comments and the event had blown over. It did, however, leave Billy forewarned about what could happen so he was prepared for the eventuality if one of the women made her move.

If he was honest with himself, Billy didn't think it would happen to him. He didn't know his predecessor but Billy didn't consider himself to be a player. He was always slightly surprised when a woman, any woman, showed the slightest interest in him. He did not think of himself as "God's gift" to womankind.

Everything appeared to be normal for the first few days and then the weekend arrived and with the coming of the Sabbath so things had started to heat up. Apparently, there were several of the regular residents who lived and worked elsewhere in Israel who only descended on Eilat for the weekends.

Their husbands, high powered businessmen during the week came down to Eilat to visit the Casino at the Taba Hilton or take a trip out on one of the Casino Boats, their wives and in some cases their daughters were left to amuse themselves. Of course, there was only so much shopping that one woman could engage in and being ladies of leisure they had plenty of time to visit the much better stocked Malls and shopping centres in other parts of Israel so when they arrived in Eilat and were promptly abandoned by their high-roller husbands they very quickly became bored and it was then that the trouble started, at least it did for Billy.

He was completely unprepared for the level of attention he received and being at heart a trusting young man he quickly fell victim to these predatory ladies.

Maybe his naivety played a part in it or maybe they were just used to getting their own way. Whichever was the case, Billy was out of his depth from the start and as a pool boy that was not a safe or comfortable place to be.

He was clearing up at the poolside of one of the properties on the first Friday when one of the residents showed up at his shoulder. She placed an arm on his bicep and Billy could have sworn she gave it an experimental squeeze before she gushed in heavily accented English that she needed some help to carry some groceries upstairs to her apartment.

This was not strictly part of Billy's job description but a quick look around told him that he was alone in the complex at that precise moment in time. He dropped his broom and followed the lady in question out to her car. The bag of shopping looked neither large nor especially heavy but Billy did not feel that after only a few days in the job he was in any position to point this out to the lady. Instead he leaned into the boot of the car and collected the bag. He then followed the woman upstairs to her apartment.

She fiddled with her key and then pushed open the door. This was the first time Billy had been inside one of the apartments and he was overwhelmed by how luxurious and well-appointed they were inside. The lady waved an arm in the vague direction of the kitchen and Billy went to place the groceries on one of the granite worktops.

He returned to the main room and was confronted by the woman concerned who had used the few seconds he had been out of the room to divest herself of her outer garments and was stood in the middle of the room wearing only a pair of stiletto heels and a wide saucy grin. Billy stopped dead in his tracks. The woman stood there with her hands on her hips.

"So do you want to hang around here for a little while? I am sure we can keep each other company."

Billy could not resist giving the naked woman a long look over. She was gorgeous to look at. She clearly worked out and when she was not at the gym she obviously spent plenty of time sunbathing naked as there was not a tan line on her anywhere. Billy was fighting hard not to let arousal take over. This beautiful woman could only have been a couple of years older than he was.

"I can pay you for your time, the same as I did for Peter. He and I had a very nice arrangement. Very mutually satisfying."

So that was the temptation. Aside from anything else there was the possibility to make extra money. No wonder this Peter guy had thought it worth the risk. He wondered for a fleeting moment just how much these women were prepared to pay for sexual favours and whether it could be financially rewarding.

The woman opposite him had obviously got bored waiting for his answer and had taken his silence as tacit agreement because she was slowly advancing across the room towards him, her hands still firmly on her hips and her high heels, whilst enhancing her body posture, clacked menacingly on the stone floor.

Billy eyed up all the angles and calculated possible escape routes and as soon as there was a chance he went around the other side of a coffee table and fled towards the front door of the apartment. Over his shoulder he made what he thought was the politest of refusals and bolted out of the door. He tore down the stairs and back into the open area in the centre of the block and collapsed down in the shade of one of the trees. After he had regained his composure and his breathing had returned to normal, he went back to his cleaning.

About half an hour later the woman arrived poolside in an outrageously small bikini, gave Billy a very sexy conspiratorial wink and then stretched out on one of the sunbeds. There was not a shred of embarrassment about her earlier nakedness or Billy's rejection she just lay there in the sun whilst Billy finished his cleaning job, trying hard not to stare at her body.

Billy was grateful when he had finished off the task in hand and was able to beat a hasty retreat to one of the other properties.

It would have been acceptable if this had been an isolated incident but as the days wore on there were more indecent proposals.

These took many different forms some were subtle, a note left on the sunbed where Billy and only Billy would find it with an invitation to drop by the apartment when he had time, others were more blatant and took the form of direct proposals delivered face to face. Each time it was hard for Billy to refuse and maintain any degree of composure.

He slowly became a nervous wreck, jumping at his own shadow, dreading going to work in the mornings, and growing increasingly short tempered. He knew that it was only a matter of time before he over reacted to a simple and innocent request from one of the residents and caused someone major offence.

He tried to make an appointment to talk to Eli about the problem but his employer was always too busy to see him so instead Billy just withdrew into himself, focused on getting the work done as quickly as possible and getting out of the properties as quickly as possible.

Without the unwelcome attentions of the female residents the job would have been quite pleasurable. He was outside in the sunshine all day and the work was for the main part different from the hard, physical labour of the building sites and the gardens.

The end when it came was not a total surprise to Billy but the circumstances did leave him with questions regarding the actions of his predecessor and whether he had really been the lothario that everyone had painted him to be.

When Billy arrived at the first property one Sunday morning there was a message for him to call Eli. Billy was pleased as he thought that finally he would have a chance to put his case to his boss and ask for his advice. On the note was a number for him to call so Billy went to the site office, picked up the phone and dialled the number. It rang once before it was answered. It was the main man himself who took the call.

Billy introduced himself. Eli asked him which property he was at and when Billy told him Eli instructed him to wait in the office as he would be right there.

Billy sat on a hard, plastic chair and waited for the ten minutes it took for Eli to arrive.

When he arrived Eli had a face like thunder.

"Billy, I thought I told you that when you were on duty at my properties and wearing my uniform, you were representing me. You have let me down."

Billy stood there mute. He was wondering what exactly Eli was driving at.

"So how come you feel it is acceptable to proposition one of the female residents, offering her sex in return for money."

Billy's mouth dropped open in shock.

"I never.." he was cut off before he could finish.

"That kind of behaviour has no place in my organisation. I am disappointed with you and I am going to have to let you go."

Billy toyed with the idea of speaking up in his defence and trying to explain the circumstances that had led to where they were now, but one look at Eli's face told him it would be a fruitless exercise.

The cool determination on his face told Billy all he needed to know. Eli was too focused on his personal reputation and that of his company to allow a potential scandal like this to get out. His clients were all powerful people, most of them capable of ruining him both professionally and financially if they chose to do so. Billy shrugged his shoulders, so there it was, tried, found guilty and executed in less than fifteen seconds. It was a personal a best for him.

Eli escorted Billy to the curb outside the property and asked him to deliver the uniforms to the lettings office in the city centre where he would be given the balance of any wages owed to him. He then climbed into his air-conditioned Mercedes and drove away.

Billy stood for five minutes on the curb before he turned on his heels and walked back across town to the beach. He stopped to buy a bottle of Vodka at one of the supermarkets and even though it was only just after nine in the morning he cracked the seal on the bottle and drank deeply.

As he walked he began to wonder about his predecessor. Had everything he had been told about him and his behaviour been an invention. Maybe he had simply fallen victim to some rich woman who he had rejected once too often and who had felt it was necessary to invent some claim of sexual harassment to mollify her bruised ego.

As the alcohol began to take its toll Billy drifted to another extreme where he regretted not taking the money and performing for these women, not because he particularly fancied any of them but because if he had known he was going to get fired anyway it might have been better to have taken the money. Better to have been hung for a sheep rather than for a lamb, or in this case no lamb at all. The extra money might have made all the difference.

He was already half pissed when he arrived back at the shelter and changed out of his uniform and into his own clothes. He put the three uniforms in a bag and slung the bag towards the back of the shelter. He would drop them by the office in the morning.

He sat down outside the shelter and lit a cigarette. He didn't know why, but he had taken up smoking again. He had smoked as a schoolboy but had quit when he started work. Just lately he had decided to take it up again. It seemed that everyone he knew smoked and there were always packets of cigarettes on the tables in the evenings. It was just too easy. It was a filthy habit and Billy kept telling himself he would have to quit again, but that was a job for another day.

So, he sat there in the sand with his bottle of Vodka and his packet of Time and drank and smoked. He was well gone by the time Mel found him a few hours later. She guessed exactly what had happened just by looking at him and she went into one of her best mothering routines, but for some reason the sympathy instead of soothing him made Billy angry and they had a huge fight which only ended when Billy chucked his empty bottle at Mel and stormed off down the beach. The bottle missed but Mel was so shocked by the event that she just sat on the sand outside the shelter and burst into tears.

Billy stalked furiously along the sand not really focusing on where he was heading, just walking and cursing under his breath. The sudden anger and the resulting burst of adrenalin had taken the edge of Billy's drunkenness and the alcohol from earlier had left him with a dry mouth so inevitable his wandering took him in the direction of the Peace Cafe and the prospect of a refreshing cold beer.

It was still only mid-afternoon and the place was largely deserted. The main crews from the Wall had not returned from work so there was just the usual crowd of vacationing Volunteers and other deadbeats who hung out here during the day.

Billy ordered himself a large beer and took a table on his own. He didn't feel like being social at the moment and he knew that if there was anyone who even vaguely knew him then he would have to answer questions about his sacking or come up with some story about why he was in the bar in the middle of the afternoon. Neither of these things appealed to Billy right now. Instead he would sit alone and try to figure out how he could apologise to Mel and make things right with her again.

He really didn't want to make polite conversation with anyone so he was annoyed when a shadow blocked out his light and a voice asked him if the chair on the other side of the table was taken. Billy looked up briefly and saw a large man standing over him He waved his hand in the direction of the vacant chair indicating, he felt, that the chair was available, but hopefully communicating to the new arrival that he was not in the mood for idle conversation. Judging by the brief glimpse Billy had got of the man standing over the table and considering the man's attire, he was a newcomer to the Eilat scene and maybe even to Israel. He wasn't dressed like a volunteer. His clothes were too clean and tidy. Maybe he was a tourist who liked to slum it. Billy really didn't care as long as the newcomer didn't want entertaining he could occupy the seat on the other side of the table.

Billy continued to sip his beer in silence whilst the newcomer fiddled first with his bag and then with his camera all the while taking intermittent sips from a large glass of coke.

"Are people always this friendly?" the newcomer spoke.

Billy rolled his eyes but due to the angle of his head this was not apparent to the guy sitting over the other side of the table. Billy thought he detected the vaguest trace of an American accent in the voice. Billy relented.

"No not always. Sometimes we are quite friendly. I have just had a bad day. I got fired."

"Oh that's not good. What were you doing?"

"I was a pool boy at an apartment complex full of rich bitches with too much time on their hands, and husbands who didn't pay them enough attention in the bedroom." Billy tried to keep the bitterness out of his voice but it was impossible. He didn't want the newcomer to feel sorry for him.

Unfortunately his words had exactly that effect.

"I don't suppose you would let me buy you another beer?"

Billy looked up for the first time and made eye contact with the man sat opposite.

"Yes, that would be kind of you."

"What are you drinking?"

"The draft beer would be fine."

"Is it alright if I leave my camera and my bag here?"

"Yeah sure. I am not going to steal them and run off if that's what you are worried about."

"I am glad to hear that." The man stood up and walked over to the bar.

This gave Billy a chance to study the man without being observed. From behind he had all the outward appearance of a well to do tourist.

He was wearing tailored shorts and a polo shirt and his feet were encased in a pair of soft leather moccasins. As his hand went to his pocket for his wallet or bill fold Billy noticed what looked like an expensive watch on his wrist. His hair was cropped short and was

bleached blonde, Billy guessed by the sun, and his skin was well tanned. He looked fit and healthy, like he worked out regularly, and was careful about what he ate and drank. As if to confirm this he returned with another soft drink for himself as well as Billy's large beer.
He placed the drinks on the table and re-took his seat. He raised his glass in a silent toast to Billy and took a sip. Billy who had just finished the last of his own pint while he waited picked up the fresh pint and took a mouthful.
"I suppose some form of introduction should be in order." The stranger obviously thought the time had arrived that they became better acquainted. Billy, who was still a little buzzed up from the earlier Vodka and now mellowed off a little by the beers, felt it would be churlish not to respond.
"My name is Christian Jensen, I am originally from Denmark, but for the last couple of years I have been living and working in Los Angeles. I am here in Israel working and touring around."
Billy hadn't guessed at the Danish connection, although now it was mentioned Billy could see the classic Nordic features in the man sitting opposite him, not least of which were his piercing blue eyes. A hand was extended across the table towards Billy.
"I am Billy Randell, originally from a small town just outside London, now gainfully unemployed, but you already knew that."
The two shook hands.
"So how does a lad from London end up working as a pool boy in Eilat Israel?"
"It's a long story."
"I have time. I am not due to be anywhere today."
"Well," Billy exhaled, wondering where to start and what to leave in and what to leave out.
"I came to Israel to volunteer on a kibbutz and that didn't exactly work out the way I planned it. There was a bit of a misunderstanding and I was asked to leave."
He decided to skip over the finer details of his expulsion.
"So, I drifted down here and took various labouring jobs and then one day this guy asked me if I was interested in being a pool boy and I was, and so I became a pool boy and everything was great, at least until this morning."
"What happened?"
"It's complicated."

"Ah OK. I won't ask any more questions, except maybe one. What does an unemployed pool boy do next?"
"I have absolutely no idea. I guess I will be back on the Wall in the morning."
"What's the Wall?"
Billy pointed to the stone structure a few metres away.
"That's the Wall. Basically, if you are looking for work you come and sit here and if someone is looking to hire workers they come by here and the two of you reach an agreement."
"So it's like an unofficial labour exchange?"
"Yeah, I guess so. It seems to work well though. There are plenty of people who get work here every day."
"So what kind of jobs are on offer?"
"Mostly it's manual work, labourer jobs, building sites, gardening. It's all pretty informal, all black economy, if you get my meaning. It's mostly cash in hand."
Christian nodded his head to show he understood the concept.
"So what about hiring people onto longer term contracts, maybe a couple of weeks at a time? Can you do that through the wall?"
"Depends what you want them to do. I guess people might agree to long term work, the only problem might be with permits. I doubt any of these guys have got proper work permits and some of them might not even have valid tourist visas."
Billy thought again about his own predicament where, without Passport and accompanying visa he could, if caught, be expelled from the country. He had not thought about this for several weeks now, but he knew that ignoring the problem would not make it disappear.
Billy knew that there were no questions asked when you worked the Wall but anything better paid or more stable was out of the question whilst he lacked the proper documentation.
Working for Eli had given him a taste of what life could be like with a regular pay packet at the end of the week rather than the hit and miss of daily cash in hand work.
"So, if you could get around the problem with work permits and visas then people might be interested?"
"Like I said, it will depend on what you want them to do."
"Oh it is not manual labour, exactly the opposite. Would you be interested. I could use a smart guy like you who knows his way

around. Maybe you could work for me as liaison person. Would you be interested?"

What Christian was saying sounded interesting to Billy, even in his slightly befuddled state, but at the back of his mind there was single red warning light that was flashing.

What was a smartly dressed guy like Christian, who clearly had money, doing slumming it in a bar like the Peace Cafe, looking for guys to work for him? What exactly was it that this guy did for a living?

Billy took the opportunity to raise his glass and take a drink while he used the break in conversation to study the guy sitting opposite him. There was something that was bothering Billy about this guy and with all the alcohol coursing through his body he was having difficulty putting his finger on exactly what it was. And all the time the red light was flashing.

He noticed that there were certain mannerisms about his new friend that struck him as odd. The way he was dressed, the way he sat, his body leaning forward towards the table, legs crossed at the knee, hands resting in his lap, fingers slightly interlaced. The way he spoke, the forced diction, the enunciation of every syllable. There were other mannerisms that Billy also noticed. He was forever smoothing the material of his shorts with his hands or picking at imaginary lint on his clothes or patting his hair or swiping his hand down the side of his head to replace hairs that weren't even out of place. Billy couldn't help thinking that if they had been in a slightly smarter establishment, one that contained mirrors, would Christian have spent the whole time checking his appearance in the nearest available mirror. He seemed vain enough for that.

Billy was aware that the silence had extended into that zone where it becomes embarrassing so he felt he had to break the silence or get up and walk away.

"So what is this job you are seeking recruits for?"

"I am looking for half a dozen tanned, good looking and well-muscled men."

The red light stopped flashing. It was now on permanently as the penny dropped for Billy.

'He's gay.' That simple thought explained everything in two short words. All the mannerisms and affectations were clear indicators. Billy had very little experience and almost no interaction with homosexuals but Christian seemed to be displaying all the text book signs. Billy felt a small shiver pass down his leg from hip to ankle, almost as if someone had tricked a nerve in his thigh. He shuffled his backside around on his seat closing his body off from Christian. It was an unconscious action but clearly part of a subconscious defence mechanism.

"We start shooting a film up in the Negev desert in two weeks. I am the second Assistant director with responsibility for extras casting. It's a futuristic crime drama and the extras will be part of a gang of bounty hunters on a desert world. Think a bit of Mad Max meets Sherlock Holmes."

Billy almost screamed with laughter as he realised his mistake and had to struggle not to blurt out, "So you're not gay." He knew that this was not proven beyond all reasonable doubt, there were plenty of gays in the film industry, but he was now not certain that Christian was one.

Instead he settled for the more socially acceptable.

"So you're in the entertainment business."

"Yes," said Christian, clearly unaware of the turmoil he had just caused. "Didn't I mention that before."

"Er no, not that I recall."

"Oh sorry, maybe I should have mentioned that earlier."

Billy barked a short laugh, more at himself and how easily he had been fooled.

"So, what do you think. Could I find the people I am looking for here in Eilat?"

Billy considered the question carefully. He had a few candidates in mind from among his fellow ex-volunteers. However, he was not convinced that they wouldn't have the same problem, form the same wrong conclusions, if he was to introduce them to Christian. And ultimately, knowing these people, that could lead to some ugly scenes.

He decided to remain upbeat but at the same time fairly non-committal.

"Sure, if the project is sold to them in the right way. I could have an ask around and see what the general feeling is. How long are we talking about?"

"Well the initial shooting schedule is for three weeks, but with re-shoots that could extend to a month or more."

"And the pay rates?"

"Well ordinary extras, the crowd, get about 50 US dollars a day."
Billy let out a low whistle. He could see a few people jumping at that sort of money, particularly if it was guaranteed for a number of weeks. He would have to fight them off.
He thought that he would try and get ahead of the pack.
"Well I would be interested, if you think I have what you are looking for."
"Of course, you do. That was why I approached you in the first place." Christian smiled across the table and Billy felt the red-light flick on again in his sub-conscious. He shook his head to dispel the thought and instead returned the smile.
"Great."
"Although I must confess that after speaking to you I might have something else I could use you for."
Pling, the light was on again. This time he struggled even harder to switch it off.
"There is actually a small role that we haven't cast yet and I think you would be perfect for the part. Have you done any acting?"
"None at all."
Christian paused for a moment as if this was not good news then he in turn shook his head.
"Well never mind I am sure we can work around this. We will need to get you a SAG card."
"A what?"
"Membership card for the Screen Actors Guild. It's the union for actors."
Billy liked the sound of that.
"And of course you would get more than the basic rate of the other extras."
Billy liked the sound of that even more.
Mentally he was now almost climbing over the table, waving a pen and demanding to be shown a contract.
In reality he was still sat on the chair, one hand clutching his half-finished drink.
"So what are the next steps?" he asked as casually as he possibly could.
"You come to my hotel."
The red light was back on again. Every time he felt he was making progress, Billy got the distinct impression he was being taken for a

ride and that Christian was trying to seduce him. Christian hadn't finished what he was saying.

"I will need to get on to the production office later and get them to fax over the necessary papers for you to sign, contracts and the like. So, if you drop by the hotel in the morning we can have breakfast and sign all the papers then I can fax them back Stateside and we can get the ball rolling."

It was a breakfast meeting, that was all.

Christian was writing an address on the back of one of the beermats off the table. He finished with a flourish and slid the mat across the table. Billy picked it up and read the name of the hotel.

"The Ambassador, suite 1704. Is that the big hotel out on Coral Beach?"

"Yes, that's the one. Just come to reception in the morning and get them to call up to my room. I will tell them to expect you."

Christian was on his feet now. Billy stood up. A hand was extended across the table towards him and Billy took it.

"It has been a pleasure to meet you Billy. I look forward to working with you."

Billy mumbled something non-committal but cool, or at least it sounded so in his ears, and watched as Christian left the bar before sitting down again heavily. He played with the beermat with the address scrawled on it, spinning it around on the table top.

Was this really true? Was Billy about to embark on a new phase of his life? Would he make a success of it? Would he fail to pass even a basic audition? For the first time in a long time he wished he had Mike here to discuss things with. He missed his friend at times like these. He liked to share his successes and his failures with his oldest friend. Now he only had Mel.

And with that thought his whole life came crashing back in on him. The reason he was sitting here in the Peace Cafe, slightly drunk in the middle of the afternoon. The fight with Mel, the flying bottle, the tears and the screaming. He knew the first thing he had to do was fix things with her and what better way to do that than to go and tell her his latest news.

He paused. Maybe he should have one more drink just to summon up the courage. He went and ordered another beer to celebrate his good fortune.

#

Back at the camp a while later he spotted Mel sitting outside their shelter talking to a couple of the other girls. She was feeding small pieces of wood into a campfire.

He had stopped by the supermarket and bought some drinks for them to share as a celebration and he had decided to take Mel out for dinner later that night but first he had a special surprise he wanted to spring on her so he skirted around the shelter, trying to avoid being spotted and went in search of a couple of confederates to help with his plan.

Billy knew exactly who he was looking for and hopefully where he could find them and fortunately he was not disappointed. The two people in question were willing and able to help him out so the three of them headed back towards the shelter.

Mel was still sat by the fire with the other two girls as Billy stepped out from behind the nearest shelter and stood before her. He looked back over his shoulder to check that his confederates had not deserted him and when he saw they were both in position he nodded his head.

The one on the left played a single chord on the guitar to give Billy a start note. Now Billy was no singer of any talent, his voice was OK but he figured out that this might be a fun way of breaking his news to Mel. His voice was a little uncertain at first.

"They're gonna put me in." Mel looked up annoyed at the disturbance.

"They should put you in a strait jacket." She jibed before looking away

The two guitars played the second chord in the sequence.

"They're gonna make a big."

"Randell you are making a big fool of yourself." Mel was not giving up. But then neither was Billy.

Again, the guitars played the next chord.

"We'll make a film."

"Oh, and I suppose you get to play the big man again." Mel was really getting annoyed.

Final Chord.

"And all I gotta do is"

"All you gotta do right now is fuck off and leave me alone." She folded her arms and pulled a sour face.

The two boys picked up the rhythm as Billy went into the chorus.

Mel had looked away after each rebuke but as the three lads went into the chorus of Act Naturally, and Billy started to caper backwards and forward singing his heart out with gusto she finally cracked a smile.

The commotion had attracted some attention from round and about so when Billy came to the final lines of the song and the guitars played what was a rather overblown finale there was an outburst of enthusiastic applause and whistles from the assembled crowd.

Mel was now grinning from ear to ear as Billy went over and pulled her to her feet and crushed her in a tight hug.

"Billy Randell," she said out of breath from the crushed ribs. "What on earth are you talking about?"

"Just exactly what I said in the song. I am going to be in the movies."

Mel pushed him away to arm's length.

"Have you gone completely mad or are you just pissed again?"

"Charming." Billy said with mock offence, hamming it up like the worst Shakespearian thespian, back of his hand to brow. He dropped the hand.

"No, I am a little buzzed I admit but not plastered. I met this guy in the Peace Cafe who has offered me a part in a movie, or a TV show, we actually didn't discuss the details."

"Well if I was you I would get a few more details before you start writing your Oscar acceptance speech." She grinned at him.

"Well I will, tomorrow. We have a breakfast meeting at his hotel so I can sign the contract and apply for my union card."

"Just like that?"

"Yeah, just like that." Billy did a bad impression of the TV magician Tommy Cooper, although without the actor's trademark Fez it kind of fell flat, that and the fact that among his audience a fair few foreigners would never have heard of the TV comedian.

"So, you aren't being hired to do impressions?" Mel was still smiling.

"No there is a small role that hasn't been cast yet and Christian thinks I would be perfect for the part."

"Oh Christian, is it? On first name terms with the director? It will be Steven this and George that next."

"Christian is only an assistant director." Billy was starting to get stung by Mel's negative comments. "Look, can't you be happy for me?"

Mel pushed herself away from Billy and turned away, then as if changing her mind, she turned back and took his hand.

"Billy, you have to understand I have been here a bit longer than you so I will let you into a secret. These "Directors"", she made the quote marks in the air with her fingers, "they come through here all the time, looking to sign people to work as extras and most of the time the projects have not even got the green light from the production company. I am just saying don't get your hopes up too high until you have something signed on paper and you are on the bus to the location."

Billy realised as always that Mel was speaking the truth. He would reserve his high spirits until he saw the signed contract. But he still felt it was worthy of a small celebration so he returned to the carrier bag that he had discarded when he started singing and handed round the tins of beer. Everyone who was there was handed a beer and they all toasted Billy's success, while some of them asked for details of the job and where they had to go to get signed up.

Later that evening when they returned to the shelter both stuffed to bursting point with Pasta and Cheese sauce and lying, in slight pain from over eating, on the top of their sleeping bags Billy propped himself on one elbow and looked at Mel through the darkness.

"I know nothing is signed yet but I need to ask you. Are you OK if I take off into the desert for a month to do this film job?"

"You haven't signed anything and you haven't passed the audition yet, but what makes you think you are escaping into the desert alone?"

"What? You want to come with me?"

"Well every great actor has to have a personal assistant. They even get a mention in the credits at the end of the movie. Anyway, if you are so thick with this director fellow then I am sure you can persuade him to find me a job."

"I will mention it to him at our meeting tomorrow."

\#

Billy kept his word and did raise the subject of Mel at the meeting the next morning. Christian was a little annoyed that Billy was already coming with his own terms and conditions but when he realised that this was a Go/No go thing for Billy he promised to give it his full consideration.

The rest of the meeting and most of the morning was taken up with going through the contract and filling out forms. Christian had some bad news for Billy. Apparently SAG already had a Billy Randell registered on their system so Billy had to come up with a new screen name. Christian was sat with a laptop computer that was connected to the SAG system so they could do searches on any possible names that Billy suggested.

"What about Billy McCartney?"

Christian typed in the name.

"No already exists."

"What about Billy Harrison?"

"Nope."

"Billy Lennon?"

"What is it with you and the Beatles? Are they your favourite group or something?"

Billy began to sing Act Naturally again and received some funny looks from other diners around the terrace where the pair were sitting.

Christian looked up.

"Well it's certainly lucky this isn't a musical, or you would have just failed the audition." He grinned at Billy. Billy stuck out his tongue in reply.

"Mel thinks I have lovely singing voice."

"Ah so now we get to the root of your request. You are bringing her along to keep your ego inflated. Trust me on this. The girl is lying."

Billy didn't respond, he just stuck out his tongue again. Christian wasn't looking anymore. Instead he was reading from the small computer screen in front of him.

"Oh, hold on a minute. Billy Lennon came back blank. No name found. So that's it." He tapped a couple of keys on the keyboard. "Congratulations you are now officially listed as Billy Lennon on the SAG system."

"Billy Lennon, Billy Lennon, Billy Lennon." Billy repeated the name to himself a couple of times just so he could see how it sounded. He tried it a few more times in different voices, each progressively more serious in tone. The last time he made it sound like he was the host of an award show announcing the winner of the Best Actor Award.

"Don't get ahead of yourself." Christian had clearly recognised what Billy was doing. Billy took this as a positive sign. His capacity of acting was obviously improving. He didn't say anything though he just went back to reading the draft contract that was in front of him. It was filled with paragraphs of legal jargon most of which went right over Billy's head.

"Do I need to get a lawyer to look over this contract before I sign it?"

"Do you know any lawyers?"

"No."

"Can you afford a lawyer?"

"That would also be a no."

"Then my suggestion is that you just sign it. It is a standard contract. No one is trying to rip you off."

Billy finally got to the last page of the document, picked up his pen and scrawled his name across the bottom.

"Oh shit," he said as he put the pen down. "Should I have signed that as Billy Lennon?"

"No it's OK for legal reasons you need to sign that contract in your own name. The time for signing stuff as Lennon will come later on."

"You mean like autographs?"

"You're getting ahead of yourself again."

"Has anyone ever told you, you are no fun."

"Plenty. Remember I am the second Assistant Director. I am not supposed to be fun."

"Well you are certainly fulfilling your job description there then."

"Right I just need to go and collect your SAG contract off the fax machine and we can get the last of the paperwork signed and sealed."

Christian got up from the table and headed off in the direction of the hotel lobby and the business centre where there was a bank of fax machines.

Billy got up from the table too and made the short trip over to the breakfast buffet where he helped himself to another large glass of fresh orange juice and piled a couple of mini croissants into a napkin.

He was munching his way through them when Christian returned with the contracts. He laid the papers on the table in front of Billy. Billy picked up the pen and then hesitated. He looked up at Christian.

"Lennon or Randell?"

"Either it doesn't matter."

Billy put pen to paper and signed his name for the first time.

                    Billy Lennon.

CHAPTER nineteen

Mike saw Yossi approaching in his jeep followed by a Police SUV that was clearly having problems with the uneven terrain and giving the Officers inside a bumpy ride.
He pulled the tractor over and applied the handbrake as Yossi's jeep pulled alongside. He climbed down from the cab and met the Volunteer leader as he got out of his jeep.
Mike had wondered why the Police were accompanying the Volunteer leader and the stern look on Yossi's face did nothing to allay any worries.
"What's happened? Why the Police?"
"They need to talk to you."
"Me? Why? I haven't done anything wrong, have I?"
"No Mike, you haven't done anything wrong. I think they need your help with a case. I will let them explain."
The two officers had climbed out of their SUV and were waiting by the front of the vehicle. Yossi turned and beckoned the two men over. They crossed the dirt and came to where Mike and Yossi were both stood.
"Are you Mike Spencer?" The taller and older of the two officers was obviously the senior of the two policemen.
"Yes my name's Mike Spencer."
"Do you know someone called Billy Randell?"
"Sure I do. Billy and I are old friends. We went to school together and came to Israel together. Unfortunately, he was expelled from the Kibbutz over six months ago."
"Have you had any contact with him since that day?"
"As a matter of fact I haven't?"
"Do you know where he went after he left here?"

"No, I don't. He disappeared. I thought he was going home to England but he never got there. Why, what's happened is there a problem?"

"We don't know yet. Our colleagues in the Police in Eilat have discovered a body and the identification papers say it is Mr Randell."

Mike sat down heavily on the grass clearly in a state of shock. When he had left Billy at the bus stop that day he had assumed that Billy would take the bus to Tel Aviv and book a flight back to England. He knew that it was unlikely that Billy would return home, not while he still owed money to Delchie Matthews. That would have been plain suicide. He also knew that Billy was unlikely to contact his mum for the same reason, but he had hoped that his oldest friend would have got in touch wherever he had ended up. Now it looked as if Billy had not even left the country and had instead drifted down to Eilat.

Mike looked up at the two officers wiping a tear from the side of his eye.

"Do you know how he died?"

"The autopsy report is pointing to a drug overdose. Now we know all about his drug use here on the Kibbutz, but."

Mike cut across the officer, his eyes flashing with sudden anger.

"Billy Randell was no junky. He hated drugs with a passion. Anyone who grew up where he did could see what drugs did to people. And as for the stuff found in his bag, it wasn't his."

Mike was furious and he stood facing off to the two Police officers ready to fight them if necessary. Yossi intervened to prevent an ugly scene.

"We did discover the truth about the drugs a few weeks later. They didn't belong to Billy but to another volunteer. I cleared all this up with your superiors many months back."

Yossi was speaking the truth. A few weeks after the incident with the dawn raid the truth of the matter came to light when the four English volunteers were caught smoking weed. In an attempt to save their own skins and prevent their prosecution they had all, separately confessed to planting the drugs in Billy's luggage. All four had been dismissed from the Kibbutz and given a Police escort to Tel Aviv where they were deported back to the UK on the next available flight. In return for their compliance in the matter no formal charges were filed. Unfortunately for Yossi it was too late to put matters right with Billy Randell, but he had asked the Police Inspector who had lead the case, to update the records of the earlier case to make it clear that Billy had been framed. Clearly, he had not got around to doing this yet.

"Well the toxicology report stated that there was a large amount of nearly pure heroin in the lad's body. He died of a massive overdose."

Mike shook his head in disbelief. It was impossible that Billy had started to take drugs and that he had escalated to the hard drugs so quickly. Mike had known Billy since they had both started school and there was no way that the Billy Randell he knew would have gone down that path. But now he was sitting here being told a body, identified as Billy had been found dead from an overdose.

"Are you sure it's Billy?"

"Well," the older officer continued, "that's why we are here. We need someone to go to Eilat and formally identify the body. They found among his documents a Visa renewal stamp for this Kibbutz so we were asked to come here and find out if there was someone who knew him. When we asked at the office they told us you two had travelled here together so you would be our first choice. If you don't want to do it we understand but we would need to then contact next of kin in England and get someone there to formally identify the body. Do you know who is his next of kin?"

"Well that would be his mother. She is his only kin I know of."

"We would have to reach out to her then, fly her here to Israel to identify her son's body."

Mike winced at that prospect. Being here and not taking responsibility would be childish. He would much rather he identified the body and then they collectively reached out to Billy's mum and helped her through the difficult process of repatriation of the body and the funeral. It was the adult thing to do.

Yossi could clearly see the internal struggle Mike was having with himself. He reached down and placed a reassuring hand on Mike's shoulder.

"I will come with you to Eilat."

Mike reached up and covered Yossi's hand with his own.

"Thanks."

Mike quickly came to realise just how important his wellbeing was to everyone on Tel Boker. Nothing remains a secret in a community like a Kibbutz for very long and when news of the reason behind the Police visit inevitably leaked out, Mike was inundated with visitors from among the Members and young members of the Kibbutz.

There were those who came to offer their condolences, knowing that Mike and Billy had been friends, others came to offer Mike support in his own grief. Some even came by to reminisce about Billy.

The oddest visit Mike had was from Daphna, who arrived distraught and beside herself with grief. In this particular case, the tables were turned as Mike had to step in and comfort Billy's former lover. He found that to talk about Billy and tell stories about some of the things that had happened to the pair of them while they had been growing up was what most people wanted to hear and Daphna was no exception. At least she had stopped crying and had the faintest trace of a smile on her lips when she left him an hour later.

Yossi, who was clearly feeling guilty for his part in Billy's expulsion and afraid that his actions had lead in some way to Billy's demise, was never far away and he organised everything for their trip to Eilat.

Volunteers were not allowed to borrow Kibbutz cars so Yossi stepped in and made the arrangement. He even said the Kibbutz would pay for the petrol.

Mike, who had very little time alone to grieve, as a result of all the attention, felt he was on an express train heading towards the buffers and that the communication chord to stop the train had just come away in his hand.

The day of the Eilat trip dawned like any other day and Mike, feeling sick to his stomach, went to meet Yossi at the dining room. They left early to make the journey to the southern city where they were expected at the city morgue at midday.

For the first part of the journey very little was said but after a rest break and a coffee the conversation picked up. Yossi was asking Mike for stories about Billy and also admitted, at long last, that he had always doubted Billy had been the owner of the drugs but that in the presence of the Police that morning he had felt stupid and his pride had prompted him to expel Billy. Mike, for his part, was quick to reassure Yossi that it was not his fault and that Billy had been fatalistic about his expulsion. This made Yossi feel slightly better, as if a weight had been lifted off his shoulders.

Mike noticed it most because Yossi relaxed more behind the wheel. When they had set out it had been the middle of the morning rush hour and Yossi had been freely cursing, and hooting his horn at other drivers. After their little talk, he adopted a much more relaxed attitude to the vagaries of other motorists. This was most noticeable when they became ensnared in a huge traffic jam on the main highway to Eilat.

At first it was unclear, what was causing the hold up. Yossi expected there had been a traffic accident but as they got closer to the seat of the holdup it was clear that there was something else going on. There was a fleet of large articulated lorries stopped by the side of the road and each one was taking it in turns to pull off the road and disgorge their load.

As they drew parallel Mike was able to see a huge crew were working to offload what looked like scenery and lights and other film equipment from the back of the lorries.

"What's going on here?" Mike asked. "Are they making a film?" Yossi glanced up briefly. He was busy focusing on the traffic and trying to see if there was a possibility to pull out and pass the long convoy of parked lorries, without risking the two of them ending up as fellow inmates in the Eilat mortuary.

"Certainly, looks like another film. They do them from time to time out here in the desert. Everything from historical dramas like Masada to Sci-Fi. The last one they made here was one of the Rambo films I think. There were plenty of volunteers used as extras. If you had blonde hair then you got to play a Russian conscript. If you had dark hair and a beard you were an Afghan Mujahedeen fighter. All ended up as cannon fodder for Rambo in the film if I recall, but they had plenty of laughs making the film and it paid good money."

Mike had never been a big fan of action films so Rambo had not been on his 'must see' list although he now thought about adding it just to see the sequences that had been shot here in the desert.

As they got closer to Eilat the conversation waned and eventually petered out as the two of them withdrew into their own thoughts. The small medical centre that served the city of Eilat was their destination and they pulled into the car park at just before midday. In a place this small, it was not difficult to find the waiting Police officers. This time there was one older male and a younger female officer. She seemed nervous and Mike wondered if, like him, this was her first time identifying a body.

The older officer who looked like he was well on the way to retirement introduced himself and his young colleague by presenting their credentials. This action was largely unnecessary as their uniforms gave them away. Mike stared blankly at the squiggly intelligible lines on the document before shaking his head.

"Sorry I don't read Hebrew."

"I am Sergeant Gabriel Wiesenthal." The voice was rich and deep, the English heavily accented as Mike had come to expect from Israelis and an uncertainty in his diction that told Mike he was not used to speaking the language.

Mike looked expectantly at the younger female officer waiting for her to supply a name. Nothing was forthcoming which left Mike a little disappointed.

Mike had seen his fair share of cop dramas on TV so he had a fixed idea in his head of how bad the experience was going to be. In the event the room they entered was brightly lit and had only the faintest trace of an antiseptic smell in the air. Mike had been expecting the strong smell of death and decay that seemed to be portrayed in these dramas so the absence of almost any smell was a pleasant surprise.

Mike had also been expecting rows of bodies lined up under sheets on the various autopsy tables but these were all bare and their aluminium surfaces were scrubbed and shone in the fluorescent lights.

The mortuary attendant was a small man with thinning hair and heavy eye glasses. He greeted them and then made a big display of wiping his hands on the front of his green operating theatre scrubs before he offered his hand to each of them in turn. He seemed to have no command of English, he spoke only Hebrew to the group as he explained the process. This left Yossi and the female Police officer to provide an English translation for Mike.

Although she had not yet introduced herself the female officer was clearly more comfortable speaking English than her older colleague and Mike detected only the smallest trace of an accent in her gentle melodic voice.

The delay while words were translated meant the whole process took slightly longer but eventually they were stood in front of the row of fridges containing the bodies.

Standing there in front of the small metal doors everything suddenly became horribly real for Mike. He knew that behind one of those doors lay the body of his lifelong friend. The names of the occupants were written on white paper cards but as all the names were written in Hebrew, Mike had to wait for the Assistant to show him which door to concentrate on.

The Assistant said something as he consulted the clipboard.

"What did he just say?" Mike asked no one in particular. He was getting more than a little agitated now and it was beginning to show in his reactions.

Yossi spoke first. "He says they have quite a number of residents at the moment as they still have the bodies of the volunteers from the terrorist attack. They are waiting for instructions on repatriating the bodies."

Mike had read about the attack a couple of months earlier when it had been plastered all over the front page of the Jerusalem Post. The general reaction to the story had been one of immense shock, given that so many of the victims were foreign and for the most part ex-volunteers. A couple of the more adventurous souls on Tel Boker had been planning a trip to the Sinai via Eilat but had, on hearing the news of the attack, changed their plans and instead headed to the North of Israel. Mike who was neither planning a trip nor aware that he had any friends in the Eilat area had read the story and been shocked by the details and then promptly forgotten about the whole incident, until it had been mentioned again today. Mike was surprised that the victims' bodies were still being held here in the Morgue in Eilat and had not been repatriated to their home countries.

This gave Mike something else to consider while he waited for the inevitable. What should he do with the body. He assumed that Billy's mum would want to have a funeral in England but he doubted that she would have the finances to pay for it. He resolved to ring his parents up and ask them if they could help. They had both liked Billy so maybe they would be able to help out. Of course, he would also have to fly home for the funeral if there was to be one.

Eventually satisfied that he had the right door the Assistant stood and placed his hand on the handle of one of the fridges.
"Here we go," thought Mike. "Be strong."
Before he pulled on the handle the Assistant said one final thing. He was looking straight at Mike as he spoke.
Mike looked sideways at Yossi for help and the Volunteer leader obliged.
"He said that the body was out in the desert for a long time, weeks or even months before it was discovered so it is in a bad way. It has become dried out and also the animals have been feeding on it."
Yossi had gone pale as he listened to the Assistant's words now it was Mike's turn. The colour drained from his face and he swayed slightly. He felt a hand clutch his elbow and he turned to see the female Police officer had placed a supporting hand on his arm. She smiled as if to give him some moral support. Mike looked around the room quickly calculating the fastest route to the nearest bin or receptacle that he could vomit into if the need arose. There was a sink about ten feet away. That would serve the purpose.
The door clicked and Mike felt the cold draft from inside on his face and chest.
Behind the door Mike could see there were two bodies both covered with white sheets. A silly thought crossed Mike's mind. 'Well at least you weren't alone in the dark by yourself Billy-boy.' The Assistant reached for the lower of the two trays and slid it out of the fridge. He pulled it out until the table the body was resting on went click. Fully extended Mike looked down at the form under the sheet, hoping and wishing that there was some way he would be able to identify the body without actually having to see it.
The tableau was now set up. Mike and Yossi were stood on one side, the male Police Officer and the Morgue Assistant on the other. The female Officer was stood at the head end of the trolley between the two groups. She was still holding tight onto Mike's arm.
The assistant reached for the corner of the sheet. Mike almost by reflex screwed his eyes tight shut. He knew in that split second that he would not be able to see the shattered remains of his best friend and that would make a positive identification impossible. His mind was reasoning with him to open his eyes and look, however briefly but his eyes remained firmly shut. He heard, rather than saw the

sheet whisper away from the body. He knew it was now. He had to open his eyes. He had to look. But he couldn't. It seemed like an age but it was only a matter of seconds. He opened his eyes slowly. He looked. And.

"No." he blurted out.

"No what?" Yossi said.

"No" repeated Mike, this time more forcefully.

"No what?" Yossi said again. This time he reached out for Mike's arm as if physical contact would make a difference.

"It's not him." Mike said simply, turning his head to avoid looking at the grizzly sight in front of him.

Then everyone started to talk at once.

The Assistant was gibbering away in Hebrew. Wiesenthal, who was obviously the only one who was still on script was asking in heavily accented English if this was the body of Billy Randell. The female officer was asking Mike if he was absolutely sure it wasn't Billy and Yossi was pulling on Mike's arm and demanding the same.

"I tell you it's not him now please cover this poor sod up." Mike pulled away from Yossi and moved out of the circle. He reached out for one of the metal tables to steady himself and took several deep breaths to try and conquer the nausea that was churning his stomach. Mike had no idea who that shattered face belonged to but it was definitely not Billy Randell. The feeling of relief and euphoria bubbled up from deep inside him and on its way, it supressed the feeling of nausea and left him instead in a state of euphoria. He could have punched the air and done a little jig if the surroundings had not been so sombre.

Over his shoulder he heard the rattle as the table was slid back inside the fridge and the dull thud as the door was slammed shut. Now he felt able to turn around and face the group.

They were lined up facing him with puzzled expressions on their faces.

Wiesenthal recovered his tongue first and although he spoke haltingly at first, with short pauses as he searched for the right words, he spoke in English.

"So that is not Billy Randell?"

"No sir, that is not." Mike confirmed.

"Are you sure? Remember his body was out in the desert for a number of weeks."

"There is no way that was Billy."
"How can you be sure?"
"Well Billy didn't have afro hair."
The use of the word Afro obviously confused the Israeli policeman so he looked at the younger police officer for help. She supplied the correct word in Hebrew and Wiesenthal nodded his understanding.
This was the first thing that Mike had taken in when he opened his eyes. Maybe his eyes had made an adjustment and naturally he had started at the top of the body. But even as he tracked down the face, which was horribly disfigured both by dehydration and by the attention of desert animals he had noticed that none of the facial features bore even a slight resemblance to his friend.
Once this small detail had been understood by Wiesenthal his face darkened with anger.
A furious discussion erupted between the Mortuary Assistant and older Police Officer, none of which Mike could follow. Yossi and the female Officer were clearly listening in and focusing on the exchange. Mike looked at Yossi hoping for a translation but none was forthcoming. Mike was left to his own devices while the argument raged on. There was plenty of shouting and arm waving going on now. Mike just stood leaning against the metal table as the storm raged to its natural conclusion.
When it was over Wiesenthal spoke briefly to the young female who in turn spoke to Mike.
"Let's continue this interview in more pleasant surroundings." She led the way out of the Mortuary and into the corridor. Yossi followed on and just as the door was closing Mike saw Wiesenthal hurl a final parting sentence at the Assistant, who snapped a response back over his shoulder as he strode off in the opposite direction.
Outside in the corridor as the Mortuary doors swung shut, an atmosphere of calm descended over the group. Yossi had wandered over to the window, Wiesenthal was still muttering under his breath. This left Mike and the young police Sergeant together.
"We weren't introduced earlier. My name is Nurit Sachsmann. Acting Police Sergeant." She indicated the new shiny decals on the sleeve of her uniform as if Mike knew and recognised the different insignia. Mike looked at the hand extended in greeting. He took the hand and shook it.

"Mike Spencer". There was a brief pause as they shook hands formerly before Mike added.

"Acting slightly confused, actually I am not acting, I am bloody confused."

Sergeant Sachsmann nodded her head in understanding before she continued.

"Mr Spencer, you are absolutely sure that the body was not Mr Randell."

"100% sure. I couldn't be more, even if I wanted to be. I am no expert on forensics but even I could tell that the body I saw was probably Negroid." Mike shuddered even in the warmth of the corridor when he recalled the damage that had been done to the facial features by weather and small animals. The soft skin around the nose had been chewed away but that had not been enough to disguise that the nose had been broad and flat. And then a question popped up in Mike's mind.

"Hold on a minute. How did they identify the body in the first place?"

"That was what Gabriel, sorry Sergeant Wiesenthal was asking the Lab Assistant," said Sachsmann, "and it appears that they found your friend's passport with the body."

At the mention of his name the older Sergeant joined them standing patiently listening to their exchange.

"Did nobody check the photo in the Passport?"

"That was another question he asked."

"And what was the answer?" Mike was keen to get to the bottom of this.

"Well that was where it all got interesting. The Assistant went on the defensive, saying that he was just responsible for administration and care of the bodies. He had nothing to do with the post mortem process or formal identification, that is down to the Coroner, or the person carrying out the post mortem."

"So somebody else dropped the ball?" Mike tried not to sound too sarcastic but failed.

The two Police officers either missed this nuance or chose to ignore his sarcasm. Yossi who had now also joined the group to listen in, picked it up and he looked sharply at Mike as if warning him not to take this too far.

"I don't think we should start playing a blame game just yet." He offered, playing the role of Peacemaker. "I know this has been a traumatic experience for you Mike."
The two Officers picked up on this.
"Yes," said Sachsmann, "and we would like to offer our sincerest apologies." She continued in a lighter vein. "Does anybody fancy getting a cup of coffee? The canteen is just around the corner."
They all agreed it would be a good idea and they made their way to the canteen which was still busy as it was the end of the lunch hour. They managed to find a table and Wiesenthal went off to get four cups of coffee. He returned with a tray with four steaming cups of coffee and four glasses and a large bottle of water. He shared out the coffees and then poured each of them a glass of water.
He had just finished this when the Mortuary Assistant appeared from behind them and slammed a plastic bag down on the table before stalking off without uttering another word. The female officer reached for the bag and unzipped it tipping the contents onto the table in front of them. Mike saw the familiar passport among the assorted papers and reached for it. He stopped his hand midway and looked over to the two Police Officers.
"Is it OK? I don't need to wear rubber gloves."
Sachsmann smiled and her face lit up. Mike thought she looked gorgeous when she smiled.
"No this is not evidence anymore. But ten out of ten for asking."
"Too many Cop shows as a kid." Mike grinned. Now that the awful incident was over some of his natural charm and humour was returning. He picked up the Passport and opened it to the picture page. His friends face starred back at him. It was an awful picture, but then, Mike thought, who is ever proud of their Passport photo. It was usually a source of amusement whenever the document had to be produced.
Even so, there was no way anyone could have mistaken the photo he was now looking at for the body he had just seen in the Morgue. Never in a million years. He showed the photo to the two Officers and asked them the same question. The two, obviously already entering some form of damage control mode and wary of any possible impending court action were both rather non-committal. Yossi on the other hand was fully behind Mike and he said so.

"So, my next question is this. If this is Billy's passport then why was this guy running around with it in his possession and where exactly is Billy?"

Now that they were free to speculate without any fear of incrimination the two Officers were prepared to offer opinions. The general consensus of that discussion was closest to the truth. Billy had probably had the Passport stolen or he had mislaid it, most likely the former. The Officers agreed to check their records and find out if Billy had reported the theft. They also suggested that they contact the British Consul in Eilat to see if they had issued a temporary replacement document.

"So, my final question is this. Where is Billy now?"

"That is a very good question," said Sachsmann. "And given the circumstances I think we owe it to you to try and help you find your friend."

There was no immediate disagreement from Wiesenthal.

"Good," said Mike draining the last of his water, "When can we start?"

"When was the last time you saw or heard from him?"

"Well he was expelled from the Kibbutz about six months ago now and I have not heard from him since. I didn't even know he was in Eilat. I thought he had gone home to England."

"Well it looks like at some time in the past six months he was here in Eilat and I guess we can try and ask around and see if we can find anyone who has seen him."

"I want to help if I can." Mike looked over at Yossi as if seeking confirmation that he could help in the search.

Yossi nodded his head.

#

Mike screwed the cap off the bottle of water and took a long swig. It was hot work trudging around the streets of Eilat and he had been doing just that all week. The Police had been kind enough to provide him with a list of all the hotels, boarding houses and hostels in Eilat and Mike had visited every single one of them asking after Billy. The police had also provided him with a photocopy of Billy's passport photo so he could use it to show to people. So far, he had drawn a blank.

He had to admit that the photograph was a bit outdated. Billy had really short hair in the picture, so unless he had had a haircut since arriving in Eilat, and a severe one at that then the hair was all wrong. Haircuts were not something offered to the Volunteers on the kibbutz so unless a hairdresser or barber was among the volunteer group then everyone just let their hair grow. Mike's hair was now well down past his collar and Billy's had been getting on the long side when Mike had last seen him.

Nevertheless, he was disappointed that he had not come across a single person who recognised Billy or could give him any idea where he was. He got the impression that there was a very transient community in the city but at the same time there seemed to be a fair few people who had been around Eilat for a while and he was surprised that none of them had crossed paths with Billy. He had not totally given up hope of finding someone who could give him some information but he felt that time and the places left to look were both running out. He now had the last few hostels to visit and then he was going to head back on the bus up to Tel Boker.

Yossi had been kind enough to grant him a few days of leave but he really couldn't take it much past another day at the most. He had the last few hostels on the list to visit and then he would go up to the bus station and buy a ticket home. He was disappointed to be leaving Eilat without having found Billy but he had secured a promise from the Police that if Billy did show up after he had left they would ask him to contact the Kibbutz and let them know he was alright.

Mike had kept in contact with the Police through Nurit Sachsmann who had appointed herself as unofficial liaison officer in this case. They only met when she was off-duty so she was not acting in any official capacity but she seemed prepared to bend the rules and pass on information about the case. This was how Mike discovered that unlike his own search the Police had met with some success in identifying the body they had in the morgue. After Mike had informed them that the corpse was not Billy Randell they had employed a sketch artist to make a drawing of what the person would have looked like. By showing this around they had come up with a name, or at least a nickname.

According to Nurit, the man in the morgue went by the nickname of Dusty and he was a known face in the twilight community of the city. This was where the petty criminals, drug dealers and users all existed. Enquiries in this community had highlighted the fact that Dusty had, in fact, gone missing several months back, but given the transient nature of the community and its inhabitants, no one had thought to report his disappearance to the Police.

Based on this information they had developed a timeline which had Dusty, at some point robbing Billy of his passport, documents and money and then using the money to buy drugs, overdosing on those drugs and dying as a result of the overdose. Nurit furnished some details about Dusty, all off the record of course and she had pointed out the camp where most of these transients lived on the North Beach.

Mike had ventured there one afternoon to take a look. He didn't bother to enter the camp but merely passed it by on the beach. There were a few people visible inside the camp area but their general appearance was enough to dissuade Mike from entering the place alone. Instead fearing that he might become a victim of a mugging as Billy clearly had, he had given the place a very wide berth, observing only from a distance.

From the outside the camp looked like a dismal place, a mishmash of tents and crudely built shelters dotted around. There were several open fires smouldering, filling the air with hazy smoke. The few inhabitants, rough shaven, dirty and clad in rags and blankets looked like the victims of some natural disaster. Mike wrinkled his nose at the smell of smoke and decay that emanated from the place and after making a single pass of the place, he had turned on his heels and headed back into town to continue his search for Billy or signs of his whereabouts.

He had three hostels remaining on his list and as he walked he checked his watch. He had discovered, by trial and error that there was only a short window of opportunity to visit the hostels and ask questions. If he arrived too early in the morning then the hostel staff were busy cleaning and preparing the place for the incoming guests. Too late in the afternoon and they were busy booking in and welcoming the aforementioned guests.

At both times, the staff were too busy to even bother looking at the photocopy Mike was carrying. But there was a short period in the middle of the afternoon, when the staff were finished with their cleaning and preparations and before the first guests arrived when they had time free.

This was one of the reasons it had taken Mike so long to make the rounds of all the hostels on the list. To approach them at any other time was a waste of energy.

He double checked the name and address on the list and looked up at the street sign. Along this street lay the Peace Hostel and Mike had no difficulty locating the front door. It was open so Mike pushed his way through and went inside. Mike hadn't really paid too much attention to the names of the places he had visited until now. They were all pretty much the same in concept and layout. This place struck him as slightly different. The place really was peaceful. The atrium was quiet and cool after the heat from the street. Mike took a moment to let his eyes adjust to the softer light.

"What do you want? We're not open yet." The Australian accent was harsh, combative and a complete contrast to the tranquil surroundings. Mike searched for the source of the voice.

A tall, lanky, blonde haired guy was advancing towards him from one corner of the open space. His arms were rigid by his sides, his fists clenched in an aggressive and challenging manner. He was flanked by two young women who looked equally ready to do harm.

"We're not open yet. Did you hear me? Do you speak English?" The Australian was not going to leave off.

Mike was struck instantly with the dissimilarity between the name of the place and its surroundings and the welcome he was being given.

"We don't open until four." One of the women piped up in heavily accented English, repeating the phrase in what Mike thought was probably her native German tongue.

Initially Mike had been stunned into silence by the hostile welcome but now he took a step forward into the open and found his voice.

"It's OK I don't want to stay here." Mike had taken a room at a small hotel on the first night and satisfied with the hotel and its surroundings, location and facilities had paid for a whole week. He was definitely not looking to move and certainly not to an unfriendly place like this.

Now he had spoken up the three had paused and taken up position on the far side of the row of tables.

"What were you hoping to sneak in here and do some thieving?" The Australian had folded his arms across his chest and was looking accusingly at Mike.

"No actually I just want to ask you some questions."

"You want answers about Eilat then go to tourist information near the Bus station." He was definitely the most unfriendly person Mike had encountered in many months.

"It's about a person. I am looking for someone who has gone missing."

"Missing persons, best talk to the Police." The Australian was not giving any ground and he had taken a couple of steps closer to Mike as if he was intending to physically eject him from the place. Mike stood his ground.

"I just want you to look at a picture of someone I am trying to find."

Mike held up the photocopy in front of him as if it might prove he was genuine.

The third person in the group now spoke for the first time.

"Come on Ian, it won't hurt us to look." Her accent placed her as English.

"Well I don't know Blossom. You know what Yoram is like about people hanging around here during the day."

"It won't hurt, just for a few minutes. And we are finished with all the cleaning and prep work."

The Australian didn't seem happy with the prospect but he relented and stuck out his hand for the piece of paper. Mike handed it over and he took the briefest of glances at the paper and handed it straight back.

"No, never seen him before."

"Hold on Ian, let me and Trudi take a look." Blossom had stuck out her hand and waited for the paper to be handed to her. Ian passed the paper over and the two girls studied it for a moment.

"Billy Randell." Blossom said slowly

"Yes that's his name." Mike assumed that she had read the name from the passport page. "Did you know him?"

At mention of the name the other two members of staff had stiffened. Blossom seemed to be the only one of the trio not affected by the name. Ian looked like he had swallowed something sour and the other girl had gone white with shock.

Ian found his voice first.

345

"We knew the guy. We sent him packing. Why what's he done now? Who has he upset this time? What is he to you?"
Mike chose to ignore the blatant hostility and just told them the truth.
"He was my best friend. We came to Israel together and I am just trying to find him."
"Wait a minute, are you Mike?" Blossom looked at him enquiringly.
"Yes, I'm Mike, Mike Spencer."
"Oh my god." Blossom's hands shot to her mouth and her eyes sparkled like she was meeting her all-time favourite Pop Idol in person for the first time.
"I never thought I would meet you in the flesh. Billy used to talk about you all the time."
"So you know Billy? Do you know where he is?" Mike had zoned out the other two and was focusing all his attention on Blossom. He studied her for the first time and saw that she was rather good looking under all the hippy clothes and hair. Just Billy's type he thought.
"Billy disappeared several months back. We had a fight and he left." She looked sad now.
"And we made sure he didn't come back." Ian added with a note of satisfaction in his voice.
"What happened to him?" Mike turned his attention to the tall Australian.
"Yes Ian do tell." Blossom was standing with her hands on her hips. Her attitude had changed in an instant from one of sadness to one of simmering anger.
Ian, unhappy to be the subject of two withering looks, had the good grace to squirm a little.
"We made sure he couldn't get a bed to sleep in."
"You did what? How?" Both Blossom and Mike spoke together, over each other.
Ian was now very uncomfortable and both his arrogance and confidence were rapidly draining away.
"It wasn't my idea. It was Yoram's idea. You know how he feels about you."
"What did that fat smelly bastard do to Billy?" She shuddered at the thought of his attention.

"Well he called up all the hostel owners in the city and got Billy blacklisted."

"He did what? Why?" Blossom was now clearly outraged.

"Like I said he has always held a torch for you. He just wanted to protect you."

Blossom now looked physically sick.

Ian was now in full on panic mode frantically trying to put the blame squarely on the shoulders of the Hostel owner.

"Yoram made a few calls to the other owners and told them Billy had been caught stealing and that it was his recommendation that he not be allowed a bed anywhere."

Blossom looked horrified at this latest revelation.

"Mike, you have got to believe me I had no idea. I thought he had just drifted away, left. I didn't realise he was run out of town."

"I believe you." Mike said. He was still processing the news that he had been so close to finding Billy but now he had reached a dead end.

"Do you have any idea where he might have gone?"

"Well a lot of people leave Eilat and go south into Sinai, end up in Dahab or Sharm."

"That's not likely as he doesn't have his passport." Mike tapped the paper.

"Well maybe he headed off to one of the other cities, Tel Aviv or Jerusalem, both places have large numbers of ex-volunteers working the black economy like here."

This seemed to be a logical enough explanation. Mike decided that there was nothing further for him to do here in Eilat. He had at least got some of the answers he came for, so now it was time to go home.

He had not managed to find Billy and it now appeared likely that he had left town. It was time for Mike to do the same.

He thanked the three for their time and then headed back onto the street. He looked at his watch. He had enough time to get back to the hotel and collect his stuff and then make the evening bus back to Tel Boker.

"Mike, hold on a minute."

The voice behind him made him stop and turn around. Blossom was stood in the doorway of the hostel.

"If you find Billy would you give him a message?"

"Yes of course."

"Tell him I accept his apology."
"Is that it?"
"Yes that's all. He will know what you mean."
"Well if he turns up again I will deliver your message."
"Oh I am sure he will turn up again. People like Billy always do."
"I wish I had your confidence." Mike thought to himself as he turned and walked away up the street

CHAPTER TWEnty

Billy dropped the sun visor into place to shield his eyes and pulled up the cotton shemagh to cover his nose and mouth and protect him from inhaling all the dust. He climbed onto his adapted All-Terrain Vehicle and gunned the engine. With all the extra weight of the space-age modifications the vehicle handled like a wallowing buffalo but Billy had quickly got the hang of the extra weight and was quite comfortable in the saddle.

At the beginning of the shoot they had all been riding ordinary All-Terrain vehicles and then some bright spark in the design department had come up with the idea of altering them to make them look more like they came from the twenty-fifth century. All of the vehicles had been modified with aluminium and wooden additions which had changed their looks but also added the extra bulk.

Under Billy the engine was humming away nicely. He was ready to go when the Director shouted action and he risked a glance to left and right and saw that the rest of the team were all in the saddle and ready too. Now they had to just sit and wait.

For all his acclamation of his Jewish roots and heritage, Stanley Kaminsky was uncomfortable in the desert heat. The Director of Banquo PI 2025, the current working title of the project they were filming, spent most of his time inside his air-conditioned Starliner trailer, only emerging when he got the call that the cast and crew were ready to shoot and, more often than not, beating a hasty retreat to the cool interior as soon as he uttered the word "cut." But after three weeks in the desert most of the cast and crew were becoming accustomed to the somewhat idiosyncratic behaviour of this novice director.

Kaminsky for his part viewed the location shooting as a necessary evil and longed for it to be over so he could return to his luxurious lifestyle in his Pacific Palisades home, the arms of his high maintenance girlfriend, and shooting on the backlot in downtown Burbank. Los Angeles was hot in the summer but it was different type of heat. Out here in the desert it was dry, and everywhere was infested with flies.

Billy sat and waited patiently, his head and body slowly boiling in the leather and PVC costume he was wearing. Some of the other extras were lucky as they were wearing nothing more than leather loincloths or kilts but as a senior member of the gang of marauders, Billy found himself clad in more substantial garments, more fitting of his character's status.

Christian had been true to his word and Billy had actually been cast with a speaking role in the movie, even though his dialog primarily consisted of repeating orders issued by the leader of the gang or simply agreeing with him with a smart salute and a prompt "Yes sir".

Privately he wondered how much of his dialog would end up on the cutting room floor, but the lines he had been given meant he was officially a cast member and therefore entitled to a bunk in one of the air-conditioned huts set aside for the senior crew and junior cast members.

The executive staff and the stars were all allocated their own Starliner trailer, and rooms at a five-star hotel by the Dead Sea. Junior crew were confined to a set of tents whilst the extras at the bottom of the heap had to either sleep rough or arrange their own accommodation. The one leveller on the whole production was the commissary where cast and crew of all stripes ate together. If an army marched on its stomach the same equally applied to a film crew.

The commissary had also been the site of the first conflict when only a few days into the first week of shooting, the alcohol supply had run out. The commissary staff were very apologetic but they had not factored in the high demand for alcohol among the extras. Billy had managed to ride to the rescue. He borrowed one of the ATV's used by the production crew and paid a visit to a nearby Moshav.

After some tense negotiations with Members and the owners of the Supermarket, he had managed to secure permission for the production staff to use the supermarket situated at the heart of the settlement. The Supermarket owners were wholly unprepared for the influx and demand for beer and spirits but unlike the commissary crew they had swift access to local suppliers and were therefore able to replenish their stocks within twenty-four hours. The Supermarket manager became a close friend of Billy's and offered him substantial discounts on all his purchases. He was slowly watching his profits sky-rocketing, as a result of the new customers and he knew exactly who he had to thank for that. Billy was just pleased because everyone was happy again and particularly the extras, many of whom had been hired on his recommendation or had applied for the jobs at his suggestion and he didn't want to fall foul of Scouser and some of the others from the building site crew who were part of the group.

After he had signed the contract with Christian and the documents had been sent off and notarised Billy was put straight to work. As had been suggested at their first meeting Christian had been keen for Billy to act as an intermediary as he was familiar with the local scene and knew how things worked already. Billy quickly realised that his new position was a double-edged sword. On the one hand people, as soon as the rumour slipped out that there was a film project hiring and that Billy was the go to guy, were hounding him to be considered for a job, but at the same time there was a certain amount of conflict with people if they felt they were not even being considered.

Christian had been quite clear about the type of people he was seeking to fill the roles of the marauder gang. He had some casting notes that he had let Billy borrow so that he could read them and Billy had decided to take a break and retire to the Peace Cafe and read through the pages while drinking a cold beer. The notes, closely type written were very specific in their description and as Billy read them he looked up and around the room which was just starting to fill up with the first of the returnees from the Wall crew. He was reading the character descriptions and looking for people in the room who could fill the roles. After this length of time hanging out in the Peace Cafe he knew most of the regulars by name so he could pencil names next to the typed descriptions and make up a list that way.

It seemed the most logical and methodical way of doing things. He began to write some of the names in the margin.

"What's cooking Billy my old friend?" A pair of spade like hands were planted on Billy's shoulders from behind. Billy swivelled his head to see who it was even though it was not really necessary. The broad liverpudlian accent could only belong to one person he knew. Scouser took a seat at the table opposite him. As Billy watched the rest of Scouser's crew filed into the bar and occupied a table close by. They were all dusty and dirty after what had probably been another long day on some building site somewhere. Two of the team were up at the bar window ordering drinks for everyone. One of the team came over and placed a couple of large cold beers on their table. Scouser took one and pushed the other across the table towards Billy.

"Drink up and you can tell me all about this high paying gig your recruiting for."

Billy accepted the fresh drink and took a mouthful.

"So the word is out then?"

"You know this place. It's hard to keep anything a secret. Come on man, spill the beans."

" I have been asked to make a list of names for Christian; people who I think would be good in the roles, and most importantly look good on the screen."

"And of course, your old mate Scouser's name is on that list somewhere."

"I haven't really started writing any names down yet."

Billy had only scribbled a couple of names on the paper so far, so nothing was finally decided.

"Come on Billy. Remember I gave you your first break off the Wall. It's time to repay that debt."

Scouser was right. He had given Billy his first break and invited him to join the crew working on the building site and at a time when Billy was desperately in need of money. Maybe it was time to repay the favour.

"I will put your name on the list, but the final decision isn't up to me."

"Come on man, if they have asked you to prepare a list then you must have some input to the process, some kind of influence."

Billy wasn't sure exactly what influence he would be able to exert but he knew that one good turn deserved another so he would make sure that Scouser was given a fair chance.

"It's all I ask for Billy, a fair chance."

Scouser pushed himself away from the table and went to join the rest of his crew who were grouped together around an adjacent table. Billy looked over at them and watched the dynamics of the group. They were a bunch of misfits but as Billy sat there he imagined them clad in costume and to be honest he couldn't think of a better group of individuals to play a scary bunch of desert marauders. He wished he had a polaroid camera so he could capture an image to show to Christian. He wrote Scouser's name on the list and added '+crew' in brackets afterwards.

He could see Scouser now from where he was sitting astride his modified ATV. He was the passenger in one of the marauder gang's pickup trucks, again heavily modified by the scenic designers to make it look more futuristic, its most striking feature was a lethal looking laser weapon array mounted in the truck bed. Scouser was strapped into the control pod for the weapon and was practicing aiming it as he waited for filming to start.

Billy could always easily spot Scouser on set, mostly due to the fluorescent green Mohican wig that he had to don every morning during their time in the make-up caravan. He had bitched about it at first until Christian, who had remained calm and resolute throughout the rather vociferous complaint when a weaker man would have beat a hasty retreat, actually pointed out that by donning a wig everyday he increased his daily pay rate. At that point, all complaints mysteriously evaporated. And Scouser was usually first in the queue for Hair and Makeup in the morning.

They had been rehearsing this short scene all morning and now the message had gone to the Director that they were ready to shoot it. It was not a very complex scene, merely part of a chase across the landscape with some gun action but with the Special Effects of the laser weapons due to be added later, along with some of the explosions it was crucial that the drivers hit certain marks.

There were a couple of special effect explosions that would be triggered and the armoury and special effects guys were hovering about nervously talking into walkie-talkies coordinating the various teams working on the shot.

Eventually the waiting was over and Kaminsky arrived at the Directors position. After conferring briefly with the First Assistant Director and with Christian as Second Assistant Director they called everyone to attention and the call went out, "Action."

After the shot was completed Kaminsky paused briefly to check something on his monitor then hoped aboard his golf cart and was

whisked away, his horsehair flyswatter wafting ineffectually in the breeze. It made him look like some African potentate.
Christian and the First AD were conferring for a while and everyone else on the set was relaxing.
Cigarettes were passed around and lit up and one of the runners did the rounds with bottles of cold water. Billy noticed Scouser was sipping secretly on a can of beer, trying to hide the fact from the men in the Directors position. Billy knew that when Scouser had been assigned the role as the co-pilot on the Land Cruiser he had spent some time with the driver modifying the tool chest in the back and installing a cold box. Every morning he managed to get a couple of freezer elements from the Commissary and loaded the cold box with beer. On a long day, by the time they had shot the final frames, he would already be well buzzed. Billy had to be a little more circumspect in his drinking habits as the ATV was an unwieldy beast in the sand and this had been made ten times worse by its twenty-fifth century upgrade.
He didn't want to have an accident and have to miss filming. Already a couple of extras had been injured in one scene, not seriously, but needing medical treatment at the local hospital which effectively ruled them out of any further filming. Also, the prospect of minor injury was magnified up to life threatening when you factored in the weight and bulk of the ATV and the fact that the costume he was wearing and the part he was playing ruled out any chance of wearing protective headgear of any form.
When you added in the treacherous terrain, common sense ruled out drinking anything but soft drinks during the working day.
Once, however, the working day was done and they were not required for any night shooting then Billy was ready to party with the best of them and often he did. In that part of the production site which had been set aside for the extras there was usually some form of party rolling on into the early hours. In that respect, it was not very different from the camp back on the beach in Eilat or indeed the volunteer quarters back on Tel Boker.
The two AD's had finished reviewing the film that had been shot during the day so they called everyone together and gave them the details of the "call" for the morning. This was a list of the personnel, actors and extras alike and the times they would be expected to be on-set, in full costume and make-up. It was up to the individuals to work out what time they would need to wake up

in order to go through the laborious process of hair, make-up and wardrobe in order to be ready on time.

A production of this magnitude cost thousands of dollars a day to keep going so even a short delay was expensive. Late arrival on set due to over sleeping was not something that could be afforded or tolerated so everybody did their best to ensure it didn't happen. With that last administrative detail out of the way, they were released for the day. The extras all queued up to get their timecards stamped by Christian or a member of his team. This was the only way they could ensure that they would get paid. Billy began to make his way back to wardrobe to return his costume.

He knew the staff in that department would be working long after the rest of them had clocked off, but they were not alone. There were other members of the crew who worked through the night. Lighting staff would be rigging lamps and any green screens needed for the following day, the transport team would be servicing and repairing machines, set decorators and builders might work through the night to get some piece of scenery finished. There was always something going on twenty-four hours a day.

As Billy ambled through the caravans a voice behind him startled him.

"Hey mister, are you a movie star, can I have you autograph?"

Billy turned around wearily. It was part of his life these days. He reached out his hand for the pen.

"Have you got a pen?"

"I have got a black marker pen. Would you sign my boobs?"

Billy looked up at the autograph hunter. Mel grinned at him from behind a huge pair of mirrored aviator shades. Christian had come good on his promise and found her a job as part of the production staff. Billy was not sure what she did but she was always around set looking important and carrying armfuls of paper or a clipboard.

"I bet you say that to all the stars." Billy enfolded her in an embrace and they kissed.

"Careful Billy. Some of us are still working." Mel pushed him away and he saw she had an armful of closely typed, photocopied sheets in a stack.

"I have to distribute these script changes to all the principals before I can call it a day."

"And there was me thinking you were hanging around their trailers hoping for a date."

Mel pulled a face at him, sticking out her tongue.

"What are we doing tonight?" She asked.

"I dunno, probably the usual. Have a few drinks and something to eat and then sit talking bollocks under the stars."

"Sounds like a plan. Are you heading back to the hut?"

"Yeah just as soon as I have dropped off this costume."

"Well don't use all the hot water."

"I will wait until you get back and then we can shower together." Billy said with a lascivious grin.

"That's a deal." She leaned forward and pecked him on the cheek. "See you in a bit."

They parted company, Mel heading off towards the trailers set aside for the stars of the film and Billy in the other direction towards the wardrobe.

\#

Billy instinctively ducked his head and turned his head to one side, scrunching up his eyes. The downwash from the helicopter rotors was already kicking up dust and small pebbles from the desert floor. He aimed for the open ramp at the back of the aircraft. Inside he could see Mel was already sat in one of the seats, strapped in and with an unusually large set of headphones in place on her head.

There were a couple of other members of the film crew dotted around in other seats all wearing headphones. At the front of the aircraft there was a pile of suitcases and rucksacks, their luggage, which was being arranged into cargo nets by a loadmaster.

Billy tossed his small pack, his worldly possessions, into his open arms and watched as it joined the others in the net. Billy took his seat as another crewman showed him how to buckle himself in and handed him a pair of headphones.

He placed those on his head and was surprised at their ability to instantly cancel out the noise in the cabin. This was replaced by the calm clipped and educated tones of their pilot. Billy could see him sitting up front with his co-pilot as together they completed the pre-flight checks and contacted the Air Traffic controllers to file their flight plan details.

He listened in to the conversation, while he looked around the cabin at his fellow passengers. Most of them were sitting blank faced and he suddenly realised why. The conversation over the audio circuit was in Hebrew and he was probably the only person, beside the crew, sitting back here who spoke the language.
It was hardly surprising the crew were conversing in Hebrew, this was a military aircraft and the Air Traffic in this part of the Negev was probably controlled by Military rather than civilian Air Traffic Control.
Filming on this part of the movie was now complete and the production would resume, after a two-week hiatus on the studio lot in Burbank.
Billy glanced sideways at Mel. She was sat with her eyes fixed on the opposite wall of the cabin. They still weren't talking. They had fallen out. Billy settled back in his seat and waited as the crew completed their final checks and the ramp was raised.
He knew the reason that communications had broken down between him and Mel and it was all his fault. Relations had broken down when, with a week of filming left, Christian had called Billy to a meeting in his trailer. Mel had invited herself along as Christian had offered to make them both cocktails and she was not about to miss out on the chance of some free drinks.
In the calm, cool interior of the trailer Christian had dropped his bombshell. The script editors had been at work and had written some new scenes. These new scenes were interior shots and would be filmed on the back lot in Burbank and as Billy was one of the actors in those scenes he would be flown to California in time to start filming at the end of the month.
Christian was pleased that Billy's character was developing, Billy was euphoric about flying to LA and having the chance to work on a real film set. Only Mel seemed to be negative about the whole idea and Billy had called her out on this later when they were walking back to their lodgings. She had stopped dead in her tracks and turned to Billy barely able to conceal her anger.
"I know I am the only one working on this project who knows but, aren't you forgetting one thing? You don't have a passport."
In all the excitement Billy had been swept along and had clearly forgotten the one detail that could scupper his budding film career. He couldn't fly to the States, he couldn't fly anywhere. He didn't have any valid travel documents.

"Now do you want to be the one to go back and tell Christian that fact, or shall I?"
Billy hunched his shoulders in a sulk.
"I will tell him." He admitted in a rather sulky voice.
"When?" Mel was not going to let this lie.
"Soon."
"I would suggest tomorrow morning." With that parting shot Mel had set off again through the desert landscape. Their relationship had slowly deteriorated since that point.
Billy had not found the courage to tell Christian about his missing passport and now they were almost at the point of no return. The previous evening Billy had been handed a travel voucher to be exchanged for an airline ticket at the American Airlines desk at Ben Gurion airport.
Reading the small print, he quickly found the section that stated that valid travel documents would need to be produced in order for the ticket to be issued. He had avoided showing the voucher to Mel, knowing that she would immediately jump on the missing Passport again and use that to beat Billy up, verbally at least.
He also knew there was another reason that Mel was so negative with him at the moment. She had relished her job as a runner on the film and had talked openly about her desire to continue in the job when the film relocated back to California.
In part encouraged by the feedback she had received from colleagues she had expected to be on the list of personnel being shipped back to the States and when her name had failed to appear on any of the lists she had approached her boss for an explanation. Apparently, she had been told, the studio had a plethora of staff already under contract in the US, anyone of whom could fulfil her role. It had been hard for her to swallow but at that point there had been no talk of Billy continuing in his role and the expectation had been that the two of them would therefore, drift back down to Eilat and pick up from where they left off, their brief careers in the film industry being chalked up to life experiences.
So, when Billy received the news that his role was being expanded and new scenes written for him it had upset Mel. It was not so much that they would be separated, Mel was not naïve enough to believe their relationship was going to be a forever relationship, she had known all along that it would run its natural course and

then falter and die, it was more that she was not ready for it to end just yet.

If this thing with Billy was going to end she wanted it to be on her terms and not decided by some outside forces. It was selfish and she didn't need Billy to point that out, and it certainly didn't help that he did. So, the two of them had been freely tearing emotional chunks out of each other for the last couple of days and now they were both, at least on the emotional front, utterly exhausted.

Billy was troubled by the news he had received that morning that he would need a full UK Passport, with at least six months remaining before its expiry, to get a Visa to enter the US. A temporary travel pass, that he could obtain from the British Embassy in Tel Aviv would only allow him to travel a single journey, back to the UK.

He had spoken by telephone to the British Embassy that morning and been told that it would take at least a month to get a new passport issued, too late for him to make it to Los Angeles for the remainder of the filming. The lady on the other end of the phone had assured him that there was no way she could fast track a replacement passport. She had been asking for details so she could cancel his current document when Billy had hung up. He didn't want anyone knowing who he was or the fact that he didn't have a valid Passport just in case the Embassy felt they had to report him to the Israeli authorities.

He was in enough trouble without the Immigration people hunting for him as well. He had entertained the idea of trying to get a fake passport but had dismissed it when he had discovered firstly how much one would cost and secondly the length of the prison sentence he would face if he was caught entering the US on a forged document.

Billy now faced a serious dilemma. He knew that he would have to contact Christian at some point in the next five days and tell him about the stolen documents. He had about a week before the bulk of the cast and crew flew home to the States.

They had been given the vouchers so that they could book their flights to any destination they chose, as long as it was within the Continental United States. If they wanted to return home and visit with family or friends they were free to do so. Likewise, if they chose to remain in Israel and enjoy the sunshine or see the sights that was also allowed. The only fast date was the scheduled production start-date in two weeks and everyone was expected to be in Los Angles and ready to work by that date.

For several days leading up to the end of filming, a popular subject for discussion in the Commissary and often late into the night was what was there to see in Israel. Some of the crew who had flown in for filming picked the brains of the locals, including the extras, about what was worth visiting. The younger members of the cast and crew were keen to explore the nightlife and the holiday spots on offer, the older members were looking for more of the historical or religious experience. Scouser and some of the older Israel hands among the extras were enjoying their new-found position as local experts where for so many weeks they had been the ones having to learn.

One of the cameramen had negotiated this helicopter trip. The machine had been used intermittently throughout the filming process for aerial shots and the pilots had been persuaded to give those interested an aerial tour of the country. The final destination was to be Ben Gurion airport where the passengers would be disembarked, but not before they had enjoyed a comprehensive tour of the country from the air. The first flight had departed at eight this morning and this flight was the second and final opportunity. The flight this morning had been full, this time though there were several empty seats.

The engine noise rose to a high-pitched whine which penetrated even through Billy's headset and suddenly the machine lurched into the air as if breaking free of the earthly shackles of gravity. Once off the ground the pilot dipped the nose and the aircraft started to move forward. There was a grating noise beneath his feet as the landing gear retracted and then free from the drag of the undercarriage they started to gather speed.

Billy glanced out of the nearby window as the Pilot circled the site waiting for permission from Air Traffic Control to climb out to a cruise altitude. From above, the site was already markedly different from even a day ago. Billy had managed to blag his way onto a flight a few weeks before when they were going up to check on some camera angles for aerial shots.

On that occasion, they had made several passes over the whole site and then it had been like looking down on a settlement in the middle of the desert. Now it was different as if some giant hand had descended and simply erased parts of it. The whole area which had housed the commissary trucks and the dining tents was now empty. The trucks had packed up and left that morning after serving a simple breakfast.

The area where the stars and senior staff had been quartered in their Starliner trailers was also empty. They too had pulled out in a long convoy in the early hours of the morning. Most of the principals had left in a group of exclusive SUV's after the wrap party the previous night bound for various luxury hotels around the country. As Billy watched one of the huts that had housed the crew was being hoisted onto a flatbed truck, while two others stood ready to leave the site, their engines running and smoke curling up from the exhausts of the rigs pulling them.

There was another fleet of trucks already heading for the highway. Billy guessed they contained all the technical equipment, like lights and cameras.

Finally, they passed over the tent encampment that had been home to the extras and the other camp followers. This camp ground was now largely deserted with only a couple of tents still pitched. From above the people looked like ants and Billy spotted a huge group heading down towards the highway where there were buses waiting to whisk them away to Tel Aviv, Jerusalem or Eilat. Billy knew that among that phalanx of people would be Scouser and the rest of the Eilat people heading back south to resume their lives in the southern city.

The pilot made one final circuit of the campground before pointing the nose of the Helicopter northwards and climbing out of the valley that had been Billy's home for the past six weeks.

After reaching their cruising altitude the radio chatter between flight crew and Air Traffic Control diminished and instead the Pilot was able to start giving his passengers the full tourist experience in the form of a non-stop commentary. The two crew chiefs were also more relaxed and didn't intervene if the passengers released their seatbelts and moved to one or other of the windows to look out and admire the scenery as it passed by below them.

Their course took them almost directly across the Arava region of the Negev to the southern tip of the Dead Sea and then up the western edge passing the fortress of Masada and the settlement of Ein Gedi and then on past Qumran, the site of the discovery of the Dead Sea Scrolls. Passing over the city of Jericho they picked up the track of the Jordan River following it north to the Sea of Galilee, flying low over the Lake and round the northernmost tip, before turning south again and flying a direct course for the city of Jerusalem where they were given permission to make a low pass over the Old City.

With Jerusalem in the rear-view they set course for the Mediterranean coast and finally landed at Sde Dov Airport in the North of Tel Aviv.

Those who were disembarking were ferried off the tarmac by minibus. There were only five passengers left in the cabin when the ramp was raised and the helicopter climbed back into the sky. Their final destination was a Kibbutz, the idea being that those remaining on the flight would have the chance to experience something of the life on a Kibbutz for themselves. Billy had already spent time in a Kibbutz but for him it was the destination rather than the concept that was appealing. It was the Pilot who had first suggested the idea and Billy had been lukewarm about it until he had heard the name of the Kibbutz they were going to visit.

The Pilot had been part of the planning team who had organised the round Israel air-tour and it was his idea to offer the possibility for a short stay on a Kibbutz for anyone interested in seeing these unique settlements from the inside. He had mentioned that he was a child of the Kibbutz movement having been born and raised on one of the settlements and it was to his home Kibbutz that he was no flying now, the name was Tel Boker.

It came as a complete shock that the Pilot was not only a child of Billy's former Kibbutz but also that he was the offspring of Yossi the Volunteer leader.

Billy didn't think Yossi looked old enough to have a son in his mid-twenties but apparently, he was older than he looked.

Billy had grabbed the pilot, Dov and taken him on one side to explain his particular dilemma with regards to his expulsion from Tel Boker and the full circumstances surrounding it. Dov had taken a moment before answering. He had peeled the Ray-Ban aviator shades off his face and placed them in the front of his uniform shirt before studying Billy with his dark eyes.

Obviously satisfied with what he saw there he pronounced judgement.

"Listen Bill, all of you are coming to Tel Boker as my guests so I will vouch for every single one of you. I think if my father had paused for a minute and studied you, just as I have done he would have seen no tell-tale signs of drug usage and could have made his decision accordingly. You must however understand the huge burden of responsibility that comes with being Volunteer leader and having responsibility over that many foreign visitors."

"Dov, I never once blamed your father for the decision he made. Yeah, sure I was mad because I knew who the guilty people were but I knew there was no way, given the circumstances, that I could prove it. In the end, I just had to accept my fate, but I certainly never blamed your father for it."

"Well maybe your arrival back on the Kibbutz this way can help to rehabilitate you and reconcile the pair of you."

"We can only hope so, but if there is anyone who needs rehabilitation it's Mel. She is desperate to get back onto a Kibbutz."

"Why?"

"Well she made a mistake, had an affair with a married member and was expelled when the affair became public." Billy skipped over the small matter of the argument in the kitchen and the waving around of the carving knife. He didn't think this was important.

"God I really hate the hypocrisy of some people. It takes two to tango and only the Volunteer ends up paying the price leaving the Member to carry on where they left off as soon as the dust settles. There are no real sanctions against them, they are left to continue their philandering unchecked."

Billy thought about his own brief dalliance with Daphna but decided to keep that little piece of intelligence to himself. Dov might already know about the affair but if he did or if he had made the connection to Billy he didn't give anything away.

"Anyway, in Mel's case she has been living a lie for the last year, pretending she is on a Kibbutz when all the time she has been living rough in Eilat. Her parents have been sending her money and now they want to visit and see what wonderful place has kept their daughter enthralled for the last year."

"And she needs to be on a Kibbutz for the visit to happen." Dov filled in the obvious blank

"Exactly."

"Well like in your situation I can vouch that Mel is a hard worker and provided she restricts her amorous exploits to single men I can't see there being any problem".

Billy had hoped this piece of good news would thaw the frosty relations between him and Mel. He had been sorely disappointed on that score, she was still angry with him and his prevarication over the Passport issue. She felt Billy was being irresponsible in not confronting the issue and confessing to Christian.

After all that he had done for Billy, Mel felt it was the least Billy could do, given that it would be Christian who would be left looking stupid when Billy failed to show up in LA. Billy found there was nothing he could say to mollify Mel but at least she was on the flight as they flew south towards Tel Boker in the last of the afternoon light, so Billy had not totally given up hope of a peaceful solution.

After a short flight at cruising altitude Billy felt the helicopter begin to descend. He looked out of the window and saw the desert landscape suddenly turn to green fields and orchards as they crossed over onto the land farmed by the Kibbutz.

Dov was clearly happy to announce his homecoming as he steered the aircraft through a series of low passes across the Kibbutz.

The result of these aerobatics was that when the helicopter finally flared out and dropped lightly down on its wheels there was a large crowd of people gathered to welcome home the hero son.

The open space where they landed was just outside the front gate of the settlement so to see a great wave of people surging towards them as they walked down the rear ramp gave Billy grounds to pause. The last time he had been in the company of some of these people he was being driven, in shame, down to the end of the road, expelled from their presence and lucky to have avoided being arrested by the Police.

Dov who was right behind him on the ramp noticed his uncertainty. He placed a fatherly arm around Billy's shoulder and steered him down the ramp and onto the ground and then left his arm lightly on his shoulder as they crossed the ground to where the crowd was assembling.

Dov, as the returning hero was in front leading the group to where the members of the reception committee were waiting. He was forced to tighten his grip on Billy as soon as the former caught sight of the figure who stood foremost in the welcome party. Yossi was stood front and centre as the proud father of a returning decorated Airforce Officer.

Yossi's wife, Dov's mother was stood just behind her husband and his youngest sister who had just started her military service was also present in her new uniform. Dov released his grip on Billy to embrace his father and Billy took the opportunity to try and fade back into the rest of the group but there were only five bodies in the following group so disappearance was impossible and it as therefore inevitable that he would come face to face with Yossi within a few seconds of Dov releasing his father and bending down to enfold his mother and sister in a group hug.

"Hello Billy, welcome back to Tel Boker." A big paw of a hand was extended in greeting. Billy offered his own and had it crushed in the firm grip.

Billy took some encouragement that the greeting was so warm and friendly and did not involve the sentences, "What are you doing here?" or "When are you leaving?"

Billy still couldn't be absolutely sure that this greeting was not playing to the crowd and that in a few moments he would be singled out and escorted off the Kibbutz and dumped back at the end of the access road. He searched the bearded face but saw only warmth behind the eyes.

"I need to talk to you when all this balagan has died down." Yossi released his hand and turned back to join the family group who were slowly making their way back to the Kibbutz.

"Come and find me in half an hour." Yossi offered as a parting shot over his shoulder as he disappeared into the crowd. People were surging forward to greet Dov with handshakes, hugs and kisses. He was like a returning Messiah, parting his way through a sea of humanity accepting greeting from left and right as he did so. Billy stopped in his tracks and looked around him. The rest of the passengers from the Helicopter including the three-remaining crew, were all stood in a loose knot on the outskirts of the crowd. Billy felt that as a former resident of the Kibbutz he could at least take over and show them all the way to the Kibbutz dining room where they would hopefully find someone who could help them with accommodation. Mel was stood on her own to one side looking miserable. He went over to them and offered to act as guide. They all accepted so they began to make their way into the

Kibbutz following the great herd of people who were in turn following Dov and his family.

In the Kibbutz dining room, they had held up the evening meal so that they could welcome their guests formally. Dov had managed to shake off the welcoming committee and was there to take charge of things, and introduce the group to Judah who was ready to show the newcomers to their rooms and get them settled. Billy was not expecting any such special treatment and was looking around the faces of the volunteers present to see if there was anyone he recognised. He was disappointed that he couldn't see Mike among them and he assumed that Mike had completed his stay and returned to the UK or was currently off the Kibbutz travelling.

A hand on his shoulder startled him and he spun around not sure what to expect. Mike was stood in front of him. Looking leaner than he had when Billy had last seen him, but also more muscled from all the hard, physical work and also hairier. His blonde hair now uncut and unchecked for over a year was well down his back in a long mat of blonde curls. He kept it from his face and eyes with a colourful bandana. His hair was still a little damp from a recent shower.

The two old friends grabbed each other in a fierce embrace, clinging to each other in unselfconscious pleasure.

"God Billy it's good to see you again. I have missed you."

"I missed you too Mike. How have you been?"

"Good, just working hard, playing hard. You have been the one having all the adventures."

"Yeah one or two." Billy agreed, releasing the close hold on his friend whilst holding him at arms-length so he could study him.

"You want to get out of here? I have a few cold ones in the fridge. The food here hasn't improved one jot and I heard rumours that there might be a welcome barbecue later."

"Yeah let's do that. Hold on a second there is someone I want you to meet."

Billy went over and tapped Mel on the shoulder. She was looking increasingly lost and isolated from the group of newcomers who were now receiving the lowdown from Judah on life in the Kibbutz.

"I have someone I want you to meet. We are splitting from here to have a few drinks. You are welcome to join us."

Mel looked around her, uncertain over what was expected of her but as no one was really paying her any attention she readily agreed and the three made their way towards the exit.
Billy made the introductions.
"Mike I would like you to meet Mel, she has proved to be my rock for the last few months."
Mel visibly warmed at Billy's kind words.
"Mel this is Mike my lifelong friend."
The two shook hands. And the three left the Dining Hall together.

\#

From the comfort of the old swing set Billy sat and enjoyed the company of old friends, a cold glass of Arac and water in one hand and Time cigarette in the other. Mike had been slightly surprised that his Billy had taken up smoking again, but after the initial surprise he said nothing more. Yara, who was still together with Mike, and appeared much more relaxed around the Volunteer quarters than she ever had been in the past, had joined them and now the four of them sat around drinks in hand and talked.
Billy had been talking virtually non-stop, recounting the story of their recent exploits in the desert on the film shoot and what the future held for them. Billy had been doing most of the talking, with Mel only occasionally chipping in when she felt Billy was exaggerating his importance or misleading his audience. She seemed to have relaxed a little and her frosty attitude towards Billy also seemed to be thawing as well, albeit slowly.
Billy was keen to catch up with the news. Were there any volunteers still remaining from when Billy had been here before? Was life still as crazy as it had been back then? Was there still a party every night?
Billy was clearly keen to pick up where he had left off, Mike on the other hand had other ideas.
When he managed to get a word in he told Billy, briefly, but succinctly about his trip to Eilat He started at the beginning with the arrival of the Police Officers and then the trip to Eilat with Yossi. Billy was smiling throughout, but his smile quickly faded when Mike began to describe the interior of the Morgue and the process of identifying Billy's body and his emotions as he stood there waiting for the Morgue Assistant to remove the sheet. Billy

quickly put himself in Mike's place and realised how unamusing the whole incident would have been if the boot had been on the other foot.

The whole incident had clearly shaken Mike and he was close to tears as he described looking down on the ruined face of the corpse and realising that it wasn't his best friend lying there.

"I found out later from the Police that the guy was a known face in the petty crime scene down in Eilat. His nickname was Dusty."

"Did you say Dusty?" It was the first thing Mel had said in a long time and there was a seriousness in her voice.

"Yes, they didn't know his real name, just a nickname, Dusty."

"And you say this guy was Black?"

"He might have been Black or Half-caste. Why?"

"I knew him." Mel seemed suddenly overwhelmed with grief.

"Mel?" Billy was concerned and he slid across to her and put a hand on her arm. "What's the matter?"

"Don't you remember when you moved into the shelter? I told you we had a space because someone had left."

Billy nodded his head. He vaguely remembered that some stuff had been thrown out to make way for his gear. But Mel had made so little fuss about it at the time that Billy had let the whole matter pass and he had certainly spared no thought about it ever since.

"That was Dusty. He was there one day and gone the next. We never did find out what had happened to him. He just disappeared."

Billy was stunned that the circle had completed itself in such a bizarre way but there was one detail he was still missing. What was the connection between a dead person in Eilat and him. Why had the Police come looking for Mike to identify the body?

"But Mike, why did the Police come here looking for you? Why did they think it was my body in the Morgue?"

"Because he was found with your passport and documents in his possession and no one bothered to check the Passport picture."

"My Passport? Are you sure it was my Passport?" Billy simply couldn't believe what he was hearing.

"Yes Billy, I held the thing in my hand. I had a photocopy of the picture page that I used to try and find you after we had established that the body wasn't yours."

"So who has my Passport now?" Billy was starting to shake a little as the full import of what Mike was saying was slowly getting through to him.

"The Police in Eilat have it in their evidence locker, or they did last time I spoke to Nurit."

"Who is Nurit?" Billy asked getting very excited now.

"She was the young Police Sergeant who helped me when I was looking for you."

Billy had noticed Yara stiffen when Mike had mentioned the name Nurit and he wondered if there had been more between Mike and the female Police Sergeant than he had admitted or whether it was just a small case of the green eye on Yara's part. In any case it was irrelevant. If the Eilat Police were still holding his Passport then he could reclaim it and still be able to make the trip to the States.

"You know what this means?" Billy said with a huge smile on his lips.

"That Dusty was the guy who robbed you." Mel said flatly.

Billy's smile melted away in an instant. "Well yeah, I suppose so." It was definitely not what he had meant. But he had to concede the point.

"And with the money he stole from you, he brought some good quality dope and went off on his own and killed himself."

There was silence as the full impact of Mel's word sunk into the consciousness of everyone present.

"You seem to be taking this rather personally." Billy knew it was the wrong thing to say as soon as the words were out of his mouth and Mel reacted with a sudden flash of anger. She pushed his hand off her arm and stood up, turning on Billy as she did.

"I loved that guy as much as I loved you. In fact, maybe even more." They were harsh words and they stung Billy. He had not given any thought to Mel's romantic attachments before he came along. Everyone of a certain age had a history, baggage, skeletons in the closet. It was part of life and you only ended up paranoid if you let any of the past effect the present. Old girlfriends and boyfriends were memories for the person concerned. To even begin with comparisons or to ask for too many details was the start of a rocky road that led to a breakup.

"I never knew." Billy started.

"You never asked." Mel wailed cutting him off.

"Why would I?" Billy was starting to get angry now and his voice started to rise.

"Exactly Billy. Why would you?" Mel burst into another flood of tears and stormed off, stopping a short distance away to cry on her own.

Billy looked at Mike for support, a confused look on his face saying 'Help me out here mate.'

Help came from another quarter. Suddenly into the midst of this tableau Yossi appeared, like a silent ghost out of the evening dark. "I thought I might find you all here." He said perching himself on the arm of one of the chairs. "I need to talk to you all." He looked over to where Mel was still shaking a little as she sobbed her heart out.

"Melanie, would you come here I need to talk to you."

Mel looked around when her name was called and noticed Yossi for the first time.

"Come and sit down," he waved in the general direction of an empty seat. "I have some good news for you."

Mel used the bottom of her vest top, lifting it up to dry her eyes. They were all treated to a brief flash of flat stomach.

She sniffed a couple of times for good effect as she returned and took her seat on the swing beside Billy. He made no attempt to touch her. He was focused on Yossi and what the volunteer leader had to say.

"Right let's get the easy stuff out of the way first. I have spoken to the Police in Eilat, a very helpful young lady called Nurit Sachsmann", he paused and looked directly at Mike, "she says to say Hello to you, by the way Mike."

Billy noticed Yara stiffen again at the mention of the name. He made mental note to interrogate Mike when they were alone to find out what had happened between those two while Mike had been in Eilat.

"I told her that Billy has returned to the Kibbutz. She is very keen to interview you and of course return your documents and other possessions to you."

"There has been a bit of development in the case." Mike sounded like a Police Officer when he said this. Yossi nodded his head indicating Mike should continue.

Mike explained about how Mel had known this Dusty character before. He didn't go into the details of their relationship just the basic facts.

"Well I am sure that the Police will be keen to speak to you as well then Mel. They still have no idea of the poor chap's real identity or where he came from or if, indeed, he has any family. Do you know much about him?"

"Everything, I know everything." It was obviously still upsetting for Mel to talk about her former lover so Yossi, seeing this, decided to change the subject.

"OK well I suggest we all make a trip to Eilat in the morning. And yes Yara," he said with an evil grin, "You can come along too and keep an eye on Mike."

Both Mike and Yara had the good grace to turn the brightest shade of red. Billy burst out laughing as did Yossi. Even Mel managed to crack a small smile.

"Right Melanie. I have some good news for you. I contacted the Kibbutz office and asked them to look up your records. From them I got the phone number of your former Kibbutz and spoke to the Volunteer leader there. He gave you a glowing reference."

Mel looked up surprised at the news particularly in light of what had happened there.

"He did mention the matter of your indiscretion but said the person concerned was a serial womanizer and chased volunteers for sport, that was the main reason that he and his wife had separated in the first place. He had actually been unhappy about expelling you but the Members council had been adamant that you had to go. In the light of this I would like to formally welcome you to Tel Boker as a volunteer, of course if you want to stay that is."

Mike and Yara both raised a small cheer. Mel was overcome with emotion and looked on the point of collapsing into floods of tears again. Billy just smiled knowing how important that piece of news would be for Mel.

Yossi held up his hands for quiet and waited for a moment for things to settle down.

"There was one small thing he mentioned. He said it was not a good idea to ask you to work in the kitchen. Do you want to explain?"

"Er n, no I'd rather not." Mel spluttered blushing a furious crimson Billy burst out laughing. Mike and Yara looked confused.

"It's OK," Yossi smiled obviously he knew the facts but he was keeping them to himself.

"But I take it you are happy to join us here on Tel Boker?"

"Yes, I would like that very much." She stammered a small shy smile playing across her lips.

"Excellent. Well when we get back from Eilat we can sort out the relevant paperwork."

"As for you Billy, I have reached a decision." Yossi sounded stern and Billy feared for the worse.

"I knew all along that the drugs weren't yours and I also guessed who the real owners were. This was confirmed shortly after your untimely departure. Unfortunately, by the time we discovered our mistake the damage had been done and you were long gone. I have to admit that when I was asked to travel to Eilat to identify your body I was overwhelmed with guilt. Thinking that I might have played a part in your death was not something I ever want to experience again. Anyway, to cut a long story short, you are also welcome to re-join the Kibbutz as a volunteer. This decision has been ratified by the Secretary and the Members Council at a special meeting just now. That is if you are not too busy jetting off to LA to be a film star."

Billy hadn't really thought too much about what he would do after the filming finished. He could just as easily return to Israel as anywhere else in the world.

"I think I will come back to Tel Boker after we wrap."

"Wrap?" Yossi was clearly not familiar with film jargon.

"Wrap," Mel offered, "It's a technical term for finishing the filming. Billy just being a snob."

Billy thought he detected the first sign of a truce in her voice. He didn't want to hold out too much hope but he was secretly pleased that he might still be able to return to Mel's affections if he put in the groundwork.

"Right." Yossi stood up. "That's all settled then. I hope you will all drop by the house later as we are going to be grilling some steaks in honour of my son's return."

They all chorused that they would be delighted to drop by later.

"Don't get too drunk between now and then." Yossi departed.

Mike stood up from his chair.

"I don't know about you but I am going to get another drink. I think we should celebrate."

There was a general chorus of agreement and even Mel joined in.

CHAPTER TWEnty one

There were a couple of very tender heads when they assembled in the Dining Room the next morning. After several drinks in the Volunteer quarters they had all moved up to Yossi's house in the main part of the Kibbutz, where on the green outside the house a large barbecue had been set up and steaks were grilling on the hot coals. The delicious smell of cooked meat made everyone's mouths water. As soon as the steaks were ready they all descended like a pack of hungry dogs.
There were salads, pitta and cold drinks on a table adjacent to the grill so everyone congregated around them, helping themselves and others to food and drink. People peeled away from the tables and assembled in groups, most of them sitting on the grass, but others, particularly elderly family members and friends were furnished with garden chairs to sit on. There was a friendly buzz and hum as people chatted and ate then chatted some more.
When things broke up at Yossi's the four of them drifted back to the Volunteer quarters where there was the usual nightly drinks and music taking place.
Mike had arranged to spend the night at Yara's so Billy and Mel could use his room. Billy was expecting them to sleep in separate beds but obviously the news of the return of his Passport together with the invitation for her to join Tel Boker as a volunteer had mellowed Mel's mood so when they finally arrived back in the room she was happy to climb into bed beside Billy and cuddle up with him.
Billy awoke once a little later and the bed was empty. He sat up quietly because he detected there was someone else in the room. In the gloom, he could make out the figure of Mel sat on the other bed, her knees drawn up to her chest. She was rocking slowly back and forth and Billy thought he heard her crying. He lay back down

quietly, not wishing to disturb her private grief. A short time later he felt pressure on the mattress as she climbed back into bed beside him. She reached across with her arm and pulled herself close to his body resting her head on his chest.

She was still in that position when Billy woke up in the first light of dawn.

Billy was gentle with her when she woke up. He had never experienced the vulnerable side of her personality. Since they had first met all those months ago Mel had always struck him as someone who was totally in control of her life and comfortable with the hand that she had been dealt. To have witnessed her total desolation in the depth of the night made him feel slightly uncomfortable, as if he had been prying into something secret and highly personal, but it was an image he could not un-see so he had to take it as part of Mel's personality that, until now, she had managed to keep completely hidden.

It also shook Billy to realise that this character, Dusty, had clearly meant more to Mel than she had been prepared to admit, at least to him.

He was sensitive enough to realise that the next couple of days could be very stressful and emotional for Mel so he was extra careful and attentive to her when they got to the dining room for breakfast.

The food on offer had not changed and Billy was at the hot food counter ladling fresh scrambled eggs onto his plate when Mike came up behind him.

"Morning Billy boy, did you sleep?"

Billy took the childish question with all its innuendo in his stride.

"Like a baby mate. You?"

Mike pulled a face.

"Always do these days, it's like being married."

Billy pulled a similar face in sympathy but neglected to comment as Yara was suddenly right behind Mike looking over his shoulder, taking a keen interest in what was on his plate.

"You need to make sure you have plenty of salad with that." She offered

Mike pulled another face which Billy could see but Yara from her position behind could not. Billy struggled manfully to avoid bursting out laughing. He stifled a giggle and turned away, this failed attempt caused Mike to giggle.

"Why are you two giggling like small children?" Mel had joined them with a plate of salad on her tray as well as bowls of cream cheese and yoghurt.
"I'll tell you later." Billy went off in search of some tea and toast to go with his eggs. Mike was railroaded back to the salad bar by Yara, a rather forlorn look on his face.
Yossi arrived just as they were finishing up their breakfast.
"I have managed to get a car for the trip. Shall we meet in the parking lot in fifteen minutes?"
They all agreed that would be the plan and went their separate ways to prepare for the trip. When they assembled later there was an almost holiday atmosphere among the small group. Mike and Yara were clearly relishing the idea of a day off from their respective jobs and although Billy was excited at the prospect of retrieving his passport he was trying to temper his enthusiasm out of respect for Mel's feelings.
Of the four she was the most silent, only speaking when she was directly asked a question. For the rest of the time she sat silent, obviously wrapped in her own thoughts.
Mike was quick to point out the contrast between this trip and the last trip to Eilat. He was riding up front with Yossi. The others were squashed in the backseat.
As he reminisced about the last trip Billy was frantically trying to get his friend's attention. He knew where Mike was going with this conversation and he wanted to avoid any embarrassment. Mike carried on blissfully unaware of Billy's vain attempts from the backseat.
"I remember how depressed I felt last time. Can you remember how you felt?"
Yossi with the added benefit of the rear-view mirror was able to pick up on Billy's facial expressions so he remained rather non-committal with his responses.
Mike continued to prattle on about the desolation he had felt to be travelling all this way with a horrible task awaiting him at the end.
"It was if I was a condemned man on the way to execution."
Billy having failed with his subtle attempts to attract attention now moved to more overt tactics. He broke out into a fit of coughing. Mike glanced over his shoulder.
"I guess those fags still don't agree with you. You ought to quit again."

After this quick aside, he faced front and continued with his reminiscing. Billy smacked his head sideways on the window, in despair. There was just no getting through to Mike. Billy drew in a breath ready to talk over Mike.
"And then to be standing in the morgue starring down at a sheet and wondering what lay underneath."
Billy didn't want this to go any further so he simply lashed out with his knee, clattering into the back of Mike's seat. Mike was propelled forward.
"Ow, what the fuck Billy."
"Sorry mate, I have a cramp in my thigh from sitting back here."
"Well did you have to kick me in the back so hard." Mike had now sat forward and turned slightly so that he could massage his lower back. Facing this way, he was able to see the three friends ranged across the back seat. All three of them were looking very disapprovingly at Mike.
"What? What's up? What did I do now?"
"A trifle insensitive in your choice of subject matter." Billy nodded sideways indicating Mel who was sat in the middle seat between him and Yara.
Mike looked at Mel for a moment and obviously confused, replayed the recent one-sided conversation back in his head. Realisation suddenly dawned on him and his hand shot to his mouth in horror. Behind his hand Billy saw Mike's mouth was forming a large O.
"God, Mel I am so sorry. I didn't really think."
"You never do." This came from Yara on the far side of the car.
"That's not fair."
"Kids," Yossi's deep voice intervened "Don't make me stop this car and make you all walk".
"Talking of stopping," said Billy, "I could do with a comfort break and a cold drink. Anyone else?"
There was a general chorus of agreement so Yossi pulled over at the next service station.
When they got back to the car Yossi suggested that Mel ride up front with him as he wanted to get to know her. The other's agreed and despite Mike's extra height they all climbed into the rear seat and Yossi pointed the car in the direction of the highway.

#

Mel seemed to be shaking as they all got out of the car outside the Police station. She had spoken mutedly to Yossi throughout the remainder of the journey south, only answering his questions, volunteering nothing further and lapsing into long periods of silence in between. She was clearly troubled and Billy now moved in taking her by the elbow and steering her away from the group.

"What's the matter? Something is eating you."

"I can't do it Billy."

"Can't do what?"

"I can't look at Dusty."

"Nobody will ask you to."

"Can you be sure of that?"

"Not 100% but look at it like this. His body is at the hospital, in the morgue. We are at the Police station."

"Yes but what if they ask me to identify the body."

"It won't come to that and if it does I will do it."

"But you didn't know him."

"I'll lie."

"You'll get into trouble."

Billy thought about that for a moment. He didn't want to overcomplicate things today. For him today was all about getting back his Passport so he could leave Israel with the others when the time came.

"Listen," he said putting his arm protectively around Mel's shoulder. "I will think of something."

Reassured by his words and the arm around her shoulder Mel allowed herself to be steered inside the Police station where Yossi was already talking to the Officer behind the reception desk.

Mike and Yossi both stood up when Gabriel Wiesenthal came out through the door from the back office. In his shadow, the much younger Nurit Sachsmann was busy tying up her hair with a scrunchy.

Mike and Yossi both shook hands with the pair before introducing the rest of the group. When Yara and Nurit shook hands Yara held on for a moment longer than necessary as she said something to the female Officer. Billy thought it sounded like "Mike's mine", but it was said quickly, in Hebrew, and he didn't catch it all. Whatever she hoped to achieve with this possession play was wasted as Nurit just smiled sweetly and moved on to shake Mel by the hand.

With the introductions completed Sergeant Wiesenthal escorted them all to a conference room which had been prepared for them. There were cold drinks and fruit in a bowl in the centre of the table and strong coffee and mint tea in pots on a side table.
They all helped themselves and then sat down.
Wiesenthal who was at the head of the conference table began by outlining what he hoped to achieve at the meeting. He spoke for a couple of minutes in both Hebrew and his own limited English before he handed the chair of the meeting over to Nurit Sachsmann.
She seemed a little uncertain as she stood at the head of the table and looked over the assembled group. She glanced down at her notes in front of her before she looked up again and began to speak.
Almost immediately Billy raised his hand.
"It's OK Mr Randell, you don't have to raise your hand we are not in school."
Billy looked at his hand as it hung in the air and placed it back on the table.
"I just wanted to say that I hope it will not be necessary for Mel to identify the body."
Mel looked sharply across at Billy as if by mentioning it, it would somehow become a necessity.
Sachsmann looked quickly over at Sergeant Wiesenthal for assistance and Billy glancing at the older Police man thought he detected a slight shake of his head. It seemed to be enough for Nurit to answer him.
"No. You can relax, Miss Bishop, that will not be necessary. We are satisfied that we have identified the body although we still don't have a real name, just a nickname. Unless of course you can help us out with that."
Mel who was very uneasy at being the centre of attention so early on, reached under the desk for her handbag. She placed the colourful fabric bag on the table in front of her and undid the rope string at the top. She reached inside and produced a slim black booklet. It looked like one of those pocket diaries. She placed it flat on the table in front of her before she spoke.
"Dusty's real name was Joshua Ogafemi," she looked at the two Police Officers who had both extracted notebooks and were keenly writing down every detail.

"He was British by birth, although I think his parents were originally from Nigeria. He lived with his mum and a sister in South London, New Cross. I don't have an address but I am pretty sure there will be an address in here." She patted the small book on the table.

"What is that?"

"This was Dusty's address book. I kept it when we chucked all his stuff out. Just in case he came back."

"Can we see that?" Wiesenthal put out a hand.

Mel kept her hand firmly on top of the book. "That depends."

"On what?"

"What you intend to do with the contents of the book."

"What do you mean?"

"Well I am pretty sure that Dusty wouldn't remember the names and phone numbers of all his suppliers. He was not very good with numbers. So, there is a strong chance he wrote them down in this book. If I give you this you will have access to all the main drug dealers in Eilat and across Southern Israel."

Wiesenthal looked sternly at Mel. He spoke briefly, but privately to his colleague and as Billy watched the two he noticed them both casting longing looks at the leather book on the table top.

After a few minutes Nurit spoke directly to Mel.

"Whilst we respect your loyalty to your friend, maybe I should point out that those so called 'Dealers' you are trying to protect now, well at least one of them was responsible for the death of your friend. Maybe you need to think about that?"

The words came as a slap in the face to Mel, who had obviously not considered this and as Billy watched he saw Mel's lower lip start to quiver. She fought her emotions for a moment and then she looked directly at Nurit.

"This book should have been destroyed on the fire along with his other stuff. It was just sentimentality that made me hang onto it."

Mel seemed to be regretting her actions now and her hand was still firmly placed on top of the book. Billy, knowing Mel as well as he did could see they were at an impasse and neither side was likely to back down any time soon. He suggested a compromise.

"What if one of us looks in the book to see if there is a home address in there and then we can read it off to you?"

The two Police officers looked annoyed at the proposed compromise. Both of them had clearly hoped they could exert enough emotional pressure on Mel so she would part with the book and that this book would, in turn, help them to clear up some loose ends in the war on drugs. It would have meant masses of kudos from their fellow officers and a whole heap of praise from their Station Commander and this was before the potential long-term effect of making the streets of Eilat a safer place and maybe, just maybe, saving some poor soul's life.

The more immediate problem was to find an address for the one poor soul whose body was lying in their morgue so at least they could find out what was going to happen to the body. They would have to be satisfied with closing this one case. The other stuff would have to wait for another day. The two conversed briefly in Hebrew, aware that Yossi and Yara would both understand what they said but unaware of Billy's command of the language. Mike was about to open his mouth to ask for a translation when Billy shot him a look that said. Let it wait.

The two officers were agreeing with Billy's proposal but he waited until they said as much to him, in English, before he acknowledged them. There was no point in letting on that he understood every word and he hoped the Hebrew speakers around the table or indeed the non-Hebrew speakers would not blow his cover.

Billy put out his hand towards Mel and she rather reluctantly removed her hand from the book and allowed Billy to pick it up. He turned to the first page and sure enough in rather childlike script was the name and address of the book's owner. Then Billy realised. The book had probably been in Dusty's possession since he was a schoolboy, hence the childlike script.

He read the address out and the two Police officers wrote it down.
"25 Florence Gardens, London SE14 2TQ."
"Is there a phone number?"
"Not on the title page. But Directory Enquiries will probably be able to help you out there."

The two officers conversed in rapid fire Hebrew before they reached a decision and Wiesenthal left the conference room. He returned a few minutes later with a London telephone number scribbled on a piece of paper. Obviously, the Police Service of Israel didn't have to rely on the vagaries of the British Directory Enquiries service.

Gabriel spoke in hushed tones to Nurit before handing her the piece of paper. She placed it down on the table top on top of her notes.

"That was quick." Billy was surprised at Gabriel's speedy return. Mel looked up as Billy spoke. "Are you going to call ?"

"We don't think we can." Gabriel had re-taken his seat and Nurit was back on her feet.

"Sergeant Wiesenthal just checked with the Superintendent and there are apparently rules regarding this in the UK. Any news like this has to be broken to the relatives by a local Police Officer. We can't just ring the mother and tell her. This number," she tapped the paper on the desk, "is for the local Police Station in New Cross. They will have to send an officer around to the house and break the news. But first we need to get some more information so we can confirm that the body is actually the right person before we contact the next of kin. We don't want to repeat past mistakes."

Billy saw Mel stiffen. She was now really worried that as a punishment for not surrendering the address book the Police would make her identify the body. Billy reached over and took her hand and squeezed it tightly.

Nurit, like any good Police officer noticed the movement and interpreted it for what it was.

"Ms Bishop, you don't have to worry. We will not be asking you to identify the body. We have already had a positive identification. What we need now is something that will confirm the bodies identity, like DNA, fingerprints or dental records. These we should be able to get from the local Police in London."

Mel breathed an audible sigh of relief.

Sergeant Wiesenthal stood up from the table, collected his notebook and placed it back in his shirt pocket. He addressed the group in his broken English.

"We have some phone calls to make. You stay here". He pointed to the table top before stalking out of the room.

Sergeant Sachsmann was a little more pleasant.

"We will be back as soon as possible. Help yourself to tea and coffee and if you need to smoke you can do so in the atrium in the middle of the building."

She looked around the table for agreement and hearing no objections she followed her older partner out of the door, shutting it firmly behind her.

Billy was gasping for a smoke so he got up and made his way outside into the sunshine. Mel chose to join him, although she didn't smoke, or at least she only smoked when she was drunk and she was very sober right now.

"Do you think I did the right thing?"

"What? By not giving them the address book?"

"Yes."

"Look I never knew this guy so I can't comment on what he would have wanted."

"I know, but what do you think?"

Billy did Mel the courtesy of actually considering her question at some length as he sucked nicotine into his lungs. Finally exhaling a large quantity of smoke, he turned to her.

"Honestly, if it was me, I would hand over the book. But then I have seen first-hand some of the absolute devastation that drugs have caused to families. It was part of my childhood."

Mel looked gloomily over at Billy. Billy took another drag on his fag before he continued.

"Not something you were likely to come across growing up in the leafy suburbs of Bushy?"

Mel shook her head. "No, we had the odd pothead in school but that was it. Anything harder and people would have freaked. As it was the potheads got expelled."

"So, if you want my honest opinion I would give them the book or alternatively hand it over to the family and let them decide."

"But if I give it to the Police to return it to the family, what is to stop them looking through the book before they return it."

Billy smiled. "You read my mind. Look at it like this. If you have returned the book to Dusty's family and the Police use the time they have the book in their possession to extract information from it then who is really to blame?"

Mel didn't seem entirely happy with Billy's idea.

"I think I need to think about it for a while longer."

"You do that." Billy stubbed the cigarette out in the ashtray and turned to go back inside just as the door swung open and Nurit appeared.

"Ah Billy, just been looking for you we need to go through these." She held up a clear plastic bag that was wrapped up with tape marked 'evidence'.

Billy's heart flipped over with joy as he examined the contents of the bag, waving in front of his nose, and saw through the clear plastic the tell-tale blue cover of his Passport.

Nurit turned on her heels and walked off down the corridor, the bag was draped over her shoulder like some lure or bait and Billy had no alternative but to follow her back to the conference room like a donkey following a dangled carrot.

Back inside the conference room, nothing much had changed. Mike, Yara and Yossi hadn't moved further than the table with coffee and now they had three steaming cups of the thick black liquid set on the table in front of them. Wiesenthal had proceeded Nurit into the room and he was already back in his seat at the head of the table. Mel and Billy filed in last and took their places. Nurit remained standing and placed the sealed evidence bag on the table in front of her. She fished in her pocket and pulled out a knife. It had a slim silver encased handle and when she pressed the button a four-inch stiletto blade shot out. She saw the looks of amazement on the faces of the civilians dotted around the large table.

"I took it off a teenager." She grinned conspiratorially. "He had no right to be carrying such a blade. They are illegal in Israel."

Wiesenthal harrumphed his disapproval. He felt this was too much information to be sharing with civilians.

"It's OK," Nurit concluded, "he got a receipt." As if this made it all acceptable in her eyes.

She used the blade to slit the top of the plastic bag along the line of red tape that bore the legend 'Evidence', then spilt the contents onto the table top.

She then used the point of the knife to separate the pile out into its various component parts.

Inside the bag was a folded sheaf of papers. An inventory list so she picked this up and read from it.

"One United Kingdom Passport in the name of William Randell." She pushed the blue covered document to one side.

"One TSB Cheque Card in the name of William Randell." The card joined the passport

"One ATM card also issued by TSB bank, also in the name of William Randell." This was also moved to the other pile.

"One hundred and ninety-eight dollars in assorted small US currency notes." The roll of notes was moved aside.

She had to pick up the papers next and open them to check which was which.

"Various Licences for Forklift Truck driving." She placed them down again.

She paused for a moment before picking up the next item as if she was unsure what to do with it.

"One business card for "The After-Dark Strip Club.""

Mel tutted disapprovingly.

Mike burst out laughing, "You got a business card from that dive?"

Billy had the good grace to blush scarlet before stammering, "I only went there once."

There was a pause before Nurit continued.

"One VIP Membership for the After-Dark Strip Club."

This time there was a sharp intake of breath from both Mel and Yara.

Billy looked from one to the other. "Look I can explain."

"Don't bother." Mel folded her arms in a gesture of finality.

Billy looked over at Mike for support. Mike was gazing away into the corner of the room refusing to meet his friends eye. He was chuckling to himself under his breath.

"Mike, come on mate you were there."

"Hey Billy don't involve me, leave me out."

"Come on mate, you know we all had to get those VIP cards to get in to the bar area. It cost me about ten quid for the privilege."

Mike looked at his friend and decided he had suffered enough.

"You mean it cost me ten quid if I remember. Yes, all right we did only go there once it was for someone's twenty-first birthday. There was group of us."

"Doesn't excuse it. They degrade women in those places." Mel was still not impressed.

"They didn't look very degraded to me." Billy offered and got a swift punch on the bicep for his trouble.

"Ow, Police," he wailed half joking, "I would like to report an assault."

Nurit had moved the VIP Membership card on to the other pile. There was not much left for her to process now.

"There is a library card, an Organ Donor card and a Medical card all made out in the name Billy Randell." She moved the last items over.

"Is there anything missing."

Billy paused for a minute.

"Well it was a while ago but I seem to remember there was about another hundred and fifty pounds in Sterling in my wallet. I guess that got spent."

"Most likely." Nurit agreed with him.

The last item was the wallet itself and the plastic folder that had contained his licences and documentation.

Sachsmann flipped a clipboard around and skidded it across the table towards Billy.

"We need you to sign to say we have returned the items to you."

Billy looked down the form which was all written in Hebrew. He looked up hopefully at the two Police officers.

"Where do I sign?"

"You can't read Hebrew?"

"Not a word." Billy lied. He knew exactly where to put his signature but he was still not prepared to reveal his knowledge of Hebrew to the two Police Officers.

"You do know that lying to the Police is obstructing justice and therefore a Criminal Offence." This statement was delivered in rapid fire, colloquial Hebrew. The objective was to see if Billy reacted to the severity of the situation when confronted with it. Billy was the picture of innocence as he looked over at them with big wide eyes.

"I beg your pardon." Billy looked at Nurit and Yossi as if asking both of them for their help.

Sachsmann cleared her throat and repeated the sentence in English.

"Really?" Billy looked shocked at the statement.

Sachsmann held Billy's gaze for a moment longer than was necessary trying to will the lad to look away and confirm her suspicions. Billy's gaze was totally level and unflinching.

"At the bottom of the form, last box on the right." She said.

Billy signed his name with a flourish and then pushed the clipboard back across the table.

In the interim Nurit had been placing all his possessions back in the evidence bag which she now handed across the table to Billy. As Billy's hand touched the plastic Nurit tightened her grip on her side of the bag reluctant to release it.

"We have just one question. Why didn't you report the theft of your possessions to the Police when it happened?"

Sitting beside him Mike looked up at his friend wanting to gauge his reaction. Billy had half risen from his seat to accept the bag. As Mike watched him the colour drained from his face to be replaced by a fevered rosy flush across his cheekbones. Billy let go of the bag and collapsed back into his chair, clearly rattled by the latest turn of events.

"Well I," he began but got no further. His mind was furiously working processing all the possible answers and their possible impact on the audience present.

Eventually common sense prevailed and he decided to stick with the truth.

"I was worried about getting expelled from the country for not having a Passport or the requisite work permits. At that point because all my money was stolen I was effectively a penniless vagrant with nowhere to stay and not more than a hundred shekels to my name. I had one recent brush with the Police over drug possession, of which I was completely innocent I might add. So, to be honest I just didn't want to flag myself up on the Police radar."

Nurit and Wiesenthal had listened intently to Billy's explanation and now a look passed between the two of them as if they were silently deciding what to say next. Eventually after a couple of moments Wiesenthal ducked his head indicating that Nurit could continue the questioning.

From the folder in front of her Nurit pulled out a large map of the local area. It was a detailed Ordinance Survey Map of the whole district around Eilat, including large parts of the desert to the north of the city. She folded it out onto the table top.

"Can you show me on the map approximately where the robbery took place?"

Billy looked confused. He shot a quick panicky glance first at Yossi, then at Mike. He stood up slowly.

"Er, why?"

Nurit looked at Billy as if the answer to his question was obvious.

"We are trying to establish a timeline for Mr Ogafemi's final hours."

"And what exactly has that got to do with me?"

"Well at some point in his last hours Mr Ogafemi did steal your backpack and all your possessions. And then a few hours later he ends up dead."

"You don't think? You can't think?"

"Can't think what Mr Randell?" there was no kindness or bonhomie in Nurit's voice now.

"Hang on a minute Nurit," Mike intervened on his friend's behalf. He could see Billy was slowly slipping into full panic mode. "You can't think Billy had anything to do with Dusty's death?"

"It's Sergeant Sachsmann, thank you Mr Spencer." Nurit suddenly sounded all formal as if the next thing out of her mouth was going to be the Miranda warning. "And I am the one asking the questions here."

Billy picked up on the vibe as did all the others around the table. Despite the fully functioning Air Conditioning unit in the corner of the room he felt the sweat break out between his shoulder blades and start to trickle down his back. He licked his lips nervously, now on his guard about everything he said and did.

"There is something I feel you all should know at this point before we go any further. Following Mr Spencer's visit to us and as part of our enquiries we reopened the case file on Mr Ogafemi. In these cases, it is procedure to request a second Post Mortem. When the Coroner re-examined the body, he made some interesting discoveries. He found injuries and lacerations at the base of the skull. Now these could have been caused by the victim falling and hitting his head while intoxicated or equally they could have been as the result of a blow to the back of the head with a blunt object. The Coroner was unsure which was most likely. Furthermore, he was unable to determine whether it was the drugs or the blow that was the cause of death, or whether one contributed directly to the other. Therefore, the reason we need this information is because we could at this point to investigating a homicide."

Now Billy was really scared.

"And you think I am responsible?"

Wiesenthal now intervened. "That's why you must show us on the map. Where were you robbed?"

Billy stood up slowly, unsure of whether he could trust his legs to keep him upright. His knees felt suddenly wobbly and there was a knot in his stomach.

He knew from what he had heard about Dusty's death, he still couldn't get his tongue round the guy's real name, that it had taken place in the desert and that the body had lain undiscovered for a long time. What he couldn't know was whereabouts the body had been found or if the body had been buried or hidden. That it had remained undiscovered for so long pointed to one or the other scenario. If the body had been found in the same area of desert as the robbery then obviously he would be a prime suspect. He wished, and not for the first time, that he had never succumbed to the stupid petty jealousy and taken himself off into the desert and got drunk. Until now his regrets had been mainly formed around loss of his money and possessions, now, however, there was an even bigger problem. He could end up being charged with murder. He poured over the map tracing the route he had walked that night from downtown out past the apartment buildings and houses and on into the desert.

On the map after the last of the properties the desert was just an empty space of white on the map with a few gradient lines crisscrossing the white to show some elevation but apart from them the map was featureless.

He pointed his finger to the blank white space.

"It was somewhere in this area here, although whereabouts exactly I cannot be sure."

Nurit followed Billy's pointing finger.

"I see. Very interesting." She showed no trace of emotion. Blank, stony-faced, she was giving nothing away.

Billy flopped down again in his seat and wiped the sweat of his forehead, painfully aware that the sweating and general nervousness made him look guilty.

"Do I need to get a lawyer?"

He said to the room in general.

"Why don't you take us through what happened?"

"Well," Billy paused regathering his thoughts and reaching out for the distant memories from that night. "I had been on the beach all day and I was feeling depressed so I went to one of the supermarkets and bought a bottle of Arac and some water. I mixed a strong mixture of Arac and water and headed into the desert alone. I built a small fire and then sat down." He paused looking at the two Police Officers. Wiesenthal was scribbling away furiously on his notepad. Nurit was watching him intently from over steepled fingers pressed against her lips.

Billy thought her lips looked very kissable but he had to dismiss the thought immediately and focus on the rest of the story.

"After I lit the fire I carried on drinking and then I must have passed out from intoxication."

"You blacked out?"
"Er yes, I guess so."
"So you have no recollection of what happened next?"
"No not until I woke up later in the night."
"So anything could have happened and you would have no memory. You could have woken up when Mr Ogafemi tried to steal your backpack and fought with him and struck him a blow and you would have no memory of the struggle."
"Well yes, I could have, but I don't think I did."
"How can you be sure?"
"I can't," Billy was aware of where this line of enquiry was leading and he was not in the least bit pleased by it. In fact, he was starting to shit himself with worry.
"But if I had been in a fight, even while I was unaware of it I am sure I would have been bruised or had some injury to myself. I was not injured at all, just my pride took a beating that night."
"Your pride?"
"Yes, I was stupid. I stormed off for all the wrong reasons and I awoke to find my backpack and all my possessions had been stolen so as well as making a fool of myself I was also made to look the fool, that was real retribution."
"And you claim it all took place in this part of the desert?"
"Yes I woke up and the fire had gone out. My backpack was missing along with most of my money and my other possessions. I walked back towards town and discovered my backpack discarded about," he stood and studied the map again, "about here." He pointed to a place on the map where the first of the houses started to appear adjacent to the desert.
"I then walked back downtown, stopped at one of the all-night gas stations to buy a bottle of water and then returned to my hostel."
"I thought you were sleeping in the beach camp?"
"No at that time I was still staying in the Peace Hostel."
"Can someone confirm this?"
"Well the manger might have kept records." Billy offered hopefully.
"What about the girl at the hostel?" Mike chipped in, "What was her name? I met her when I was looking for you."
"Blossom." Billy supplied the name. "Is she still living at the Peace Hostel?"

"Well she was there a month or so back when I was down here searching for you. And she definitely remembers you."

"So go talk to Blossom at the Peace Hostel or the manager I am sure they will be able to confirm my story. I got back around breakfast time with a screaming hangover."

"We will go and have a word with them later."

Billy was reluctant to ask the next question but he really had to know the answer as so much depended on it.

"So what happens next?"

Nurit and Wiesenthal exchanged glances. Wiesenthal nodded towards the door and the two officers rose as one and left the conference room pulling the door firmly shut behind them. Neither of them had responded to Billy's final question and somehow that made things even more ominous.

There was silence in the room for several long minutes when the only sound was the ticking from the Air Conditioning unit in the corner of the room.

"Bloody Hell." Billy swore loudly and thumped the table with his fist for emphasis.

"You can say that again." Said Mel.

"Bloody Hell." Billy said a second time although this time he omitted the emphasis with his fist which was still smarting from the first blow.

"I was talking hypothetically." Mel said flatly.

"I wasn't. If I was talking hypothetically I would have said "I'm fucked"". Billy sounded angry and scared now, but Mel was not going to cut him any slack.

"How is that hypothetical. Do you even know what hypothetical means?"

"I don't think either of you really do," Mike interjected, "And tearing strips off each other is not going to help the situation. Seriously Billy how bad do you think this is?"

"To tell you the truth mate I don't know. They reckon Dusty could have been murdered and as far as I can see they think I might have done it. That sounds pretty bad to me."

"What do you think Yossi?"

"I don't know. To be honest I have never been in this situation before and I can't really tell where this whole thing is going. All I can suggest is we wait and see what happens next."

"Do you know any good defence lawyers?"

"Never needed one. Look Billy the only thing I can say is just tell the truth and it will be all right."

"I tried that last time and look where it got me." Billy was half smiling when he said this.

Yossi looked up and saw the smile playing on Billy's lips and he returned the smile if only to keep the lad's spirits up.

"Good point."

Billy pushed away from the table and stood up.

"I need another cigarette." He headed towards the door.

He was reaching for the handle when the door was pushed open from the other side.

The two Police officers barrelled into the room. Billy took two steps back from the door to allow them access.

Billy slunk over to the window and leaned on the frame folding his arms across his chest and crossing his legs.

The two officers took their seats again and Nurit opened the brown file folder she had been carrying.

She looked over to where Billy was standing, leaning against the wall.

"You might want to come and sit-down Mr Randell."

"I am fine here, thank you."

"Don't be difficult Mr Randell, just come and sit down." She had a more forceful tone the second time, like Billy had no alternative so he pushed off the wall with his shoulders and crossed to his empty chair.

As he slumped down in his chair Mel spoke up.

"Before we go any further can I ask a question. Is all this hostility and hassle because I wouldn't surrender Dusty's address book?"

"What hostility?" Nurit looked the picture of innocence as she spoke.

"You just about accused me of murder, and I still don't know if I am going to walk out of here or into a jail cell." Billy tried to keep his voice steady but the stress of his position was difficult to supress and his voice cracked slightly at the end.

"We came down here to collect Billy's possessions and he ends up being accused of murder. That's pretty hostile in my eyes, but if it means so much to you here take the book. I had made up my mind to pass it on to you anyway. If it can help you to catch and lock up some dealers and prevent more people like poor Dusty dying then it's a good thing and it will be worth it."

Mel tossed the book on the table and it skidded across towards Nurit, only coming to a halt when it cannoned into the brown folder she was holding open in front of her.

"Thank you for your help Ms Bishop. It is very public spirited of you." Nurit gathered the small book off the desktop and put it to one side.

"Right if we have all finished maybe I can enlighten you a little about what we have discovered." Nurit looked at each of them in turn as if seeking their assent to continue.

Nobody offered anymore objections so she looked down at the papers in front of her as if refreshing her memory on some of the finer points before she began to speak.

"Right well you are probably all desperate to know the outcome of our findings. While we were out of the room earlier we made a couple of phone calls. Just now we have been back to collect the replies. One was from the Medical Examiner, the Coroner who performed the post mortem. He was quite clear in his conclusions. He stated and I quote," she paused and looked again at her notes as if she wanted to be as accurate as possible. "Anybody who had been in close proximity to Mr Ogafemi when he was struck on the head would have been covered with blood due to cast off from the injury. Now if you don't know what that means I can explain." She paused and looked around the room. Everyone was sat stony-faced at her description of the injuries, all except Mel who had turned white with shock. Billy noticed this and reached out to her to take her hand. She reacted to his touch by shying away from him like his touch had burnt her hand and she folded her arms across her chest and slumped lower in her seat.

Nurit noticed this reaction and paused for a moment.

"Miss Bishop, would you like to leave the room? What I have to say next might upset you."

Mel looked across the table and hesitated as if she didn't quite trust her voice.

"It's OK, you carry on. I am already upset and I want to know the truth."

Satisfied that there were going to be no further interruptions the young Police officer consulted her notes one more time and then continued.

"When a weapon is used on a victim and blood is drawn some of that blood splashes back as the weapon is drawn back and forms a

distinctive pattern of spray called cast off. In the case of head wounds like the one sustained by Mr Ogafemi, there would have been, according to the Coroner, extensive blood flow and considerable cast off as a result. So, in conclusion Mr Randell, if you had struck the blow that may or may not have killed Mr Ogafemi then you would likely have been covered in blood or at least have had blood on your clothes. Were your clothes covered in blood that morning?" She looked over at Billy.
Billy didn't have to think very hard to remember that the clothing he had been wearing was not covered in any blood at all, not even his own.
"No, they weren't. I have to confess," at this point Billy's cheeks flushed scarlet, "I might have pissed myself in the night, but no there was no blood."
Given the seriousness of the situation nobody laughed at Billy's embarrassing admission.
"The second call was to the Police in New Cross and they have confirmed that Mr Ogafemi was registered with a local dental practice so his dental records have been faxed to the Medical Examiner and we can confirm that the body is definitely that of Mr Ogafemi, so there will be no need for you to examine the body Miss Bishop."
Billy heard a huge sigh of relief escape from Mel and her body deflated slightly as she clearly relaxed at that piece of good news.
"So, we now come to the most recent phone call we made. We spoke to the manager of the Peace Hostel just now and to your friend Blossom, who sends her best wishes and both of them confirmed that when you returned to the hostel, although you appeared in distress you were not covered in blood. I guess that backs up your evidence. There is one final piece of evidence that actually exonerates you completely. The Forensic team have completed their analysis of the clothing and from articles found at the site where Mr Ogafemi's body was discovered and together with the Coroner's report it is most likely that Mr Ogafemi died at the scene, probably instantly, or shortly after he was struck on the head. As this location is on the other side of the city out near the Water Treatment plant it is unlikely that you played any part in his death. So, Mr Randell, you are free to go."
Billy let out a whoop of delight and punched the air. He stood up and he turned to Mel who also stood up. The two grabbed each

other in a tight embrace. Billy realised he was almost on the point of bursting into tears, so great was the feeling of relief.
Mel having finally discovered that Billy had clearly played no part in Dusty's death and was going to be free to walk out of the Police station by her side, even managed to crack a small smile.
Mike was close behind him now slapping him on the back.
"Never doubted you for a minute Billy boy."
"Mr Randell, just one final question." Nurit interrupted the celebrations. She switched into her native tongue and asked the question.
"When were you going to tell us that you spoke Hebrew?"
Billy was not to be deterred from the levity he now felt so he cracked a half smile at the young Police sergeant.
"Can't a boy have some secrets?"
Nurit smiled at first then pulled a stern serious face. "Not from the Eilat Police Force one can't. Not if you want to stay out of jail."
Rebuke delivered, she cracked a smile again.

#

Outside the Police station in the heat of the mid-afternoon sun Billy felt exhilarated that he had in some ways dodged the hangman's noose and was a free man. It had definitely felt a bit touch and go back there in the conference room but now he stood on the pavement and drank in the air.
Everyone else was hunting around in bags and pockets for their sunglasses to shield their eyes from the harsh sunlight. Billy found his own and slipped them on. He turned to look at the rest of the group.
"I feel like celebrating, anyone care to join me."
Mel, now that the ever-present spectre of having to identify Dusty's body had been lifted and despite the harrowing details of her former boyfriends last moments was now trying to put a brave face on things so she raised her hand and hopped up and down. "Me, me, me." She sounded like an excited child being offered a tour to the candy shop.
Billy realised the strain that she had been under for the past few hours and knew that a few drinks among old friends would be a good cure for her blues.

"You're on the team." He smiled at her and she did a little twirl of delight.

Mike shuffled his feet. "Would love to but I promised Yara we would go and check out the shopping mall." He had the good grace to look apologetic.

Billy with his new-found sense of freedom decided to be magnanimous.

"It's OK mate. I know that shopping opportunities are limited when you live in a Kibbutz. You two enjoy yourselves. If you get bored we will be in the Peace Cafe. You know where it is?"

Mike nodded and then headed off in pursuit of Yara who was already striding off in the direction of the large downtown mall which loomed in the distance at the other end of the airport runway.

Billy didn't expect Yossi to agree to join them and sure enough the Volunteer leader produced a large piece of paper from his pocket. "I have a few errands to run. The price I had to pay to get the loan of the car at such short notice. I will come by the Peace Cafe and pick you lot up later." He headed off after Mike and Yara to fill them in on his plans.

Billy turned to Mel. "Guess it's just you and me kid". He bowed his arm and Mel slid hers through the gap and together they wandered off down the street arm in arm like old friends should.

With money in his pocket, his Passport and other papers returned to him Billy felt like a different person when he walked into the Peace Cafe that afternoon. There were a couple of the other former extras from the recent shoot still dining out on stories of their escapades in the deep desert.

The money they had received for the work would soon run out and they would no doubt be back on the Wall again touting for work with all the other drifters. For now, whilst the money lasted, they could enjoy the life of Riley and bask in the collective spotlight of their fifteen minutes of fame. No one would begrudge them the attention and they all knew they had one man to thank for their success. So, when Billy walked into the bar a ragged cheer erupted from the group. Billy acknowledged them with a wave and set about buying a round of drinks for everyone.

His magnanimous gesture did not pass unnoticed and a place was quickly made for both him and Mel at the table.

They were still in the same seats a couple of hours later when first Mike and Yara and then a short time later Yossi arrived in the bar. Mike and Yara had accepted a drink but Yossi was anxious to get on the road back to Tel Boker. So, the four of them finished their drinks and then with promises to keep in touch and names and addresses scribbled hastily on beer mats the five of them left and got in their car and headed north on the highway in the direction of Tel Boker.

Billy looked back over his shoulder at the sun setting for the last time over the Red Mountains and wondered if he would ever return to Eilat again. It was city that sucked you in and only the lucky ones escaped. That was the very nature of the Eilat Trap.

epilogue

"Do you think Dusty ever took magic mushrooms?" Billy looked over at Mel who was sat beside him in the passenger seat of the Jeep he had hired for the weekend. She was dressed in some loose fitting Arab trousers and a matching kaftan top, recently purchased on a shopping trip to the souk in Jerusalem. Billy was clad in a new pair of Levi's and a pair of sliver tipped cowboy boots he had purchased while in the States. He had stopped short of buying a black Stetson afraid of the parody he might have become.
Mel grinned at Billy's attempt at levity.
"I see where you are going with this and knowing Dusty as I once did I am sure he did indulge in a few psilocybin at some point in his life."
She reached across and squeezed his leg through the denim.
"It's alright Billy I am OK. You don't have to wrap me in cotton wool. I will be fine."
Billy and Mel were back together and enjoying each other's company. After the scare they had both suffered at the hands of the Eilat Police Department they had spent the rest of the time remaining before Billy's departure to LA in each other's company, except for the time they had both been working at their new jobs on the Kibbutz. Billy had taken a job on the Irrigation crew and had acquitted himself admirably. His new-found strength and resilience to the heat after his hard work on the work gangs in Eilat had played a big part in contributing to his overall fitness. Mel had

been placed in the Citrus Orchards away from any sharp knifes except the small pruning knives they used to manage the trees. Mel had accompanied Billy to Ben Gurion when it was time for him to leave and the two had written or talked on the phone almost every day while he had been stateside. Mel had also been at the Arrivals gate when Billy had returned making a huge scene by vaulting the fence and leaping into Billy's arms nearly knocking him on his back. She had been reluctant to let go of Billy ever since and kept touching him just to make sure he was real. This was acceptable when they were alone but embarrassing when they were with friends as they were right now.

Mike and Yara were occupying the two rear seats, both were casually dressed and had their eyes encased in mirrored aviator shades. The wind in the back of the Jeep made conversation almost impossible unless you put your heads very close together but they were grateful for the lift that Billy had provided for them and the chance to see some of the beautiful Israeli landscape at close quarters.

The four of them were crossing the Arava desert on yet another trip south. The purr from the V8 engine was drowned out by the whine from the off-road tyres on the blacktop of the highway, which was in turn drowned out by the classic rock that was blaring from the exceptionally powerful in-car entertainment system.

Mel had the map folded up to the correct section and a quick glance at a passing road sign, confirmed with a cross check of the map told her they were swiftly approaching their destination.

"The turn for the park should be just down here on the right."

She was not wrong and a few hundred metres later they came across the tell-tale orange sign for the Timna National Park.

Billy slowed down and turned off the highway. They didn't look like two volunteers from a Kibbutz but more like two wealthy tourists on a sightseeing trip, but their reason for being in the park was far from that of casual tourism. They were there for a much more serious reason.

When Billy had arrived back at Tel Boker the previous weekend he was tired from the flight but excited to share his latest news with Mel, Mike and the rest of his friends.

Studio Executives had reviewed the footage already shot and decided that instead of a single two-hour feature film they would in fact commission a one-hour TV pilot and follow this up with a full series of thirteen shows.

This announcement, made on the final day of filming in Burbank, had caused an uproar as contracts and availabilities had to be negotiated for all of the principal actors involved. Billy, although not on the principals list had been asked to reprise his role in the series and had been offered a sizeable retainer, negotiated in part by his newly appointed Hollywood agent, the inimitable and aptly named Miss Tara Shade.

With her Pamela Anderson figure, her ever present Shih Tzu lap dog, and her hardnosed style, she had burst into Billy's trailer on his first day in Burbank and offered to represent him. She was not prepared to take no for an answer and after consulting with Christian and getting his feedback Billy had agreed. She had come good with an instant pay rise and then the offer of a retainer while the series went into pre-production development. Billy and Christian had been dispatched back to Israel to try and round up as many of the original extras used on the film and they had, after many calls to the Peace Cafe managed to locate and speak to most of them. Scouser had been particularly willing to re-don his green Mohican, especially when he had seen the figures on the contract that Christian had dangled in front of him.

The Producers had decided to return to the Negev to shoot as they had loved the futuristic light and colours offered by the desert landscape and felt nothing in California, Nevada or Arizona could compare to it.

Billy was so hyped up by his latest stroke of luck that even the arrival of a message from Nurit Sachsmann hadn't managed to dampen his spirits.

She had called Yossi and he had been the one to bring the news to Mike, Mel and Billy. They had been sat as usual in the late afternoon, outside their room enjoying the last of the afternoon heat and a few drinks.

Yossi stood there for a moment and watched the easy chatter between the three friends, unwilling to be the bringer of serious news. He had spent a difficult quarter hour on the phone as Nurit gave him the latest news from Eilat. It had not all been good news but she had asked if he would pass the information on to Mike and Mel. She didn't know that Billy was back in the country until Yossi told her.

Billy had noticed the volunteer leader lurking uncertainly in the background and called him over, offering him a cold beer from the fridge. Yossi had accepted the drink and sat on one of the free armchairs.

"Listen, I don't know how to break this news to you but I just had a phone call from Nurit Sachsmann in Eilat. She wanted me to tell you that they have made arrangements for a funeral and memorial service for that fellow, Joshua Ogafemi. It is the day after tomorrow."

Yossi looked at each of the three friends in turn.

"Of course, you will be allowed to take the day off to attend the funeral."

Yossi had outlined the rest of the details of the arrangements and then finished his beer and taken off back in the direction of his house.

Billy had showed up there a bit later asking to use the phone and Yossi had waved him inside to where the phone was located. Billy emerged a half hour later and dropped some money on the table in front of Yossi.

"That's for the phone bill".

Yossi had opened his mouth to complain that it was too much but he stopped dead when his wife shot him a warning look and scooped the money off the table and tucked it into her shirt pocket. Billy's phone calls had been first to Christian who was holed up in a hotel in Tel Aviv. He was hoping to get down to Eilat for the weekend to tie up the last of the extra contracts. Billy told him that he and Mel would be in the city at the weekend if he needed any help. The next call was to a car rental company to arrange for them to deliver the Jeep in time for Billy and his friends to drive south. It had not been a cheap rental but Billy had got used to driving the powerful machine in America where the Studio kept a fleet of them so he would rather have the extra power and durability over rough terrain, particularly given their destination. The third call had been to make them all reservations at the Ambassador Hotel out on Coral Beach. Billy had booked two rooms for the weekend. The first part of the road into the Timna National Park was an ordinary tarmac road but once you passed the visitors centre it all got a little wild and off-roadish. This was where the Jeep came into its element. They had stopped briefly at the visitors centre to pay

the admission fee and to pick up a guide map to the park and it was
this that Mel was using to navigate to their ultimate destination.
The map, in itself, proved unnecessary. Their destination was not
only well signposted but was one of the most famous locations in
the park and even on a normal day there would have been a steady
stream of cars and minibuses heading towards it.
This was not a normal day and the road through the park was filled
with vehicles of all ages, shapes and sizes. Billy looked at the jam
of traffic and was reminded of the opening scene from the
Woodstock film where all the hippies are trying to get to the
concert site and the rural roads around the town of Bethel in
upstate New York are brought to a standstill by the sheer weight of
traffic. In this case the roads were not blocked but there was an
overwhelmingly large stream of traffic heading in the same
direction as they were.
Their destination today, along with all the others, was the world
famous Timna Mushroom.
This had been chosen as the site for the memorial celebration for
Dusty, or Joshua Ogafemi.
The rest of Nurit's message had been rather upsetting. They had
managed to contact Joshua's relatives but far from being upset at
the sad news of his death, they had seemed almost relieved and
when the matter of burial had been discussed they had absolved
themselves of any responsibility and involvement.
When news of this had leaked out to the ex-volunteer community
in the city there had been a conscious effort to collect money to
give him a proper send off. Pictures of Dusty were placed in every
volunteer bar and cafe in the city with a collecting tin and the
money gathered was enough to pay for a cremation and for this
party today at the Mushroom. When news of the event had got out
there had been a further wave of donations and offers of assistance.
The urn containing his ashes had been ferried north from the city in
the middle of a convoy of assorted vehicles including motorbikes,
vintage cars and even a couple of old buses. All of them packed to
the gunnels with people determined to wish the young man bon
voyage.
When they arrived at the Mushroom the area resembled pictures
Billy had seen of the Arts fairs that were springing up in the
deserts all over the Western United states.

With the tall stone monument as its centrepiece a large camp had sprung up around the site radiating in every direction.
Everywhere you looked there was something to catch the eye. There were kites of all shapes, sizes and colours flying in the breeze. Some were swooping in deft circles performing tricks and stunts, others merely hung majestically in the air their long tails streaming out in their wake.
The breeze was also causing the many flags and banners to flutter. The deep blue and white of the Israeli national flag was among one of the colours but there were equally as many hand dyed bedsheets in the full panoply of rainbow colours.
As they parked the Jeep on the edge of the crowd the noise of the gathering broke through replacing the engine noise.
Close by where they had stopped the Jeep there was a group of musicians and their audience sat in a large loose circle. There were three acoustic guitars enthusiastically hammering out a wild gypsy jazz melody while other exotic instruments added depth to the music and a counterpoint to the guitars. Two wild dreadlocked guys played digeridoos, their whooping sound providing a throbbing bass undertone while at other points of the circle people kept time on a range of percussion instruments. The lead melody was played by a striking woman with wild red hair and Celtic face markings. Clad in a silver sheath dress she swung her violin back and forth brandishing it like a weapon as she coaxed forth the haunting melody.
All the faces in the extended circle were alive with excitement and concentration, both the musicians and the bystanders in the audience, as the music wrapped itself around them and seeped into their very souls. The music was fast approaching a crescendo that suddenly exploded in an orgasmic final elongated note that slowly dissolved into an uproar of cheering and clapping.
A quick count in and they launched into another tune.
Moving past the musicians and deeper into the crowds a thought struck Billy. He bent his head close to Mel to share it.
"I reckon looking around here that Eilat must be empty today".
Mel touched Billy's shoulder to keep his head down and stretched up to place her mouth close to his ear in order to be heard above the general din around them.
"I guess most of the interesting people have made the trip."

They were both accurate in their assumptions. These were the people who entertained the tourists along the sea front and manned the stalls on the markets along the boardwalks. They were the artists who painted portraits, the silversmiths who made jewellery, the weavers and the knitters who sat there day after day creating the crafts that they sold. Everyone had made the trip and some had brought their wares with them. Others were just enjoying a day out and one group were sat producing friendship bracelets of cotton thread which they were giving away for free.

Billy was handed a woven necklace with one of the Israeli telephone tokens woven onto it. The guy who handed him the item offered to tie the necklace in place and Billy stood still and lifted his hair to expose his neck to make the job easier.

Someone handed Mel a photocopied piece of paper and Mel read it and then handed it to Billy.

"It's the programme for today."

Billy looked and saw that the organisers had devised a loose program for the day. The main event, the scattering of the ashes by the Mushroom was to take place at sunset. Billy looked up in the direction of the sun, shading his eyes against the glare. There were probably a couple of hours of daylight left.

"Well I don't want to miss the main event but we can certainly have a look around and enjoy ourselves for a couple of hours before that."

They moved through the tightly packed crowds soaking up the party atmosphere. There was food and drink to be had and people were taking advantage of the free alcohol as well as the free barbecue food. Billy was touched that so many people had made the journey out here.

Whether their intentions were to pay their respects to Dusty or just to come out here and get wrecked in the desert, the fact that they had turned up was testament to something, a feeling of community, a sense of belonging to something bigger than oneself.

Billy did notice that despite the fact that Dusty had died of a suspected drug overdose there were still plenty of people openly pedalling drugs of all stripes and strengths.

Billy noticed Mel observing the brisk trade that they were all doing.

"Looks like the Police haven't made use of the address book yet."

"I was thinking the same thing. Just as long as today doesn't lead to any more casualties."

"I think there will be a few people with very sore heads in the morning." Billy said as he put his arms up to fend off a couple of semi-clad males who were staggering through the crowd cannoning of every other person.

Mel stopped dead in her tracks and Billy looked around realising she was no longer close by his side. Mel raised her arm and pointed.

"Do you think they are undercover or is there going to be a raid?" Billy followed the direction of Mel's outstretched arm and saw exactly what she was driving at.

Emerging out of the crowd, looking a little square and very much out of place was Sergeant Gabriel Wiesenthal of the Eilat Police Department. Following behind him and by virtue of her age and her attire, blending in slightly better was Sergeant Nurit Sachsmann. The two Police Officers spied Billy and Mel and came over. There were handshakes from Gabriel and brief hugs from Nurit for all of them, although Mike's embrace with Nurit was so quick it almost didn't happen and he was under observation the whole time by Yara.

The group continued together through the crowds of hawkers and dealers with Gabriel and Nurit choosing to turn a blind-eye to the drug deals that were taking place in the open. Billy secretly wondered if the two cops were mentally taking notes or trying to remember faces for future use.

Knowing that he would be driving them into Eilat later that evening in the Jeep, Billy was restricting his intake to food or soft drinks only but the others were able to partake of the full feast. On the far side of the Mushroom away from the gypsy jazz musicians the music was a little more hard-core with a mother of all sound systems pumping out rave music and dancing couples gyrating to the driving beats.

As the light started to fade the intensity amongst the crowd increased. The music got louder and the fires were lit casting fiery and devilish colours on the faces and bodies of the dancers.

"Billy?" The voice behind him sounded familiar, he spun on his heels and found himself face to face with Blossom. Billy had wondered if she would be among the crowd today and here she was standing right in front of him. He looked either side of her head to see if she was with her friends from the Peace Hostel but there was no sign of the others. Blossom noticed where Billy was looking and moved to reassure him.

"The others are not here today. Yoram wouldn't give them the day off. He owed me a couple of days so I was able to come here. By the way congratulations on your new-found fame. Now to be a TV series."

Billy looked surprised that Blossom had heard about the new TV series.

"You looked surprised?" She said.

"Only that news has travelled that fast. We only found out about the decision a short time ago."

"Eilat is a small city and as soon as one person knows something it quickly becomes common knowledge. Just look at the turnout today. This didn't take long to organise. Are you here alone?" Blossom moved a step closer to Billy entering his personal space. Billy looked hurriedly over his shoulder trying to locate his friends. They had been distracted by one of the stalls and had stopped about fifty metres away among the crowd. None of them were looking in his direction so he couldn't attract their attention.

"Er No," he stammered, "I am here with some friends."

Blossom looked to the left and right of Billy trying to identify these missing friends. No one was close enough to Billy to fit the description and a look of slight disbelief spread across her face, replaced by one of sympathy. She reached out a hand towards Billy to touch his arm and Billy recoiled as if he had been burnt.

"So how did you know Dusty?" Billy asked desperately trying to shift the focus of the conversation away from him and his supposedly imaginary friends.

"He was a former resident at the hostel." Blossom didn't have to be more exact. They both knew which hostel she was talking about.

"Another evictee?" Billy asked

"Yes, as a matter of fact he was chucked out, but only because Yoram caught him dealing drugs. How did you know him?"

"He was a former resident of the shelter I stayed in at the Beach Camp. Although looking back he was probably already dead before I moved in there." Billy still hadn't really come to terms with the part he appeared to have played in Dusty's death. It was his money that had enabled Dusty to buy the drugs that had killed him and he had moved into Dusty's bed space shortly afterwards. That alone had left him feeling guilty and that was even before he got around to the fact that he was also now dating Dusty's former girlfriend.

"I never got the chance to meet the guy. What was he like?"

"He was a nice guy."

"So why did Yoram kick him out?" Billy couldn't help but feel resentment towards the owner of the Peace Hostel. He had been singlehandedly responsible for the worst few days of Billy's life.

"Because he was dealing drugs from the hostel."

"So why not just warn him. Why kick him out?"

"Billy I know what happened to you and I swear I played no part in it".

Looking at the earnest expression on her face Billy found himself almost believing her.

"Yoram was behind the whole thing. He has some sick twisted fantasy about me and him being an item."

"Well are you an item?"

"No fucking way." The earnest pleading look was replaced by a sudden flash of anger.

"There are things no one else knows about Yoram Cohen."

"And you do?"

"Yes as a matter of fact I do."

"Like what?"

"Like he is one of the biggest drug dealers in the city. He controls the flow of drugs to the street dealers. Dusty was threatening his business. He had to go."

Billy looked startled at Blossom's candid revelation. Aside from the obvious indiscretion on her part, a revelation of this nature, if it became general knowledge could eventually find its way to the ears of the authorities and lead to Yoram's arrest, the closure of the Peace Hostel and the end of Blossom's current cushy arrangement. Blossom couldn't know that he was on first name terms with members of the Eilat Police force. Billy filed this little piece of information away to be passed on to Nurit and Gabriel when the chance presented itself. He was sure the chance to nail the Mr Big of the Eilat drug trade would be a feather in both of their caps, or Police berets or whatever headgear it was they wore these days.

"So, Billy what about us?" It was the question he had been waiting for. He would have been slightly disappointed if the subject had not arisen.

"What about us?" Billy kept his tone as flat as possible.

"Well now you are a TV star I am sure you can afford to move back into the hostel if you wanted to."

"I don't. So obviously the rumour machine is not without flaws. I have moved back to my old Kibbutz, I am back with Mike on Tel Boker."

A brief look of confusion passed across Blossom's face. She obviously had not heard that particular rumour.

"I met Mike when he came looking for you. Did he give you my message?"

"What Message?"

"That I had found it in my heart to forgive you."

Billy put his head on one side as if trying to recall receiving the message. The pose was straight out of the Introduction to Acting text book. He held the position for a brief moment before he straightened up. "No I never got that message. Mike did tell me that he got a rather frosty reception at your hostel."

This caused Blossom to frown. She was disappointed that her message had not been delivered and the fact was written clear on her face. Billy for his part remained neutral.

"So how come you were allowed back on Tel Boker?"

"Well it turned out my expulsion was a mistake and the council reversed the decision."

At that point Billy felt a warm arm snake around his torso and Mel stuck her head under his arm so Billy's fell naturally across her shoulder.

"Who is your friend Billy, are you gonna introduce us?"

Billy was relieved that Mel had found him and that relief probably showed a little too clearly on his face. Blossom had taken a step back at Mel's arrival, taken a further moment to appraise the easy body language between the two of them and now looked for all the world like she had sucked a lemon.

Billy did the introductions and almost immediately Blossom made her excuses and left disappearing back into the crowd.

"Is that the "Blossom"?" Mel asked watching the retreating figure.

"Yes." Billy said.

"Not very friendly, was she?"

"I think she has a lot on her mind today."
"Bullshit. She still fancies you."
"Ah my sweet your female intuition is fully functioning as always." Billy grinned at her.
At that moment a fight was avoided as the others caught up with them.
Billy passed on the intelligence about Yoram to Gabriel and Nurit. Nurit was about to reach for her log book from her handbag to take notes when Gabriel hissed at her in Hebrew.
"Not here, you will get us both lynched."
Nurit had the good grace to look embarrassed.
"I will come by the station and make a statement if it will help."
"You will be wanting paying as a CI next." Gabriel grinned.
"My rates are very favourable."
Gabriel growled at Billy.

\#

As the sun set a silence fell over the assembled throng as they carried the urn containing Dusty's ashes to the centre of the gathering.
All eyes were on them as Mel unscrewed the cap and upended the container. The ash poured out in a long stream immediately caught by the wind and whipped up into a whirlwind cloud that settled slowly over the desert sand.
Instead of sadness a ragged cheer erupted from the throats of those present and hugs and kisses were exchanged among the throng.
In the aftermath of the silence a single drum began to beat coming out through the speaker system mounted on top of one of the buses. Increased by the amplifiers inside the vehicle the pulse wave could be felt in the chest like the beating of a gigantic human heart. The beat intensified until it was just on the cusp of painful then the bass came in vibrating through the desert floor and up through the legs. The two, combined, made it almost impossible to stand still and people began to move to the rhythm. When the lead instruments joined the mix, the whole place was lit up with lasers and fireworks and the crowd, with an animal roar began to dance wildly.

It was a fitting last tribute to Dusty and as Billy and his friends left a few hours later the party was still in full swing and looked set to continue throughout the night.
"It was a shame Dusty's family didn't want to be a part of this. They would have been impressed."
Mike was a little drunk and a little high but he meant what he said. Mel was more thoughtful.
"I am glad my Mum and sister are arriving next week. I really miss my family and I am looking forward to showing them this mad place."
"What about you Billy. Have you contacted your mother?" Yara was trying her best to keep Mike upright and just about succeeding.
"Yes Yara, I sent her a letter last week telling her all the news and inviting her out to visit, all expenses paid. And this morning I got a reply and she has accepted."
"That's good" said Mel sliding her arm through Billy's
"Very Good" He agreed

The Beginning:

ABOUT THE AUTHOR

Nick Cree is the creator of the popular blog site "It Shouldn't Happen to a Volunteer" (ISHTAV) which has been active since June 9th 2017 which incidentally was the 30th Anniversary of Nick's arrival on a Kibbutz in Israel. The site has so far had over 25,000 visitors, reading some 50,000 pages.
He denies he was running away but life until that point had been pretty meaningless with a round of dead end jobs. In Israel at the time the most popular song was from U2's album the Joshua Tree. I still haven't found what I'm looking for might have been the case when Nick finished his stint on Kibbutz but by that time he had at least figured out what questions to ask.
He moved into the lucrative IT contract market and worked for the next 20 years in the IT Industry. A break to raise his son gave him a chance to start writing and he has produced a number of novels in draft form which he has promised to publish in the near future.
The Eilat Trap was not a cynical move to cash in on the success of the website, honestly, but because he realised that whereas the work on ISHTAV was all personal stories, over the years he had amassed a huge body of other stories told to him while he was there, and over the years since, about things that had happened to other volunteers.
So, in a way the Eilat Trap is a tribute to those people who took the time to tell him about their adventures.

As for Billy, Mike and Yara, we don't think their stories are quite over yet and certainly Billy Randell will be back.

Printed in Great Britain
by Amazon